# *The* LATER ADVENTURES *of* TOM JONES

## Bob Coleman

LINDEN PRESS/SIMON & SCHUSTER

NEW YORK 1985

Copyright © 1985 by Robert Coleman
All rights reserved
including the right of reproduction
in whole or in part in any form
Published by Linden Press/Simon & Schuster
A Division of Simon & Schuster, Inc.
Simon & Schuster Building
Rockefeller Center
1230 Avenue of the Americas
New York, New York 10020
LINDEN PRESS/SIMON & SCHUSTER and colophon are trademarks of
Simon & Schuster, Inc.
Designed by Eve Kirch
Manufactured in the United States of America

1   3   5   7   9   10   8   6   4   2

Library of Congress Cataloging in Publication Data
Coleman, Bob, date.
The later adventures of Tom Jones.

Sequel to: Tom Jones/Henry Fielding.
I. Fielding, Henry, 1707–1754. History of Tom Jones.
II. Title.
PR9199.3.C586L3 1985      813'.54      85-16017
ISBN: 0-671- 54643-0

*To Marjorie Williams*

# CONTENTS

# BOOK THE THIRD

# BOOK THE FOURTH

# BOOK THE FIFTH

# BOOK THE SEVENTH

# BOOK THE EIGHTH

# BOOK
# THE FIRST

# I

## *A New Bill of Fare to the Feast*
### *or,*
## *on Second Helpings*

Reader, I do greet thee heartily! Where have the years flown since we parted along that great London road, site of so many shared adventures? May we not pause here for reacquaintance? Harsh time has treated thee gently. Thy features look as firm as when last we met, thy eye and smile as bright. And thy judgment—remains it as shrewd as when thou wisely chose to praise my first account of the life of Mr. Tom Jones of Somersetshire?

If, indeed, thou art as eager to hear as I am to tell, we shall travel most pleasantly these coming days, for I have tales to share with thee of a wildness scarcely to be imagined. Yet must I ask thee to attend forgivingly; for though the years have touched thee lightly, I, perhaps, have fared less well. An author's life is never easy. If a weakening memory hath introduced error into what follows, then, reader, thy charity hath found its nearest object. Should any small inconsistencies appear, thou must act mercifully: nod thy head, and grin; toss another log upon the fire, but keep this volume in thy hand. Read on, you will discover something to your taste: for here will you find virtue rewarded, villainy punished, and chastity—treated as it deserves.

Some twenty-six or -seven years have passed since last we spoke of the early life of Mr. Jones: how he was left as an infant in the bed of Mr. Allworthy, the richest and best-hearted gentleman in Somersetshire; how Mr. Allworthy raised him almost as a son; how, when Tom was a young man, the lies and treachery of his half-brother, the wicked Mr. *Blifil,* cost him the friendship of Allworthy; how he wandered half the length of England, coming finally to London, where his warm spirits sank him to most desperate straits; how at last his friends' efforts and his own repentance overthrew the plots of Mr. Blifil, and brought Tom the forgiveness of Allworthy and the love of his dear Sophia—to say nothing of saving him from an early death by hanging. And so at journey's end we parted happily (or so I have always believed), secure in the knowledge that all-wise Providence had at last repaid the young lovers for all their sufferings.

And yet Providence grants us nothing permanent while we walk this earth. Mr. Allworthy, full of years and honours, was laid soon after to his well-earned rest, while tenants and friends competed to speak his praises and mourn his passing. Tom, his only heir, rose to be squire of Paradise Hall, where he so benevolently exercised authority as to be universally acclaimed a blessing to the county.

And Tom in turn was blessed by Sophia with a son, Hacksem, a daughter, Amelia, and a second son, Rob. Of these it was said that, in Amelia lived the image of her mother; in Rob, the spirit of his father; and in Hacksem, the temper of the devil. To the raising of these children, Tom and Sophia devoted all their energies. In the popular opinion of the county, they succeeded very well in two cases of the three; and eventually, even bad-natured Hacksem was persuaded to abandon the igniting of small animals in favour of architecture. Thereafter (while Amelia passed her time with books, and Rob squandered his with dog and gun), young Hacksem enjoyed building clever little models of Paradise Hall—which he would then, however, generally explode with gun-powder.

Alas, just when familial joy seemed nearest to flowering (for Rob and Amelia were delightful children), that joy was cut at its root. In her thirty-eighth year, Mrs. Sophia Western Jones fell ill of the influenza and, shortly joining the angels she so nearly resembled, left poor Tom bereft of consolations, though not of challenges.

For six full years did Mr. Jones, widower, labour to raise these children, 'til Hacksem was twenty-one, Rob, eighteen, and lovely Amelia— the apple of his eye—an innocent creature of nineteen. Regrettably, Hacksem, without the restraint of his mother's kindness, grew to proclaim an absolute right to reorganize Paradise Hall as he saw fit. In one stroke Tom found his parental duties more than doubled, even as his home became a battlefield, more awful than Culloden, providing him two willing allies, but one implacable foe.

In all his labors, a single principle guided Tom: that he would teach virtue by displaying it. How well he succeeded must be known by what followed—for virtue is nothing until it is tested.

---

It hath wisely been observed—precisely where, I do not recall—that an author ought to consider himself as one who keeps a public eatery, at which all are welcome for their money; and that, in fairness to these guests, ought to publish at the outset his *bill of fare.* Accordingly, reader, be advised that it is our intention to serve a main course of *Adventure,* set off by various side-dishes such as philosophy, and comedy, and romance, all cunningly dressed and carefully served.

Whether such a menu may tempt thee, reader, thou alone knowest. But I would urge thee to persevere, for Tom Jones, as thou must recall, is no ordinary country squire. Though we begin on a harmless May morning of the year 1774, thou had best keep thy raincape and thy pistol about thee: rougher times lie ahead. At this inn are to be found as much brawling and swordplay as metaphysics and *repartie;* as much salt beef and ship's biscuit as fresh-buttered rolls and fine wine.

Therefore, Reader, only nibble, or sip, here, and thou shalt, methinks, discover much to thy taste. But come! The tab is small, the dining long and varied. Second helpings are often best! We begin!

## II

### *A Short Description of Squire Jones, and of His Family*

On one particularly warm and breezy morning early in the month of May, Squire Tom Jones, of that part of our kingdom commonly known as Somersetshire, stood upon the terrace of his house and discontentedly surveyed a very beautiful scene.

Beneath him stretched the broad lawns of his estate; these yielded gradually to a fine grove of old oaks, at the bottom of which, near the center of the valley floor, lay a lake, about a quarter of a mile distant. This lake was fed by many cascading natural waterfalls, which ran spectacularly down Mr. Jones's hillside, and which provided that morning a music almost as sweet as that of the thousand birds singing in his park.

From this lake flowed a river, which wandered smoothly past woods and meadow and farmlands until, some miles away, it emptied into the sea, the far prospect of which marked the furthest point of Mr. Jones's view. It was the sea, indeed—and not the river, or the valley, or the valley's several villages or old ruined abbey—which fixed his attention this fine spring morning. The sea, and all beyond it, had begun to mean to him freedom, freedom from both the considerable ill, and the considerable good, of his life.

On this, the morning of his forty-fourth birthday, Mr. Jones (for so we must call him, as he possessed just then so little of the spirit of our old friend Tom) suffered from one of those states of mind in which it is far easier to count one's blessings than to enjoy them. He had indeed many things to be thankful for: good health, great fortune, and as clean a conscience as any of us may hope to claim in our forty-fourth year; and a fam . . .

But there he halted, for into the blessing of his family some admixture of sorrow had crept. The old Jones restlessness had now affected each of his children: Amelia was discontented, Rob in trouble, and Hacksem— well, Hacksem was a deep pond, a nest of unfathomable and unsavoury plans.

Above all, the absence of his Sophia—now six years gone—was a weight about the heart of Mr. Jones, and a wash which faded the colours of the morning. He had felt her absence every moment of the six years passed, and would feel it until he died.

Here Mr. Jones rubbed both hands lightly over the silver hairs gracing his temples, then tugged smartly at his turquoise waistcoat and drew himself erect. Thus did he habitually answer his sorrow with overnice-ness. Since her death, he had honoured his absent Sophia by a rigid discipline, indulging neither his sorrow with tears, nor his amorous long-ing with the company of women. He showed his love by making himself miserable, as though this were a kind of amends for the sin of living on after her.

Such self-denial had, of course, demanded other outlets for imprisoned feeling, and Mr. Jones had striven to become a second Allworthy, not merely passive, but active and sweeping in his goodness: he read much, prayed faithfully, and represented the county very skillfully in Parliament. At the end of his six years, he was accounted by most of his neighbours a scholar, a statesman, and a minor saint. Their natural hatred of such a paragon was, however, much tempered by the universal knowledge that he was not a happy man.

When this Mr. Jones—in many ways a different Jones than you, Reader, may recall—had spent about half an hour in a condition combining conscious prayer with unconscious resentment, he called for his breakfast to be set upon the glass table of the terrace. He then seated himself gingerly, for his fine suit of clothing was tight: hard riding, hard walking, and much martial exercise had kept his figure robustly powerful; yet he would not indulge himself in anything more comfortable. By such Puritanism he made himself, oddly, a temptation to just those women he intended to avoid.

This birthday morning, Mr. Jones ate a breakfast of only bread and toasted cheese. When he had done, he made an uncharacteristically sour face and instructed Mrs. Limeslices, his worthy housekeeper, that he would now see his son Hacksem.

That a person of Mr. Jones's frank and open manner might deny his own son at breakfast ought to warn thee, reader, that this young Hacksem was no person to be met unawares by the innocent. Prepare thyself, therefore, for what villainy thou mayest read hereafter. As Mr. Jones's own manner attests, the sight of Mr. Hacksem Jones was an experience which only a strong stomach, lightly filled, could prepare thee to endure.

# III

## A Doleful Conversation

When bright Phoebus, lightly bussing the rosy cheeks of Dawn, did bid her adieu and commence to climb the steepest portion of his diurnal rounds; when, in plain English, the clock had just struck eight, Mrs. Limeslices stepped again onto the terrace to pick up Mr. Jones's breakfast tray, and to announce in grudging tones, "Mr. Hacksem, sir."

Of all reasons possible for Mrs. Limeslices's dislike of Hacksem Jones, one at least—disappointed love—might, I think, be safely dismissed.

Black-coated and dour of demeanor, this Jones could perhaps have won the love of a mortgage, writ, or bill of execution; for that would have been merely the return of his own great affection. But among the few *women* of his acquaintance, the sole feeling he raised was an overwhelming and justifiable revulsion.

An ambulatory cloud, a thunderhead, a fog, a dark night, a—what you will, this young gentleman approached his own father with a very proper sense of calculation and mistrust. As he advanced, he shifted from hand to hand a large roll of documents which, finally, he placed on the glass table before Mr. Jones. These were documents, we must say, which our hero had seen often enough before to have grown thoroughly to detest.

"Father," began this promising young man, "I hope your birthday morning finds you well."

"Well enough, sir," Mr. Jones answered. "At least, well enough to settle what business we may have before us."

Realizing that further compliments would be amiss, Hacksem Jones untied the cord wrapping his roll of documents, and spread them politely before his father.

"Here, Father—if I may—are the details of my project for your consideration."

"These are, I suppose, the very plans whose preparation I opposed?" asked Mr. Jones with some firmness.

"All prepared at my expense, Father."

"Very good of you sir, I am sure. But how am I to enjoy the reading of plans whose drawing I resented?"

"They've been polished, Father."

With irritation quite unlike him, Mr. Jones nearly shouted, "Polished, sir? Why cease there? Varnish 'em, bronze 'em, and be done with it, sir. Be done, I say."

This outburst frightened Hacksem as much as the sparrow does the goshawk. He went on evenly, "You will be pleased to witness, sir, that the situation of our lands offers three distinct advantages, *viz.*:

"That of materials: we have in plenty timber, brick, coal and iron ore.

"That of situation: by a simple campaign of drainage and canalization —not above two miles' worth of digging, I warrant you—we shall move our goods by river to the sea, and thence to any commercial port in the world.

"That of population: as our lands are rich, our needs of workers, both manual and mechanical, may be easily supplied.

"In short, we are nothing lacking for the introduction of the manufacturing arts to our estates."

And so, with a neat summation of parts worthy of Mr. Hume, Hacksem paused for reply.

But Mr. Jones, to whom love of the land unspoilt was next to love of life itself, could not easily respond. Before him were spread twenty vellum sheets covered with steel engravings, produced for the enticement of investors and describing his lands as a new center for manufacture. These dire pages seemed to turn the bright May sun as cheerless and cold as any late Winter's afternoon, and nearly froze his heart.

Yet so strongly ingrained were the instincts of goodness and charity in Mr. Jones, that he began to conceive that his poor son might be merely thoughtless, and not malicious. When he spoke again, therefore, the old, familiar kindness returned to his manner.

"Hacksem, you have proved these last three years a great help in the administration of our lands. What you have done in the ordinary course, you have done well."

At this, Mr. Hacksem, as was proper, bowed.

"Yet," continued Mr. Jones, "beware the dangers of too wild and presumptuous a tampering with the settled course of life. Though some innovations, to be sure, enrich life and ornament society, we may too easily by recklessness squander our peace and happiness, and even our lives. Whatever changes we contemplate, we must consider first the well-being of our fellow men, then the just order of society, and only lastly our private profits. Proceed slowly, sir, and dispense with these speculations, and you may yet do much that you propose."

Reader, we shall not often in this narrative have cause to sympathize with Mr. Hacksem Jones. However, in fairness—for fairness is to be our hallmark—might not his father's remarks have tried the patience of the best-natured child in the world? Whatever we may think of Hacksem's plans, might we not grant something here to youthful enthusiasm?

Still, even Mr. Hacksem's firmest advocate must admit that only a little patience here—a hint of grace—might, in time, have given him all he desired. Yet such was his nature that he must force the issue. "May I speak frankly, Father?"

"Frankly, sir, or not at all."

"Father, your world is passing. There are men upon the 'Change in London who command a million pounds of capital; our poor ten or twenty thousand a year is nothing to them. They mean to convert England into a commercial and manufacturing power, and when it suits them, they will drive down corn prices until our land is worthless, and then buy it from us for a song. Other men will industrialize Somersetshire if we will not. We may choose the actors, but not the play."

It hath been very aptly observed that nothing hurts so much as the truth; and Mr. Jones, like most of us, tended when injured to react without much thought. His response, therefore, was sharp.

"And how, sir, if some players dislike their parts? How shall we persuade our tenants to forsake the health and security of agriculture for the grime and smoke of manufacturing?"

Nothing so charmed Mr. Hacksem Jones as a practical query concisely phrased. A smile—though one shaped as if his teeth were too hot for contact with his lips—formed upon his features.

"There, indeed, Father, lies the true strength of our position. By an escalation of our rents, we may secure a dual benefit: those who choose to pay will enrich us by so much more each year; those who find the new rents insupportable will have no choice but to leave off cultivation and seek work in manufacture. In either case, we gain."

"Very generous, sir. Very nicely calculated. And if they protest, I suppose we may play the magistrate upon them, and send them to poor house, or to gaol—those we do not transport, I mean."

"We may, sir, if necessary," answered Mr. Hacksem, a little uncertainly.

"Their wives may protest a little, but women are easily silenced."

Mr. Hacksem said nothing.

"Their children may be a burden to them—for we must keep wages moderate—but troublesome children may always be sent profitably to London, the little boys to steal, the little girls to whore."

For perhaps the last time in his life, Mr. Hacksem Jones had the grace to blush—though immediately thereafter his face became exceedingly hard.

But Mr. Jones had not concluded. "Then there are lesser problems. When we drain our lands and clear our forests, some ducks may die, and deer, and foxes. Yet we shall form burial details, and so increase employment. Some animals, indeed, may not die immediately, and so trouble us with their calling and burrowing. No matter. We shall poison them handily enough."

"You are pleased to make a jest of me, Father."

"I am pleased with nothing about you, sir."

Mr. Jones, though rarely choleric or irritable, felt he had been tried beyond patience. He stared down at the documents, which the morning breezes made flutter with an undeserved life. He gazed at the distant cool promise of the ocean, and his annoyance grew apace. No one, he believed, had ever been as tired of parental life as he was.

Just before bursting forth in wild anger, however, Mr. Jones recalled how he himself had once been horribly misjudged by his own beloved Mr. Allworthy. Unwilling to duplicate such an error, he paused, and in that moment, began to formulate a solution to both his own restlessness, and his son's.

"Now hear me," said Mr. Jones calmly. "Your plans may have some merit; at least, I may hope you propose them through no malice of heart, and that only impatience makes you phrase them so harshly.

"I believe we may, if we are careful, find some means to test your fitness to govern Paradise Hall and its possessions.

"Nay, sir, do not gloat too soon. Whatever test I design will turn upon your charity and fairness. Some third person—such as my friend Dr. James—shall judge you. If you succeed, we shall speak again of your proposals, but if you fail, then, sir, we shall reconsider your place as heir to my estate."

Hacksem, after hearing this in uncertain silence, seemed about to press for details, but Mr. Jones forestalled him with raised hand. He therefore only nodded meekly, saying, "Your will, Father, I shall never question." Stiffly gathering his precious documents, he bent down and made to kiss his father's hand. This granted, he re-fastened the binding of his papers, bowed perfunctorily, and was gone.

Behind him, the Mr. Jones who surveyed the countryside found his anger rapidly diminishing. For the first time in many years, he felt nearly at peace with himself, nearly, indeed, like old Tom again. At last he slapped a palm upon the terrace railing, glanced affectionately at the blue sky and lamb-soft clouds, and started at a marching pace back indoors to see what preparations he might make. For springtime is travelling time, and Tom Jones, with all his old impulsiveness, had decided to go adventuring again.

# IV

## Recording a More Natural Conversation

Imagine, Reader, that the lawns of Paradise Hall, light-green and long-grown, and blown by the brisk May breezes, as they were that spring morning, resembled in their billowing the waves of the seas themselves; why, then, that swift brig crossing them was none other than Tom Jones himself, who, having stopped only a moment to write a note to his friend, Dr. James, had now set ink and quill aside, and ventured out to vent his excess of spirits in brisk exercise. He carried a fowling piece, and had slung powder horn and shot pouch over his shoulder in rural fashion—and so, in truth, our metaphor might appear more just were we to compare him to a majestic man-o'-war rather than any more peaceable craft.

If so rich a figure of speech be granted (and I trust that it may be), then how are we to name that second ship, lighter of displacement and swifter of sail, which, leaving harbour in one of the estate's glass houses, now raced to intercept our hero?

This ship, or rather (to dispense with all metaphor), this second person was none other than Tom's second son, Rob Jones, a young man as fair, open and bold as his brother, Hacksem, was dark, secret and sneaking. And so it was quite natural that, seeing his father about to disappear into the nearby oaks, Rob Jones broke into a run while calling aloud to Tom.

Of that great truth that children surpass all other creatures in blending our fondest hopes with our deepest fears, this history contains no surer proof than the emotions which Rob Jones inspired in his father. Narcissus gazing into his pond was not more delighted than Tom with what he saw. Rob was a trifle slenderer than his father. His bare head rose about to the lace atop Tom's tricorn hat. Yet in color, in brightness of eye and shape of feature, they were as near alike as twins.

Alas, Rob resembled Tom in nature as much as in feature. Like his father, Rob Jones was loyal to friends, generous to a fault, and—oh, perfect weave of identical cloth!—a little prone to hastiness in love. Where a more hardened gallant might have offered his cape to keep his darling's feet out of the mud, poor Rob would never rest until he had thrown down his money and his principles as well—and so began his sorrows.

Late in November of the preceding year, new-come to the University, had Rob met the beautiful Miss Knox, a woman of pink, soft skin, sapphire eyes, and two other charms at least. Believing himself to be at Oxford for an education, he had beseeched a private interview, where he might be said to have died in ambush. That afternoon, while he innocently watched her delicate hands pouring out the tea, the blind little god had suddenly shot him more full of arrows than one of Robin Hood's straw targets. In this grievous condition, he may—though fever fogged his memory—have made some unwise promises in return for favors rendered.

However rapidly we chase after sin, punishment is certain to overtake us from behind. Miss Knox had perfectly satisfied his desires, but complications were not long in following. Rob did, it is true, avoid that particular heat in the amatory parts which requires a surgeon's care to cure. But some ten or eleven days after his bliss with Miss Knox, as he sat quietly in Wills's drinking coffee and reading a little volume of the *Rambler* essays, his light was suddenly obscured by the hulking form of a notorious Oxford bully named Danfield Whipsblood.

This Mr. Whipsblood—son, as you, Reader, probably have guessed, of the far more notorious Captain Whipsblood, of Mayfair and the House Guard Blues—was a young man of equal fortune and cruelty, who earned money tormenting country squires by insisting—as he did now—that they had betrayed the most innocent girl in the world, and must give satisfaction.

Mr. Whipsblood commanded nearly all the brawlers' arts: he knew very well how to curse, how to threaten; how to pin challenges to a door and to utter them in public places; how to tweak a nose and to slap a face. For more than a year, he and Miss Knox had shared the profits of her charms and his ferocity. But they had found a different sort of customer in Mr. Rob Jones. No sooner had Mr. Whipsblood threatened to take Rob's nose between his fingers than Rob stood and addressed his fist to that same part of Mr. Whipsblood's own anatomy. Mr. Whipsblood, who was knocked back some five or six paces until he crashed against a table, said nothing at the time (for, to speak through so much blood as gushed from his nose could only have been inelegant). Early the next morning, though, Mr. Whipsblood's second graciously called upon Rob to enquire as to his choice of weapons.

I have said that Mr. Whipsblood understood nearly all the skills of bullying. His few deficiencies were, however, noteworthy: namely, that he could neither fence nor shoot worth a fig. His (or, more properly, his father's) reputation had heretofore kept these limitations from becoming public knowledge, but Rob Jones feared no man's reputation. Accordingly, on one arctically cold morning early in January, about fifteen seconds after a queasy undergraduate had dropped the baton separating their two swords, Rob ran Mr. Whipsblood painfully through the shoulder.

Mr. Whipsblood had then turned pale, looked heavenward, dropped his sword, fallen to his knees, and sworn bitterly that Rob had done his business. Mr. Whipsblood was premature in his blasphemy, for surgeons easily dressed the wound, and he suffered no worse after-effects than to spend the following University term confined to his bed, a circumstance generally rated by his classmates a blessing, and by his tutors, little less than a miracle.

Rob's private duel, though it did not concern the courts, displeased the University, and he was—as the term is—rusticated for the remainder of that academic season. While preparing to depart Oxford temporarily, he received two disagreeable pieces of news. The first was that, as she could not abide violence, Miss Knox refused ever to see him again. The second was that young Whipsblood's father, the truly-dangerous Captain, intended shortly to call Rob out for a duel.

This second piece of news (which came as a rumour, not in a letter) inspired in poor Rob the greatest possible anguish and alarm, for he was now obliged to wait in Oxford upon the pleasure of probably the deadliest man in the realm. His suffering continued nearly three weeks, until at last the London post brought an envelope bearing the return address of Captain Desmond Whipsblood. With what a pounding heart poor Rob opened this, you, Reader, may readily imagine, but to sympathize with his subsequent disappointment will require a strong compassion for the follies of youth. Within the envelope, Rob found three or four scant lines acknowledging that young Mr. Whipsblood had apparently given the first insult, and stating that, as Rob was a mere boy,

Captain Whipsblood was disenclined to sully his hands with his blood.

Such a reprieve, had it been granted a besieged city in the Lowlands, would have occasioned the ringing of churchbells and the celebration of many a thanksgiving mass; but in foolish Rob, it inspired only a regret that he had lost so rare a chance. Never mind that this was really a chance to watch his own blood leak from his chest onto some deserted patch of ground; it was a very disappointed Rob who finally boarded the stage-coach home for Somersetshire.

Returning prodigals, whether grumbling or not, have traditionally been accorded a warmer reception than their achievements would seem to merit. So it was with Rob, whose mid-winter arrival at Paradise Hall was warmed first by the tenderness of his sister, and then gradually thereafter by the reviving affection of his father. Tom had, indeed, delivered at the outset some stern parental words upon the recklessness of youth, the value of time & etc., but as Rob had made a full confession, and was in fact one of the best-natured and most likeable fellows in the kingdom, this chill passed with the winter, and by the first of April, father and son were again on terms of perfect ease.

Now, however, the Rob sailing—or rather, running—toward his waiting father appeared upset. Since he clutched to his breast a letter, he plainly had received worrisome news. Yet Tom could conceive of no likely crisis.

Rob halted before him and asked, "Father, may I speak with you? On an urgent matter, and one of some delicacy?"

There existed no surer way to Tom's heart than simply to request his help, for he, like Allworthy before him, was more pleased to be asked for aid than to be offered it. Thinking words unnecessary, he placed a hand upon Rob's shoulder, and nodded encouragement.

Instead of addressing the matter directly, Rob blushed and whispered that he would prefer some more private place to speak. They therefore walked on silently until they had entered the nearest path coursing through the grove, and had found a quiet and secluded bench where, sheltered from the bright sun, Rob might confess his difficulties.

At last, uneasily, he began, "You will remember, Father, a certain Miss Knox of Oxford?"

"Who? Oh, she of the golden ringlets. The darling miss you wrote about. Something returns to me. She . . . wait, you wrote that she . . . how did it go?—that she 'walks not upon the ground, but upon shining cl . . .' "

If there is a more certain way to embarrass a young person than that Tom had now undertaken, no great author records it. A discomfitted Rob interrupted hurriedly, "Father, I have had a letter from Miss Knox. She says that she—that we—in short, a child is due."

"You owe someone an infant?"

"Father, please! Miss Knox has lain upon me obligations of the gravest sort, and . . ."

Tom considered and dismissed several jests concerning where exactly Miss Knox had lain. A little annoyed to have his pleasant mood disrupted by new troubles, yet understanding the seriousness of the situation, he responded, "Well then, sir, let us be solemn. Do you come to tell me your wedding plans, or do you not?"

Tom's directness inspired, not a matching frankness, but a flood of stammers and flushes. Only after several moments' utter confusion did Rob manage, "Miss Knox is a charming girl, and I am desperately fond of her, sir, but as for marriage—"

"As for marriage, sir, it is an holy estate, and not lightly to be entered into?"

"Exactly, sir."

"I begin to see." Tom assumed his gravest manner; and none of it was acting, as he was of a heart tender enough to sympathize with the difficulties Rob had created for this young Miss Knox.

"Lookee, sir, have you any reason to doubt you are the father of this alleged child?"

"In truth, Father, Miss Knox is warm-blooded, and may have had many other suitors."

"Many suitors. And yet she positively charges you?"

"Her letter is a little ambiguous."

"But you owe her something, you feel."

Hanging his head as low as his breeches, Rob answered quietly, "Aye, sir. Her—and the babe."

For a moment, thinking perhaps of his own unlucky birth and abandonment, Tom was touched, and a sigh escaped him. "Indeed, Rob, no blame—and no undeserved misery—must come upon the infant." More firmly, he continued, "Well, sir, this is a costly little caper of yours. Yet we shall see what may be done."

---

So strong was the bond between these two, and so brilliant was Tom's record of benevolence, that no firmer assurance was needed. Rob seized his father's hand and kissed it fervently, declaring him the noblest of parents.

Now that the crisis had passed, Tom felt himself correct in administering a few words of stern council; and indeed, any wise man would have done as much, so that Rob might understand he had been rescued out of love, and not invited to further wickedness; and that his father might pity what he never would condone.

Therefore, Squire Jones squared his broad shoulders and pointed a finger directly at his son's nose. "But mark ye, sir. You have begun down a dangerous road. Turn back before destruction."

"Indeed, sir, I have been foolish."

"Foolishness, sir, and wickedness, are two entirely separate matters. A wicked man will blur the distinction, and a foolish man will not see it. Much better for you to keep them separate. And pray do not pretend that you were seduced. We only seduce ourselves."

"I simply meant, Father, that I had been foolish in my precautions. A simple, ordinary French sheath might have made all apologies redundant."

Perhaps poor Rob meant merely to recover some of his damaged pride by showing himself a man of the world. Yet he could have chosen no worse way to proceed, for he seemed to make all Tom's kindness nothing, and all his preaching less than that.

With some restraint did Tom manage to keep his voice level. "How is that? Will you hide your wickedness behind a French contraption? Ye heavens, I had imagined a simple youthful error, not a hardened corruption. Tell me no more of your contraptions, sir; indeed, do not speak to me again until it is to tell me of your repentance. *French* contraptions! If you will pull the trigger with your ramrod in the barrel, you must accept what follows, and there's an end on it."

Now certainly contrite, poor Rob struggled to reply, but was silenced.

"Nay, sir, no more just now. Next time, shoot your whore and marry her lover; we'll have less expense and no more shame; and as for the sin of it, well, all's one. Now, good-day."

Tom's passion had betrayed him into a manner of speech better suited to his own late, hot-tempered father-in-law, Squire Western. Even as he spoke, he hoped Rob knew how hollow his anger was; indeed, ashamed, he was already contemplating some softening words.

But suddenly both he and Rob were startled by a loud rustling in the thick hedge of shrubbery behind them. It was the movement of a body, not a wind, and too large and bold to be a squirrel or even a deer. To discover what it was in fact, requires the space and license of yet another chapter. Do you, therefore, Reader, go ahead one chapter, and I shall join you presently.

# V

## Of an Embarrassment, and of the Nature of the Beautiful

The crashing through the underbrush which had so startled Tom and Rob now revealed a sight entirely as embarrassing as the earlier noise had been alarming.

For, just as certain Greek authors of doubtful authority tell us that the martial goddess Athena sprang full-formed from the forehead of Zeus, so now did the near-goddess of our story crash full-formed (Reader, I do not deceive thee) from the *Hydrangea quercifolia* of Mr. Jones's hedge.

It hath often been observed that wise persons speak always as though before a public audience; and that, doing so, they need never fear being overheard. Had Tom been fortunate enough to heed this injunction, his ears at this moment might have blazed less redly, for he now observed, trailing twigs and not clouds of glory, the unlooked-for appearance of his lovely daughter, the peerless Miss Amelia Jones.

Reader, thou must have sometime or another heard that commonplace about woman's beauty, that "she is never lovelier than when angry." The origins of this expression must, I think, remain obscure. Certainly, there is a kind of nobility in some righteous anger, but that seems little to the point: few ever speak of the beauty of Brutus when he assassinated Caesar. More apt critics of things feminine (or rather, of language) have claimed to see some connection with the wild beauty of angry nature, with thunderstorms and with high waves crashing upon mighty boulders.

Such reasonings appear to me forceful precisely in that degree that a woman resembles a vapor or a rock; that is to say, not at all. As a woman is in fact a human being, and as human beings are unhappy when they are angry, we mean nothing else by saying "she is beautiful when she is angry" than that we enjoy her unhappiness. Idle cruelty has no place in our narrative; accordingly, let us say of Miss Jones at her first appearance here that she was beautiful *and* angry, or that she was beautiful *despite* being angry—or anything else you may please, Reader, so long as it implies no automatic connection between anger and beauty.

For certainly Miss Jones was beautiful. Reader, restrain me, lest I wax poetical!—yet surely all I shall say of Miss Jones shall be strict fact, such as may be offered for evidence in any court of the land. Miss Jones, then, reached the upper limits of middle height, standing about five feet, six inches tall. Her hair was very blond, her eyes were very blue. She possessed a womanly figure, full, red lips, and a nose which was small and regular. She moved gracefully, but without those artificial restraints French dancing masters teach; and there was, as her willingness to penetrate hedges attests, something of the Jones recklessness about her.

Equally certainly, she was angry. With two quick strides she advanced to confront her brother and, especially, her father. All her usual gentleness had departed her. Her features were flushed, her hands were clenched. Pausing only to pluck a stray twig from her hair and to cast it irritatedly at her father's feet, she began as follows:

"So, sir! This is how you conduct yourself in private. This is your conversation of virtue and propriety—this your high regard for the role and rights of woman. That ever I should hear my own father voice such *low* thoughts!

"Are we then so little to thee, Father? Are we troublesome problems, infinitely less valuable than the children we bear?—are we simply recreational expenses, as, '*Item*, one pair tickets Covent Garden, eleven shillings; *item*, one woman, made with child through neglect of precautions, fourteen pounds, annual payment?' "

Since, with anger as with the steam engines of Messrs. Watt and Boulton, the greater the heat, the greater the speed, Amelia now approached a vast velocity of just condemnation. In reply, her father only expostulated once or twice, pleading softly, "Amelia . . ." Such mildness (which, to be sure, any classical orator would have scorned) achieved almost nothing, except that Miss Jones gradually shifted her attention from father to brother. So effectively did she recite to Rob his own remarks of some few minutes earlier, and so cuttingly did she analyze, annotate, and correct them that he passed the latter part of her discourse firmly convinced that he would rather have endured an equivalent number of whip lashes than any more sentences from her.

Poor Rob, indeed! For years, he had held himself up to his dear sister as a model of propriety. Partly from vanity, but mostly from true concern, he had wished for her sake to be better than he—or any young man of spirit—was ever likely to be. Until he had left for Oxford, his speech, his reading, even—so far as he could control it—his private life, had all been given over to virtue. This, indeed, much resembled dressing a bear in a silk gown; but, though impossible, it had been well meant. Now, revealed as mortal, he felt a shame almost unbearable.

Amelia was not naturally harsh; and when, after eight or nine minutes of uninterrupted condemnation, she believed her point to have been made, she softened her tone, and seemed ready to admit replies. But suddenly, one last irritation occurred to her—and though she spoke again to Rob, her words seemed mostly to strike her father.

"Worst of all, sir, you have wasted a University education for which many would have willingly begged upon hand and knee."

Here indeed was one—perhaps the only—long-standing trouble between Tom and Amelia. Tom, in bold disregard of the wishes of his friends and neighbors, had let Amelia, as a child, enjoy precisely the same lessons in Greek, Latin, and Mathematics as had her brothers. If, as a result, she had garnered more facts than Rob, and better principles than Hacksem, her education still brought as much sorrow to her as ridicule to Tom; for the gates of Oxford, which had swung wide for her two brothers in turn, had remained eternally locked against Miss Amelia Jones.

More than once had Tom heard angry words on the topic of her disappointment; yet never once—to his credit—did he regret, even secretly, having given her what education he might. If his punishment had been the sly laughter of his neighbours, his reward had been a companion of sense and intelligence, and a daughter he could trust.

Yet now the old awkward topic had been raised again, and in a context tending greatly to his discredit. While Rob had endured his time under fire, Tom had reconsidered what Miss Amelia had said of himself; and, while granting that free discourse glorified a family circle, he now wished to see a due respect for persons—and his own person in particular—preserved.

Before brother and sister could properly engage upon the field of *education,* therefore, Tom thought fit to draw off Miss Amelia's charge. Raising an admonitory finger, he said firmly, "Daughter, have a care before you speak too freely of the morals of others. What are we to think of a young person who hides within bushes, spies, and eavesdrops? Are we to think her a proper candidate for education, or rather a miscreant and a plotter?"

Believing himself solidly in the right, Tom had expressed himself with great emphasis. Miss Amelia, however, was ever eager in her own defense; like fair *Grimalkin,* she could absorb hard blows, land squarely upon her feet, and return unto the fray. Accordingly did she pause but a moment to formulate her reply.

Her eloquence, alas, was long deferred, for even as her lovely mouth opened in response, a single plump raindrop, having woven its way through the canopy of leaves above, plopped wetly upon the upheld paternal finger of Mr. Jones. Only then did the three notice what they had too long neglected; namely that, while they had argued with natural fervor, nature had herself turned angry. The ordinary shade of the grove had been darkened into positive gloom by the arrival, unseen, of black rain clouds; and now those clouds were discharging upon our three the full measure of their woeful burden. The winds blew up, the thunder cracked, and torrents of water battered against the trees and then dripped down impartially on Tom, and Rob and Amelia.

When the nation is attacked, all internal dissent is suspended, and politicians who yesterday were at the point of blows now link their arms and stand united against the common enemy. So now amid the downpour did our three heroes—who were indeed infinitely nearer in heart and mind than any rascally set of politicians ever to live—instantly abandon their dispute and, helping each other to rise and to run, begin a hasty charge for the shelter of Paradise Hall.

They ran across the wide lawns, which so wisely bowed before the biting wind and slashing rain; they pulled each other up when they fell; and so, for all that wind and rain and mud could do, they made a good —and, methinks, laughing—progress towards their home.

And we, Reader, shall allow them to make such shelter there as they deserve, and not join them again until, warmed and newly-clothed, they may make a better reception of the guests bidden to Tom's birthday celebration. Meanwhile, let us pause briefly to consider (and to illustrate for the benefit of all critics) the many literary beauties herein contained. I mean particularly the use of metaphor, especially the comparison between anger and a storm, by which—as you will recall—we first introduced the usually-amiable Amelia, and which, with great economy, did so artfully foreshadow the morning's coming weather. By such excellencies are true works of Art distinguished.

And so, Reader, must you be ever-alert for such craftsmanship, for there exist within this story many meaning things which appear at first merely words. Metaphors are meaningful; storms are meaningful; and as for our three heroes' abandoning their quarrel in the face of common need, why, who knows? Even that, too, may have its small significance.

# VI

## *Upon Households, Friends and Celebrations*

About seven that evening, when the setting sun's light had turned golden and shaded, there appeared before the Jones manor the single carriage bearing Tom's birthday dinner guests.

As Tom Jones was now a man of very great wealth, it may safely be assumed that the circle of his acquaintance was extremely large; for the identical reason, it may be assumed that the number of his true friends was extremely small. Accordingly, the party arranged to celebrate with him his forty-fourth birthday numbered only seven: besides his immediate family, there were his old friends the Jameses, and a young man in whose career Tom had long taken an interest. This young man was a cleric to whom Tom had not long before awarded a living in his preferment. His name was Adams.

The name of Adams in connection with the clergy must strike a familiar note to all readers of our earlier histories; and this young gentleman was in truth none other than Hezekiah Adams, eldest son and heir to the late, ever-lamented Mr. Abraham Adams, who, besides his many other services to the peace and religion of Somersetshire, had at last become both friend and advisor to Mr. Allworthy.*

From his father, young Mr. Adams had inherited an ox's strength, a lion's heart, an eagle's eye, an owl's wisdom, a pauper's fortune, and a child's knowledge of the greater world. He resembled his father in nearly everything, but especially in learning and in courage, and for that, and for his father's sake, Tom had gladly helped him through the University, and into the nearby parsonage. Of Mr. Adams's simplicity and unsuitability for modern life, we need give no other example than that he had, these past two years, repaid Tom's generosity with nothing but loyalty and kindness.

The two persons riding beside Mr. Adams (and, indeed, nearly crowded from their seats by him, for all that they appeared not to mind), were Dr. and Mrs. Richard James. Dr. James had, I believe, acquired in his youth a modest fortune by the practice of *physick*, but, having concluded that much of his practice resembled armed robbery (for he extracted money from persons in fear of their lives), he had retired in his early middle age to Somersetshire. There he had undertaken farming with a success which enabled him to live quietly as a gentleman. He had married, too, a very good, sensible woman, of whom, more later.

These three, then, made up the party guests; and they were met upon the portico without ceremony by their hosts, Tom, Rob and Amelia—for Hacksem had sent word he would join them presently. These six were all unfeigned and unaffected friends, and they walked into the house all chatting together happily.

Paradise Hall, noble specimen of the *Gothick* style that it was (and is), contained few of those modern devices for the regulation of temperatures, and was, in short, a windy old pile. The dining room, however, largely overcame this by reason of its two fireplaces, upon which, for several hours now, generous fires had burned, so that hearth and room pleasantly drove off the growing chill of the evening. These fires, moreover, emitted a light considerably more charming than that of the chandeliers just lit; and so Amelia had ordered short candles, which would burn themselves out about as the meal ended. Amelia had also ordered a meal served in the French style: six separate courses, of which the first—the soup, a fiery

*Those readers wishing the entire story of this epic clergyman will be well advised to acquire our earlier work, *The History of Joseph Andrews*, wherein they shall find it told with glorious detail.

---

33

mulligatawny—appeared as soon as Tom's health had been drunk the second time.

Simultaneously with the tureen came Hacksem Jones, slight of figure, mincing of manner, who wished his father a happy birthday in a fashion appearing coldly to correct the rest of the company. Notwithstanding this, the others kindly welcomed him, and the conversation soon became again genial and, indeed, so innocent that only two matters deserve mention here.

The first was a strange clumsiness about Mr. Adams, who, though generally accounted a most athletic gentleman, managed during the first three covers to spill half a bowl of soup in his lap, tip over his wine glass, and (by too great a downward pressure of his knife) launch half a toasted almond onto his neighbour's, Amelia's, plate. Amelia's solicitousness seemed only to worsen his confusion; for certainly when, on two occasions, she brushed his arm reassuringly, his face turned as red as an apple.

Mr. Adams's curious behaviour apparently went unnoticed by the others, but the second event could not be ignored. Hacksem Jones, after some minutes of seeming to enter the spirit of the conversation, attempted suddenly to lure Dr. James into his argument with his father.

"Do you not think, Doctor, that we shall have excellent chances of profit by manufacture here in Somersetshire?"

At this, Tom, colouring, gripped his knife and fork more tightly, but said nothing; Dr. James, who understood how he was being used, answered non-committally: "That's not a matter I've studied, Hacksem."

"But surely, sir," Hacksem persisted, "a man of your ability must have an opinion upon the matter."

As few of us savour admitting we are devoid of opinions, Dr. James was obliged to answer grudgingly, "There may, I suppose, be prospects, but not for years to come."

"You sound like my father, sir. But surely we have immediate prospects for the manufacture of weaponry? Is war not likely soon—with either the French or the Americans? Both are insolent peoples, and both are violent."

"Come, sir. Another topic, if you please," begged Dr. James.

To which, Mr. Adams added, "It is not Christian, Hacksem, to anticipate gain from the shedding of blood."

Hacksem drained the remainder of his claret; then shook his head emphatically. "While it might indeed be thought un-Christian to encourage men to fight, it is simply imprudent not to profit once they have chosen to do so. If the Americans provoke us, then it is both our duty, and our great opportunity, to help our countrymen punish them."

"The Americans are our countrymen, sir," replied Mr. Adams, who though assuredly no great political authority, began disliking immensely the blood-thirsty drift of this talk.

Hacksem Jones smiled unpleasantly. "Be good enough, Mr. Adams, to confine yourself to those few matters you understand."

"I meant no offense, Hacksem."

"You cannot avoid it, sir. And do not sit so close to my sister."

Suddenly Dr. James, who had attempted manfully to endure this discourse, roared out, "Be still, sir! Your language is impertinent, and your ideas are shameful. Remember the occasion!"

At such a challenge, another man might have thrown a goblet at Dr. James's head, or called him out to a duel, or—if he were a very good man —admitted his error and begged pardon of the company. But Mr. Hacksem Jones, rodent-like in his behavior as in his features, was more inclined, when challenged, to hiss and then withdraw until a better opportunity appeared.

"Oh, Doctor, I shall indeed remember this occasion. Thank you for your kind words. Mr. Adams, thank you for your geographical wisdom; Father, thank you particularly for defending me. A very happy birthday. Good-night to you all."

Mr. Hacksem Jones's outbursts were so common as to be generally ignored; in this instance they troubled the assemblage no more than would the howling of a distant wolf trouble travelers safe and snug within an inn. Indeed, just as the door at one end of the room slammed behind Mr. Hacksem, the door at the other end opened quietly, to admit Grimes carrying an oversized platter of smoking meat. At the sight of this, Mrs. James said happily, "Ah, the roast beef." Hearing these cheerful words, the others perked up immediately, and muttered together something which sounded greatly like, "Huzzah."

And so, with much burgundy and growing mirth, the dinner drew near its close. Just as that point was reached, however, when the ladies ought to have withdrawn while the gentlemen smoked and reflected, Tom instead asked Dr. and Mrs. James to join him privately in the library.

The conversation survived their departure, for the three young persons turned immediately to topics they liked better. Amelia in particular began upon the charms of Mr. Charles James, the absent son of the Jameses, from whom she had just had a witty, high-spirited letter.

Amelia's discourse raised polite interest in her brother, but more complex feelings in Mr. Adams, who loved to sit near the woman he worshipped but hated to hear her warmly praising his rival.

(Reader, no doubt I have stunned thee in revealing this great secret of Mr. Adams's heart, by which his former strange clumsiness is entirely explained. Pray, do not thank me—for, if penetration be the first duty of an author, generosity is the second, and I account it my pleasure to keep thee perfectly informed.)

Poor Adams! Not in his wildest dreams could he imagine himself wealthy enough to claim Amelia's hand. Since, moreover, Charles James was his friend, as well as an extremely likeable fellow, he was denied even that relief of spiteful thoughts. Indeed, for more than a year now the good parson had played the manly part, boosting his friend at every chance in the estimation of the woman he loved.

Surely, Reader, there is much to be admired in this portrait of mild loyalty and friendship. Yet must we now follow the custom of the world, and leave impoverished merit to make its own way as best it can, while we step into the next room to record the more striking conversation of Tom and his two friends.

---

# VII

## In Which Mr. Jones Speaks Frankly

---

When his friends were comfortably seated before him, Tom opened his topic with a directness which staggered them.

"Dr. James—Mrs. James—you know I have not been particularly happy these past six years."

Dr. and Mrs. James exchanged glances, but said nothing.

"Another man in my position," continued Tom, "might pretty easily have gone, with explanation or apology, to live in London, to indulge himself as he pleased—you know it is common enough policy."

To this, they both nodded.

"As best I could, however, I have stayed at home to fulfill my obligations—until now. Now my children—except perhaps Amelia—are grown, and I would like to be off."

"Off to do what?" asked Dr. James mildly.

Tom now looked very uncertain. "Something in government, I think. Hacksem is right about one thing: weakness with the Americans is leading us into disaster. We require a firm hand there.

"I've done well enough in Parliament, and believe I may claim a post in the colonial administration. I thank Heaven, our government is not yet so overwhelmed with place-seekers that a gentleman may not serve his King with credit. If nothing else offers, I may seek a diplomatic post upon the Continent."

This awkward self-appraisal ended, Tom continued more forcefully. "And yet I would never depart without leaving my lands and family perfectly secure. And so I would ask a favor of each of you.

"First of you, Richard. Hacksem's plans for this estate have lately grown both unreasonable and cold-hearted. He is a young man of great parts, but possesses neither judgement nor compassion. Until he learns those, I fear he is unworthy of trust.

"Will you, therefore, help to supervise Hacksem in my absence, for a period not to exceed three years? I could grant you legal authority over the estate as my trustee. Hacksem would manage the day-to-day details, with assistance from Mr. Sinamore, my present steward. But you would have the ultimate authority to suppress any of my son's more rabid schemes."

At this, Dr. James blushed, and apologized for his earlier correction of the young man.

"You were entirely right, Richard; and I, rather, ought to apologize to you," replied Tom.

Dr. James spread his hands, and bowed depreciatingly. "Say nothing of that, Tom; and as for the rest, well, though I think you overestimate me, yes, of course I shall help."

"Thank you, Richard, and now, madam, my request of you. Will you take Amelia into your house, to look after and guide her?"

Mrs. James was not quite so hasty to answer as her husband had been.

———

These two, indeed, offered several contrasts: both were above sixty years of age, and silver-haired, but where her husband was short, plump and lively, Mrs. James was tall, remarkably thin and so studied in her movements as to seem often only a marble recollection of herself.

Yet Mrs. James—though she lacked her husband's volubility—was entirely as warm-hearted and responsive. Having considered, she answered, "Sir, we have never had anything but pleasure from Amelia's company, and would be happy to have her with us as long as may be.

"But will not some awkwardness arise when our Charles returns from Cambridge? He is, after all, a trifle reckless; and he and Amelia have been noticeably fond of each other these past few years. Who knows what may develop? *We* may think well of them, but people will talk. Understand me: for my part, she is heartily welcome, yet . . ."

Through the afternoon and evening, Tom's desire to be upon the road had swelled almost to a mania; now he felt little inclination to debate. As, moreover, he had fair confidence in Charles James, and pure faith in Amelia, he chose to dismiss all doubts.

"In truth, madam, people will talk however we conduct ourselves; about so innocent an arrangement as we propose they can say nothing of concern to us, or even of interest to themselves. Therefore, my dear Stella, if you are willing except for that one worry—"

Mrs. James nodded her head.

"—then I thankfully accept your offer."

And so Tom disposed of what he considered his only obstacles. To abandon so rich an estate might have worried another man far more, but Tom was of a sanguine, cheerful nature; and persons so constituted always imagine the world a mirror, or rather a companion, ever anxious to return their smiles.

By this time, the prettily-twirling gilt clock which Sophia had brought from France years before had completed its twelfth chiming, and Tom's forty-fourth birthday had passed. Dr. James yawned good-naturedly and said it was time he was abed. At once, Tom got to his feet.

"Please, friends, speak of this to no one, except perhaps Mr. Adams. Doctor, you surely consider me mad as a hatter for wishing to go adventuring at my age?"

"Not at all, Tom," replied he, adding, with a complacent smile at his wife, "Were I twenty years younger, and single, I'd sell Meadowlands and go with you."

. . .

In the dining-room, meanwhile, the candles of the chandelier had all burnt down, and Rob, Amelia and Mr. Adams had moved their chairs into a semi-circle before one of the two fires, to continue conversing very happily. Amelia, after some twenty or thirty minutes of steady encomiums, had pretty well exhausted the charms of Mr. Charles James, and had allowed the conversation to drift easily towards other, more generally-genial topics.

These three young people, then, recognizing by the return of their elders that the party was ending, all stood. Tom rang the bell, and a few minutes later Grimes—who had evidently been sleeping soundly in the kitchen—appeared carrying a tray full of glasses brimming with hot rum punch.

When they had toasted out the evening, Rob and Amelia excused themselves, and Tom walked out with his three guests. Their approaching departure brought upon him a melancholy feeling, as he considered how many good things he must soon leave; and this mood persisted at least until the brisk air of the out-of-doors assaulted him.

The night sky, dark but very starry, looked suddenly an ideal backdrop for lively encounters. Yet such was Tom's affection for the Jameses that he withdrew his thoughts from all heroic topics, and took the good doctor by the hand.

"You know, sir, how extensive is my gratitude to you. Whatever contract we may draw will, I promise, be fair unto your labors, but for your kindness, I can make 'no thanks but thanks,' as the poet says. I . . ."

Here, lost for words, Tom might have hung sadly, but that Dr. James assured him that he would look faithfully after his interests; and that if he could ever render any other service, Tom had only to ask.

Before Tom could respond, Mrs. James stepped forward to hold his face in her hands, and then to kiss him lightly upon the cheek. "Goodnight, Tom. We shall always be your friends."

These gentle professions sent Mr. Adams (who understood not a syllable of their specific meanings) into raptures. The moment Mrs. James stepped aside, he seized Tom's hand, and, tears forming in his eyes, declared that he would have gladly walked fifty miles to see such loyalty displayed. Only reluctantly then—scattering appreciative phrases thickly about him—did he raise himself up to take the reins of his carriage.

A minute later, with Dr. and Mrs. James seated beside him, ever waving farewell, he was gone, and Tom stood alone beneath that velvet sky. He watched the carriage until it was a scarcely-darker smudge against the dark grounds; then, with a shrug and a sigh, went in to his rest, or rather, to his bed.

Aboard his carriage, meanwhile, Mr. Adams was filling the night—and his listeners' ears—with a splendid oration upon friendship. As his speech lacked nothing of learning, eloquence, or flattery to themselves, the Jameses permitted him to continue some time before explaining to him what Tom really intended. This news he heard with amazement, and then accepted with silence: though he once or twice thereafter opened his mouth, he formed not a single word until he bid them good-night outside their home.

When, at last, they had crossed their own threshold, Dr. James whispered sadly to his wife that Tom had been half-mad ever since Sophia's death. This Mrs. James seconded, adding kindly but decisively that no creature so weak as man ever could live sanely without a woman's guidance.

# VIII

## Of the Sadness of Departures, and of
## One Departure in Particular

Of the many ways in which human beings protect their feelings from injury, none is so often employed as *denial.* It did not happen, it is not happening, it will not happen; all these convenient phrases we habitually throw up as barricades between ourselves and that sorrowful thing which is the world. Yet as these phrases—like most other barricades—serve more often to obscure our view than to protect our safety, wise persons will, so often as they are able, endeavor to tear them down, to look about themselves, and to find whatever course of action will most nearly correct that situation they dread.

This particular brand of wisdom, if no other, was widespread within the Jones family, and thus it was that, the very next morning, as Rob and

Amelia breakfasted with him upon the terrace, Tom found the scheme he most cherished for himself already adopted by his son.

For while Tom spread jam upon his toast, Rob announced quite forcefully, "Father, I have considered our talk of yesterday, and tried—if I may say as much—to anticipate those talks we are likely to have in days coming.

"I'm a younger son, and the world expects that I make my own way. I would never speak ill of Hacksem; yet he and I . . . never like each other so well as when we are far apart. Well, Paradise Hall is to be his, and so I must be the one to travel, and to seek my fortune elsewhere."

Hearing only firmness, without a trace of bitterness, Tom and Amelia said nothing.

"Above all, Father," Rob continued, "I care for no learned profession. We have spoken, indeed, of the law, but I promise you that I would rather appear at Newgate with a noose about my neck than a powdered wig upon my head. None of the other academic callings has any greater appeal. Amelia, you have had occasion to envy my education; believe me that I heartily wish you might have had it in my place, for I have hated every moment of it."

To say that either Tom or Amelia was much amazed at this would be, in the words of Dr. Swift, to "say the thing that is not." For some minutes, though, these three only looked at one another wordlessly, until at last Tom ventured to ask, "What plans have you made, Rob?"

"Indeed, sir, though I blush to mention it, my plans shall depend greatly upon your generosity.

"I have, as you know, some debts, of about three hundred pounds' value, as yet unsettled in Oxford and in London. Those I mean to settle, either by your help, or by my own labours, before I leave England—"

At Rob's mention of departure, both Tom and Amelia grew several shades paler; not appearing to notice, Rob went on almost instantly.

"—for Ireland or perhaps America. India and the Sugar Islands I have ruled out as unsuited to my temper."

"And you will make your way there, I suppose, by seeking an officer's commission?"

"That was my plan."

"Then you found so much to enjoy in wounding Mr. Whipsblood?" Tom asked.

A little agitatedly, Rob answered, "I found nothing to enjoy in it, sir. Yet my choices do not appear numerous; and as for that, there are officers aplenty in London who do no more fighting than a *debutante.*"

"How think you that peaceful life will hold once we have war with the Americans?"

"I think that war most unlikely."

"Do you, sir?"

"Indeed, I think it the most unlikely thing in the world; yet, should it come about, I expect I shall defend my King and country as well as any other man."

To this, of course, Tom could make no reply, and so he let it pass. Upon first thought, he could discover no suggestion to offer which, in that final test of advice, he would be willing to take himself. At length, however, one possibility did occur to him.

"Have you not considered, Rob, that we might purchase for you some small estate—of perhaps five hundred pounds a year—in some distant, yet genial, part of the kingdom? You are young. By careful management, you might make it in a few years' time into a considerable fortune; yet the gift is not so great as to enflame your brother's envy. Surely this might serve?"

Rob looked down, abashed, and perhaps a tear or so stood in his eyes. Yet he answered resolutely a moment later, "It may be, Father, that in a year or so I shall have cause to regret my declining, or even to return home and beg the repetition of your offer; but for now, I am resolved to go."

Tom—having time to consult none but his own heart—answered him generously.

"Lookee, sir, I'll do nothing irrevocable with my own children. You shall have instructions to my bankers to settle your outstanding debts, including what is owed your unborn child; you shall have two hundred pounds in ready money; and you shall have my assistance, if you finally decide to purchase your commission. If, after a year's trial, you are content with a military life, you shall have an allowance made you; if not, then we shall speak again of small estates."

Before Rob could throw himself at his father's feet, Tom halted him, saying firmly, "Nay, sir, conclude your breakfast."

Amelia, who might have once or twice cherished—for such is the foolishness of woman's heart—some vague designs for adventure in her own life, had thus far said not a word. Now, however, wishing to see sentiment replaced by other, less oppressive topics, she tried to raise happier prospects.

"You will not, I suppose, Rob, be leaving before mid-summer?"

Greatly perplexed, Rob replied awkwardly, "I had hoped to go this morning."

"This morning!" exclaimed Tom, nearly trembling with dismay.

"Or, if that is inconvenient, Father, then this afternoon."

"Afternoon?" Tom echoed weakly, for confusion had entirely overwhelmed him.

"My valise has been packed since early this morning. Grimes helped me. Quite eagerly, I must say."

Tom groaned; Amelia sighed.

Some wise man or woman—I forget which—hath observed that each joy is unique, but all sorrows are alike. So, Reader, if ever thou hast lost a wager upon a horse, or missed a meal thou hast specially anticipated, or been denied entrance to some popular play, then wilt thou understand the pains of despair then penetrating Tom and Amelia.

For some long while, accordingly, those three made no sound louder than their breathing, while from nearby mulberries, the birds mocked them with joyous song. Finally, Rob, who had meant to do cleanly what he dreaded to do at all, rose, set his napkin upon the table, and went hurriedly indoors. Amelia followed some moments later; and lastly Tom, discovering his appetite had been replaced with a sort of numbness, stood and walked after them.

Agreeing with that famous Scots gentleman that, "If it were done . . . then 'twere well it were done quickly," and wishing that Rob, if he must travel, might travel while the weather held fine, Tom strode directly to his writing desk. An hour's labour produced all the needed bankers' drafts and instructions, plus two letters of introduction to gentlemen of sound situation in London, gentlemen not only of means but of steady judgement, upon whose advice Rob might safely rely. That done, Tom took candle and sealing wax, and set his mark upon the envelopes. The sunlight fell most warmly through the eastern windows as he finished; he stood there a moment steadying himself, then went to find his son.

Rob, meanwhile, had spent his hour in farewell to all in house and stable. Not a young man in the county was better liked than he. The serving girls cried, and the stable boys wished him well. Grimes gave him only a cool shake of the hand, but Grimes was Hacksem's man; that was generally known, though the price of his procurement remained uncertain.

Mrs. Limeslices cried most loudly of all, and amid her tears warned Rob sternly against the wiles of London hussies. This Mrs. Limeslices had been Amelia's, and then Rob's, nursemaid, and was desperately fond of them both. She was a short, round, white-haired old woman, who bore a strange resemblance to fluff. Being very prone to express her emotions loudly at their first occurrence, she was generally as little regarded as lint —tho' it may be, I suppose, that persons who so dismissed her did a little underestimate her capabilities.

When the hour had ended, Tom and Rob met a final time before the great drive of Paradise Hall, and waited without speaking as Highboy, the misnamed little groom, led Rob's bay mare from the stables. Rob, unassisted, slung and fastened the heavy leather saddle-bags, and then turned to receive from his father the oilskin pouch holding his precious papers. These he locked carefully into the saddle-bags; as he turned again, Tom pressed into his hands first a sheaf of Bank of England notes, and then a bag of guineas of above two pounds' weight. Rob, struck by this generosity as if by lightning, seemed about to stammer his gratitude when Tom clasped arms upon his shoulders and hugged him near. "The world grows daily more costly, and more dangerous, sir. I've provided for your expenses; do you look likewise to your safety. Give no insult, and refuse no kindness, and you will do well enough.

"Now go, sir. Wax or wane, you will always find a home here."

"Good-bye, Father."

Rob had placed one foot into the stirrup, when the great door flew open, and Amelia ran towards them both. She appeared to smile most willingly, and as for any redness about her eyes, well, it was springtime then—let us attribute it to the hay-fever.

When she had kissed his cheek, and hugged him, she sought for words to say. But as nothing occurred to her except to assure him that she did not really envy him his education, and as she knew that would be redundant, she only whispered, "Good-bye, brother. You cannot write too soon, or too often."

Rob answered that he would be as frequent a correspondent as was in his power; then, a little clumsily, he held his sword to his side and mounted the horse, which Highboy still patiently held. He called, rather wistfully, "Good-bye!" to no one in particular, and began at a near-gallop down the drive, and towards the lane which would lead him to the London road. He travelled swiftly, and they behind could watch him only a minute or two before he disappeared into the trees.

Well may you imagine, Reader, the tender feelings of those left behind. They had lost friend, companion and kinsman; and though they knew it might be best for him, such is the perversity of human nature, that—however much we love—we never believe that another's gain quite matches our own loss.

# IX

## *Of Still Another Hasty Resolution*

Not since those sad days when first he mourned the passing of his Sophia had Tom spent so doleful a time as that morning of Rob's departure. The warm sun, the gentle winds, seemed made to torment him. He was not malicious enough to wish nature as unhappy as he; yet he greatly resented a beauty so indifferent to his own unhappiness.

Sorrow, we are often told, may form the mold in which our boldest plans are cast. Whether this mighty profundity or some other acted upon Tom, about two o'clock that afternoon, having grown tired of his library, he took up his walking stick and started for the headwaters of that cool stream which flowed through his summer-hot estate.

He had no sooner finished his climb, and found a shady seat, than, with a great rush of spirits, he began to recall that no universal law reserved the Miss Knoxes of this world exclusively to *young* men. This inspiration, tho' perhaps it does no great honour to our hero's reputation for perfect morality (assuming he ever had such a reputation), was, I believe, perfectly natural—and we shall never deny thee, Reader, any portrait drawn from nature.

Tom, therefore, had scarcely seated himself upon a mossy stone beside his mountain spring when, forgetting all his former melancholy, he leaped to his feet, swept up his walking stick, and began back down the hill at a break-neck pace.

He did not cease running until he had whipt across the threshold of Paradise Hall, while shouting for Grimes to bring his pistol and riding coat.

Tom's riotous cries immediately drew, all aflutter, Mrs. Limeslices, who clapped her hands together and roared piteously, "Oh, sir, I have feared as much. Mr. Rob is dead upon the road! Robbers have had him!"

"My son, Mrs. Limeslices," Tom answered in some amazement, "is now about twenty miles down the London road, in perfect health, or he is nowhere at all. Compose yourself, madam."

"La, sir," said Mrs. Limeslices (who, indeed, dried her eyes at once, though she looked back at Tom most aggrievedly), "you must take the blame upon yourself, if you will be raising the household with such terrorous shouts of ruination."

Seeing Grimes coming toward him with cloak in hand, Tom only replied meekly, "Your criticism is just, madam, and I am sorry. Grimes, tell my daughter I am going out. I shall be in Domney, and then, perhaps, shall visit Mr. Adams. I regret that I may not return home until late."

"Very good, sir."

At the threshold, Tom halted, turned back, and said hastily to Mrs. Limeslices, "Madam, I apologize." To this, Mrs. Limeslices replied with a sniff, a curtsey and (after Tom was out of sight) a well-deserved, "Marry, come up—some people, indeed!"

By the time Mrs. Limeslices had recovered her composure (with the help, it is true, of half a glass of Tom's best sherry), Tom himself was covering the still-muddy Domney road at a lively pace, and letting the thud of the horse's hooves, and the whip of the wind, blow away the worst of his troubles.

Domney was in those days, as it is today, a prosperous, good-sized town of above four thousand souls, dogs and horses not included. A market town, it had that very year opened its own bank, only the second in Somersetshire; and though Tom was far too conservative ever to leave a shilling of his own money there, he approved the theory of the thing most heartily.

Tom's business was with his solicitor, and so, passing by the haberdashery shop with its cherry-ribbon'd bonnets so perfect for Amelia, he handed the reins of his horse to the valet who appeared from within the office door of Mr. Hastings Sinamore, Esq., attorney at law.

Of the brilliance of this Mr. Sinamore, we need only note that he was considered by those who employed him the greatest lawyer, and by those who faced him, the biggest rascal, in all the county. He had, alas, been a little known for harsh dealings in his early days—at least, if the testimony of widows and orphans is to be given much credence—but ever since Tom had risen to be the most prominent man in the county, Mr. Sinamore had appeared much amended. His generosity nowadays raised many a hymn of praise; in which singing, to be sure, Mr. Sinamore's own fine bass was often heard above the chorus.

In the waiting-room of Mr. Sinamore's offices, Tom was obliged to cool his heels no more than three minutes before Mr. Sinamore himself, augustly solemn in black garb of priestly cast, drifted out to meet him.

This Mr. Sinamore was an original, standing barely five feet, five inches tall, and measuring as much around; though he was corpulent now, he had been in his youth one of the best boxers and cudgel players in the North county of his birth, and a certain athletic vanity still clung to him. He possessed, moreover, black eyes set deep behind a broad nose, a complexion which seemed rather inflamed than florid, and massy dark eyebrows which were knit and re-knit more often than a poor man's stockings.

Harsh and unsmiling, Mr. Sinamore admitted the superiority of no man; and in all the county, accepted only Tom as something like an equal. Accordingly, he condescended to shake Tom's hand, and to enquire after his health before showing him into his *sanctum sanctorum*.

In this nearly-subterranean domain, where the single dusty window admitted a thin light which fell with a hazy sheen upon black leather and dark mahogany alike, there huddled (as if for mutual consolation in their sorrow), half the cruel deeds and uncharitable acts done in the county over the past thirty-nine years. Here were neatly copied and carefully filed all the displaced families, foreclosed farms and lengthy embittered law-suits of four decades' hard labor—along with, admittedly, a few real moral victories in those cases where wealth and right happened to coincide.

How Mr. Tom Jones ever came to sit in such a den, reigned over by such a creature, may be easily explained: Somersetshire in those days contained no one but Mr. Sinamore capable of managing the affairs of so large an estate. As, moreover, Mr. Sinamore never acted without his client's approval, and as Tom was never malicious, Tom felt (with considerable justification) that he was serving as a leash upon this legal pit bull.

When, therefore, Tom's eyes had grown somewhat accustomed to the murk, he spoke as follows.

"Mr. Sinamore," said he, "I wish you to prepare for me a power of attorney, by which my son shall replace you as steward of my estates, but only under the strict supervision of my friend, Dr. James. This authority shall include all but my London sterling accounts, and shall run for three years—with, of course, my right to void it at any time explicitly reserved."

During this brief period of instruction, Mr. Sinamore had sat in his ebony leather chair entirely unmoved, with eyes half lidded and multi-layered chin upon his chest. Jones, surprised to find his orders accepted so stoically, still attempted to soften the blow. "Of course you understand, Lawyer," said he, "none of this reflects in the slightest upon your perform-ance. My son hath simply reached the age of responsibility. Other duties will, I promise, make up your loss of steward's fees."

Only this last appeared to rouse the Lawyer from his contemplations. First licking his lips, then smiling faintly, he finally stood and offered his hand over the desk.

"Be assured, Squire," said he, "nothing concerns me except the for-tunes of yourself and your family. I shall, of course, execute your instruc-tions. The task is, however, complex, and I am bound to leave tomorrow morning for London upon urgent business. May we say that I shall bring the documents, and one other witness, to Paradise Hall on this date one month hence, at one o'clock exactly?"

"And stay for lunch, I hope," replied Tom, who had begun to think a month scarcely enough for all his farewells.

Mr. Sinamore bowed his acceptance.

Tom took his hand. "The twelfth of next month, then. Good-bye, Hastings. I know my way out."

So Tom meant to conclude the most difficult business of his career in some half-a-dozen lines. He had felt, as always, uneasy in the presence of his lawyer, but he went on his way light of heart. As for Mr. Sinamore, he waited until he heard his outer door close, then reached into his nearest drawer and withdrew a large vellum document, carefully prepared and running to six or seven pages, on which the name of Mr. Jones appeared in many places.

How Mr. Sinamore happened to have such a document, or with what intent it had been prepared, time may, perhaps, reveal. For now let us only note that he appeared to have had early warning of Tom's intention; whether that information was satanic, fortuitous, or a result of espionage, let others surmise. For ourselves, we mean to report nothing but sure fact, and to permit no speculations to approach our bench of judgement.

# X

## *Pages More Genially Spent*

For many years, Jones had avoided alehouses; yet he left Mr. Sinamore's offices so content, and so thirsty, that he determined to break his long embargo. Upon a convenient side-street, he found a pleasant enough place to drink his tankard. Companionship, however, being scanty there, he was soon enough again upon the street. The time was a little before five of the afternoon; as the sun would not set for three hours, and as he had no fear of travelling home in the dark, he decided to call on Mr. Adams, who lived about an hour back along the road he had come, and then about a half-hour farther out of his way.

The parsonage of Mr. Adams, though a bit inconvenient for regular contact with the rest of humanity, occupied a lovely patch of grounds of some six or seven acres, well covered with oaks and elms, and watered by a cheerfully murmuring brook. The charm of the place was perhaps slightly tainted by Mr. Adams's living there alone, attended only by his housekeeper, Goody Barnes, a taciturn widow of about sixty. This hardly comprised the happiest life for a robust young man of two-and-twenty; yet Mr. Adams possessed a nature well constituted to face deprivation without complaint.

That is not to say Mr. Adams was complacent. Most of the past eighteen months he had spent campaigning to end his bachelorhood. In that campaign, he had suffered the aforementioned wound from the eyes of Amelia Jones, from which he only now imagined himself recovering. Like many a veteran, he found his taste for battle diminished; yet he carefully scanned the congregation each Sunday, and had lately even exchanged obligations with neighbouring clergymen, so as to widen his prospects. If he still returned home each Sunday evening with a sigh and the name of Amelia on his lips; well, such are the follies of youth—even clerical youth.

Notwithstanding this disappointment, Mr. Adams—especially on so fair an afternoon, when the weather was mild, and the sun just beginning to cast long-stretching shadows—was a happy young man. He delighted in his garden and in his library; his elevated calling was still a novelty to him; and, when every other resource failed, he could find contentment dangling hook and sinker from any nearby river bank.

Now he greeted Tom from the midst of his yard, rising from his pea-patch like Neptune from the green depths and, somewhat absent-mindedly, brushing the soil from his breeches.

Mr. Adams was the most modest of men, and yet, if he said so himself, his garden was worthy of praise. Jones had nearly half an hour's labour to lure him into the cottage. Once there, however, Mr. Adams remembered his hospitality, offering the most comfortable carpeted chair in the parlour and sending his housekeeper for two pints of his best ale.

After he had seated himself, and lit his pipe, Mr. Adams said, "I hope you'll stay for supper, Squire."

Tom shook his head. "I have much work ahead of me, and little time."

"Then you've settled upon your plan?"

"I have."

For some minutes thereafter, as though Mr. Jones had taken his leave, Parson Adams puffed meditatively upon his pipe, until a bluish haze surrounded him like the mists about *Mont Blanc.* At last, rather shyly, he resumed, "I wonder, sir, whether you have entirely thought through your actions. God Almighty gives a man an estate like yours as a powerful obligation. Just order and social peace are yours to maintain; nor can you lightly abandon what God himself has placed in your care."

"Indeed, sir, my own son has lately challenged my competence to develop what God has granted me."

"All the more reason, sir, to hold firm. Mr. Hacksem—for I conceive you speak of none other—is hasty, and ill-suited to govern."

"Yet govern he shall, sir, whenever it pleaseth God to take me. How much more necessary, then, that he be broken to the harness now, while Dr. James may hold the reins with necessary firmness.

"Indeed, sir," continued Jones, "it is a mystery to me where a young gentleman—even such a one as Hacksem—may acquire such mad, industrial notions."

"Why, sir," replied Mr. Adams, "Mr. Hacksem hath, I hear, been often in *London.* I have long believed that London may do a young gentleman incalculable harm."

After this shrewd observation, Mr. Adams fetched a sigh, then nodded, and again withdrew in thought. When the thick blue haze had been renewed, he once more fixed Tom with a sharp glance.

"And you have no other reasons for wishing to be gone?"

Somewhat abashed, Tom immediately repeated the *apologia* he had delivered the night before to the Jameses. At no point did he mention his rekindled enthusiasm for the female portion of the human species; nor did Mr. Adams at any time suspect it, for the innocent young Parson in those days viewed humankind from so lofty a perspective, that the true facts of its behaviour occasionally became invisible to him in the distance.

Having so eloquently explained (or rather, disguised) himself, Jones ended by saying, "I have today taken steps to protect my lands; I would be grateful to you, Mr. Adams, if you would watch over my daughter."

"*Amelia?*" blurted the Parson, with a revealing blush. "How may I help?"

"Only by being there for counsel should she need it; and, as she will be living with the Jameses, by speaking firmly to Charles James should the situation require it."

Asking Mr. Adams to watch Amelia might be thought to resemble inviting the wolf to dine with the flock. Tom, however, had a perfect (and perfectly justified) faith in his friend's ethics—and an even handier ignorance of his desires concerning the young lady.

"Yet, sir," Mr. Adams replied, "I have scarcely more years than Mr. James. Will he obey me?"

"Mr. James, like us all, has a due respect for your gravity."

Whether Tom meant by this, gravity of manner (as befits a cleric), or something nearer to Mr. Newton's gravity—for Adams was as massive a cleric as any in England—I do not know. In either case, the Parson replied forcefully, "Whatever advice or protection I can offer, I certainly shall. I shall; I shall—you may be certain of that."

For some reason, this heavy responsibility strangely lightened the countenance of Mr. Adams, who seemed almost prepared to skip about the room. Perhaps to restrain himself, he called for Goody Barnes, to say —after first pressing Tom until he received an affirmation—that there would be two to dinner.

Mrs. Barnes heard this news with "an eloquent silence"; having apparently weighed her words and found them lacking, she at last permitted herself a little nod, or rather, wobble, and went away.

Whatever energy Mrs. Barnes conserved by speaking so little, she evidently lavished upon her cooking, for within the hour there appeared upon Mr. Adams's table a pair of fine game birds, skins crisp and golden;

a large bowl of fresh-picked peas seasoned with mint; a still-larger bowl of mashed potatoes upon which the butter ran in streams; a loaf of bread still warm from the oven; and another pitcher full of the parson's strong, dark ale.

As they dined, they spoke of many things, of Ogden's sermons, Hume's history, and Edmund Burke's Parliamentary speeches in favor of American independence. On religion, Adams discoursed wisely; on history, he listened intelligently; but on Burke, he held forth, or so Tom thought, rather too freely. Indeed, it had always been Tom's conviction that, as a politician, Mr. Adams made the best of divines.

Their disagreement was small—Mr. Adams said only that it was hard for the Americans to be at odds with England—and left no ripple upon the surface of the evening. Just then the quarrels of (as they seemed) greedy, distant men mattered little to Tom and his friend. Mr. Adams, moreover, delighted Tom by his bright (if at times collegiate) wit, and by a manner in which respect and affection contended, so that Tom was now "Tom," now "old Tom," and now—when authority was recalled— "Squire, sir."

About eleven o'clock, stuffed with ale and fowl, courtesy and philosophy, Tom mounted his horse and began homeward. The night was chill, and he was glad for his cloak; yet he sang as he rode some six or seven of his favorite ballads again and again, and sometimes he laughed aloud.

# XI

## In Which the First Book Ends

Exactly one month later, Tom Jones, hands held politely behind his back, and cheeks reddening from the beaming sun, awaited his guests upon the steps of Paradise Hall. About twenty minutes past noon, a very block-like horse, carrying the equally block-like form of Mr. Sinamore, rode stolidly into view, trailed by a labouring, sway-backed rag of a pony which hung its head and bore Mr. Sinamore's clerk, Will Stumpling.

Tom, whose morning had been lost to anticipation, grinned to see Will

Stumpling, for the frail clerk's wit and good humour made him welcome everywhere. Yet Will dismounted stiffly, untouched by the sun, and seemingly bleached by his solemn pending business.

That business was soon concluded. As Tom sat at his study desk, Mr. Sinamore, hovering above him like some Archbishop of Jurisprudence, ceremoniously delivered each of the seven sheets for his consideration. Tom, with his usual haste, devoted perhaps three minutes to the first three pages, then dipped a new quill in ink, intending to sign wherever instructed. "Your efforts, Hastings," said our good-natured friend, "will no doubt protect my every interest."

In response, Mr. Sinamore bowed with the expected gratitude, but (less expectedly) Will Stumpling's features were suddenly marred by a look of sharp pain, which shot diagonally across his face like a lightning bolt. Tom, though amazed, recalled the parsimony of his lawyer, and attributed this contortion to simple hunger: after a moment's pause, he returned to his signing with all possible speed.

When the two witnesses had likewise added their marks, Tom sanded and blew the sheets dry, placed his copy in a drawer, and with a formal shake of the hand, returned the other copy to Mr. Sinamore.

"Gentlemen," Tom said, speaking with particular kindness to Will, "thank you both very much. Our lunch awaits us upon the terrace."

Amelia had ordered the table spread with cold ham and chicken, cucumber salad and fresh bread, and many ripe fruits of the season. Alas, Tom, already thinking of his journey, largely ignored his company. This slip allowed Mr. Sinamore, after mounding his plate with Miss Amelia's delicacies, to seize for himself the far rarer morsel of her conversation, and so to steal from the gathering its sweetest treasure. While Amelia endured this, moreover, Will Stumpling caught Tom's eye, and by urgent gestures arranged to meet him in a quiet corner of the long terrace.

When they had drawn aside, Will, normally quick-witted, seemed to consider wordlessly half a dozen topics before, speaking low and plucking at his coat buttons, he began, "Squire, my apprenticeship to Lawyer Sinamore expires tomorrow, on my eighteenth birthday. Lawyer says he will retain me as clerk, and even make me a partner when"—here he laughed as if speaking of the magically impossible—"I have satisfied him."

"Congratulations, my friend, and happy birthday," replied Tom rather briefly, his own eagerness making him a little impatient with the worries of others.

But, shrugging, Will continued, "Squire, it would be wicked for me to stay on with Lawyer Sinamore. Now, I have not sixpence to pay, but —might you consider finding room in your coach for one more? I mean to go to London any way I can."

It happened that Tom was too occupied with his own pleasant thoughts to wonder why it should be wicked for Mr. Stumpling to stay on in Somersetshire. Charity, however, was the core of Tom's nature, as generosity was its ornament; and as, moreover (for I would not over-praise him), he was loath to travel some hundreds of miles without a companion, the request was convenient. He therefore replied easily, "If, sir, you will be good enough to stay at Paradise Hall next Tuesday night, we shall depart at dawn the following morning."

Mr. Stumpling had, I believe, denied himself the great relief of speaking his whole mind; yet he was clearly grateful for Tom's benevolence, and when he had made his thanks, the two of them rejoined the company. The sun had dropped so low that shadows cooled the terrace. Amelia, finding Mr. Sinamore's attentions tending towards some very unwelcome intimacies, signalled to her father that the party might conclude; and Tom, who could assert his authority when necessary, stood to offer a final toast and to wish his guests good-day.

At length, the horses arrived, and the two legal gentlemen departed, both declaring themselves delighted with their entertainment, though they appeared much less happy with each other.

On the appointed Tuesday, Mr. Stumpling reappeared. He arrived quite late, so that the reddish light of the sunset tinged his straw-coloured hair a laughable pink, but Amelia, seeing his old broken mare, the one poor roll of his belongings, and the same neat suit of black clothing which he had worn on his earlier visit, felt her heart go out to him. As Will approached the steps, she whispered to her father that he must in London help the young clerk's career, which Tom promised he would.

At supper that evening Mr. Stumpling continued his strange, worried awkwardness, but Tom, who could no longer ignore it, put it down to gratitude and to concern for the future. Tom and Amelia had their own reasons for heaviness, Amelia in particular having swallowed considerable annoyance at being left home while her father and brother enjoyed excitement abroad. Indeed, only old Grimes appeared content—for Grimes had appeared content ever since Lawyer Sinamore, leaving Tom's study with the signed papers in hand, had given him a slight confirming nod.

The roasted meat, as little scarred as a drawing-room colonel, was withdrawn about eight o'clock; perhaps an hour later, Tom paused at Amelia's chair by the fire to hand her a letter addressed to the chambers of two distinguished London lawyers, and to say that if she would post it early the next morning, it would precede his own coach into London. Then they went slowly to their separate bedrooms, to wait until the light outside their windows should tell them it was dawn.

In the morning, there gathered (besides Mr. Stumpling, who early placed himself discreetly in the coach) five persons, Tom and Amelia, Dr. and Mrs. James, and Parson Adams, to prepare for their separation.

Reader, fearing too much sorrow of parting hath already marked this our first book, I shall forbear to draw that most affecting scene in any detail. Indeed, if thy imagination should show thee the tears upon the cheeks, the trembling lips, and the arms unwilling to end their embrace; why, pray, do not lose thyself in sympathetic agonies. Better than to indulge in that pleasing game of sharing others' griefs, is to think how soon we ourselves must part forever from those dearest to us; and so thinking, to resolve to do them every kindness in our power while we may.

When *thou* hast so considered, and so resolved, thou hast permission to begin our next Book, wherein thou shalt find adventure of robuster sort. As for that scene of tender parting now hidden from thee—well, perhaps we may see more of it another time.

# BOOK
# THE SECOND

# I

## *That This Is a Logical Story*

Certain criticks (whose own lives may be as tangled as a bramble-bush, but who demand geometric order in an author's work) have no doubt noted that this story hath, so far, progressed most strangely. I mean in particular, that it hath begun with a beginning made of endings. Tom and Rob especially, but also Amelia and Mr. Adams in smaller ways, have all ended their old ways of living, their old hopes and satisfactions, and gone to try newer ones.

This may indeed appear an error in our plan; yet hath not great *Homer* begun his *Odyssey* upon the very same scheme? Nay, may we not appeal to still a greater authority? Doth not life itself show us how sacrifice of the old—as painful as it may be—prepares the ground for our future lives? What is known and comfortable must be set aside upon nothing more than the hope of a better world. There is a time for loving harvest, but a time as well for the difficult, dangerous ploughing.

"Well," thou may protest, Reader (for I shall pay no more mind to the criticks), "this is much too grand a sentiment for poor old Tom, whose actions surely had their origins in another part of his anatomy than either head or heart." And concerning the motives of Mr. Jones, there is, I concede, a certain ambiguity.

Yet, Reader, is not all action in life ambiguous? Suppose our hero, in travelling, was responding to instincts certain moralists might consider *low*. Are we then forbidden to ask what other, higher purposes he might have had?

In truth, no contradiction (or, at most, one very human one) underlay our hero's actions. We should no more force Jones into a single motivation to please the criticks, than show him in a cylindrical coat to please the geometricians. Let us say, therefore, that Mr. Jones's new history began with the end of his old, and that he went abroad for a variety of reasons, some (such as his desire to help his country in her troubles) very noble, and others, at least natural. Nor shall we despise his politics because his mind was sometimes elsewhere.

How well Tom will succeed, time alone will tell. For now—in this instant before yielding the stage again to Tom and his affairs—I would only urge thee not to let trivialities prevent thy consideration of our hero's profounder nature. For (whatever the theorists say) such is human dexterity, that we may any of us, man or woman, hold a grand moral purpose even with our back to a wheel, our fist in a belly, or our cheek to a lover's breast.

## II

### Concerning an Adventure

It shall ever be our practice, Reader, to value thy time most highly, and, like a good banker, to lay it out for thee where it may earn the greatest interest. Those adventures of Mr. Jones we think most likely to please thee, we shall record at length; all others, we shall omit.

Accordingly, let it be merely noted that Mr. Jones passed his first day upon the London road in complete and tiresome ease, and slept that night at an inn barely forty miles from his own home. The next afternoon, however, brought a change in his fortune. Following a morning of fair late-spring weather, and a too-leisurely lunch arrayed upon a blanket in a meadow beside the road, there befell about three o'clock an unlucky accident to one of the wheels of Mr. Jones's carriage. The coachman required about two hours' hard labour to restore the rim, and no sooner had the wheel been remounted, than the sky darkened and began to send down showers. This meant not only inconvenience for the poor coachman—who rode exposed to the worst of the elements—but mud, ever thicker, upon the road. This last seemed nearly impassable, especially as the final two miles before the Biting Whale (that famous inn) ran entirely uphill, over road too rocky to be a credit to our country.

Progress became moment by moment slower. Joseph, the postillion, hopped down and put his shoulder to one rear wheel; young Mr. Stumpling excused himself, opened the coach door and went to apply his strength to the other. Not a minute passed before Tom, with very little reluctance, stepped out to assist. The rain which drenched him was not bitterly cold, but rather so warm it appeared to melt the road about him, until he and Will were coated with mud like two macaroons dipped in chocolate. They slipped and sweated, and tore their clothes. Ahead of them, the frothing horses spread their bits as the driver forced them on, one struggling, panting inch, and then another.

For nearly two hours they laboured, 'til even the long near-summer's day began to fade. At last, exhausted, they blocked the wheels and sat to rest, pausing in the midst of the ascending road. To their left, a stand of oaks lined the road, and to their right, the hillside dropped steeply away.

They had rested so but a few moments when there came the clatter of riders, and a moment later three horsemen turned hastily into the road perhaps twenty yards ahead, and galloped towards the coach. These three horsemen had not quite the awful countenance of their four more famous brethren; yet they rode so fast and looked so hard that Tom—who had learned caution with the years—stood at their approach and reached carefully inside the coach to grip his walking stick.

In truth, Reader, these three gentlemen—one bare-headed, one wearing a broad black hat, and one with his head wrapped in a silk handkerchief, but all dirty and unshaven—were none other than riders of the dark paths or, in the popular usage, highwaymen. As soon as the hatted man reached the coach, he withdrew from his cloak a pistol, which (after some indecision, for Tom and company were so muddied and torn that master could scarcely be told from servants) he correctly levelled at Tom's belly. With that false jollity which hath marked the thief since old Falstaff's day, he called, "Good even' to thee, gentlemen. Lighten your pockets a little, and your trip will go easier." This he followed with a slight leer and a prompting motion of the pistol barrel.

Even heroes must bow before overwhelming force, else they are simply fools. Tom, therefore, held forth his purse and pocketwatch even as the silk-headed rascal, pointing sternly at Will, ordered him to bring down the lock-box from the back of the coach.

Reader, the contrivances of humankind are but folly! The ship's mast snaps, the dike gives way explosively before the flood!—and so were the rogues' plans destroyed. A mighty lightning bolt lit the sky above them, accompanied by a thundering louder than a hundred old pistols. Tom's coachman, who had endured the robbers' appearance only with the greatest terror, leaped to his feet upon the coach, each hair on his head rising in wild alarm. Suddenly, with a shout, he tumbled to the muddy ground and, wasting not a single base thought on the wages owed him, bolted nobly into the woods, showing thereby how much he scorned the petty danger of the highwaymen when the grander challenge of the unknown awaited him.

In the confusion which followed, Will Stumpling, offering a cry of defiance, lowered his head and charged the chief rogue. Whether Will was a hero or a fool, or whether he had simply noticed that rain-water was beginning to soak the pistol's pan and flint, I do not know; but advance, he did.

For one horrifying instant, Tom became the very statue of Amazement. As Will closed to within two feet, the rogue aimed the pistol squarely between his eyes, and screamed, "Halt!" The pistol snapped— but only snapped—and young Stumpling grabbed his would-be murderer by one leg and carried him out of the saddle.

Now the bare-headed villain produced his own pistol, but Tom, our English Achilles, had regained his courage and, with one rising blow of his stick, knocked this drier weapon skyward, where it discharged with a crack and a pale yellow flash. One hand crushed, the villain tried to draw his sword with the other, but Tom dissuaded him by seizing that wrist as a lever and flinging him from his horse.

Before the remaining mounted scoundrel could spur himself either to retreat or attack, Tom's postillion, having scrambled to the roof of the coach, threw himself down atop him, so that both of them were carried in a thrice directly into the mud.

Then did six of God's noblest creatures struggle to do each other's business in the very thick of the grime and rain and enclosing night. Long the battle hung in the balance, as blows (ever slower and weaker) fell in equal numbers upon each side. But though Joseph (Tom's postillion) and Will were hard pressed, Tom eventually gained the advantage of his man, and, driving his fist eight or nine times deeply into that tender part known as the *bread-basket*, at last persuaded him to lie still. That proved enough, for the other two rogues, seeing their chief fallen, gave one parting hard blow apiece and, without further ceremony, turned and ran away.

Reader, how hollow is every victory once it is won! Tom and his two allies now stood, or rather swayed, perfectly covered over in that cement of mud and blood by which, it seems, all true heroes are held together.

Too tired even to grin at each other, they merely slumped in a trio against the side of the coach, which was now itself sunk to mid-wheel in the rain-softened road. So weary and afrighted were they that when the last of the highwaymen staggered to his feet and ran, they let him go without a word.

When they had recovered a little, they agreed to walk for help to the Biting Whale, whose lights they could now discern about half a mile away.

Many is the traveller whose miseries have been relieved, whose comfort hath been enhanced, by the worthy landlord of the Biting Whale, Mr. Timothy Nautley. Our torn and bloody friends had no sooner entered his well-kept domain, than a serving-girl—as level-headed and amiable as she was pretty—showed them to chairs by the central kitchen-fire. She then begged them to excuse her, and scarcely two minutes later returned, followed by a red-faced, white-haired gentleman of ordinary height but trim and athletic frame. His dress appeared a trifle odd, for beneath a respectable coat he wore an open-collared sailor's blouse, devoid of any neck-cloth whatsoever; yet his manner and his walk bespoke authority; and indeed, he was none other than Mr. Nautley, the landlord of the Biting Whale. This good man strode directly to the chair occupied by our hero, peered closely into his soiled face, and asked softly "Whether he was not Mr. Jones?"

Tom, who had by this time much recovered, opened his eyes and replied gratefully, "Mr. Jones it is, sir, and most happy to see you. Mr. Nautley, you must forgive my imposing as well as my appearance."

But the landlord was already in motion, roaring out commands in a voice which had served well during many an Atlantic storm. Within five minutes, a team of draft horses had been dispatched to haul up the coach; Stumpling and Tom's postillion had been found clean clothing; and Tom himself was sipping contentedly from a tankard of hot punch.

This much accomplished, Mr. Nautley bowed genteelly and, saying he looked forward to Tom's company in the Red Porpoise as soon as possible, left the little maid to show Tom upstairs. We, in turn, shall—as is our custom—leave Tom to his washing and dressing. As some minutes must now transpire before we are all met together again, Reader, thou mayst well pass thy time contemplating this prophetic truth: that in shaping our lives, the most violent brawl in the world rarely counts half so much as a single, proper, quiet word.

# III

## In Which Tom Joins the Company

Good Mr. Nautley was one of those lucky men who have made their art their fortune. His great art was none other than *sociability,* in which nature and travel had well qualified him, for he combined an agreeable person, a knowledge of the world, and very polished manners, with a genuine concern for his fellow men, traits which quite compensated for his being a seafarer, and a self-made man. Indeed, though I cannot promise that three anonymous persons appearing in his kitchen in rags would have been so grandly treated as were Tom and his companions, many a wanderer will attest that Mr. Timothy Nautley hath never turned away the needy from his door.

A part of Mr. Nautley's success, to be sure, stemmed from the fact that, as he never hesitated to aid the needy, so he never hesitated to charge the rich. As expensive as the Biting Whale was known to be, however, it offered good value for its fees, for besides both French and English chefs (and a board which might, by request, run fifteen or twenty courses), it provided elegant furnishings, comfortable beds, and conversation as good as any in the realm.

A very old custom underlay the charming talk of the *Whale.* While today, you will in too many inns find persons of quality dining alone in their separate rooms—Milord bored in the Admiral Vessey, the Squire retired in the Canton, and the Reverend Doctor gloomy in the Peach—Mr. Nautley, as was once universal custom, still encouraged the best of his guests to dine together in his finest room, the Red Porpoise.

Into that rosy mammal, then, was Mr. Jones shown about forty-five minutes after his arrival at the inn. During those forty-five minutes, he had washed and new-dressed himself with clothes fetched from his coach. Now he blazed forth in an emerald suit, its waistcoat well-woven with silver; and the vapours of victory had risen between his ears, to brighten his eye and, perhaps, to lighten his head. He was shown the way by that kind little maid Betty, who immediately returned to her colleagues with the news that, having accidentally seen Mr. Jones washing, she could declare him to possess, from head to toe, the whitest skin and manliest figure of any mortal alive.

This cool early-summer evening, the Red Porpoise shone with only moderate splendour. Though the windows were shut, barely a wisp of a fire burned upon the grate. The silverware glistened, the table-lace was clean and of its famous pinkish tone, but the company was sparse. Mr. Nautley having stepped out, the apartment contained but two persons, a rather unprepossessing-looking officer of some provincial regiment, and the most beautiful woman Tom had seen since his dear Sophia had died.

I do not mean to imply any precise resemblance between this new lady and his late lovely bride, for where Sophia had been black-haired and petite, this was a brown woman of some good stature. Her skin was sun-touched, her mouth was full; her whole posture and manner shone with intelligence and self-reliance. Her eyes were dark brown, and no light was as startling as that which shone from them as she contemplated her companion. Her ardent look seemed to Tom at first distressingly like love, and he only gradually understood that she was angry.

As Tom, with an unanswered bow, assumed his place at the table, the military man was patronisingly saying, ". . . that, as for myself, I dislike harsh measures, but if the Americans will persist in their wicked unreasonableness, then forbearance will be wasted. You must never forget, madam, that you are the children, and we the parent; and if nothing else will answer, then the military will." Noticing Tom for the first time, he turned toward him for confirmation. "What think you, sir? Shall we settle with these impertinent Americans once and for all? I say, let us send over a Captain Whipsblood with a few regiments of dragoons and let the firing squads and the noose inspire a proper love of their mother country in these vicious ingrates."

Our hero (who had been using his eyes more than his ears) had heard this speech with casual approval, until one particular name startled him. He then turned toward the major, and asked frostily:

"Do you know me, sir?"

"Indeed, not, upon my soul," replied the gentleman uncertainly, for he detected something dangerous in Tom's voice.

"My name is Jones."

"So? What of it?" demanded the gentleman, gaining a little confidence from the obscurity of the remark.

"There have been certain difficulties between Captain Whipsblood's family and my own, and I wish to know whether you meant to provoke me."

As the marks of his recent brawl still stood redly upon Tom's countenance, the gentleman thought a meek answer proper, and accordingly said that he had meant no offense whatsoever.

To this Tom, who desired no other quarrels that evening, replied with a bow. He was about to return his attention to that woman across from him, whose beauty seemed every moment more striking. Before he could speak, however, the visionary creature, her cheeks now glowing with spots of red, burst out emphatically:

"If you have given no offense to this gentleman, sir, you have angered me mortally. If we Americans *were* your children, how much greater the shame that you have exploited us, have shackled our ports and suspended our legislations; have treated us, in short, like your chattels, not your children.

"And, sir fool, your children have grown. Today we are your ships and sailors, your ironworks and your infantry, your tobacco crops and a hundred things more. You may send your dragoons and your Captain Whipsblood"—at this name, Tom started involuntarily—"but they will fail as your governors have failed.

"Sir, we in America will fight you forever, will sacrifice everything for liberty, will drink ditch water and eat muddied oats, asking no more sustenance than our horses until we secure all the rights of free human beings. If you send your troops, be ready to follow them yourselves, for we will oppose you by every means, every man and woman of us."

These words, uttered in something of a choking tone, appeared indeed to throttle her opponent. That *gentleman*—if we may so cheapen the term —finding himself unable to reply, contented himself with the sorry consolation that her speech, though unanswerable, had still sprung from a skull smaller, and breast softer, than his own. So let us leave him to his contentment.

Mr. Jones, meanwhile, felt himself half-mad. Suppose, Reader, that he had walked into the Red Porpoise only to hear the Devil saluted, wickedness praised, and damnation recommended as the cure for all earthly ills. What would have been his shock and horror?

By surrounding himself with Tories in London and retainers at home, Tom had, since rising to his estate, almost perfectly isolated himself from

American politics. So had he granted his own conservative beliefs almost the sanctity of religion—and so may we account for his first horror at this woman's tirade.

Yet politics are not, like morality, immutable; and it sometimes happens to us (perhaps once, perhaps twice, in our lives) that a moment unexpectedly opens a new world. Such a dizzying world had Tom discovered before the end of her speech; and—Reader, do not laugh!—he suddenly, almost drunkenly, wished to ride beside this eloquent, mysterious woman, to share with her (if absolutely necessary) oats and muddy water, and to defend a cause he had five minutes before liked less than witchcraft. Are we to blame all of this upon fatigue? Or even upon his having so long been faithful to his Sophia's memory? "Well," you will say, "this woman was beautiful." Yes, to be sure she was, but so, in a curious way, were her ideas and her courage.

Tom's contemplations had cost him, for while he sat dazed, this woman of his hopes had risen and left the room. He asked the Major (who was gulping wine with broad red face perspiring and wig askew), "Does that lovely lady happen to be your companion?"

"Indeed, sir," replied the officer fiercely, "she is so far from being my companion, that I heartily pray I may never see her again."

Satisfied that he risked no duel, Jones dashed from the room, and found his desire just mounting the stairs. Looking humbly towards her, he half-whispered, "Madam, may I say that your speech has inspired my warmest admiration?"

She had looked back angrily, but now seemed mollified; and even appeared to like the sight of Jones. "Well, sir. You are kind."

"May I offer you a glass of wine, and introduce myself?"

Instantly, her anger returned. "Indeed, sir, you may not. And as for your warm admiration, if you will pour cold water upon it, and rebutton your trousers, all will be well, and so good night."

Then, moving quickly, she was gone, while Tom looked somewhat stupidly after her, and sighed.

Reader, thou hast no doubt observed the sudden decay of our hero; and, in truth, a chance encounter doth appear to have undone both his spirits and his intellect. Perhaps thou wouldst prefer one of those steady *German* heroes with lead in either fist, and a large quantity of the same metal behind his eyes. Pray, let us not desert Mr. Jones on account of his humanity! Love and action are not at odds; they are line and colour in every picture we draw from life!—and, Reader, when we sneer at Love, we balance upon a single tall stilt, and only laugh until we fall.

With many an oblational murmur, then, did Tom mount the stairs to his sea-green room. So heated was the night (or perhaps our hero) that he parted the curtains surrounding his bed, and even cast aside his comforter. He lay submerged in bed-down an hour or more, having nothing to distract him but a statue of nymphs and swordfish upon the mantelpiece; and after as much of this as he could endure, he rose to summon Betty, with what effect you shall read hereafter.

# IV

## An Interview Between Tom and Betty Concerning Several Matters

Betty appeared at Tom's door as swiftly as if she had been hovering nearby for just that purpose. Pleased with her alacrity—for a strange eagerness had overtaken him—Tom tugged her hastily into his room.

"What is your name, Miss?"

"Betty, sir."

"And, Betty, will you be kind enough to help me with some enquiries?"

She nodded in a manner meant to agree to this, and to whatever else Mr. Jones might propose.

"Well, then: what is the name of that most-exquisite lady I saw this evening in the Red Porpoise?"

A little glumly, Betty answered that the woman went by the name of Mrs. Wilson, but that the landlord had said confidentially that he doubted whether that might be the strict truth.

"And where is she from?"

To this, Betty only shrugged and said petulantly that she did not know, but that such persons—who were surely no better than they should be—most often came from London, but wound up in Hell.

"Betty, I am shocked to hear such language," responded Tom, having finally garnered some idea of the young woman's interest in the issue. "But I pray you: can you give me no other information about her?"

"Not any, Squire, except that she and her servant called for their horses about a quarter-hour ago. If you listen hard, you may hear them galloping away even now," concluded Betty, with sudden pleasure in her voice.

The mildness with which Betty gazed up at Tom scarcely explained his own look of consternation. He dashed to the window and raised it, in time to witness the outlines of two caped figures disappearing into the darkness, then raced back towards the door while calling distractedly for Betty to have his carriage drawn up.

But Betty intercepted him, pressing her hand against his chest and saying, "Nay, sir. Your coach will not be here 'til morning; 'tis stuck deep in the mud."

"Horses, then," cried Tom.

"None to be had at this hour, sir."

Our hero groaned so very dispiritedly that Betty brought herself to say, "Poor Squire. Does it console you to know she asked your name before she left?"

Reader, I believe this news restored our hero entirely, for no man was better disposed than he to hope and dream upon the slightest pretext.

Betty, however, had not yet withdrawn her hand from Tom's waistcoat; now, indeed, she began to move it lightly, three buttons down, then three buttons back up; to the pocket at the left, then, gently, towards the pocket at the right. Tom himself was not unmoved by this kindness, for there are some passions (in some persons) which, once raised, are fairly easily re-directed. Tom felt the greatest desire for Mrs. Wilson, but Mrs. Wilson was gone, and Betty was—in a word—handy.

Somewhat urgently, therefore, he asked her to be certain he was called before dawn, that he might ride once his carriage was ready. Putting her lips very near to his, Betty promised this would be done; then, reaching out two moistened fingers, she deftly snuffed the wick of the room's sole taper.

Darkness must therefore conclude our report, though anyone passing in the hall during the next hour or so might have heard issuing from Tom's room several distinct cries, of which "Oh, Squire!" was one, and "Oh, Betty—*dear* girl!" another.

# V

## *In Which Our Hero Leaves Somersetshire*

June nights are brief, and June days warm, and when Tom, broadly smiling for reasons which escaped him, awoke the next morning, the hot sun was already steaming the muddy roads dry. His coach stood in the court-yard, and a groom, in neat sailor's garb, was leading down his horses.

Downstairs, Mr. Stumpling, a plaister affixed above one eye, awaited and grinned at him, and the light which poured through the opened windows made the room seem magical and fine.

"Morning, Squire. All our gear's stowed, and Mr. Nautley will attend you at your convenience."

Tom having ordered an early start, his breakfast—a mere snack of eggs and bacon and sausage and toast—was set before him as he took his seat. The brawl—or something—had given him a yeoman's appetite, and he had devoured half the plate before saying that he would gladly see Mr. Nautley.

This worthy man entered directly, and with cheerful courtesy told Tom how pleased he was to see him recovered from his injuries.

"My old friend," answered Tom, "once more I am in your debt."

Mr. Nautley, ducking his head and spreading his hands, muttered that it was nothing. After a moment, he added more forcefully, "We couldn't catch your highwaymen, Squire. You must have put a right scare into them—we'll not be troubled hereabouts again anytime soon. So that's all one—favor given, and taken."

Tom drained his tea cup, and put it back in its saucer. As nothing else edible lay within range, he began, "Timothy, I met a woman in the room last night, and wish to find her. Her name, I believe, is Wilson."

Mr. Nautley heard this revelation without surprise; nor, I believe, did much of importance transpire under his roof without his knowledge.

"To be sure, Squire, Mrs. Wilson is a Massachusetts woman, recently landed in England. Her politics may be little to your liking . . . or, if it matters, to mine. Yet she paid in sterling like an honest gentlewoman and seemed (except concerning politics) a most civil lady. Her stay, however, was short, and I believe I can tell you nothing more."

Mr. Nautley now hesitated, for he well understood that confidentiality is the cornerstone of the world's great inns. Few persons, however, can resist an opportunity to hear themselves praised for their own sagacity; and so, after a moment's hesitation, during which he several times rubbed his chin, he continued.

"I can say nothing more than this: that when we talked, which was only once, Mrs. Wilson used terms only a sailor would use; and in such a fashion that I'd say she is, or was, a smuggler . . . either that, or I'm a devil's eyelet."

Mr. Jones roundly praised his friend's intuition, and, in truth, was extremely pleased with what he had learned, for this notion of Mrs. Wilson's exotic career was a perfect sauce to his appetite.

Mr. Nautley, meanwhile, had stood, only first discreetly placing the reckoning beside Tom's plate. "Well, Squire," he said, "a pleasure seeing you, as always. If Mrs. Wilson reappears . . . any message?"

"Only that I'm on my way to London, and that my house is in Hanover Square."

"Good enough." Timothy Nautley stretched forth his arm, and the hand which showed beyond the ruffles was hard and horny. "Squire, the ocean's wide and dangerous. When a man gets to be our age . . . well, be careful, will you?"

"Good-bye, Timothy. My thanks for everything."

Tom took a moment to settle his bill, then securely twisted five guineas together in a slip of paper, which he meant to hand to Betty for a dress or shoes. But she was nowhere to be seen, and, fearing that she might misunderstand so impersonal a gift, he substituted within the packet a signet ring. The day was growing extremely hot. Meaning to hand the keepsake to Mr. Nautley to convey, he stepped out into the blazing sun. He had not, however, gone more than three or four paces when he heard a whistle behind and above him. He turned, and there saw Betty leaning saucily out the second storey's window, the sunlight glistening on her white cap.

Instantly his hand went into his coat pocket and retrieved the paper packet, which, in a neat flat arc, he tossed carefully toward her.

"Here, Betty. For sweet friendship's sake."

She caught it from the air with one hand.

"Sweet friendship's sake, Squire," she answered, pressing the packet to her lips. She detached the chain and small locket she wore about her neck and, with a sad little smile, dropped them down to Tom. "Travel safe, darling Squire."

Holding this rare souvenir tenderly in his hand, Tom stepped into the already-stifling coach, let down the near glass, and called out, "Aboard, Mr. Stumpling. We're London bound."

# VI

## A Political Chapter

Across Westminster Bridge, along the edge of St. James's Park and the Abbey, and thence North on Swallow Street, the coach rolled, at last reaching Hanover Square, and the London home of Mr. Jones.

That commonplace, that "*nobody* is in London between June and October," may once have held some truth, but by 1774, the growth of Empire had made the governing of our land and colonies a year-'round task. Though booby squires may have all returned home (leaving place-holding rascals to poach upon their interests), though City families may have left their countinghouses to vacation elsewhere, the real concerns of Empire continued unabated, and those of the Nobility with any useful function to perform generally travelled, not to family estates in Suffolk or Scotland, but only to villas some few miles away. Settled comfortably upon the north shore of the Thames, they remained even more comfortably near to the ever-growing centers of policy, the Foreign Offices and the Admiralty. Even arriving when he did, Tom might expect to meet powerful, influential persons.

Tom's connections with influential men had declined since he had left Parliament on Sophia's death, but he could still claim important friends. This, combined with his proven abilities (for he had, during his active years, authored three well-regarded bills and a treaty with the Dutch), made him certain he would be offered a good post. It was with high spirits, therefore, that he climbed the broad stone steps of his house.

Mrs. Guerdion, Tom's housekeeper, was a neat, forceful woman of about fifty, with steel-coloured hair and unblinking grey eyes. She possessed every attribute to keep a property secure and a house in good order. If any small flaw marked her character, it was, perhaps, an excessive devotion to Mr. Jones. The occasional follies inspired by this loyalty, Tom had, however, learned to accept—especially as she was otherwise a very sane woman, and justly proud of her knowledge of politics, government, and trade.

This morning, once Mr. Stumpling had left them to walk the Square, Tom invited her to sit in the parlour and talk.

"You've had a second letter from your friend Colonel Askew, Squire," she began. "No doubt he wishes to see you very soon."

"I shall leave my card for him later this afternoon," said Jones. "I like no man better than he."

"Indeed, sir," said Mrs. Guerdion, suddenly lively, "I cannot but love him for his courage. For his decision to side with Mr. Burke and the Duke of Richmond—tho' it is not made public yet—is certain to bring upon him a great storm of foolish, wicked criticism."

"I beg your pardon, Mrs. Guerdion?" said our hero uncertainly.

"Why, sir," she answered. "To be sure you are yourself so brave and firm a friend of the Americans, that you will scarcely notice the hazards. But for a military man to speak against the Coercive Acts (for so most knowing persons are calling our laws strangling the noble port of Boston —and, I fear, our own immortal souls)—"

"Madam," said Jones, unheeded.

"—Tho' you are certainly right, Squire, that we shall never harm the gallant people of Boston, as aid is now reaching them from every part of the colonies—"

"MADAM!" cried Jones, very loudly. "What nonsense are you speaking?"

"Why, Squire," answered Mrs. Guerdion, a little uncertainly, "are you not in agreement with Colonel Askew?"

"Mrs. Guerdion," replied Tom, "the Colonel is my friend, and I respect his opinions; but if he is now upon the side of the Americans, then there I utterly oppose him."

Mrs. Guerdion now turned somewhat red, before crying, "You are very right, sir. I should no more wish to see the wretched Americans prevail, than I should wish to turn your house over to ruffians, for to be sure, they are only thieves who would claim what is rightfully ours."

If Mrs. Guerdion's sudden reversal hath surprised thee, Reader, the explanation for it was by no means complex. This good lady, while very fond of facts, had absolutely no interest in opinions, and very willingly altered her own to suit her audience—at least where her employer was concerned. She had first assumed Tom knew of, and shared the Colonel's opinions, and had formed her own accordingly; but upon learning her error, she had as expeditiously reversed her course.

Whatever embarrassment she may have felt was now, however, conveniently ended by the reappearance of Mr. Stumpling, just at the moment the tea was placed upon the table.

Mr. Stumpling, his face glowing with his travels, made a much heartier tea than did Tom, and spoke almost unbrokenly of his plans. Finally, he summarized, "Squire, I believe I shall burden you only a few days. I go this afternoon to meet with Messrs. Curtis and Hayfield, and hope I may join their firm within the week." Mr. Stumpling had discovered in his room a most encouraging letter from this firm, in the composition of which, Tom's influence had played no small part. Tom supposed Mr. Stumpling guessed the nature of his debt, for he concluded softly by saying, "Squire, I should horribly regret doing anything leading to your discomfiture."

Having ended so, Mr. Stumpling placed his napkin upon the table, and walked from the room, leaving Jones behind him to muse upon those pleasant sensations which come from a knowledge of having done good.

# VII

## Of a Dinner

"It was perfect luck, Tom," Colonel Askew said, as he refilled the wine glasses, "your arriving here this evening. Another evening in such dreary company as I've kept these last three weeks, and I'd've been quite desperate. Well, here's your health."

Bob Askew stood a little below the middle height. He had a full, florid face, slightly prominent eyes, and a good deal of lank blond hair tied back with a plain black ribbon; in a country governed by Hanoverian kings, these were not bad features to have. He had proven his valor in the Seven Years War, and his good sense ever since. Though still an officer of the Household Guards, he performed the greater service to his country in amending quarrels, and building friendships, among the powerful—at which he worked with such an easy good nature, and with such a thorough devotion to the gentle arts (and the gentle sex) as to seem himself scarcely a power at all.

Yet he could speak directly, when so required. "But what's all this you've written about wanting the government service?"

Tom shrugged. "I suppose I've had enough of whatever I've had these last six years. I need a change. But now, the news is limited in Somersetshire. Tell me: how bad's this situation in Boston?"

"Well . . . even Gentleman Johnny says we're cutting our own throats, and when General Burgoyne's against a fight, you know it's a form of suicide. That's the military sense of it; as for the morality, oh . . . the Ministry has its case, and no doubt the Americans have often been provocative and irresponsible, but . . . nothing could be worse than that we kill our countrymen over so small a fragment of the right.

"There's an opposition, of course—the City's money men favor the Americans, and Burke, Chatham and Richmond have all been eloquent—but every day the rhetoric grows more ghostly. There's a cavalryman's nightmare, Tom, that retreat has been sounded, but one's own horse still charges on, regardless of the reins, into the cannon-fire. Why, Tom, that's how Parliament has seemed these last months."

Jones, I suspect, had wished to hear that the Americans only wanted a few fair-minded country squires to solve all their problems. As it was, surprised by Askew's ending so passionately, he waited nearly a minute before asking, "But . . . are there opportunities for someone like me to help . . . in the administration over there?"

"You really want to go?"

"I do."

Askew observed him curiously. "Well . . . Lord Suffley has been offered the governorship of Maryland, and will likely need an aide. That's beneath your rank, of course, but if Suffley decides to take you, I might be able to wring some sort of special appointment from his Majesty to make it more respectable."

Jones, growing excited, raised his hand slightly. "My stature's not so important, as long as the work is interesting."

"Too," the Colonel added, "whether or not he takes the governorship, Suffley's to go on a mission to France very soon. We need to dissuade Louis from helping the colonies in case of war. For this delicate job, his lordship has (so far as I can see) no other qualifications than a fierce temper and an unreasoning hatred of all things French. Perhaps he's supposed to terrify the boy-king—Lord knows, he terrifies me. And don't be fooled by that beautiful wife of his."

Jones now found his prospects every moment more interesting.

"Still," Askew continued, "the more I think of this, the more sense it makes. You think you're a staunch Tory; so did I. Visiting America may change your mind, but even if it doesn't, I can count on you to temper the Suffleys' blunders. Anyway, it's worth a try. I can introduce you to the Suffleys next weekend."

Tom very eagerly expressed his gratitude for this assistance, then, embarrassed, asked, "You wouldn't know anything about one American in particular, would you? A lovely creature by the name of Mrs. Wilson —some sort of patriot, I'm sure."

The Colonel's laugh was surprisingly loud, and not entirely happy. "No, Tom, though there are many beautiful American women, I know none by that name. But I understand you at last."

Askew's great complaisance and fondness for Tom now struggled against his sense of duty; and, indeed, his features displayed the agonies of this struggle. His earlier signal for the waiter being finally answered, in the few moments of privacy remaining, he leaned forward, and spoke urgently.

"Look'ee, Tom. If there's someone you want to find in America, go there and get her quickly. Last December, when we lost our tea, the King told Lord North that the Americans must be made to submit unconditionally, or be crushed. His Majesty thinks we'll have a short, bloody battle, and win. I know the Americans pretty well. I say we'll have a long, bloody war, and lose."

Colonel Askew set money upon the table, and rose. Only then did his weary features remind Tom of what he had callously forgotten, that the Colonel had a brother who was younger, much-loved, and a planter in Virginia.

# VIII

## Tom's Evening Continues

Before starting toward the hackney-coach stand across the street, Colonel Askew paused to square his uniform, and to inhale the cooler air outside the restaurant. It was then a bit past eight o'clock, and the sky had enough darkened in the east that a false night was forming beneath the trees of St. James's Park. A breeze blowing from the west carried fresh country scents to replace the London stench. The Colonel was pleased, for he felt he had told Tom just enough, honouring his obligations to a friend without compromising his duty to his Monarch.

"Well, my friend," said he, "in olden day, I'd have given thee a choice, either to call upon some pair of lovely actresses, or to visit a bagnio and share the embraces of its young 'priestesses of Venus.' Tonight, I should add a third possibility: if we care to admit our age, we might walk the lighted paths at Vauxhall, and talk, and overhear some inoffensive music."

As Tom had always abhorred his undeserved reputation as a whoremaster, he shrugged politely, and answered that he would prefer simply to walk at Vauxhall.

Askew then rubbed at his upper lip and, having first asked whether he might trust Tom with a secret, announced, "Well, then, you may take me for a greater fool than any in *The School for Scandal*, but this September I am to leave the army, and wed. To Miss Carlylse of Dorsetshire, a clergyman's daughter of beauty and virtue and no fortune at all."

Tom's delight at this could not be contained. Seizing his friend's hand, he gave it several hearty shakes; then, not content with that, he threw his arms around him and bussed him upon the cheek. "Well, my boy!" cried he. "No bagnios for us. To Vauxhall, then, to speak of honesty and virtue!" With that, Tom waved towards the hackney-stand, and began tugging his friend into the street, to the great annoyance of two gentlemen traversing it upon horseback. These two, indeed, seemed about to resent the interruption of their travels, until Colonel Askew, with his hand upon

77

his sword and a look of martial ferocity upon his face, persuaded them to accept their inconvenience like Christians.

It was Askew's festive notion that they cross the Thames to the Vauxhall Gardens not by Westminster Bridge, but by boat. Accordingly, just as the sun had reduced itself to a pale red band along the western sky, Tom found himself seated in a comfortable sort of barge, called a "small lugger," which, its single sail barely filled by the breeze, made a gliding progress over the smooth water. Their talk was leisurely, and the boat's crew, red handkerchiefs bound tightly about their heads, and tiny earrings in their ears, added a charming touch of the exotic. And Tom, for the first time in London, but scarcely the last time in his life, thought, "What a perfect time this is—if only *she* were here."

They reached Vauxhall at full dark, as the park's two thousand lamps began to cast their full glow against the night. The grounds shone most strikingly, clear beams shooting here and there from beneath the trees and illuminating small figures. As they stepped ashore, the music of the orchestra drifted out over the water, above the gentle rush of the water upon the quays.

The crowd—or rather the procession—hath ever been considered the highest joy of such pleasure gardens as Vauxhall. The procession that evening could not but please, being in every regard well-dressed, well-mannered, and well-ordered. I do not mean that in Vauxhall's "dark lanes" one less woman of pleasure embraced one less impassioned young swain. Yet, strolling the lighted paths, Tom and his friend savored the usual, democratic mix of Quality and commoner; Noble, business-man, and sailor. Our two friends found many acquaintances to whom it was proper to bow; they bantered cheerfully with the prettiest of these, and at last retired by themselves to one of the booths lining the grand promenade, far enough from the stage that the music of Mr. Haydn (or Mr. Mozart, or some other foreign rascal) came agreeably, rather than noisily, across the grass, to blend with the lovely sounds of crickets and owls.

When their refreshments had been brought, Colonel Askew, whose seat faced away from the central stage and towards one of the dark paths, suddenly cast his shadowed gaze downward and asked uncertainly, "You know, I often think that in my life I've never done one entirely admirable thing? I don't mean that I've been wicked, but that if I were to die tomorrow, while it might be said that I was a decent enough fellow, or a jolly dog, or some such, no one would recall a single time I rose above myself to some act of genuine courage, and . . . dignity."

This, to be sure, hit more directly upon the theme of virtue than Tom had expected; as, however, the drift of his own thoughts had been toward the same river's end, he merely nodded.

Askew mused silently before resuming, "Well, Tom, here's another secret for you. If, after my wedding, I'm returned to Parliament by my neighbours, then I mean to side with Burke and the rest, to keep us out of war."

Of course, this revelation contained no hint of surprise for Tom, who had been informed of it that morning by Mrs. Guerdion. Yet Colonel Askew had long been the most honourable of the King's go-betweens; and now he was preparing to sacrifice much for a doubtful cause.

Whatever response Tom might have made to this confidence was, however, swept away half-formed by the shocking vision which now approached him.

Reader, thou hast often enough upon the stage seen such ghosts and sprites as best become the sickly *drama* of our day; but rarely, methinks, hast thou encountered such an oddity of a man. Quite wildly drest, standing no less than six feet, four inches tall and proportionately as massive in its other dimensions, it did not walk normally, but rotated uncontrollably about the hips, while its hands waved, powerless to assist it. It carried two eyes unable to focus together within a face entirely disfigured by the scrofula; and it was accompanied by two gentlemen almost slavishly attentive. It—or rather, he (as unfamiliarity never permits us to deny humanity) seemed a common fixture at Vauxhall, for he attracted no stares save that of Mr. Jones.

"Lord help us, Bob," said he. "Here comes a great idiot led by two gentlemen."

Colonel Askew glanced carefully around, kicked Tom sharply upon the shin, and whispered harshly, "Quiet, for G__d's sake." He then stood (for the idiot had approached very near), and said respectfully, "My dear Dr. Johnson. May I have the great pleasure of introducing to you my old friend from Somersetshire, Mr. Tom Jones?"

The great *idiot*, having remarkably stabilised himself once he stopped walking, now held out a firm hand, and said very politely that the pleasure was entirely his. Some more compliments may very well have been passed, but poor Tom heard nothing, for he was utterly bewildered by his own failure to recognize the celebrated author of the *Dictionary*, *The Rambler*, *Rasselas*, and a hundred other works which had carried the glory of English letters to the corners of the globe.

Deftly filling the silence left by Tom, Colonel Askew told the Doctor how sorry he had been to learn of the death of Oliver Goldsmith, one of the greatest of comic authors, and Dr. Johnson's close friend. For two or three minutes in reply, the Doctor spoke with a sincere, melancholy eloquence upon his late friend's merits and tribulations, before rousing himself manfully to say, "But, gentlemen, I keep you from your own pleasures. Bob, I believe we shall see each other soon, at the Suffleys', this Friday fortnight."

He laughed with sudden cheerfulness. "As we shall be the only two there not avid for positions, or terrified for our reputations, we shall be the happiest dogs about. Do you spend your days wisely, and bring me many amusing tales."

"Doctor, I shall."

"Mr. Jones, your servant."

"And yours, sir."

The Doctor resumed his strange rolling gait and, flanked by his two silent companions, disappeared into the crowd. Looking after him, Bob Askew said rather sadly, "*He* invited to the Suffleys'. There's a fine gilding for scheming and wickedness. Poor gentleman: to possess so clear a genius, and so fine a character, and to be obliged to root about for scraps of patronage. Well, you and I would do the same if it were necessary; 'tis the way of the world."

With these sympathetic thoughts, Mr. Jones entirely concurred, and the two sat silently for several minutes. As, however, the object of their pity had gone off to enjoy the fair; and, as few of us care to fire our guns once the target is out of range, they soon recovered their spirits. Colonel Askew called for more mulled wine, and in a little while, they were merry again.

# IX

## At Edenfield, Two Weeks Later

A little over two weeks later, then, Tom found himself in a coach along with Colonel Askew being borne the short ascent from the Suffleys' dock to Edenfield, their villa. Tom and his friend had travelled together the eight or nine miles from London by barge, then transferred to the elegant chariot provided by their hosts. It was now about half-past nine in the evening, and nearing full darkness; the sky was overcast, and the air, alas, a little too warm and stuffy.

Colonel Askew had daily proven an invaluable source of information concerning London and politics; now he presumed to offer a quick word of counsel concerning Tom's ambitions.

"Look here, my boy," said he. "You may safely count upon the Duke's support: any gentleman of fortune, appearance, and Tory politics will satisfy him; and your ignorance of diplomacy is rather a recommendation to him, as it makes you less likely to interfere with his prerogatives. If you meet him, try to appear a little greedy and not too bright: speak of hunting, and such things.

"The Duchess is the real power you must please. She is said to favor Sir Richard Garrick's son, a handsome boy of twenty or so: you must be persuasive as you can. . . ."

This advice was accompanied by so sly a tone that Tom felt obliged to enquire as to the nature of the Suffleys' marriage.

"Why, Tom," answered his friend. "It is as with most fashionable marriages. Ellena Newley was the most faithful of wives all the way to the altar, but the pipers may as well have played, 'Good-bye, My Bonnie Lad' on the processional home. Once she had secured her fortune, she let her eyes wander; or, more accurately, she apparently decided that, as her interests lay elsewhere, her body may as well, also."

The carriage had now rolled smoothly to a stop. Colonel Askew glanced briefly out the window, then busied himself a moment with his gloves. "Well, my boy," he concluded, "There's the shape of the battlefield, as best I can report it. Heaven prosper your sword. I'll arrange for the body's return, if it comes to that." He looked up and grinned, just as a footman in the Suffley livery opened the carriage door.

Edenfield was a sprightly affair, constructed in the Palladian style, its front of perhaps six hundred feet augmented by secondary buildings which extended outwards embracingly, like arms or other limbs. This evening, Tom and his friend mounted the steps between a double row of smokey torches held by servants whose powdered wigs matched the silver of their livery. The flames rose straight in the still, heavy air, and the servants stood with a rigidity which made marble seem agile; and there was all-in-all a sense of witchery in the scene.

Four large rooms had been committed to the party: the two smallest (not over sixty feet by forty) were for cards and other gaming; the next largest held a lavish *buffet* and many heavy-set persons; and the very largest was the shared domain of the orchestra conductor and the Master of Ceremonies, who between them led perhaps thirty musicians and a hundred dancing couples. Innumerable chandeliers lit each of these rooms, which were accordingly very bright and very hot. As Edenfield was a summer home, it had been built with as many tall, broad windows as possible, and each of these had been thrown open, permitting much light and laughter to escape, and making it difficult to determine where hilarity ended, and darkness began.

Tom's friend led him first upon a brief tour of each of these rooms, then, upon an intermission in the dancing, directly towards a rather dimmer corner of the room farthest from the music, where three or four persons stood talking with unusual gravity.

One of these was Dr. Johnson, the most somberly dressed man in the room. He was being observed with considerable admiration by two quite young ladies, and was speaking seriously with a slightly older woman. This elegant lady was, indeed, a little past the first bloom of youth, yet possessed charms to make youth seem a quality much over-rated. She possessed, besides every perfection of form, the most strikingly beautiful red hair and the palest blue eyes Tom had ever seen. This woman, who appeared to hold herself aloof from all around her, was introduced to Tom during a break in the conversation as his hostess, Lady Ellena Suffley, Duchess of Harrit.

Having made the introductions, Bob Askew immediately withdrew again into the crowd, but Tom was spared any obligation to speak, for the

Duchess, having addressed not a word to him, asked the Doctor, "Are we, then, to make no concessions to the Americans?"

"Madam," he replied, "the first rule in dealing with rebels is to listen to nothing that they say. You may depend upon it: the Americans do not wish to *end* all hierarchy, but only to rearrange it, and place themselves at the pinnacle. Do not be fooled: let their Indians or their blacks begin demanding self-government, and we shall hear no more of *universal rights*. Should the Coercive Acts be repealed? Very probably. But they exist— and we must oppose a defensible change, lest a hundred worse be pressed. A line must be drawn."

Very softly, one of the young ladies ventured to ask, whether such a policy did not mean danger for such good gentlemen as his friend Colonel Askew.

The Doctor was not naturally choleric; in a voice less strident, he admitted, "Indeed, miss, the tragedy of war is that we must hazard our best. . . ."

The Doctor then began to speak very warmly of Colonel Askew's courage and sense of duty. Tom at first followed this praise of his friend with close attention, partly from interest, and partly from resentment of what he took to be a snub on the part of the Duchess. Shortly, however, he discovered that the object of her indifference had shifted: she had begun ignoring Dr. Johnson, and had turned upon our hero precisely that look of meticulous appraisal with which country gentlemen examine prize specimens at the annual cattle show.

Yet, to say truth, something about her manner, her breathing, or her stare suggested an interest even greater than that of Squire _____ in Big Fellow or Derby's Pride. She wore a gown extremely *décolleté,* and as she glided nearer, Tom became uneasily conscious of the pulse of his blood past the tight collar of his shirt. The good Doctor was saying something highly interesting; yet it had become impossible to hear him. Finally Lady Suffley addressed her first words to Tom.

"Are you warm, Mr. Jones?"

Tom replied that he saw and felt nothing which was not absolutely delightful.

Just then the Master of Ceremonies announced the recommencement of the dance, and Lady Suffley, after slipping the strap of her fan over her wrist, held out her other arm for Mr. Jones.

During all the formal, musical steps which followed, Lady Suffley said not one word which could have failed to strike any over-hearer as insipid, or to strike Mr. Jones as inflaming. At the conclusion of the dance she left him, only pausing for a moment to fan herself, and then to suggest by certain secondary motions of her fan that if Tom would follow after her in twenty minutes, he would achieve entire happiness.

Tom suffered during those minutes an absolute agony of confused anticipation, scarcely knowing to whom he spoke, or whether his remarks made the slightest sense. At last he slipped as quietly as possible through the same doorway used by the Duchess and discovered himself at the beginning of a long dim hallway, at the far end of which rose a staircase. A pert, wordless maidservant met him there, and let him upwards (in no spiritual sense, surely!) to the second floor; where, after a short further procession, she pointed towards one particular door, and, with what a less charitable (or eager) man than Tom might have considered a leer, silently vanished.

The bedroom of the Duchess was attired in a gorgeous wallpaper of Chinese manufacture, hand-painted birds and fruits all bright with reds and greens and blues and golds, but in truth, Tom's later recollections would remain imperfect, for, during the tumultuous hour which followed, his view was sometimes of the walls, but more often of the ceiling, the floor, and the bedding (both head and foot thereof), as well as several other sorts of ornaments not proper to be mentioned in such a narrative as this.

Whether, indeed, our hero could have survived a full night of such bliss, we shall leave for the debates of the College of Surgeons (though our own opinion is that he could have, *readily*); as it was, his powers were nearly at their height when there came a sharp knock at the door. Lady Suffley then bolted upright, the bedding cascading from her just as the waves had cascaded from the rising *Venus,* and cried in a fierce whisper, "The Duke!"

Alas for Tom!—now struck stone dumb between admiration for the beauty before him, and alarm for danger outside the door. Too many years had passed since his last intrigue, and now only his mistress's presence of mind (and vast recent experience) preserved him. It was she who dragged him into a condition to face the unkind world, and who, once he had rebuckled his sword, now hurried him towards the window, as his only safety. Such is the inconstancy of the human heart, however, that, no sooner had Mr. Jones lowered himself to where his head was about level with the window-sill (he grasping that ledge precariously with both hands), than the Duchess gave him such a kiss as only the great *Michelan-*

*gelo,* or perhaps only the even greater *Hogarth* could properly have shown thee, but which we can only picture by saying that she appeared determined to haul our hero back in *by the lips.*

The sweet moment ended, Mr. Jones was left to save himself while Mrs. Suffley went to calm her husband. Tom then noticed that, because of a curious slight overhang to the window structure, he could, by gripping firmly to the ivy, conceal himself very handily from observation above, while still being able to overhear all that was said. This policy (for he was a gentleman of some curiosity) he adopted, but the ensuing conversation, which was short, only demonstrated that Lord Suffley, though not a very clever man, loved and trusted his wife almost to distraction. This discovery raised within our hero (for he was by no means entirely debauched) some pangs of shame almost as sharp as the pangs of his lust; and accordingly he hung undecided whether to climb up or down the trellis when the Duke should depart.

Yet, Reader, Nature hath means to cool, as well as to raise, our passions. The night had been, as we have earlier noted, extremely warm and muggy; and, indeed, a thunderstorm had been long pending. This shower, accompanied by distant lightning and noise, now began, and though Tom was largely sheltered from the worst of the rain, the overhang, and the ivy to which he clung, were natural conductors of the stream. They at once became quite moist, then extremely slick. When the window above was shut with a bang more alarming than the thunder, Tom's grip slipped a bit, then a bit more, then gave way entirely, and he shot down the wall, first stuffing his hands with torn-away leaves, and at last plunging freely in a drop which (had it not been for some convenient bushes, ever helpful to true lovers) might have broken his foolish neck.

Instead, he suffered only some bruises and scratches, and an injury of uncertain severity to his pride: as the moralists say, it was only when he looked up that he realized *how far he had fallen.* Drenched, and not a little discouraged, he gathered himself up, and began walking gingerly back the hundred yards or so to where the Duchess's proud row of footmen were now huddled tousled, slumping and wet, with their torches extinguished.

For several minutes, the rainfall having moderated, Tom hovered within the hedge bordering the drive, uncertain whether to re-enter the party, or whether from Edenfield to take his solitary way.

He had nearly determined to depart, when he noticed a gentleman in very plain garb walking uncoordinatedly down the steps toward him.

This proved to be none other than Dr. Johnson, who, for strong reasons having decided to leave the party early, was now resolved to find his way back to London.

Mr. Jones immediately stepped from his place of concealment to join him. Dr. Johnson's clothes, which had seemed inelegant at the ball, now permitted him to move quite snugly through the drizzle. Our hero, of course, was (aside from his sundry bruises and scratches) a sodden mass of lace; but to a scholar, such trifles excite no comment, and so the Doctor received him very civilly.

The Doctor then declared, with no apparent gloom, that, his function having been fulfilled, his services were no longer wanted at the ball; a circumstance poor Tom found perfectly understandable. Upon further examination, it became clear that the Doctor had made himself unwanted by saying of a popular cleric that he had no religion, "or that, if he did have religion, it was of no very reputable kind." A lady present objecting that no man in England had studied more theology than this cleric, the Doctor had replied that "such a man studies theology as our Generals study the intentions of the French, the better to oppose and confound them, only."

"Why, sir," continued the Doctor to Tom, "no sooner had I said that, than the room cooled considerably towards me. The chill became *palpable.*" This he said with a smile which showed how little he valued the opinions of the great; and such manful independence persuaded Tom to leave off feeling sorry for himself, at least for the while.

Tom therefore mentioned his intention of hiring a barge to convey him back to London, and asked the privilege of the good Doctor's company. This being readily granted (for, in truth, the Doctor, whose means were very limited, had given not a thought to his manner of returning home, though he would certainly have swum nine miles up the Thames rather than stay where he was not wanted), the two gentlemen fell into natural and cheerful conversation, which lasted without interruption the entire boat ride home. During this ride, the clouds all gradually blew away, and by the time they reached London, a little past two in the morning, the stars twinkled very bright in the moonless sky.

BOOK

# THE THIRD

# I

## *Of Morality in Writing*

Although, Reader, I have heretofore labored to banish every scrap of interpretive commentary, and to present thee solely with the hard facts of Mr. Jones's adventures, these are perilous times for authors, and a book without commentary too much resembles a country with unpatrolled borders, for it is thereby left open for criticks to rape, pillage and burn as they see fit. Accordingly, Reader, I must try thy patience occasionally with certain brief digressions, in which I shall explain the principles upon which my book is built; and so (with thy kind indulgence) shall I build a strong tower, from which the criticks may be laughed to scorn.

Indeed, it may not be criticks only who question one aspect of our narrative. I mean particularly those actions of Mr. Jones herein described which do not, at first glance, appear to advance the noble ideal of *male chastity*. And this, I agree, is a concern not to be lightly dismissed, for the author who promotes immorality is not a nation to be protected, but an outlaw to be hung; and the criticks in his case are but a lawful *posse*.

Yet, Reader, the first duty of the historian is frankness. As, in the loveliest garden, an occasional weed grows, so there are weaknesses in the finest character. These it is the purpose of religion to correct, of eulogy to disguise, but of history to report. Some very polite authors, to be sure, draw curtains over these unseemly details. Yet drawn curtains have ever marked the sick-room; we shall, so far as we can, throw those curtains back, to admit all possible light and air—and if, with such freshness, we also admit the stares of the curious; well, so be it.

Reader, we shall not, like some angry dissenting minister, condemn Tom to eternal hell-fire prematurely; rather we shall trust in a merciful Providence to work his reformation, as such confidence seems to us true religion, as well as better literature. Nothing in his actions so far seems to us to indicate any true wickedness of mind or soul; Mr. Jones's heart was always extremely good; but so, alas, were *all* his organs.

Some honest persons may object that we betray the confidences of Mr.

Jones and others in publishing so complete an account. These persons (understandably, I believe) expect from every author the reverent discretion they in fact should receive only from the authors of tombstones, or of those inscriptions upon public statues which are meant to turn visitors green with envy even as the bronze turns green with age.

Reader, nothing is more abhorrent than a charge of ingratitude; yet in this case it is misplaced. When the time comes (as I have no doubt it shall) that his admirers erect a statue to Mr. Jones, certainly the inscription shall praise him for being loyal to his country, kind to his servants, faithful to his friends, silent about his own sorrows but responsive to the miseries of others—statesman, patriot, and on, and on. Nowhere shall we find him celebrated for having, "seduced half the women, broke half the heads, and drunk half the beer, of a grateful nation." Censorship is in this case proper, for if such lines were permitted upon public statuary, the descriptions of great men would soon display a tiresome sameness—but it is proper nowhere else.

To our hero, then, we shall apply neither the crushing rebukes of a too-harsh religion, nor the polite dishonesties of a social tradition. Between good and evil lies folly, and it is the business of the author (as it is the life-work of most men and women) to understand such folly, and to master it. Accordingly, we shall be frank, or else silent utterly.

There, Reader! Our borders now stand secure; we may walk about this realm in safety, and though it is sometimes in the interest of an author to flesh out a scanty chapter, I shall spare thee my victory oration, and return to the affairs of Mr. Jones.

# II

## A Chapter Full of Mystery, Showing How Folly May Lead Into Wickedness

Tom's appearance at Edenfield, interrupted though it was, apparently convinced Lady Suffley that he was a gentleman whose talents deserved notice, for the very next morning he received the following brief invitation, or rather, command:

My Dear Mr. Jones,

I find that the impression of our meeting remains very vivid in my imagination this morning. My husband and I are to spend week-days until our departure for France at our house in Bedford Square, where we shall be happy to receive you.

P.S. My husband goes to the Ministry every afternoon from two until six.

P.P.S. I know you are too much the gentleman ever to betray a confidence, or to boast of your conquests over the tender and trusting.

Tom (despite certain marks about his body which led him to believe that Lady Suffley was descended from a line of the tender and trusting reaching back to Alexander the Great via *Genghis Kahn*) was delighted with this note. About five minutes past two on Monday afternoon, therefore, he presented himself in Bedford Square, where he was first scolded for his coldness and delay, and afterwards passionately forgiven.

During the next two weeks, Mr. Jones experienced the trust and tenderness of the Duchess in the park, upon the Thames, and atop nearly every sturdy item of furniture in her Bedford house. Yet these encounters only soured him. He became discontented. After the first few nights, he slept but poorly, and began almost to view his afternoons with dread. Nor, of course, had he the relief of confiding in his family, since (tho' he wrote both Hacksem and Amelia of his hopes for employment with Lord Suffley) no force on earth could have brought him to mention these awkward complications with her ladyship.

Lest thou imagine, Reader, that Tom's uneasiness sprang from a penitent spirit, we must tell thee otherwise. Colonel Askew had uncovered a promise by Sir Richard Garrick to grant Lady Suffley four hundred acres near Bristol in trade for her taking his son to Maryland; and four hundred Toms, all dressed in red silk, could not undo such a bargain. To this report Tom at first objected, but when the Duchess, returning kisses for questions, refused even to speak of America, he knew it to be true, and felt himself defeated. Our hero, in short, suffered not a bad conscience, but a disappointed ambition; and that (all doctors agree) is by far the more dangerous case, especially when, as was here likely, the infection spreads to the patient's *vanity*.

Now, any true fortune hunter, had he been so insulted, would have instantly cut his losses and turned his efforts elsewhere. It was to Tom's credit (I think) that he still felt some obligation to Lady Suffley, which would not permit him to desert her.

Yet even the noblest soul is coupled to the flesh. On Friday of the second week, slumping home from his labours, Tom finally resolved to abandon the life of tenderness, admitting sadly that if he could not secure his future, he must try at least to save his health. Upon reaching his study, though, he made a discovery which turned weariness to interest and alarm. This was a note, written in a coarse hand upon the cheapest of papers, and enclosed within an envelope bearing no return address. We here give it thee *verbatim et literatum:*

Sir:
    There is a conspiracy against you which can be neither conceived by a healthy imagination, nor defeated by an ordinary prudence. For the sake of the safety of yourself and those dear to you, it is imperative that you come to the Bloody Dog tavern, Turnbull Street, in Smithfield, tomorrow between midnight and one o'clock. Present yourself as a gamester, and for a small sum of money they will conduct you to a cock-fighting ring in a building behind the tavern. I will be there, and will recognize you.
    Please speak to no one of this, 'til you have spoken with me.

---

Recognizing immediately that the letter's style was as much disguised as its penmanship, Tom at first dismissed it as the work of a madman or a jokester. Yet he allowed no jokesters among his friends, and the style, while awkward, was not deranged; as he considered, therefore, he became concerned, and, at last, he resolved to go.

We must all applaud the courage (if we cannot admire the *brains*) of a gentleman willing to visit Turnbull Street after dark, let alone after midnight. Yet, Reader, would I offer thee this moral, to accompany thee as thou walkst with Mr. Jones: though folly may indeed hold some middle space between good and evil, we must never doubt its dangerous tendencies, especially when our folly comes not from our own inexperience, but from the active intervention of other persons. Such persons too often lead us from folly to true evil, as the tailor who sells us new breeches generally tries next to sell us new coat and all, so that we may be attired whole cloth in our new fashion.

Such a caution, Reader, I hope may give thee more comfort than a loaded pistol. Then again, it may not.

---

# III

## *A Charming Interview, and an Approaching Danger*

---

The next morning, Tom's breakfast tea was interrupted by a disapproving Mrs. Guerdion, bearing a letter written in a familiar hand but a style entirely new. Following our policy, we here give it thee unaltered:

My Dearest Tom,

For weeks now, I have avoided speaking of what most concerned you, for what I could not grant, I thought best not to discuss. Certain previous arrangements, probably unknown to you, made it impossible for me to speak to my husband about a position as his secretary abroad; and so I felt compelled to silence upon a topic as important to you as your happiness is to me.

Last night, however, I received strong intimations that the great obstacle to our happiness may, like the stone before the tomb, have been rolled away without our knowledge. If you were as sincere in your entreaties as you have been ardent in your devotions, I beg of you to visit me this afternoon about three; for, that we may never be parted by narrow Channel or wide Atlantic is the most-cherished wish of

> your fond,
> loving,
> Ellena Suffley

Reader, the feathery pigeon, when its tiny brain is pierced by the marksman's bullet, is not more staggered than was our hero when he had read this note. Indeed (since we have a vast aviary of such metaphors), his heart fluttered like a finch's wings with this news; for here, after all, he saw at once the triumph of his policy and the affirmation of his charm, and which of us would not spring from our chair upon such a double victory?

Tom's imagination instantly swept westward across the water. Yet, Reader, gratitude is a feeble thing compared with love, and we must inform thee that the lovely woman with whom Mr. Jones mentally cavorted was not his benefactress, but a certain tall, proud, brown-eyed American named Mrs. Wilson. So great, however, was the perpetual flow of animal spirits within him, that he began to feel even for the Duchess a kind of warmth he had never expected.

Precisely at the appointed minute, therefore, Mr. Jones was shown into Lady Suffley's drawing-room. That Saturday happened to be Mid-Summer's Eve, and a very warm one; however, certain screens had been set to block the excess sunlight through the curtains, and the room, which was predominantly of a green colour, was as cool as could be expected at that time of day and year.

Lady Suffley herself wore a cool green dress of very modest design: and this modesty was continued in the refreshments, which were only lemonade, accompanied by a small plate of French biscuits topped with sugar crystals.

When the maid had withdrawn, Lady Suffley (with what may have been a blush—the light was poor) said quietly, "My dear Tom, although in some ways we know each other intimately"—here Tom certainly blushed—"I believe this is the first time we have ever happened to speak at length."

Tom, who had been standing beside the empty grate of the fireplace, now bowed.

"You have several times," she continued, "hinted of your desire to accompany my husband and myself to France, and then to America. May I ask whether your interest is political, or—personal?"

"Madam," replied Tom, delighted to hear his abject begging called nothing worse than hinting, "my desire to help my country in her difficulties is quite sincere. As for my personal motives, I should have hoped these past two weeks would have given ample proof of my ardent affection."

In return (for Tom had certainly not managed the sort of passion to sweep a woman off her feet), the Duchess studied him with her light-blue eyes for above a minute. At length, apparently satisfied, she declared, "Then I believe I may advise you to prepare for a journey. We sail for France in about a month, and must be ready to leave for America shortly after our return. What I considered possible when I wrote you this morning, I consider almost certain this afternoon. Later today I speak with the gentleman whose son was some months ago tentatively promised the position. The matter is delicate, but I believe I can arrange compensation which will leave everyone happy; and you and I, my dear Tom, something more than happy."

Tom expressed his satisfaction with this; and, of course, he was extremely pleased.

Leaning forward, the Duchess went on, "I hope you really are happy, and that you will forgive me for not telling you sooner. It galls me exceedingly to be denied in anything, or to admit a limitation. Can you forgive me?"

"Dearest madam, you have been kind in everything, and my gratitude is now nearly as great as my love."

The ambiguity of this statement went happily unnoticed, and the interview ended very amiably. Lady Suffley rose from her chair to give Tom a parting kiss; her lips were indeed rather cold, but she had been drinking lemonade.

Upon the street again, Tom felt himself a trifle confused. He had in his time known several love-struck women (had, for that matter, been often love-struck himself), and believed Lady Suffley to have displayed few of the symptoms: love with her was so cool a business that he could imagine no reason for her change, except perhaps a sudden collapse in the value of Bristol land.

On any other afternoon, such a riddle would have thoroughly occupied Tom's attention. Now, however, another mystery concerned him. He still carried in his pocket the urgent request for his presence at the Bloody Dog in Turnbull Street. His decision to comply had begun to seem a little hasty, and so, for expert advice, he resolved to call upon his friend, Colonel Askew.

---

# IV

## A Long and Dangerous Chapter, Showing Some of the Value of Friendship

---

Colonel Askew was not at home, but his *valet* vouchsafed that he would return in about an hour, and had no particular plans for the evening. Tom therefore left word that he desired the Colonel's company at supper, and would wait at home for his reply.

Tom then passed nearly two hours at his own house, warding off the heat with still more lemonade and wishing he were in a shady grove near Paradise Hall. Some of this sentiment he managed to channel into lengthy replies to letters from his daughter, the Jameses, and Parson Adams. While writing, he many times paused to examine the silver plate on which Mrs. Guerdion regularly placed such mail as he received. Many long weeks had now passed since Rob Jones had ridden from Somersetshire, and not a word had been heard from him: though Tom was not yet truly alarmed, parental concern mixed with denied curiosity made him reach often for an empty plate.

About six, Colonel Askew's note of acceptance, suggesting that Tom dine with him at his apartments, arrived. The engagement was for nine o'clock; Tom spent a good part of the time before dressing at his gun-cabinet, first selecting and then carefully cleaning a good pistol. This was a highlander's weapon, long-barrelled and all of metal, so that, if it misfired, it still made a club of considerable value. Pairing this with a *shakudo* dagger more decorative than useful, and once or twice drawing his sword for practice, he set his preparations aside, and ordered his bath to be drawn.

Colonel Askew's apartments were large and airy, as befitted a bachelor of considerable fortune; yet nothing about them suggested their possessor's violent occupation. Here hung no battle prints, nor crossed ancient battle-axes; here you heard talk, not of Wolfe's struggle with Montcalm, but of Pope's tussles with Homer, for, though certain carping fops claimed that the Colonel was a good classicist *for a military man,* the truth was that he was a good scholar by any standard, and his house put you in mind of no battle save that one in a library described by Mr. Swift.

For just that reason, Tom began slightly to doubt his own judgement in asking Askew's advice. He preferred initially to enjoy the Colonel's pleasure (and surprise) at learning of the Suffleys' tentative offer. Yet, having come so far, Tom determined to proceed; and, having mentioned the note generally during the roast beef, he at last produced it after the dinner had been cleared away.

Colonel Askew, after reading it through twice (a task needing little time), said simply, "You must believe it genuine, or you would not have brought it. But can you make anything of it?"

"How do you mean?"

"No grudges against you?"

Tom nearly smiled. "None."

"Your fortunes are completely unentangled? No obligations overdue?"

"No obligations at all," said Tom, a little less pleased with this question.

"I'm sorry, Tom. It was a discourteous question."

"Not at all. But I assure you that I have, to my knowledge, neither a single enemy anywhere, nor a single debt of any sort."

"Hmmm. No trouble at all?"

Reader, our hero was then many miles from his family, seeking an adventure suitable for a man twenty years younger, and intriguing with a married woman; yet such is that sweet complacency with which we habitually treat ourselves, that he answered with an emphatic, "None!"

"I wish I could say as much for myself. Well, then, I suppose the only thing to do is to go and find out. Do you think we'll need help? I can get Jack Banfield, and . . ."

But Tom leaped to his feet in confusion. "My dear Bob, I only sought your advice; to ask you whether to attend the writer, or to wait for a second communication and question the messenger."

"I should think that anyone wishing to waylay you could have chosen any avenue in London after dark, our streets being what they are. No, your correspondent, if he is not a mad-man, is a frightened one, and if you fail to appear, you'll likely never hear from him again.

"But look'ee, Tom: this is not fair, to ask your friend to share the worry, but not the satisfaction of a part. Don't be foolish: I'm considered a brave man, but I always took my regiment with me to a war. It excited no comment, I assure you."

But Tom was not to be smiled into consent, even by one so evidently his well-wisher. "I'm sorry, Bob; I'll see you tomorrow at church—"

"In the unlikely case you're still alive—"

"—and tell you all I discover."

"Well, if we bury you at mid-night, I'll mourn 'til breakfast," said the Colonel, with another wry smile. Good breeding now prevented his pressing further, and so he shrugged his shoulders before standing. Indeed, he seemed utterly to have forgotten the matter when he held out his hand and added, "It's been a splendid visit. Thank you for coming."

"You're not angry, are you, Bob?"

"Certainly not. The decision's yours. If you change your mind, of course you'll let me know?"

"I will."

"Tomorrow morning at St. Paul's, then."

The supper had been a short one; Tom stepped back onto the street only a little after ten o'clock. A faint breeze was beginning to stir, making the night somewhat less oppressive. One part of the Colonel's advice seemed perfectly sound, and so he started home to change into less elegant clothing; for in such a neighbourhood as Smithfield, elegance is not an incitement to respect, but an invitation to insult and violence.

A few minutes after midnight, then, a plain black hackney-coach, tattered and rather foul-smelling, bore Mr. Jones towards Turnbull Street. He wore a simple countryman's suit of coarse-woven, thin wool, dyed a dark brown, an open linen shirt, and a brown tricorn hat with something of a broken crown; his hair was unpowdered, and he affected no wig. His sword was certainly the most expensive thing he carried, but a man who spends so much of his wealth upon arms is generally received with respect, if not affection.

The streets of Smithfield were dark, narrow and dirty to an extreme degree, and, by reason of overhanging upper stories, even narrower above than below. These wobbling, ill-cobbled paths trapped every sort of stench, but principally those of the open sewers and the open windows of gin-shops and low taverns, which had attracted the attendance of nearly every person in the area who was not already stretched unconscious upon the side-walk. Indeed, the only persons standing along Turnbull Street— and they were extremely numerous—were certain women intent on selling themselves upon the open market; who, in response, presumably, to the great heat of the evening, had opened the bodices of their dresses to a remarkable degree. Of that noble body called the night-watch, no representative, however sleepy or aged, could be found; for they (as is widely known) construe their duties most strictly; and, having watched the night arrive, immediately leave the streets to those who are willing to kill to possess them.

It was, in short, a region in which blood and alcohol flowed with equal freedom; and as it had often before erupted into riots which required the Army to quell, it was a region to be avoided by those who had it in their power to do so. Jones wisely rode pressed far back in his seat, so that his appearance might give no cause for a robbery-attempt. When the coach halted upon their arrival, he surveyed the ground carefully before stepping onto the street. The coachman, to whom he offered a guinea if he would wait, at once put the whip to his horse's back, and called over his shoulder that he would not stay for any price, "for even a poor man's life is worth more than guineas, sir, and I wonder that you hazard your own."

As this cry faded (and indeed the last of it drifted to him from many yards away), Tom was left to study the tavern's sign, which was a wooden carving covered in badly faded paint (almost invisible in the dark) of a large mastiff, fierce in the utmost degree, and missing one ear; from the damaged side of its head the blood streamed, to pool at its feet, and beneath the charming colophon, and over an unconscious client, Mr. Jones strode into the Bloody Dog.

The noise of the Bloody Dog, a mix of quarrels and oaths, banged tankards, song snatches and whores' cries, could not down a deeper rumble, often coming to crescendos, from somewhere nearby. This Tom recognized as the sound of the gaming pit. Finding an ill-fed, hook-nosed and red-eyed old man, whose hair seemed to have been pulled out in patches, and who wore a server's apron, Tom placed some coins on his wooden tray, and told him he had come for the gambling.

The aged bawd responded by grabbing a passing barmaid's arm, and saying, "Here, Mary; take this gentleman back, will you?" His tone was, for the place, extremely civil; he shouted just loudly enough to be heard, and she responded with a curtsey before taking Tom's hand in a greasy one of her own and leading him into the tavern's black recesses.

They climbed buckling stairs (causing Tom great fright), then crossed a walkway to a second building, which they entered by a sagging cloth door—the crowd's din becoming exceedingly fierce—to reach a rope ladder leading down to the pit-room.

This round former barn, lit and heated by several dozen bracketed torches, made Tom perspire at once. Staring down at the crowd, he saw every face flushed and dripping, from alcohol and heat. Before descending the last rung, he paused, so that anyone expecting his arrival might have time to recognize him.

Imagine, Reader, the smell of a distillery with the noise of a riot. On the dirt floor stood above a hundred persons in the highest state of excitement. The roar, of cheers and shouted wagers, was agonizingly loud, and the shoving flow of bodies made trivial the pickpocket's work. The pit itself stayed hidden from Tom, who saw only the backs of heads and coats and then, rising sixty feet, the ceiling peak, with cables dangling from a pulley at its apex. Curiosity and enthusiasm aroused, he asked, "Can you get me to the front, Mary?"

"Certainly, sir," she replied sweetly, and led him forward to the edge of the pit. Tom could now see her clearly: she was a child of about fifteen, pretty and unspoiled, though her future in such a den was certainly hopeless. Her accent was of the North counties, perhaps Yorkshire. Tom, feeling pity, asked her whether she would like honest employment in a gentleman's household. She answered cooly that she had been well treated where she was, but that she thanked him.

"Yes, Mary, I understand you," Tom said, "but if you should think differently in the morning, go to the house of Mr. Jones in Hanover Square, and ask for Mrs. Guerdion. She will have honest work for you, if you want it. Meanwhile, please take this for your troubles." He gave her some silver, knowing that anything more would harden her suspicions. Although he could never expect to save every poor girl in London, as she forced her way into the crowd, he felt a faint, tender hope that he might save her.

The noise of the room grew deafening. A fighting cock, breast-feathers all bloody, had driven a spur deep into its opponent's eye. The victim, with beak flying open, now pitched forward upon the ground, one leg out beneath it at an awful angle, and did not move again.

Thunderous joy accompanied this barbarism, and as the trainer kicked the fallen bird to certify its death (and swept up the victor to prevent discovery of its death of its wounds), money went from hand to hand, accompanied usually by grins and wry faces, but sometimes by clenched fists and blows.

Across the pit, meanwhile, a small, bearded, shabbily-dressed man was arguing. Suddenly he bolted, leaping the low border of the ring and attempting to run, as cries of "Cheat!" rose behind him. He had taken but a stride when two tall fellows, broad-backed and unshaven, grabbed and started pummelling him. Briefly he resisted, then his head lolled to one side, and immediately the ruffians lifted their hands in a signal. An unclear chant arose, while the ceiling ropes lowered a coffin-like basket to the floor of the pit. Into this basket the gentleman was forced (indeed, he resisted but little), and, amid great laughter, the basket was raised off the floor, given a spin which set it rotating swiftly, and then hoisted to the ceiling. It was saluted in its progress by many thrown mugs and tankards, and at its arrival by several loud jeers; after which it was promptly forgotten, as the pit was being prepared for a contest of rat-killing terriers.

This behaviour shocked Jones, who had almost imagined the helpless man was running towards him for assistance. Tom's sympathy inspired him to ask a nearby gentleman (who stood a head taller than he, was much fatter, and wore wooden teeth) about the victim's fate. The huge squire replied fiercely that he would be left to hang until morning, then let down and banished, but that, " 'tis too gud by haf fur 'un; shood ha' ins *stoons* coot auf fur such a welshing a bet, by God!!" Our hero, made queasy by such a surgical prospect, now abandoned any notions of a rescue, for he perceived (as we must emphasize) how gambling had destroyed the humanity of his countrymen. As, moreover, he had already waited a quarter-hour without recognition, he began to think of leaving, though he delayed another few minutes before bequeathing his place to a giddy young gentleman charmed with the legacy.

Returning alone to the Bloody Dog, Tom eased through a crowd thinned by stupor and sated lust, and had nearly reached the door before he looked back to spot Mary. She now leaned against the scratch-headed old man, who seemed to guard her with paternal care; but Tom, who knew (by report) the methods of city pimps, saw only gloom in the picture. His hopes concerning her faded, but he could do nothing more, as he now had troubles of his own.

Alas, something of the fate of Orpheus clung to our hero, for in looking back, he knocked the table of an ill-tempered cut-purse, who began pouring out curses as automatically as a dog howls when its tail is trod by a careless foot. It was then that Jones made a discovery somewhat harmful to his own peace of mind; namely that, while he had been distracted by events within the tavern, some enterprising person had relieved him of his pistol. He therefore went out the door as quickly, and as apologetically, as he could.

To find a hackney-coach in such a place at such an hour would have been only the wildest coincidence, so Tom hurried towards what he hoped would be a safer neighbourhood. He skirted alleys and doorways, avoided groaning drunkards, and held himself as one "as little willing to accept, as to offer, insult"; yet these measures offered scant comfort, for he saw the angry rogue, accompanied by two allies, was now pursuing him.

Tom's situation had become extremely dangerous, since he must soon either face these villains (who might easily draw upon him and kill him); or else flee, in which case, if he did not trip on the broken pavement, he might very well draw a mob eager to run him to earth.

Smithfield, however, was a small district, and he shortly left it behind him. No London street is safe at night, but at least bleak Turnbull now widened marginally. A dim streetlamp shone ahead upon the windows of a good-size tavern, which seemed quiet and decently lit. Tom dashed inside, meaning to fight, if he must, where the terrain (and perhaps some brave souls) could assist him. The battle he found, however, was utterly unexpected, and too complex to explain in less than a full, and lengthy, chapter. Yet, Reader, beware! I fear it shall require of thee more courage to read on, than to tweak the nose of a *Grenadier*.

# V

## *An Astonishing Encounter, with More upon Friendship*

All that greeted Tom upon entering this tavern was satisfactory, for it was neat and respectable, although scantily populated (in which blend of decency and poor profits, there may be a lesson for all tradespersons). The ground floor was divided into an open eatery, and a back room, separated by a half-wall with upper timbers but no glass partitions. Tom took a seat near the front, in such a place as gave him safe view of the doorway. The rogues who had been pursuing him had halted there, and then withdrawn across the street to wait, or to form some plan.

Grateful for this respite, Tom called for ale and a piece of cold chicken, then turned his head to survey the entire room. His eyesight was extremely good, and he noticed, sitting partially turned away from him at the farthest table to the back of the tavern, a tall woman with dark-brown hair of a particular fullness. Joy brought him instantly to his feet, for by her appearance he was encouraged, and by her manner (she was arguing with an officer at her table), he was assured, that this was none other than his long-sought Mrs. Wilson.

Now all the rogues in Smithfield might have been transported to the farthest planet for all they concerned our hero; indeed, he required every ounce of his self-discipline not to run immediately to take Mrs. Wilson's side, treasonous as her theme was likely to be. As, however, she had previously shown herself capable of spreading sedition unaided, he merely carried his ale and chicken, when they were brought, to a bench more convenient for viewing. In so doing, he was obliged to leave behind him the only occupied tables in the room, one taken by a party of butchers decently attired, and the other by a pair of Life Guardsmen of considerable bulk.

Tom, as thirsty for the gaze of his *douce dame* as ever was lunatic hero of the longest French romance, now expected to drink in at his leisure. No sooner had he taken his seat, however, than he noticed something amiss, for Mrs. Wilson's eyes, besides those sparks of anger which so became her, showed a feeling nearer to fright. The gentleman facing her, tall, black-haired, and aristocratic (or perhaps merely arrogant) in manner, appeared to make some demand, at which Mrs. Wilson instinctively drew back. At once the gentleman, with very quick hands, seized her wrist, and began to drag it towards him across the table.

What happened next, Tom did not clearly see, for already he was up and rounding the partition. Pausing only a fraction of a second to be certain that his sword was clear of his coat, he stepped directly to the offending gentleman, and demanded, "Sir, take your hand from that lady."

The gentleman ordered God Almighty to damn Tom to hell.

Tom placed his arm strongly on the gentleman's red-coated shoulder and repeated his demand.

Very swiftly, the gentleman kicked back his chair, and attempted to draw his sword. Tom, however, forestalled him by grabbing a wine bottle from the table and breaking it sharply over his head. The liquor apparently worked as forcefully outside a man as within, for the officer's harsh features assumed a sudden mildness, and he slumped *mustachios first* onto the table.

Mrs. Wilson, who had followed this with some interest, now asked calmly, "Mr. Jones, isn't it?"

"Madam, your servant."

"I see you have settled with your family's enemy."

"Madam?" asked Tom, in some confusion.

"Why, surely you knew who that was you saluted with my burgundy?"

"Who, madam!?" cried Tom in alarm, for from the corner of his eye he had noticed the two Life Guardsmen, who had heard but not seen the bottle break, rising from their table and starting in his direction.

"Mr. Jones, I commend your initiative: you've drawn first blood from Captain Desmond Whipsblood, by repute the deadliest man in England; and to my certain knowledge, the most ruthless. I hope you had good cause."

Tom had grown pale with the news, and grew paler still when he saw the two Guardsmen taking a tentative step towards him. Throwing caution to the wind, or his life into her hands (or whatever you will), he now said most earnestly, "Madam, you were my cause. Since that night I saw you, I've thought of no one, of nothing, else."

At this, Mrs. Wilson laughed aloud, though whether from affection, derision, or simple nervousness, I cannot tell. "Why, Mr. Jones, you must have the emptiest head in England. What vacuities must lie between those ears!" Then, a little contrite, she added, "But you have been kind, and I am grateful." This she followed with a loud whistle, at which there immediately appeared a misshapen figure. "Arthur," said she, "we're leaving. Find the back door." As she hurried away, she called over her shoulder (for she had evidently appointed Tom her Rear-Guard) that she must depart at once for Southern France, but that she hoped they might someday meet again.

With this scant consolation, which in truth pleased him more than a Dukedom would have, Tom turned to face the Guardsmen. Unluckily, Captain Whipsblood (whose head upon the table had been concealed from their view by the low partition) chose this instant to rise a few inches and groan; and the Guardsmen, at last understanding, charged.

Tom, though no coward, and able to give or take a drubbing as well as the greatest boxer in the realm, could not master two such giants. He hoped instead to terrify them, and then to follow Mrs. Wilson's path. The danger that a villain from the Bloody Dog might have been stationed at the alley door he would confront later, for his enemies must, like the patients of any prominent surgeon, wait their turn to be treated.

He therefore climbed atop the room partition, stepping first onto the seat of Mrs. Wilson's chair, and next onto the nodding head of Captain Whipsblood. Once mounted, he drew his sword (though he had no intention of using it) and brandished it ferociously.

Tom's boldness momentarily dazed his opponents, who were evidently none of the brightest; and who, like the Latins when they saw their leader Turnus fall, felt weakened and dismayed by the whimperings of their mighty Captain.

These goliaths were, however, fighting men from scalp to toes, and Tom's life would surely have been measured in seconds, had there not, to his utter amazement, come racing through the door the figure of a man in broad hat pulled low, who, with barely a pause, lifted one of the heavy wooden tavern benches and charged with it into the backs of the two Guardsmen; at which assault, they, caught unawares, flew forward to crash almost at Tom's feet.

The Guardsmen instantly rose, fumbling for their swords with massive hands. But the other figure, having kept his balance, met them with blade drawn, and the stern warning that they had best desist lest their blood be shed.

During this brief struggle, the stranger's hat had been dislodged, and there now tumbled out a length of lank blond hair which, with his free hand, he pushed hastily back from his rather bulging blue eyes. He was, of course, none other than Bob Askew, who now, his chest heaving with his exertions, instructed Tom to disarm the two others. When this had been done, he addressed them in the following words:

"Gentlemen," said he, "this brawling in taverns does little credit to our reputations, or our uniforms." At this they stared, for he wore ragged civilian clothes; but considering, perhaps, that a drawn sword bestowed at least a quasi-military rank, they raised no objection. "Will you give me your words the story will not leave this room?" To this they assented, as in the common interest. "Excellent. Lastly, if you'll promise me to let our quarrel die here and now, you may have back your swords." Again they agreed; and indeed, I believe they would have agreed to anything which guaranteed their never seeing the Colonel again.

Colonel Askew gestured to Tom to return the weapons, but he, having rather a more temperate view of the honour of soldiers, simply placed them upon a table several yards from their reach. The Colonel, with a shout of triumph, then called to Tom to step beside him, and, exclaiming that line of the *Aeneid*'s Ninth Book which is usually translated,

> *Old age hath slowed us,*
> *But not dimmed our spirit or our vigour*

began backing towards the front door, his sword held at the salute.

As gallant as this gesture was, it nearly produced disaster, since Tom's first adversaries, having with great patience awaited the opportunity, now chose to rush upon our friends as they crossed under the tavern lintel.

Those who moan to pay the cost of our armies would have found some satisfaction of their scruples in what happened next, as Colonel Askew, in quick order, cracked the hilt of his swords across the cheek of one assailant; drove the tip of his boot into the stomach of another, and stepped clear to allow Tom his turn at the third; all before these murderous hounds had struck a single blow. Tom, eager to return some of the favour done him already, pretty effectively (tho' not so stylishly) dispensed with this final villain by darting his head into the pit of his stomach, and then dealing him several dexterous blows as he descended to the pavement.

Our friends had, however, about exhausted their advantage, and may have found themselves in difficulties (for Colonel Askew's two were already back upon their feet) had not a fast-moving hackney-coach now reined to a stop beside them, allowing its driver to snatch up a musket from beside him and fire a shot just over the head of the nearest rogue. This driver then drew a pistol from within his shirt, and declared that he would shoot the next man to move.

Poor Tom was at this all confusion; for he had in the space of two hours confronted more enemies and friends than most of us (unless we serve in Parliament) will see in many years, and he felt at a loss to tell into which category this new arrival fit.

Colonel Askew, apparently too winded to speak, grabbed Tom's arm and steered him aboard the chariot, and climbed in after him. The vehicle rolled away, leaving the rascals on the street, once they had recovered their courage, to vent their anger aimlessly.

"Well, my boy," Askew then said, "your friends will keep you company, it seems, whether you like it or not. 'Tis the price of charm."

To this sally, Tom made no reply, for he was filled with grateful meditations upon love, Providence, and the beauties of friendship. As, however, these meditations (true as they were) have already been perfectly expressed by two or three thousand divines and one or two poets, we shall skip on to matters better suited to our pen. Think when thou wast grateful once, Reader, and the mind of Mr. Jones will be flawlessly clear to thee.

# VI

## A Concise Chapter, Containing About a Month

The following morning the weather broke, allowing rain showers to wash the smoke, and lift the heat, from the air; and immediately after there arrived one of those chill spells which make our English weather seem as changeable as the affections of Miss _____* or Sir _____.* That afternoon, as Tom and his friend walked together in the weather-made solitude of St. James's Park, the Colonel explained how he had happened to participate in the events of the night before.

*Whomever the reader wishes.

He had been playing cards at White's, it seemed, when a gentleman had mentioned some unhappy news: earlier in the evening, Danny Garrick, Sir Richard's son, had been wounded in a nasty brawl. Strolling near Leicester Fields with a courtesan of notable beauty, he had been provoked by two or three young braves. Words were exchanged, then blows, and he had unwisely drawn his sword, whereupon, he had been run through.

"This news," the Colonel continued, "taken with the note you'd shown me earlier, and Lady Suffley's strange remark to you about persuading the Garricks to withdraw their claim, raised my concern—perhaps foolishly, I admit. I supposed I would check in on you. Perry, my *valet*, is an old veteran; we hired use of an aged coach, and waited just out of sight of the Bloody Dog. I followed you surreptitiously from there to the Knave and Compass, and then . . . well . . ."

"And then you arrived most handily, for which I hope I may someday repay you," Tom said. He was, however, immensely concerned at the Colonel's information. Feeling somewhat as the deer must when first it notices the hunter, he asked his friend if Garrick lived, and whether the fight had seemed an ambush, a conspiracy.

Askew first replied that the doctors had—as always—despaired of the young man's life, but that several gentlemen calling to pay their last respects had since found him in bed very sore and bruised, with a broken jaw and a leg wound, but feverless, and in no danger of dying.

"Yet," the Colonel continued, "my suspicions were like your own, and so I spent this morning visiting the parties involved. The magistrate who dismissed the case is a fee-taking rascal; the young braves have all left London; and the young girl, who calls herself an actress, tho' she is appearing in no play just now, told me only this: that Master Garrick quarreled drunkenly with three gentlemen, was soundly thrashed for his rudeness, and then challenged them as they were departing; and so (although she was sorry to say it) got just what he deserved. At that, she tenderly wiped at that place where a tear should have been, and hinted she was unoccupied this evening.

"In conclusion, I've learned only that our streets are dangerous, our magistrates corrupt, and our prostitutes hard women; and that was scarcely worth my bustling morning's activities."

The two friends then passed beneath some laurel trees, where the shade was chilly; and that, or something else, made Tom shiver. Observing him, the Colonel said sympathetically, "Look'ee, Tom, it was natural to suspect but, having reconsidered, I see how implausible it is that the

Duchess of Harrit would have hired anyone to eliminate your rival. Surely no gentlewoman could be so wicked, especially when she had the simpler course of withdrawing her offer to his father."

So clear an argument persuaded Tom pretty well. Whether the Colonel himself believed it, I do not know, but certainly those of us who would never stoop to deception from any other motive, may be sometimes tempted to do so out of kindness.

The two friends then walked a short distance in silence, until they had come to an opening in the midst of the grove, where, after looking searchingly around him, Colonel Askew asked, "You said earlier, Tom, that you wanted to repay me for last night. Did you mean it?"

"Of course."

"Well, you could, if you will, perform a crucial service."

"Yes?"

"When you visit France, take careful notes of what you see and hear, and when you return—not before—write me a full report."

"You want me to spy?" asked Tom, in some confusion.

"Merely report your general observations, plus whatever you can learn of military, and especially naval, matters. Can the French convey an army to America? Defend their own ports? Anything you discover—particularly about their recent ship-building—would be useful."

Poor Tom!—who thought so many years before that Molly Seagrim had amended his innocence forever. Yet there are many kinds of innocence, and he, in his fondness for his country, had never imagined how much England depended upon espionage for her survival. The budget of our Secret Service stood that year at £80,000, including nothing for the voluntary contributions of such gentlemen as Colonel Askew, who informally passed on what they discovered.

But if Tom was naive, his patriotism was unquestionable. Just as Colonel Askew, though disliking the American venture, still worked for his country's true security, so Tom, despite a simple honesty which made him mistrust spying, was willing to help—if absolutely necessary. In that weak tone which generally precedes agreement, he said, "I know very little of military matters. Surely someone else . . ."

"An ignorance of military affairs is easily corrected; and is, indeed, advantageous, since our French counterparts will hardly suspect a"—here he winked—"booby country squire. Why, Tom," he continued more solemnly (for he feared his joke had miscarried), "even Joshua sent spies into Jericho; 'tis a tradition, like war itself, we must honour for all our doubts."

They walked a dozen yards in silence before Jones consented. Rain threatened, and it was time for evensong, which Colonel Askew expressed a great desire to hear. The two friends therefore turned their steps towards the barracks of the Horse Guards, where the Colonel's carriage had been left.

So Tom, having, for motives too numerous to list, undertaken a job of vast complexity, now began by far the busiest month of his life. His position as secretary to the Suffleys, to be sure, showed every sign of being a disappointment, since his lordship made it clear at their first meeting that he considered Tom merely an ornament to his own prestige and worthy of no true authority.

Tom therefore applied himself to his military studies, and at the end of his month was, I may say (not without regret), much better qualified in the theory of naval warfare than several young gentlemen who have become commodores solely because their fathers were earls.

It was, in short (despite the pompous Lord Suffley), a month Tom savoured, for besides the tenderness of the Duchess, the thought of Mrs. Wilson, and the companionship of Colonel Askew, he had acquired the friendship of Dr. Johnson. As much time as they could find during that short month, the three gentlemen spent together, and Tom, for all that he had worked himself into notable difficulties, began, as of old, to enjoy life's fulness.

# VII

## In Which Our Hero Receives a Letter
## and Leaves the Country

As the fifteenth day of September drew to a close, Tom Jones sat beneath an arbor, gazing at the small garden at the back of his Hanover Square home. The Suffleys' departure, twice delayed, was at last firmly set for the following morning at dawn, and he had passed eight hectic hours supervising the packing and transportation to dockside of his wardrobe and supplies. Those preparations had been unusually extensive for a simple trip to France, for, following their six weeks on the Continent, the Suffleys and their entourage were to return to England only briefly before boarding H.M.S. *Nonesuch* for the voyage to Maryland.

Tom, therefore, had spent a very busy September, in which all the duties and pleasures of the preceding month were compounded by endless visits to his bankers, his tailors, and a dozen of those London merchants who exist to see that the English gentleman sets out upon his Grand Tour equipped with everything but his money, which they are generally pleased to keep for themselves. And so it was that our hero, newly attired from periwig to shoe buckles, rested beside his fig-tree (or rather, beneath his grape-leaves), and contemplated with satisfaction the growing shadows of the closing day.

He had not been long lulled by the comfortable warmth (for it had been a very warm September) before an interruption appeared in the form of Mrs. Guerdion, bearing the wrought-silver letter salver. The glint of this in the fading sunlight caught Tom's attention, and his languor vanished when he recognized the handwriting of the direction. A moment later, he had turned himself in his chair so as to have light enough to read:

> Dublin, at Captain
> O'Hehir's house
> 25 August 1774

Dear Father,

    I write only briefly to tell you that all is well, but that, for several reasons, I have decided against a military career.

    I arrived here about the 1st of July, bearing letters to several persons from friends of yours, and was very kindly received by the military gentlemen I wished to meet. I passed some weeks observing the maneuvers of Captain O'Hehir's company of infantry, and tho' the company was genial, the way of life was not, for I have discovered that the soldier's great dangers, so long as we remain at peace, are sore feet, poor food, and vast monotony.

    The military here, moreover, face extreme unpopularity, not only with the poor (who are pitiable beyond imagining), but with those persons I should particularly wish to know, clergymen and merchants, as well as wits and young ladies.

    Under such circumstances, I know I will do better leaving, and so I trust I will have your blessings and approval for my revised plan, which is to depart Ireland for the West Indies, where the climate (except for a few bugs and diseases) is much better, and the prospects for a young man of spirit are much brighter.

There is, of course, nothing I desire more than your advice and counsel upon the direction of my life, and were it not that my ship departs here tomorrow morning for Kingston, Jamaica, I would certainly wait here to receive the benefit of your opinions. As it is, I shall pass every spare moment aboard ship in collecting observations, so that my next communication may contain more of value than this present poor effort of

Your loving,<br>obedient son,<br>Rob Jones

P.S.: I know you will forgive my not having written these past months, since I wished to spare you those empty, frilly letters which say nothing of substance, and which I know you despise.

Every parent must sooner or later receive such a declaration of independence as this, and Tom, though he would have given much for the lost frilly letters, sought rather to admire than to lament what he had read. There was, indeed, much to encourage him, since Rob was evidently in good health, and neither impoverished nor discouraged. Tom's concern on learning that his son was sailing eight thousand miles to a land of fevers, pirates, and rebellions, he was obliged to suppress, and he strove instead to imagine white beaches and clear blue seas. . . .

His brief reverie was cut short by Mrs. Guerdion's clearing her throat loudly.

"Ah, Mrs. Guerdion. Perhaps you would like to see this letter from my son?" Tom said, for he knew that his housekeeper was devoted to Rob.

She, snatching the letter from Tom's hand, read it with some difficulty in the spreading gloom, and then said, in a tone less harsh than her words, "Marry, it seems Mr. Rob might have remembered some persons who always had time for him. Yet the young gentleman has much upon his mind; and there is a deal of spirit to his writing."

Handing back the letter with some reluctance, she declared, "But, sir, if you still plan to attend Mr. Burke and the other gentlemen for dinner, you had best come in and prepare. And, sir, the last of the lading receipts from the *Mary Anne* have arrived. Your goods will all be aboard before dark."

"Thank you, Mrs. Guerdion." Taking one last look around the garden, which appeared in the dusk to have filled with a bluish smoke, Tom felt a curious longing for times, and persons, long gone. "I'll come in. And Mrs. Guerdion: thank you for many years of kind and faithful service."

"Why—marry—indeed—" she stammered, and, trailing a grumbling protest, scurried back into the house.

Tom had chosen to spend his last night in England at a supper arranged by Colonel Askew, to which a dozen gentlemen of diverse opinions, including Dr. Johnson and Mr. Edmund Burke, had been invited. So many political beliefs being represented, the conversation was wisely restricted to painting and personalities for part of the evening, and at length degenerated to that general hilarity which ordinarily accompanies much food, more wine, and well-assorted companions.

At length, however, the party broke upon some extremely droll remarks by a gentleman named Boswell, and the guests departed, many singing, into the night. It was then two A.M., and, as Tom was due to board the *Mary Anne* at five, Colonel Askew and the Doctor offered to accompany him to his ship's dock near the Tower. Because the loading of several vessels still continued at that hour (under the shutting eyes of those customs officers who were not snoring in their shed), the area was safe, and the three friends walked and joked with travellers' exhilaration.

They had, indeed, drunk so much ale that their locomotion was a trifle faulty. Colonel Askew declared they staggered like three sailors in a *hurricano*. Doctor Johnson (who had drunk least of all) agreed, and a moment later quietly and surprisingly added that he was soon to leave for France himself.

"Why," cried Tom, "we shall meet in Paris."

"I fear not, Tommy, for I travel at the expense, and therefore at the pleasure, of the Thrales."

Tom, guessing the painfulness of such dependence upon patrons, asked the Doctor what visits he would pay, if he were at liberty.

"Why, sir, we must all see the great churches and public buildings; those are inevitable. I think I should next like to meet Mr. Franklin," he replied, suddenly playful.

His friends, knowing his Tory hostility to the Americans, expressed amazement.

"Nay, gentlemen," said he, holding up his large hand, "Mr. Franklin is a man of talents. In general, I do not love a philosopher, for a philosopher is one who, when you are starving, will only tell you what Plato said upon hunger, and that is a piece of news you are not likely to want. Mr. Franklin may not feed you, but he will raise a committee to give you twenty pounds, and that's at least as well. He is an *energetic* philosopher."

Tom, who would have reverenced such a meeting between the two great sages, said sympathetically, "I regret, sir, your never receiving that position in government worthy of your talents, which might have made such a meeting possible."

The Doctor very genially replied, "My dear Thomas, gentlemen nearly always receive what they deserve. Indeed, tho' I may never hope to steer the ship of state, yet I feel I have been a sort of literary Marine, who in wartime mounted the rigging, and now and then hit one of the enemy's officers." This he said jestingly; yet their talk had sobered them. In the east the sky now lightened.

"Well, sir," said Tom, "you will yet do great service for your country."

"Indeed," agreed the Colonel, "he is not young. Yet gold never tarnishes."

From the time of his first fame, Dr. Johnson, who was now three days from his sixty-fifth birthday, had treated the young respectfully, and had in return enjoyed their loyalty and affection. Now he smiled widely. "Well, you dogs, you flatter me with your predictions. Indeed, though, you must avoid prophecy. Prophecy is the most certain thing in the world. Whoever attempts it is certain to fail."

As they laughed, a bustling began, first with the appearance of the crew upon the deck of the *Mary Anne,* anchored some few dozen yards off shore; and next with the arrival dockside of two carriages. The smaller of these was a simple hackney-coach, bearing the ship's captain; the other was the splendid vehicle of the Suffleys, which discharged, besides the noble couple, at least half a dozen of their servants. Tom was now obliged to take cordial leave of his friends, and to join his travelling companions, who were waiting unsociably at water's edge for the passenger barge to reach them.

Of the persons greeting Tom, only the Suffleys are to take any great part in our story, and as Mrs. Suffley is already known to thee, Reader, we shall confine ourselves to a brief description of her noble husband.

Lord Didapper Suffley, then, was a small man, with a plain, pale face, untrustworthy little brown eyes, and calves the thickness of splinters—but extremely elegant clothes. He generally observed Tom with a kind of melancholy hatred, which dissolved into polite contempt when (I suppose) he recollected that Tom, whatever his personal advantages, was still only a booby country squire with no claim upon nobility. Tom, for his part, had during the preceding weeks learned much about his employer, but never how to like him.

Upon such cozy terms did Tom board the *Mary Anne.* He went at once to examine his quarters, which (in contrast to the luxury accorded the Suffleys) were merely an enclosed cot, set at the very rear, or rather, aft, of the ship. Returning upon deck, he discovered, rather sadly, that his friends had departed. Sailors now ran to set the canvas and raise the anchor. As the white sails caught the pink dawn light, the ship moved swiftly into the current.

A crossing breeze blew pleasantly over the deck, and Tom, resolved to be cheerful, strode to the stern of the ship, where he placed his hands upon the railing and contemplated with satisfaction the numerous evidences of English maritime supremacy: the uncountable skiffs and barges and coasters, and here and there the massive *India-men;* the countless buildings and the distant bulk of London Bridge.

Tom had imagined himself to have found the one private place upon deck; yet he now heard his name called, and turning, saw the Duchess stepping near to him. Her red hair flowed from beneath a straw hat whose azure ribbon was tied loosely beneath her chin. The ship at that moment happening to lose the wind, the deck rolled slightly, and Lady Suffley stumbled, falling forward but catching herself upon Mr. Jones. Their embrace (for Tom could scarcely help steadying her) seemed to linger, and indeed one of her hands had settled rather low. The reviving wind swept her straw hat overboard. Having spent the night in one form of indulgence, Tom was a little reluctant to spend the morning in another; yet, looking down into her pale eyes, then back at the wet commercial grandeur of the Thames, and still again into her eyes, he admitted with pleasure that the English practiced superbly at least one art besides seafaring.

BOOK

# THE FOURTH

# I

## Containing the Solution to a Mystery, as Well as a Notable Credo

Before accompanying Mr. Jones abroad, we must, I believe, clarify several mysteries relating to his home-land; for I have often observed that readers who feel themselves denied essential facts travel as unhappily as doth a voyager who hath left baggage behind on the dock, and cannot enjoy present marvels for worrying about past mistakes.

Indeed, Reader, I believe we may recast this notion more profoundly yet, for, though we unhappy mortals are fated to live our lives mostly in error and darkness, we may, while we read, be spared this misery, if only our author will lay clearly before us what facts are available, as soon as he or she shall acquire and understand them.

In all the brilliant glow of our history, there remains, perhaps, a single shadowy region: why did Lady Suffley, to her apparent disadvantage, make Tom her husband's aide? Even granting our hero's very considerable personal charms, we must wonder.

To answer this question, we must call to thy attention a singularly dark night directly preceding the day when Lady Suffley first intimated Tom might have the desired post.

On that dark night (the quarter-moon having already sunk very low), a handsome equipage overtook a plain hackney-coach upon a rough and dusty by-road halfway between Edenfield and London. As these two vehicles, side-by-side, rolled slowly on, their facing windows were lowered, and during perhaps a ten-minutes' passage beneath a grove of ancient overhanging oaks, a pact was made. Only when the coaches returned at last to the open way did the faces of their occupants become briefly visible. In the matchless coach-and-six, her stunning beauty hidden by a hooded black cape, sat Lady Suffley. In the humbler conveyance, his own hard visage a sufficient protection, rode . . . Mr. Hastings Sinamore.

It was Mr. Sinamore, I suppose, who (having learned from Tom's letters to Hacksem of our hero's wish to travel with the Suffleys) first proposed a meeting to her ladyship. What, precisely, was sworn as they rode that dark path, must, alas, remain unknown; yet surely it secured for Lady Suffley a share in whatever dark schemes the lawyer had in motion; and for the lawyer, a promise that Tom Jones would be kept abroad and, so far as possible, ignorant of events at home.

The potential wickedness of such a pact may, Reader, cost thee some uneasiness; and, in truth, I fear it had thus far reached but a fraction of its final scope and malice. Yet we may now at least comprehend the behaviour of Lady Suffley, and (if necessary) steel ourselves for worse deeds to follow.

Reader, I have perhaps been guilty of unkindness in not informing thee of this meeting earlier. In truth, while it is my instinct to oblige thee in everything, I have remained silent for this simple reason: that, if thou wilt understand our characters, thou must understand as well some portion of their ignorance and confusion, by which thou shalt come to admire their courage and tenacity in enduring, much more than our own skill in recording, the events of this history. In truth, I consider an author who will usurp the glory due the persons of his or her story, to be simply a thief, as contemptible as those politicians who place upon their own heads the laurels won by the blood and brains of their distant soldiers.

For such good reason, Reader, have I with-held from thee these facts; and, as I hereby pledge to with-hold from thee nothing further, I hope I may be forgiven. Indeed, I hope I may henceforth prove a torch unto thee, to illuminate this dark world—and not merely the orange tip of a burning fuse, which glows upon nothing but itself, 'til it provides the light of an explosion, and takes all with it to perdition.

# II

## Containing the First Part of a Trip to France

As our history is neither diary nor travelogue, we must eschew the detail typical of both those forms, and concentrate our narrative upon those places or events which shaped the mind, or influenced the fate, of our hero.

On the morning of his twelfth day in Paris, the fourth day of October, therefore, Tom Jones awoke in the grasp of a painful nostalgia which had affected him from his first arrival in France, or rather from the start of his journey by coach from Le Havre.

The French countryside had then seemed unspeakably pleasant, and its fields in the golden pregnancy of the nearing harvest, had made him remember that his love for his Sophia had begun one perfect day on her return with her aunt from France. As the coach forced its rough way over that soft countryside, he heard with extremest clarity a song she had delighted to sing. It was a sad ballad, which began, "*Sans cuer, dolens, de vous departiray. . . .*" Then had he first understood how iron are the doors which time closes for us; and for the first time in his life, he felt old.

Had Tom been a monk in his cell or a philosopher in his garret, his musings upon this nostalgia might perhaps have led him to the reform of certain actions which did no credit to the memory of Sophia. As, however, he was simply an English gentleman in the bed of a French *hotel*, his contemplations (whether of our theme, or of the canopy above him) were now interrupted by the entrance, *sans* knock, of his *valet*, who first dropped a cup of tea beside his bed, and then seized the chamber-pot and heaved its contents, with every evidence of joy, out the window and onto the street below.

Thus roused, our hero went to join his patrons at breakfast, where, as he had done every morning since reaching Paris, he savoured the loveliness of the gardens behind Parisian homes. For the company, alas, he felt less enthusiasm. No sooner had Tom taken his seat than Lord Suffley began one of his addresses to the family Parliament.

"Remember, Mr. Jones," said he, "that we are in the land of our enemies, and must have no blundering amid the alien corn. Hear as much as you can, and say as little; and wherever possible, defer to one who understands these matters, meaning, of course—myself."

His Lordship made a dramatic halt, which Lady Suffley occupied by secretly rubbing her bare foot along Tom's ankle.

"In brief," the Duke resumed, "our situation may be summarized as follows: Louis XVI is an impotent boy and probably an idiot, who in the middle of the night stands out on the terraces of Versailles shooting cats when he ought to be making love to his wife. Of his two chief ministers, one is a seventy-four-year-old incompetent, and the other is a fat bourgeois —his name, Vergennes—who would sell his wife to a slave-trader to revenge the beating we gave *la belle France* in '63. Our job is to convince them that any interference in America will get them a whipping that will make them recall '63 as a Lord Mayor's banquet. . . ."

Reader, lest thou imagine that I slander our statesmen to record such rantings, I must assure thee that Lord Suffley (though he spoke precisely as I have suggested) was more temperate without his family than within. Men and women lose control of their language when they have lost control of their situations; and marriage, after all, had been for Lord Suffley what the Battle of Quebec had been for the French, a piece of gallantry that turned into a slaughter. It hath very aptly been observed that a diplomat is "a man sent to lie abroad for his country," and Lord Suffley, who was as willing to lie for his country as for any other of his interests, represented England with diplomatic grace.

Tom, meanwhile, heard His Lordship placidly enough, for he had already devised a plan of his own. Two days earlier he had sent a card to Mr. Franklin, who was then staying at the nearby village of Passy. In return, he had received an invitation—not cold and formal, but sociable and hearty—to dine with the sage at one this afternoon. This minor part of his plan, Tom felt he could conceal, but the greater part required a public discussion.

"If you have no objections, my Lord," Tom began, "I shall leave tomorrow for Marseilles. I have been requested by certain persons I need not name to learn what I can about French naval preparations."

"I imagine you are an expert upon military preparations?" His Lordship asked peevishly.

"Mr. Jones is expert at many things," Lady Suffley interjected, with perhaps too fond a smile.

Tom, meanwhile, said nothing, but merely waited for His Lordship to choke down his anger. To say truth, His Lordship, after briefly turning a dark, choleric red, immediately calmed himself, for his brains, while they might pant crossing the Alps of philosophy, moved quite nimbly through the bushes of deceit; and he clearly saw that a Tom in Marseilles would be out of the arms of a wife in Paris. "Well, my dear," he began at last, "no doubt you are right. Mr. Jones, you know your duty, and must do it. Only remember to be back here by the 25th, for we should be *heartbroken* to sail without you."

A few minutes later, having finished his *croissant*, Lord Suffley stood importantly, as he had been invited to a most singular honour, that of attending the King at his *Lever*. This odd ritual was meant to show the weight of the Crown of France, by requiring that the gentleman who wore it be helped from his bed each morning by twenty of his noblest courtiers. This was indeed the perfect occupation for those French Lords who had nothing but time and money to burn; their intellects having, I imagine, gone up in flames long ago.

The Duke's departure left his wife and Tom to enjoy one of those scenes of tenderness which, we have no doubt, are as shocking to thy morality, Reader, as they are tiresome to thy imagination.

Reader, we shall not, for pity, describe any more of Mr. Jones's encounter that morning; for, in truth, though we have always been his friend, we are at present a little ashamed, and a good deal worried, on his account. His frigidity toward the suffering Duke (tho' the Duke was not a good man) was perhaps the only occasion in his life on which he displayed coldness of soul; and in truth, it ought to be a warning to us all, no matter how good our natures, that bad habits, uncorrected by prudence and true religion, will inevitably lead us to that state which is generally pictured as a pit of fire, but which might more properly be called a cave of *ice*.

# III

## A Trip to France Continued

Following his celebrated dispute with the members of the Privy Council concerning the justice of the Boston Tea Party, Mr. Franklin had temporarily exiled himself to a house owned by a rich sympathizer with the American cause named Leray de Chaumont. The house was at Passy, a village about halfway between Paris and Versailles, set above the river Seine. The afternoon Mr. Jones dined there, white puffs of clouds dotted the blue sky, the pear trees hung heavy with unripened fruit, and the wind, wherever the sun did not shine directly, blew autumnally cold.

Eight persons sat down together at the table, but the two French gentlemen, M. de Chaumont and a friend, were called away early, and the four French ladies, who talked charmingly through the meal, took their jolly leave not long after its conclusion; Tom and his host assisted them across the lawns and into their carriages, for which Tom received many kind words, and Mr. Franklin, many affectionate kisses.

When the carriages had rolled away, Mr. Franklin first said happily, "Delightful ladies!" and then, more sharply, asked, "Well, my friend, will you do me the honour of sitting in the garden to enjoy this bracing air, or shall we huddle by the fire in the study like a pair of old men?"

In very few hours, Tom had grown accustomed to the genial provocations of his new-found friend. Ben Franklin was then sixty-eight years old. Much affected with gout, he walked with a cane, and that only slowly. The white fringe of his remaining hair he wore at shoulder length; he was plump, double-chinned, and clothed in heat-preserving beaver hat and coat. Yet no one was ever more alive than he. Youthfulness and imagination shone from his eyes, and Tom easily saw why the ladies had kissed him: he was a loving, and a loveable, man.

And yet a tart one, who must have forced mouths to pucker for reasons other than love. No sooner were they seated upon a stone bench in a grassy part of his garden than he began, "So, my friend, you work for Lord Suffley. He's the one with the gaping eyes of a poisoned pig, if I remember. I wouldn't trust him as far as I could throw him; and, given my age and condition, that isn't a compliment. *You* don't like him, do you?"

This, to be sure, was softened by a nudge in the ribs; and Tom was so staggered by the mock assault that he laughed and admitted that he did not.

"Well, then, Tom, you are an honest man, and we can talk together. Why did you come?"

In truth, this was a question Tom could not easily answer. The great philosopher was by most accounts his enemy, having recently been stripped of his colonial postmaster's position by the British government on a charge tantamount to treason.

Yet a trip inspired by restlessness, fashionable curiosity, and an honest desire to understand the arguments for American independence, had become now almost a pilgrimage. The old American reminded Tom miraculously not of one man, but of two. He seemed to blend the judgement and philosophy of Squire Allworthy with the reckless joy of Sophia's father, old Squire Western—as wild a sportsman as ever pursued the fox. Such a character must inevitably have inspired Tom's reverence and affection; and, Reader, we must believe that political enemies may sometimes find incentives of simple humanity to try the garden bench and the conference table before the arsenal and the battlefield; or else our world must be a bloody place indeed.

So thinking, Tom began, "I have come, dear sir, on no embassy save my own. I tell you frankly that six months ago, when I first thought to seek a diplomatic role, I believed that only an iron hand—indeed, one clenching musket and bayonet—might restore civility to America. Since then, having met some Americans—" (here he thought of Mrs. Wilson, and blushed)"—I began to think differently.

"And so, good sir, I would ask you directly whether you believe war with England is inevitable, and whether you can suggest anything that a poor aide to a Colonial Governor might do to prevent it."

It was part of Ben Franklin's nature that he could not seem portentous or tragic; and so he always spoke bad news with a certain dry directness.

"Tom, two years ago I told a friend that it would take a hundred fools, all pulling hard, to drag our two countries into war. Well, we were five or six fools short on our side of the ocean, but yours worked extra hours, it seems. Will you follow me, please?"

The old gentleman now led Tom through an iron gate at the back of the formal garden, and onto a field of knee-high grass which, unprotected by garden walls, shivered in the snapping breeze. This field, indeed, appeared to stretch on for a great distance, and Tom saw no object they might be seeking.

When they had walked perhaps two hundred yards along this field, they came to a shocking evolution: the grass suddenly ended at a cliff-side, and below them, awe-striking, spread the valley of the Seine River. They stood no longer upon a meadow, but at the edge of a precipice.

"Good M. Leray de Chaumont," Mr. Franklin began, "says he keeps the ledge unfenced to dazzle visitors with the majesty of nature; I tell him he means to shove me over when I've worn out my welcome." Here, unexpectedly, the sage arched his back and spun his arms like one tottering before a plummet; then, having amused himself, he folded his hands behind his back, and continued, "But understand me: this represents Britain and America these past twelve years. Too many hopeful people have been galloping across the meadow toward an abyss."

Mr. Franklin's meadow, so used, must have struck any thinking hearer as perfectly reflecting not only the political crisis, but the lives of most of our fellow beings. Our hero (tho' he rarely flaunted the fact) could think very well—and, despite the sarcasms of some envious persons, with his *brains*, too.

Therefore, as the wind whipt at the strands of his hair and drove the swift clouds high above the shadowed valley, he answered softly, "Yet, dear sir, while the horseman remains in the saddle, and the horse still touches the earth, something may be done, may it not?"

"My friend, you are asking one who has worked a decade to prevent the accident, without success. Yet every political society must embody both problems, and means for resolving them. Let the means for resolution be generally accepted, and society will survive any problem. But the long passage of time with problems unsettled will gradually erode confidence in the means of resolution; and when those are despised, anything may occur—even rebellion.

"The wise politician will therefore compromise any other principle before those principles of resolution, for they are the heart and essence of his society.

"In short, sir, this is a good time to be generous, and a poor time to be stubborn; it is time for England to show she cares more for the happiness of her colonists than for any abstract old debts. Otherwise, she may well collect her taxes, and lose her empire."

Only at the last, very suddenly, had passion entered Ben Franklin's speech; Tom, looking closely, saw him to be trembling about the mouth and breathing with some difficulty, and was sorry to have caused such trouble—especially as he had scarcely received any practical advice.

At last, Tom said quietly, "My dear Ben, you may be consoled to know there are many men in London—men of great influence—whose sentiments are exactly yours. They—"

"They had best use their influence quickly, then," the old gentleman interrupted, speaking almost to himself, "for—tho' I can tell no secrets—I fear both sides will very soon retire their men of influence, and leave the field to their men of arms."

Mr. Franklin had said this in tones of strongest emotion, but he now paused, and seemed (as most of us shall, in time, if we have lived good lives) to take some comfort, or perhaps information, from memory.

"Thirty years ago, Tom, I armed the Pennsylvania Colony. The Quaker fathers would grant no money for weapons, so I requested it for the purchase of "rice and other grains" and for *"fire-engines."* I thought myself clever. The "other grain" was gunpowder, and the *"fire-engines"* were cannon. They knew this very well, but needed some salve for their consciences—and they voted us the money.

"So, you see, I know something about these matters, and can tell you that men will always find the means for killing when they think they must. The implements of war are very easy to take up, and very hard to lay down."

Mr. Franklin then looked again over the valley, which was gradually losing its colour in the late afternoon, until the sails of the boats were as grey as the water, and the homeward-bound cattle on the distant hills seemed nearly-black dots against the dark-green of the pastures. The wind had become genuinely cold; yet he stood unmoving. "Ah, Tom," he said sadly, "it *is* a beautiful world; and we have only ourselves to blame, that we are not happy in it."

Our hero could think of no reply to this; and so, after another few minutes watching the closing day, the two gentlemen returned slowly across the meadow.

The crossing of the meadow restored Mr. Franklin's spirits. He brightened as he showed Tom through the house, and at the front door, he suddenly excused himself, and returned with a hinged box perhaps six inches long, and half that in its other dimensions. "Something I invented. I hope they will remind you of me. No, don't open it 'til you're on your way." With a smile, he added, "Perhaps they will help you see your way clear to write a line now and then to a bored old man?"

Tom promised he would write often.

"Forgive me for not asking you to supper. I expect a guest who must leave Paris late tonight, and with whom I must discuss several urgent matters."

Tom, needing no further hint, immediately said his farewells and most-genuine thanks, and hastened down the broad front steps.

By the dim half-light within the coach, Tom opened his present, and was amused to find a pair of those eye-glasses Mr. Franklin had invented, which contained two different lenses set concentrically, and which he had named "bifocals." So charmed was Tom, that he failed to observe the passage, in the direction opposite his own, of a second, rather meaner, carriage. This carriage soon halted, allowing Mr. Franklin to greet its sole passenger, who was a tall, dark-eyed woman by the name of Wilson.

## IV

### In Which Our Hero Acquires a Servant, Travels South and Sees Much of Interest

During his trip from Paris to Marseilles, a journey of some five hundred miles which he accomplished in just over six days, Tom Jones enjoyed several satisfactions, but chiefly that relief which rural travel gives to the overburdened mind.

The mind of our hero was in fact burdened by no fewer than four separate worries which, like bats, were oft-times content to leave him alone in daylight, but always returned to attack him after dark. These four worries (in no particular order) were: his longing for Mrs. Wilson; his alarm at the words of Mr. Franklin; his doubts about his affair with Lady Suffley; and his concern for his family in Somersetshire. Indeed, Tom had not received a letter from home since he took ship for France, when his correspondence had fallen under the control of Lady Suffley, and his daily post had come to consist of only the apologetic looks of empty-handed servants.

(Reader, I in turn must apologize for with-holding from thee this last information, which, I assure thee, was not done from malice or laziness. In truth, an author's task resembles that of a juggler of plates upon sticks, who, as his work progresses, has every moment more plates to keep aloft, and who, always running to maintain stability, must now and then slight one topic when another begins to wobble. Indeed, I would have thee think these wobbles are but tricks to emphasize an author's skills, and that, the more the wobbling, the greater the skill—yet I digress.)

Four problems, then, beset our hero; in his struggle against unhappiness, he was aided not only by his sanguine temper and the beauties of the countryside, but by his new servant, his *valet* from the household of His Lordship. The Duke of Harrit was never one to stint doing his fellow man a good deed—provided only that it produced a still greater benefit for himself. In loaning Tom this *valet* (whose name was Bavard, and who appeared in our story two chapters ago, dumping a chamber-pot), the Duke had indeed treated himself nobly, for he had rid himself of one of the most disreputable (though at the same time, most engaging) rogues in all France.

M. Bavard, I must tell thee, was a tall, narrow-shouldered, concave-chested, beak-nosed and black-eyed knave of somewhere between eighteen and fifty (for he had the judgement and desires of one of eighteen, and the appearance of one nearer fifty). His hair was long, black and greasy, and as for his complexion, it most resembled a glass vessel filled with burgundy wine; and this shade indeed revealed the inner man.

Tom's trip with this paragon-of-servants had been largely without incident, except that Bavard had stolen some roasting chickens in Lyon, some sausages in Paray-le-Monial, and altogether some eight-or-ten other items at nearly every stopping-point along their road. In Burgundy, to be sure, his behavior had become a trifle excessive; yet that viney province must be considered his spiritual home, and some excess of religious joy must be allowed to even the soberest man upon pilgrimage. Nothing that Tom could do—even to providing him a small purse of his own—could bring an end to the petit-pillaging, for M. Bavard used money as wise countries use their armies, to obtain their will only when all other methods fail.

Tom's patience with the troubles this entailed can be explained quite simply: M. Abelard Bavard was one of the jolliest spirits and happiest talkers in all of France. He had in his younger days studied at the University of Paris, and tho' the academic life held no charm for him (indeed, he had gone over the University's walls one night *via* rope), he still collected knowledge much as he collected roasted chickens: in some haste, but with enthusiasm. In this, he seems to me to have met the definition of a true scholar held forth by Saint Augustine (or someone) and many others: in that he sought knowledge *for its own sake*—for surely it never brought him a *sous* of profit.

Accordingly, as the coach bearing him and Mr. Jones (and some seven or eight roof-passengers) began its descent towards the heart of Marseilles on that sunny October morning, M. Bavard was pointing out the window with a joint of roast chicken, and saying (so nearly as we may approximate his accent):

"Behold, m'sieur, zee port of *Marseilles,* zee oldest tru ci-ti een *Frahns,* and eendeed een Europe, known to zee Greeks *primus* as *Lacydon* (for zat eenlet *a la gauche,* zere), and later as *Massilia.* Zat beelding, weeth zee bootefool doom, was a-built by *Puget* ahn zee sevanteenth santooree. Soon we shall see zee *Cathaydral de Sahn Lah-zahr,* frahm zee twalf santooree, so gloireous, it would make zee Dah-veel heemself une Cray—how you say?—a Christian. Zee light thoo eets weendows is a hundred sarmons, and I never see it but I wish I were a better man. . . ."

(Reader, we shall henceforth spare thee any further such transliterations of the accents of M. Bavard, for besides being tedious to record, they are really a kind of low humor. We mean to ridicule in our narrative nothing but wickedness; and to be born French [or Greek, or Dutch], while it may be folly, is not really wicked. Thou mayst, Reader, imagine henceforth whatever accent thou likest, or even, if thou art of a sympathetic nature, no accent at all.)

Serenaded by such unbroken commentary, then, Mr. Jones made his way through the streets of Marseilles early upon a Sunday morning, just as the church bells rang for a late Mass. At the advice of his *valet* (whose judgement in these matters had proven infallible), he stopped at last at an inn in the hills above the city, where the food was of a delicious freshness, and the rooms offered a view of the Mediterranean and the Islet of If, which not even the most rascally landlord on earth could entirely spoil.

The day being still extremely young, Mr. Jones only saw his trunk brought up to his room before returning to the harbour to begin his survey of French naval might. As, however, such work seems very likely to be hot, tiring, and even dangerous, may we not, Reader, like M. Bavard, remain here gazing at the wine-dark sea, ideally through half-closed eyes? So shall we leave all the glory to our hero, and have all the supper to *ourselves.*

---

# *V*

## *Containing the Moon, a Ship and Several Hints About Love*

---

As, Reader, thou hast no doubt already repented (as I assure thee, I have) of that slackness which overtook us at the close of our last chapter, I may here happily inform thee that we missed nothing of importance, or at least nothing which we may not easily enough recount here.

Mr. Jones arrived at that part of the harbour reserved to the French Navy a little after noon. He found no evidences of secrecy; indeed, the greater part of the French Mediterranean Squadron having that week returned from manoeuvres, two of its ships had been opened for public display. One of these was a graceful cutter of no importance, but the other was the pride of the squadron. This was the *Marie Antoinette,* and she represented the epitome of French nautical design, her eighty-four guns, upon three decks, offering the firepower of a fortress made to float upon the seas. Small boats were ferrying groups of respectable persons to and from her; after a few moments' hesitation, our hero asked, and was granted, permission to join this trade.

The *Marie Antoinette* was in truth a splendid piece of work, all bright brass and new-coiled ropes and decks sandstoned a blinding white in the southern noon, and had I ten thousand pages (and sufficient ink), I should describe her to thee fully. As it was, only one detail much influenced our history: for Tom noticed that, beneath the *Fleur de Lys* she flew the broad pennant of a flag-ship with her admiral aboard. Thinking he could learn more by an hour's conversation than a year's counting of cannon-balls (tho' he did count all he saw), Tom asked the lieutenant who had been showing the ship (a kindly veteran of above sixty years) to carry in his card and compliments. This the lieutenant willingly did, but he returned almost at once greatly flustered and abashed, to announce stiffly that the Admiral was occupied.

This rebuff dampened our hero's spirits, and he very soon returned to his lodgings—where our narrative may now resume.

Tom passed Sunday afternoon and evening chatting with his landlady (his landlord was an irascible bully who never spoke); and by flirting with his landlady's daughter, a sweet girl of about sixteen, named Lisette. Despite this attention, and the efforts of Bavard to be amusing, he felt extremely low, partly from the failure of his naval expedition, but mostly from the press of those worries we have earlier catalogued.

In the morning, after a night of little sleep, his breakfast was interrupted by a fierce-looking French ensign, who presented a letter with all the bellicosity of one delivering a challenge. Tom received this with some trepidation, but, upon breaking the red wax sealing the powder-blue envelope, he read as follows:

> Dear M. Jones,
>     Please forgive my not finding time for you on Sunday, but the duties of an Admiral after some months at sea are, as you may imagine, considerable. I would be pleased to have you as my guest for a small supper Wednesday evening at nine o'clock. Among the other guests will be an American lady known to you, at whose particular request you have been invited.
>                                         I am, Sir,
>                                         Sincerely yours,
>                                         François de Vernay
> P.S. Ensign Laguerre, who brought you this note, will stay for your reply.

The tone of this letter was not, to be sure, unduly gracious; yet our hero (who, whatever his faults, never squandered even the slightest chance to be happy) seized upon one phrase of it, and, forgetting the Ensign's former coldness, asked him fervently, whether the American lady was tall, and brown-haired?

The lieutenant now sneered, and answered, "I believe she is, and yet

I hope M'sieur entertains no idle hopes of this lady, as she is an American patriot, come to help fasten the bonds of friendship between the Navy of France, and the future American republic."

This retort, if it was meant to crush our hero, failed utterly in its purpose, for Jones now heartily offered the Ensign a chair and, all the while whistling a country air, begged a quill of his landlady, and dashed off his eager acceptance. The lieutenant, looking a little crest-fallen, took this with a formal bow, and departed.

The Ensign had no sooner left, than Jones began to despise himself for having neglected the obvious step of asking the lady's name. Very shortly, however, his naturally high spirits convinced him that, in a just world, the name could only be *Wilson*.

He then commenced the two happiest days of his stay in France: what had been duty, now seemed pleasure, and what had been pleasure, almost ecstasy. On Tuesday, he completed his military investigations when the local army commander, sharing a cheerful bottle, complained of having to house 1200 Marines training to conduct landings against inlet targets. That afternoon, his work concluded, Tom persuaded his landlady and her daughter to join him on a picnic into the hills above the city, where, beneath the shading trees, a great deal of innocent flirtation had helped them pass the time delightfully.

Tom's genteel behavior beneath the olive trees had so won the heart of his landlady that she scarcely grumbled when he requested a second bath on Wednesday evening. When, however, the order was given to gentle, black-eyed Lisette to bring up the kettles of boiling water, she demurred, saying, "But Monsieur is already clean and ruddy of cheek; and I promise no one could smell sweeter than Monsieur."

This she said with a hasty impatience. Tom, more surprised than angry, noticed that she wore her best Sunday-clothes and a riband in her hair, which, presumably, she feared would get wet—and was prepared to drop his request.

His landlady, however, who had a nicer sense of what was due to well-paying guests, began at once upbraiding her daughter in angry terms, which, alas, inspired only stubbornness on the part of Lisette, and embarrassment on the part of Mr. Jones. A scene appeared likely, but suddenly Bavard advanced, took the girl aside and whispered to her; she soon nodded, then said pleasantly that, "If Monsieur will take himself back upstairs, his bath will be ready very soon."

Very soon indeed, the water was brought, not only steaming, but scented with pine-essence. Our hero, despite some scruples about smelling like a tree, at last relented, and found the sensation exquisite.

Perhaps an hour later, redolent of forests, Tom stepped into his landlady's parlour, and saw to his satisfaction that Bavard was, for once, presentable, having visited the barber and donned his best clothes, the silver livery of the Suffleys. Having by this time utterly forgotten his failure to confirm the identity of the American lady who had invited him, Tom held not the slightest doubt she would be Mrs. Wilson; and to make a favorable impression was now paramount in his thoughts. He was, therefore, exceedingly annoyed when his *valet*, with a fawning expression, approached him as follows:

"Monsieur," he began, "I must tell you in perfect frankness that for me to attend you this evening will be to sacrifice my happiness, my freedom, and perhaps my life."

"How, sir? Can this be so?" replied Tom in sudden concern.

"Indeed, monsieur, tho' the tale is too long and too sordid to tell now, I am a man wanted by the French Navy. A youthful folly, monsieur, which, I promise you, I have repented a hundred-fold. Please, monsieur," says he, with his hand over his eyes, "do not ask me to explain."

This story bore every mark of implausibility; yet Tom quickly realized that leaving Bavard at home would vastly reduce the likelihood of finding a stolen ship's mast stowed away in his coach at the evening's end. As, moreover, Bavard was now displaying many signs of terror, *viz.*, clattering teeth, knocking knees, and rolling eyes, it seem'd a time for mercy.

"Look'ee, rascal: do you promise me faithfully I will find you here on my return?"

"Monsieur, on my life, yes."

"Then stay. But look to our packing. We leave the day after tomorrow for Paris," concluded Tom; and in so saying, he began to feel a certain panic himself.

Now, we have no doubt that Tom's decision will be condemned by many firm-minded persons as an unpardonable laxity, and one likely to lead to a swift unraveling of the social fabric. Against this charge, we can, in truth, make no defense but the weak one that servants are human beings, and so entitled to occasional indulgence. In all probability, however, Mr. Jones's motivation was much simpler; that, having wound himself to the highest pitch of happiness and expectation, he was unwilling to be the source of sadness and despair in another. Accordingly, a few

134

minutes later, having ordered the horses put to his coach, he placed his hat upon his head, and stepped alone into the warm night.

It was indeed one of the most beautiful nights of the year, when the *Marie Antoinette*, lit by a harvest moon in a clear sky, rode at anchor like some castle made of gossamer spires. The lights which glistened from the windows at her stern were supremely inviting. Mr. Jones was piped aboard by sailors at attention, and even the bellicose M. Laguerre seemed to have softened as he announced Tom to the others.

Reader, thou hast often, I believe, made the comparison between a war-ship and a playhouse; for the polished boards, the sails like blank scenery to be raised and lowered by the same riggings, and the actors in their costumes, all tend to this impression. Too often, alas, these floating playhouses show only tragedies, full of death and sorrow. Yet upon this warm night in autumn, the program was to be different; was to be—

Alas, Reader, I cannot say exactly what the evening was, for in the first place, none of those old terms of Mr. Aristotle—tragedy, comedy, epic— do justice to the wonderful confusion of life; and in the second, my best witness to the events of that evening spent his first minutes aboard ship in a state of the greatest possible mental disorder, for—

For, not to delay the matter further, the guest known to Mr. Jones was in fact Mrs. Wilson; and I have often found that, while lust has the habit of focussing all our power of mind (usually towards some mischief), true love tends the other way, drying our brains to dust, and then blowing that dust away in a *hurricano* of joy.

Mr. Jones, therefore, failed to notice some of his surroundings (including the very cool welcome given him by Admiral de Vernay, and the very warm handshake and smile given him by the Admiral's wife). He did, however, pay the strictest attention when Mrs. Wilson, perfumed with jasmine, and wearing a white French country gown of perfect simplicity and elegance, came forward to address him.

"I am very glad, Mr. Jones," said she, "that we meet again."

"Why, madam!" cries Jones, his brains doused with pleasure, "I have thought of nothing but you since that night I was so lucky as to rescue you from . . ."

Alas for our hero! Tom had, all unwittingly, affronted that fierce self-reliance which slightly blotted the character of Mrs. Wilson, who answered sharply, "Rescue me? Why Mr. Jones, however do you fill your time when you are not flattering yourself?

"Indeed, sir," she continued, "I must tell you that your intervention only saved the life of that wretch Captain Whipsblood, for had my servant failed to shoot him, I always carry a pistol in my bag."

Such anger utterly abashed our hero. Having brought his appearance to the peak of elegance (and the stares of the two other ladies upon deck showed how well he had succeeded), he had now nearly destroyed his hopes by accident.

"Madam," began Jones, very contritely, "I fear when we first met at Mr. Nautley's I gave you some offense, which I now seem doomed to repeat eternally. Believe me that I regret it very much."

Mrs. Wilson, while proud of her abilities, was not mean-spirited. Nor, I suppose, had our hero's past gallantry, or his present appearance, failed to make their impressions. "Indeed, sir," said she somewhat mollified; "you had only the bad fortune then to approach me when I was over-wrought; and in any case, your later assistance was kind. If we have quarrelled, let us now be friends." She offered Jones her hand, which he instantly kissed, and so their quarrel ended.

Mrs. Wilson now smiled wryly, and whispered, "I fear, Mr. Jones, that our hosts will titillate themselves by talking endlessly of war between England and America. As, however, I have spoken of nothing else for above a month, I should be infinitely grateful to you if we could confine ourselves to any other matters. Will you oblige me?" To this Jones assented, with what could only be called relief.

A moment later, the guests were invited to the Admiral's quarters, where the convenience of an English-speaking friend became very apparent to our hero. Admiral de Vernay, accustomed to enjoy only the company of seafaring men, had arranged the party for his own convenience, placing at one end of the table Tom and Mrs. Wilson, the mayor of Marseilles and his wife; in the middle, his own wife and a young playwright named M. Beaumarchais; and at the other end, himself and his fellow officers.

As it happened, I believe neither Jones nor Mrs. Wilson would have given a fig if they had been seated alone together upon the highest yard-arm; or if the steward who conducted them there, had asked all the others to walk a gang-plank. To be brief, they spent their time speaking only to each other, and tho' they neglected politics, found themselves in perfect agreement upon every other topic raised, from excellence in painting to the joys of rural life—and were soon as well pleased with each other's minds, as with their external forms.

———

From such mutual satisfaction, to the more interesting emotion of love, it is not always a very long distance. Mrs. Wilson, in short, began to hint that Tom's desires might sometime be attainable. Nor, indeed, was hers the only female heart inclining towards our magnetic hero; for Madame de Vernay, though handicapped by Tom's limited French and her own utter lack of English, wasted no opportunity to smile and nod in his direction.

When the meal had concluded, Admiral de Vernay suggested a stroll upon deck. As the cabin, despite the large stern windows, was somewhat close, the notion was accepted with acclaim.

Upon the quarter-deck, the soft glow of lanterns and the softer lapping of the waves produced a moment very conducive to romance. Mrs. Wilson was, however, commandeered by the Mayor and his lady (who had both been enlivened by considerable wine). At the same time, Jones was approached by Madame de Vernay and M. Beaumarchais. The Admiral's wife had no sooner placed her hand upon Tom's wrist, than her husband, looking furious, excused himself and, with his officers, went below.

I believe the naval gentleman had retreated unnecessarily, for Madame de Vernay, after a few small remarks, seemed to lose her nerve, and fell silent, leaving the floor entirely to Tom and M. Beaumarchais. The amiable playwright, who had a lively mind, and a hundred enthusiasms, of which America was only the latest, spoke for perhaps ten minutes upon the poetic rightness of Franco-American friendship, before declaring respectfully that Mrs. Wilson, just arrived from Paris, had endorsed Tom because both she and Mr. Franklin considered him an American sympathizer.

Tom (who was naturally honest) might have tried correcting this error, had not Beaumarchais continued, with a sigh, "Ah, monsieur, you are a lucky man. The lovely Madame Wilson is insensible to my charms, but quite taken with yours."

Tom, of course, heard this with delight. Just then, however, Ensign Laguerre returned to invite them all to the evening's entertainment, an offer Tom more readily accepted once he noticed Mrs. Wilson was nowhere upon deck.

Striding to his chair, Tom was startled to discover upon the face of his beloved a look—a pale, tremulous look—which seemed (at least to him) to express the last degree of love-sickness. Indeed, Reader, she did glance distractedly two or three times at Jones before mastering her emotions, and attending to the entertainment. Since nothing could have more encouraged our hero, he was himself uneasy until, about forty minutes later, the evening finished with singing by a quartet of sailors; good-byes were said; and there was a convivial walk back up to the deck, attended by all but the Admiral, who pleaded pressing duties. Finally the boats pulled away, carrying the five guests.

Once ashore, the Mayor and his wife were helped by their servants into their coach—the Mayor bidding a cordial good evening to one of the coach wheels, and then hiccoughing loudly—and M. Beaumarchais made a short, fierce, and very sober speech on Liberty before embracing our hero and Mrs. Wilson in turn. At last he mounted a fine white mare and, calling, "For America—sweet lady, sweet gentleman, adieu!" he rode speedily away. Tom watched him almost with regret, for his politics were blithe and honest, not bitter; yet now Tom and Mrs. Wilson were alone, in circumstances highly desirable.

Indeed, the silliest poet in France would have been hard-press'd to find a more romantic moment. The time was then just after midnight; a moon the colour of orange-blossom honey hung over the harbour; the air was cool but very still and silent. Our two friends looked into each other's eyes, and heard each other's breathing; and, Reader, if thou are not now at least half in love thyself with one or the other of our characters, then surely I have described the scene, or them, very ill.

M. Beaumarchais's horse had scarcely disappeared in the distance, when Mrs. Wilson very urgently requested our hero to step with her into her coach. Jones had now concluded that the universe was, indeed, just. His expectations may be easily imagined; but what actually transpired will likely amaze thee, Reader, as utterly as it did stagger Mr. Jones.

# VI

## In Which Jones Is Shocked, and Then Suffers the Consequences of a Noble Nature

When Mrs. Wilson had gotten Tom into her coach, she closed its window and said urgently, "Alas, Tom, remove your hands, and listen carefully. If you value your life, we must get you out of Marseilles at once. Return to your lodgings, if necessary, only long enough to gather your things."

"Dear Angela!" answered Jones (who could not, I believe, have been more staggered, had an archbishop shot at him from the pulpit). "Surely you are jesting. I have no enemies here, nor any interest but loving you. What can you mean?"

"Look'ee, Tom; you waste valuable time." Seeing him unconvinced, she now continued more slowly, "I long ago learned, Tom, not to trust military men; and when the Admiral hastily departed from the deck after dinner, I followed him.

"He went with his officers to a cabin aft of his own, where he instructed one of them to collect a ship's gang. They shall wait until two in the morning, when they suppose you will be asleep in your room, and then they are to set upon and murder you."

"*Murder!?*" cries Jones, who had now begun to believe some part of this. "What in heaven's name I have done to offend the Admiral?"

Replied Mrs. Wilson hastily, "Admiral de Vernay, who hates and mistrusts everything English, this evening concluded that you were making love to his wife to pry from her secrets concerning his ships."

Jones answered in consternation, "Why, madam, I made no effort to distinguish myself with her; nor, in truth, had I eyes for any lady there but yourself."

"Sir, that matters very little; for he is far more jealous of the secrecy of his fleet, than of the honesty of his wife. He certainly thinks you are a spy; but," she concluded tenderly, "I shall let no one harm a gentleman I know to be a friend of America."

Alas for Jones! It now at last flashed upon him how perfectly Mrs. Wilson must have been deceived; for his praising her speech at the Biting Whale and then assisting her against Captain Whipsblood, would have led her naturally to make too much of his talk with Mr. Franklin.

Now, Reader, there came upon Jones one of those harsh choices which many of us seek to avoid, but which heroes merely seek. He had now only to continue an accidental deception in order to guarantee both his safety and (he felt certain) his immediate happiness in the arms of Mrs. Wilson. Yet Jones, as we have often declared, was an honest man. The rainy world may have somewhat tarnished our hero, but he was still of perfect metal within.

"Madam," said he, very sadly, "I must be frank. Altho' I have lately reconsidered my views upon America, and may someday, I suppose, alter them, I am no friend to the rebels. My support for you against the Captain and before was personal, not political. You and I are presently at odds, and as I care for you, I cannot deceive you."

Mrs. Wilson looked at him in disbelief, laughed bitterly, and, after a silence, said, "Alas, Mr. Jones, I begin to be sorry we met. I fear something lovely hath just ended. I am obliged to you for your honesty, but you must see how this destroys our prospects. What affection can there be, where disagreement is so strong? Why, sir, I am here to *buy arms* for those very rebels."

"And yet," cried Jones, suddenly paler than the moonlight (for, Reader, I regret to say he had never imagined a woman could have so active a part in politics), "perhaps the crisis in America will resolve itself peacefully, and leave us to our own affairs."

"That, I fear, will never happen, 'til England leaves America to herself; and *that*, I fear, will take a war. Old England, sir, is a land of privilege and arrogance, and of hopelessness for the poor; and America is something better. No, sir, either you or I must come to think differently."

Had Jones found time to consider these words, who can tell what would have resulted? Mrs. Wilson, however, began shaking him, while whispering fiercely that he must go.

"Oh, madam," cries Jones (who could so little bear the thought of their parting, that he scarcely knew what he said), "will you not come away with me? How, madam, can I dare to part with you?"

Mrs. Wilson's feelings too fiercely blended disappointment and desire for her to pay Jones any great heed. She had, after all, just seen her engaging patriot friend unmasked as a vile Tory—a shock not easily endured. And yet, Reader, I suppose the unmasked Jones was nearly as engaging as before; since, had she viewed him in a strictly political light, she would very likely have taken the pistol from her purse and shot him herself.

Instead, Mrs. Wilson now commenced pushing our hero from the coach, while crying, "Why, sir, we may perhaps meet again, but go now; I would have little reason to love a man with a sword protruding from his back, and believe me, these gentlemen are in earnest. If you were dead, you would lose a major source of your charm. Go, for *heaven's* sake."

Tom realized his danger when (having been pushed about halfway from the coach) he observed upon the deck of the *Marie Antoinette* a mustering of six or seven very hard-looking sailors in civilian clothes. Stepping to the ground, he said, "Madam, if there are any powers upon earth sympathetic to love, I shall find you again; 'til then, I only beg of you one ki—"

Jones had not completed this oration when the American lady put her hand around his neck and give him such a kiss as could only be described by either Mr. Milton or Mr. Dante, both of whom have had considerable experience of heavenly glories. Mr. Jones, I believe, had almost decided that he would be content to remain and die in her arms. Luckily for him, however, Mrs. Wilson had no sooner drawn back her lips than she commanded her coachman to drive on. In a moment, standing amid the dust cloud raised by the coach's wheels, our hero was alone.

A hellish gloom now settled (like the dust from the coach) upon poor Jones. In a moment, however, he recalled his danger, and ran to his own coach, a few yards away. The instant he was aboard, it started rolling at a high pace, to carry him towards those adventures contained in our next chapter.

# VII

## In Which Jones Returns Home
## Pensive, but Soon Draws His Sword

We have already, Reader, mentioned the gloom which engulfed Tom Jones as he started for his coach; and yet, if thou hast imagined he departed the waterfront in either a panic, or a rage of disappointed lust, thou hast greatly underestimated our hero.

Perhaps because he saw no path back to Mrs. Wilson but a political one, Jones experienced during the ride a series of recollections—including the arrogance of Whipsblood, the cockfight at the Bloody Dog, and the methodical seduction of the girl Mary, being trained into prostitution—all supporting her opinions, by showing England as a brutal and uncharitable land. Very forcefully, these images shook his old beliefs; and he, for the first time, began to consider American claims seriously.

These fascinating images so occupied our hero, that he had almost arrived home before he resumed worrying about his French pursuers. When, however, the coach had stopped, he stepped down quickly, and, supposing the rascal Bavard would have gotten drunk, called to the postillion to accompany him upstairs.

The hour then being about one in the morning, Tom was surprised to find the front gate unlocked; moreover, the maid who answered the door was flustered and unfamiliar.

"I pray you, monsieur," said she, "to forgive our poor service this evening. If—"

"Please, mademoiselle," interrupted Jones, "if *you* will find the good landlady, I must settle my bill and leave here at once."

"Go up to your room then, monsieur," she answered uncertainly, "and I will see what may be done."

Tom hastened upstairs and, after looking into one or two likely closets for Bavard, instructed the postillion to start his packing. He had, however, barely spoken, when there came from below the slamming of a door, and then, from the window overlooking the rear courtyard, two or three loud crashes and a bellowing debate composed of baritone cursing and tenor cries for mercy.

Jones now ran to the open window, where he heard:

"Aiee! Mercy, monsieur, I beg you."

"Rascal! I'll teach you mercy. I'll not rip off your ears, for then you'd not hear your own screams; nor poke out your eyes, for then you would not see when I slice off your manhood. Afterwards, I shall kindly . . ."

This, Reader, was accompanied by many feinting sword-pokes upon the breast of the hapless victim, who had been backed against the courtyard wall between two large potted trees. After a single glance, Tom declared to the postillion, "Carry from here what you may. Have the coach moved a quarter-mile down the road; and I will meet you there." He stepped through the window to a ledge, and thence flung himself down onto the soft soil of the garden; for the grunting, oath-swearing assailant was his bully of a landlord, and the poor victim, his face white with unspeakable terrors, was none other than Tom's servant, the pitiable M. Bavard.

Very little time remained for reasoned expostulation; Tom raced across the courtyard, and with his fist knocked down the landlord's sword, then pushed him aside and drew his own weapon as he called, "Hold, sir! What cause?! Put up thy dull blade; this man's blood will disgrace it."

The landlord, however much he may have reverenced our hero's purse, and however un-martial he may have looked with his face flushed, his doublet unbuttoned, and his fat belly hanging over his belt, considered himself as brave a soul as any Englishman. At once he counter-lunged, but Tom (with some difficulty, I admit) bound his blade and forced it from his grip. The prospect of facing cold steel with an empty hand greatly cooled the landlord's surly recklessness, and he let his tongue pursue a battle his arm could not win; or, to speak less poetically, he now began cursing both Tom and M. Bavard with the worst imaginable language, in a torrent interrupted only by commands that his wife fetch the magistrate, the night watch, all the neighbourhood, and I know not whom else.

These commands, indeed, drew Tom's attention to the other persons in the moonlit courtyard. Besides Bavard and the landlord, there stood (a few yards away) his landlady in a state of plump confusion, and poor Lisette in inconsolable tears.

The sight of Lisette crying forced Tom (who had perhaps too hastily taken his fat host as the aggressor) to reconsider the scene before him; and in doing so, he began swiftly to think better of the landlord, and rather less well of his rascally servant. Accordingly, he now addressed the angry father as follows:

"Monsieur, control yourself. I have tried to prevent bloodshed, but you will find me no protector of crime or wickedness. If you have some complaint against my servant, acquaint me with it, and we shall seek justice together."

Tom's words somewhat mollified his outraged landlord, who, after a while, still angrily but slightly more clearly, replied, "Oh, monsieur, I believe in truth that no gentleman so well-dressed as Monsieur could ever countenance wickedness—tho' no doubt Monsieur is very successful with ladies, as it proper . . .

"But! But! Monsieur has, I fear, harboured unknowingly a viper in the breast, for that rascal, that treacherous scum cringing beside Monsieur" —in his participle, the landlord was, alas, rather painfully accurate, for Bavard, tho' a scholar, was no hero—"has undone me, has taken the innocence of my precious daughter, for even as we speak, her pure blood is upon his—"

"Well, sir!" interjected our hero, with some haste, "enough of that just now. What, I beg you, is your evidence?"

"What, monsieur, more certain than the evidence of my own eyes? Not twenty minutes ago, I am standing at my window smoking my pipe —for Madame, you know, does not permit me to smoke it in the house, and what's an evening without a bowl or two of—"

"Pray, sir! Your theme!"

"As Monsieur was about to hear when he interrupted," continued the affronted landlord, "I was at my window smoking my pipe, when I noticed a certain rhythmic stirring amid my corn-stalks. Wondering that the wind shook no other part of the garden, and feeling no breeze upon my own hot brow, I went out to investigate—and what did I find, but this half-naked, rascally knave atop sweet Lisette, and—monsieur, it is enough, I can say no more."

Believing that enough had indeed been said, Tom looked searchingly towards the house for signs of pursuit before examining his servant.

Bavard, indeed, evidenced fifty signs of guilt. His clothes disordered, his eyes rolling; sweating and tearing his hair, he displayed a genuine shame and fear quite unlike his earlier charade to avoid going with Tom.

The proof of conspiracy between this rascal and gentle Lisette seemed irrefutable; yet Tom honoured the Englishman's right to trial, and supposed a Frenchman deserved nearly as well.

Therefore, he said in his fiercest tones, "Look'ee, sirrah, you stand accused of lying to me, deceiving this good man, and debauching that sweet girl. How plead you?"

With tears forming in his half-wild eyes, Bavard answered, "Oh, my chevalier, to my vast shame, I must confess to a small deception, for I am not wanted by the French Naval Authorities. I have never been to sea in my life, and in truth there is nothing in the world I hate more than water. It should not be drunk, should rarely be washed in, and as for sailing upon it, I despise with all my life the rocking motion of it, for it is like making love to nothing."

It was with Bavard, as with certain other sad fellows, that words distracted and intoxicated him, so that he had, by this short preface, lost much of his fear and most of his reason, and now continued, almost giddily:

"Indeed, monsieur, as you and I are men of the world, we can both admit to little indiscretions. In truth, I may have been a little intimate with Mademoiselle Lisette, but if so, a mere token change in her . . ."

Alas, poor Bavard had spoken too loudly. While Tom (though no friend of vice) might have been prepared to hear him out, the Landlord's rage swelled at these words just as the mighty *squirrel's* cheeks are swelled with autumnal acorns.

" 'Token change?' thou scum! 'A little intimate?' thou rascal refuse of the worst bilge slime ever pumped into a Moroccan bay!" roared this broken parent, who never before had paid his daughter the slightest attention. "Aye, I suppose a little intimate. Well, no matter: in nine months, I suppose, she shall prove a little a mother, but you, garbage, will be a little rotted in thy grave. I'll sweeten my coffee with the powder of your liver. . . ."

So saying, he leapt forward, and it required every bit of Mr. Jones's skill to restrain him.

"Hold, sir! One minute more, is all I ask; then this immoral fellow shall be yours, to do with as you chose." Tom spoke this with some desperation, for, besides his genuine concern lest murder be committed, he realized the *Marie Antoinette*'s sailors must be near and just now, he wished Bavard, landlord, and all, in Tangiers, forever.

The landlord reluctantly nodding, Tom took his frightened servant aside, and said to him softly, "Sirrah, keep thy voice low. Nothing will save thee but an honest marriage. Art thou willing to preserve her thou hast harmed? This landlord, I own, is an arrant blockhead and a bully, who deserves whatever he suffers, but what of sweet Lisette? Some injuries, sirrah, are not redressed with clever words."

Bavard looked uncertainly at poor Lisette, who, with her mother, had begun edging into the last plot of moonlight remaining in the courtyard. At last he said, very softly, and with something of a sigh, "Ah, my chevalier, I must tell you she is everything I have wished, all the sweetness a man dreams of, and a good mind, and the common sense I have not had since I was sent to University at thirteen. With her, I think I could remake my life.

"Yet what have I to offer her? If I began today to reform myself, I might in six months be presentable, and in a year have a small fund with which to begin a married life. Alas! I see too late that vices are but footmen to the great coach of sorrows." At this he pulled his lower lip, and sighed, and looked very sad—as indeed, Reader, I believe he was.

Tom himself accepted this repentance, and so asked grimly, "Are you sincere, rascal? Will you swear that, should a living be granted, you would prove Lisette's faithful husband, so long as you both should live?"

"Oh, monsieur, should such a miracle occur, I would spend my life in the only true gratitude to God, which is to live an honest life."

Tom then, after looking hard into Bavard's eyes, and noting with satisfaction that he had not bound himself with a hundred implausible oaths, said, "Very well, then, rascal, we shall try to save you."

Tom then faced the raging landlord. "Gentle sir, I implore you to forego your righteous anger, and consider only the happiness of your daughter. My servant is prepared to make her an honest woman, and I am willing to settle upon them £100 when they are wed, and a further £40 each year they are married. We need only your gracious consent to let all end happily."

We are often told, Reader, that the alchemists of Chaucer's time sought a Philosopher's Stone, by which to turn lead *into* gold. Surely, this is a misprint, for what else could the stone have been but gold *itself*, which turns poverty to riches, despair to joy, anger to contentment, and even enemies into friends? The alchemists in their dungeons never produced a greater transformation than occurred as Tom, having finished his speech, drew forth a small bag of gold, and placed it in the landlord's hand as an earnest of good faith.

How noble, Reader, are all the healing arts! The anguished father, his wrath checked, had slumped his weary body against the garden wall in futile agitation; yet, no sooner had he hefted this bag than a faint tremor of hope began to raise his eyebrows. He at once extracted a guinea piece and—so greatly did he hunger after health—bit it. The metallic drug ended all his pain and his objections: he now skipped two or three steps about the rounds; called to his daughter to stop her crying; called to his wife to set a good table; and crossed by Tom to embrace poor trembling Bavard and call him "Son."

The universal joy which followed meant our hero's work was done. Knowing but not minding that the landlord (who otherwise gave not a fig for his daughter's virtue) had staged his outburst to extort what money he could, Tom turned contentedly from the scene and withdrew quietly across the grass.

His timing had, this once in his life, been perfect; for he had no sooner withdrawn into the shadows, than there resounded through the courtyard (every window of the house being open that hot night) the slap of heavy boots upon the inn's wooden floors.

Tom's landlord, believing, for aught I know, that these were neighbours arriving to celebrate Lisette's engagement, cried loudly, "Coming!" and, "Son—daughter—attend them!" and a dozen other such things. Meanwhile, our hero (his head full of politics, and his heart, full of *Wilson*) found a sturdy vine, and ascended hand-over-hand to the top of the courtyard wall, along which he made his frantic escape into the night.

BOOK

# THE FIFTH

# I

## In Which We Charge Our Cannon with a Double Load of Words, and Fire Them Directly at Our Reader

Reader, it is with rules very much as it is with *fleas:* once you have gotten them into your dwelling, you almost never get them out.

Among the nastiest rules infesting the great hotel of *literature* are those first dragged in two thousand years ago by a certain Mr. Aristotle. Sometimes referred to as the *dramatic unities,* these rules require that no author extend his tale beyond the space of a single day, or to more than one location, or to more than one primary character. Any author who in any way divides his story is considered to be like a general who divides his armies: and to have some critick impale him upon a pen, or lead him in a cage through the capital, is the best he can expect.

Mr. Aristotle's rules, I have no doubt, excellently governed the writings of his own time, just as the rules for undivided armies served well during the ward of Mr. Julius Caesar. But what, Reader, are we to say of our own times? Are they not much altered? Did we not, in the late Seven Years War, fight the French across the entire surface of the globe, from Canada to India? Were there not commanders by the hundreds upon both sides, and soldiers by the tens of thousands? And was it not—recall the name—a combat of well over a day's duration?

Surely, then, we must understand the great rules of literature to be no more permanent than those of warfare: for if the world to be described is altered, how can the means for describing it remain frozen? However much our instincts might favour the brief tale, the quiet hearth of the country manor, must we not sail with the fleets, man the redoubts, endure the speeches in Parliament and the card-table chatter, or do whatever else is necessary to record our story aright? Or, to speak more clearly, must we not now turn our attention from Tom in France to the family he left behind in Somersetshire?

J

The laws of nature we shall obey: here you will find no fairies, elves or witches; nor, indeed, shall you find the wicked careless of their own interests, or the good indifferent to the interests of others. But there is a vast difference between a law, which is immutable and eternal, and a rule, which is not. Mr. Newton discovered laws; Mr. Aristotle made rules. Laws instruct us how to live; rules, how to dance.

Reader, every author is in a war against ignorance and folly, and we have need of commanders, not dancing-masters. We shall press our advantage where we may, and not trouble ourselves with antique rules; and we shall fight on every front which offers, so that we may, like our armies at mid-century, gain back in America what we lose in India, and, by the grace of God, prevail at last.

We shall now observe a book's cease-fire, during which the classicists among our readers may withdraw their dead and wounded, while the rest of us pause to consider how much better this world would be, were all our wars fought with words alone.

## II

### In Which We Return to
### Somersetshire, to Describe a Paradise
### —and a Snake

We last saw Paradise Hall on that dawn, both hopeful and sad, when Tom and young Stumpling departed for London. Amelia's belongings had already gone to the James home; and Amelia and her new guardians set out after them, with Mr. Adams behind, upon horseback. Soon the awkward human stillness was replaced with ordinary animal life: a hawk called, the dogs barked in the kennels, and, as full morning rose, Mr. Hacksem Jones's footsteps scraped along the terrace stones.

That summer morning—lovely once the early fogs had been burned away—announced a month of perfect days, of picnics and boat-trips and country dances, as those left behind sought the good in Tom's absence.

Amelia, to be sure, still resented having been left in so awkward a position (for she had neither the comforts of her old home, nor the pleasure of exotic travel). Very soon, however, her natural good spirits reappeared, especially as Mrs. James was the sort of independent woman she could admire, and Dr. James, a tolerant and generous man. Mr. Adams made the usual fourth to their outings, and those who saw him remarked upon a new sprightliness to his manner.

Alas, even the sprightliest Parson must wear a black gown, and poor Adams never made a very romantick figure upon a blanket beneath a willow. Amelia reserved her warmest affections for that handsome young collegian, Mr. Charles James, whose impending visit soon replaced her father's recent departure as the centerpiece of her conversation.

Mr. James's arrival was in fact expected every moment through all of June and half of July; yet when it finally transpired on July 16th, it was a little marred by his announcing, immediately after kissing his mother's cheek, that he could stay but three days.

Those three days were, however, sufficient to complete the conquest of Amelia's heart. Given Amelia's youth, and her inexperience of the world, the reasons for this are not difficult to enumerate, for Charles James was a handsome fellow. He possessed, in the first place, curly brown hair, a straight nose, and white teeth. He was not tall, but his slight figure was considered well made. His clothes were (by the generosity of his parents) in the latest London fashion. And, surpassing all, he told amusing stories, and played several musical instruments extremely well.

Accordingly, Reader, was the bastion of Amelia's heart taken by storm. During the first afternoon of Charles's visit, she made a trio with him and Mr. Adams, but by the final evening, she and he played a duet, while poor Mr. Adams was left to his *solos*. This painful rebuff the young parson bore very well; and on the morrow, he even managed to shake the departing Mr. James by the hand, tho' in truth, the muscles which upheld his smile appeared not quite so burly as usual.

Reader, I understand very well that the innocent likings of young persons are of slight interest to thee. Indeed, I mention them here only because I am myself fond of all these young persons (including even silly Charles James), and because I dread to assume my next subject, which is a matter extremely dark.

I have told thee that the party assembled that summer at Meadowlands was a happy one—and in a way, it was. Yet surely thou knowest that no member of that party had for a moment forgotten the absence of Tom or Rob; and neither, I must say, had they been allowed to forget the other Jones brother, who now occupied Paradise Hall alone.

Even before Tom reached London, Hacksem's program for manufacture had begun, and in a matter of weeks, or at most a few months, Dr. James found himself overmatched. Hacksem installed his great machine (for so, I believe, he considered his entire project to be) one lever at a time, with the removing of which, the old doctor was at last worn down. One day he would learn Hacksem had racked a tenant's rent; the moment he corrected that, there would arrive a shipment of heavy machinery, ordered by Hacksem and charged to the estate. Let Dr. James countermand this order, and he would next find sappers and surveyors preparing to open brown coal-seams; and faster and faster the gears revolved, 'til the poor doctor—whose health was failing, and who carried one secret burden he would share with no one—was crushed between them.

There came at last a mid-September evening when Dr. James returned home in mental shock. Being pressed by Amelia and his wife, he finally explained, "This morning as I rode towards Paradise Hall, there came from the meadows at the northernmost border of Tom's lands the most hellish explosion I've ever heard. You know, my dear, that I served against the Spaniards in '39, but never did I hear—and never do I hope to hear again—such a noise.

"I galloped as quickly as I could toward it, and when I arrived, perhaps half an hour later, the dust still hung in the air, and a quarter of that little hillock on which you used to ride, Amelia, had been blown away. Mr. Hacksem Jones has found his coal-seam."

"But can we not send his engineers home?" asked Mrs. James.

"That will not repair Amelia's hillside; nor, I fear, will it much delay Hacksem." This the good doctor uttered in a tone so dejected, and with a posture so defeated, that his wife and his young friend knew they had better let him rest, and so they parted.

Much later that evening, after Amelia had gone to her room and Dr. and Mrs. James lay abed in their nightgowns, Dr. James began an uneasy speech.

"My dear, I must tell you," he started tentatively, "that I am thinking of writing to tell Tom I cannot manage his affairs with success."

Mrs. James had long found peace in being the stronger half of a very strong pair, and this sudden hint of her husband's mortality frightened her exceedingly. "But, now, Richard, will we not be able to stand against Hacksem together? Perhaps if I assume the estates books, leaving you time to—"

"My dear, this Hacksem is not an ordinary mortal; some demon or other aids him, and makes him indefatigable. Three other full-grown men laboring their utmost could not do the mischief he does."

Trying to raise him from his gloom, Mrs. James said firmly, "Dr. James, we gave our word to Tom. Let us at least make one more effort before admitting defeat. Shall we?"

Dr. James was a long time silent before he answered, first by a reluctant nod, and then by an apparent *non sequitur,* saying, "You understand, my dear, that I love you very much? And that if my life should end tomorrow, I might faithfully attest before God that I never spent an unhappy day in your company?" Mrs. James blushed prettily; her husband studied her, then concluded, "Well, I will try tomorrow to see whether I may stand against Hacksem Jones."

The late-summer's night was perfectly still and warm; yet the Jameses now put their grey heads as closely together as they could, and so huddled in just that fashion, Reader, as thou mayst sometime have seen little birds comfort each other when the great storm threatens to destroy them.

# III

## Of a Tragedy

Certain grave philosophers have now and again inquired, "whether a man may foresee his own death," and, answering their own question, have concluded that, while a *probability* of one's end may be roughly guessed, the absolute certainty of it must await either the moment of consummation, or the intervention of some Providential agent, most likely an angel.

Reader, thou alone must guess what meaning, or what inspiration, Dr. James had that evening he spoke so sadly to his wife. Yet sure it is that before five days were out, Dr. Richard James of the shire of Somerset slept with his ancestors. On the last day of September, as the first cool wind began to blow the turning leaves from the trees, little Highboy, Tom's groom, rode as swiftly as he could to the door of the James home, and tried by his tears to tell Amelia and Mrs. James what had happened.

Instead, the two women had nearly twenty minutes' work quieting down the hysterical boy, by which time a calmer, most sententiously dolorous, new messenger had arrived, in the form of Mr. Hastings Sinamore, Esq.

"Oh, madam," began this pious gentleman to Mrs. James, "would that I had lost my tongue before I had need to convey you this news. Your husband, madam, is dead. Drowned, madam."

Mr. Sinamore then paused for the expected tears. Mr. Sinamore was disappointed. Mrs. James only glared at him, and so he continued.

"You know, madam, your husband and I were engaged to hunt ducks this morning. We were some three or—four hours in the field when the doctor happened to down a straying mallard which, falling into the water, drew the attention of my spaniel, who instantly leapt after it, directly into the fastest-flowing portion of the stream. My little pup happened to land with a paw upon a pointed stone, and at once began to sink. Dr. James, seeing that, immediately dove in after him, despite my most earnest protests. Whether Dr. James similarly struck his head, or whether the cold of the stream, in combination with his advanced age, brought on a seizure, I do not know; yet in a moment he was under.

"So, madam," concluded Hastings, wiping away a tear which was nowhere to be seen, "your husband's great humanity—I may even say, his great Christian compassion, extending unto the dumb beasts—has cost us this best of men. You have my deepest sympathy." Lastly, looking down at his own damp garments, he added with a sigh that he had, of course, immediately waded in after the doctor, though, alas, to no effect.

Amelia's face was already wet with tears; yet in Mrs. James, no change was visible, except perhaps that her always steady posture had assumed some of the rigidity of metal. Taking four or five breaths (which were scarcely visible as such), she very quietly told Mr. Sinamore that she was grateful for his sympathy and for his efforts, that she would be in contact with him soon, but that for the moment, she begged to be alone. This evidently suited Mr. Sinamore very well, for after several more short expressions of regret, he bowed himself from the room.

Amelia then embraced her second mother, who returned the touch with a fervour which would have seemed impossible for her only a moment before. Quickly, however, she excused herself, saying that she had many arrangements to make.

Then, seeming to Amelia frail in a fashion entirely new, she left the room. She sat at Dr. James's desk, and lit a candle, for outside the window, the earliest autumnal fogs were blowing in, making wispy the late afternoon sun. She drew out paper, took the quill from the ink-well, and wrote and addressed three letters, one each to Tom, Mr. Adams, and her son at Oxford. Only then did she set her head upon the desk, and cry.

So, Reader, do the first heavy rings spread outward from a body cast upon the waters.

# IV

## In Which Are Discussed Both Life and Death

I have ofttimes marvelled, Reader, that a single colour, black, signifies both mourning and evil, both the emptiness of loss and the hideousness of vice. Whether this confusion shows that evil persons are themselves hollow and sad, or that the worst moments of life stem, not from holy purpose, but from the workings of such evil persons, I do not know; nor, I suppose, are such speculations really a part of our history.

Let us therefore simply note that Dr. James was buried as soon as his son Charles arrived, post-haste, from Oxford. The funeral took place at the solemn and traditional hour of midnight, under a moonless sky, in a corner of the churchyard poorly lit by four lanterns and the candles of a half-dozen mourners. The occasion was indeed grievous, and though Amelia had anticipated Charles James as bringing her great comfort, it was rather she who was obliged to be the pillar of strength, and to lead and support the shaken young man from the churchyard home.

That was upon a Wednesday; there followed several days of sympathetic callers, and then several days of silent isolation. The weather had turned cold and dark-clouded, but the rain which threatened never fell.

At last, about three o'clock the very next Wednesday afternoon, Mr.

Sinamore, ever the bearer of bad news, reappeared at Meadowlands, bringing with him Mr. Hacksem Jones. These gentlemen were at once shown into Mrs. James's study. When they had expressed the depth of their sorrow (and, Reader, I am inclined to believe them, for no two persons in our narrative are half so knowledgeable about the depths of human nature in general), they turned to the purpose of their visit.

"You will please forgive us, madam," began the attorney, "for coming so quickly to our business, but I have always found that disagreeable matters are best completed soon. Indeed, I believe it would no more be Christian in me to delay the matters at hand, than it would be in a surgeon to extend the removal of a tumour over the period of a week, in order to spare the patient the pain of sewing up the wound."

Very pleased with this simile, Mr. Sinamore made a snuffling noise, and moved his chair closer to Mrs. James. "I must first inform you, madam —as I believe will come as no surprise—that Dr. James's authority over the Jones estate ceased with his demise; or rather, according to the papers I drew up at the Squire's request, devolved upon myself. And with it, the honorarium of £100 per month."

Mr. Sinamore formed this last phrase with considerable satisfaction; Mrs. James bowed her head, but said nothing.

Lawyer Sinamore then appeared to hesitate, before beginning anew.

"There is another matter, madam, of some delicacy."

"Yes, Mr. Sinamore?"

"You may have understood, madam, that Meadowlands has been mortgaged? Rather heavily mortgaged?"

"I have heard no such a thing, sir," replied Mrs. James, with the first signs of alarm. "To *whom* has my home been mortgaged?"

"Well, madam—to myself. Over a period of years, but lately combined into a single note of six thousand pounds, all due and payable, I regret to say, on the 31st day of this month."

Mrs. James now turned extremely pale; "I fear, sir—," she began falteringly, "I shall find it impossible . . . ," but here her voice trailed away.

"Pray, madam!" interrupted the lawyer gallantly. "Let's not despair. This fine young gentleman, Mr. Jones, is, I believe, well known to you; and he has a proposal which may yet make us all happy." Mr. Sinamore then smiled benevolently upon his protégé, who spoke as follows:

"You no doubt realize, madam, that your late honoured husband was pleased to disagree with me about the development of my father's lands.

My own notions were rather too aggressive for the good doctor, who, if I may say so, represented all the best virtues of an English country gentleman of some one or two centuries ago."

Mr. Sinamore cleared his throat at this, and Mr. Hacksem continued:

"Be that as it may, I now find the new trustee of our estate, dear Mr. Sinamore, much more sympathetic to my own designs—or perhaps I should say, plans.

"Yet, madam, one difficulty remains, in the mix't feelings of my father, who, I own, has been a trifle slow to see the advantages of my ideas.

"Accordingly, I have a suggestion. Rather than rob my father of those exquisite pleasures of travel he has so justly earned, would we not be kinder simply to begin improving the estate, and only to invite him back when our works have advanced far enough that he may judge them fairly? For what, after all, can be said in defense of hasty judgement?

"And so, madam, I suggest this: if I might be assured that the development of Paradise Hall and its lands will be kept our little secret from my peripatetic parent"—a grin accompanied this filial expression—"I would be happy to settle your obligations to Mr. Sinamore. Indeed, tho' I can promise nothing, it may well be that a part of Meadowlands will fit handsomely into our project; and so, madam, you may stand to earn a *considerable* fortune."

As all huntsmen agree that the skill of the snare lies in the care with which it is hidden, I will let the reader decide the quality of Mr. Hacksem's work. In any event, Mrs. James offered no reply except to ring for her maid-servant, and upon her arrival, to ask her to send in Amelia. When Amelia arrived, Mrs. James said to her succinctly, "My dear, your brother and Mr. Sinamore have offered me six thousand pounds not to tell your father that they are stealing his estate. Do you think I should accept?"

"Certainly not," answered Amelia, with equal measures of spirit and astonishment.

"Then you may bid them good-day."

At this, Hacksem interjected, "Amelia; dear sister. I hope you at least will see the good that may be accomplished—"

"Brother, were our father here, he would certainly take a horse-whip to you. If you do not leave at once, I believe I shall try it myself."

Mr. Hacksem's liking of this proposal showed immediately in the color of his face, but Mr. Sinamore, an altogether more subtle man, simply rose heavily. "Madam," said he, "you have, as you know, my condolences."

Amelia then escorted the two gentlemen to the front door, showing them roughly that hospitality the press gang shows to newly-recruited sailors. It was then about four of the afternoon, and raining hard. The sky was black, Amelia's dress was black, Mr. Hacksem's coat was (as always) black; but nothing on earth, I assure thee, Reader, was as black as the expression on the face of Hastings Sinamore.

---

# V

## *In Which Several Persons Act with Courage and Spirit*

---

Although Mr. Sinamore and his ally had properly charged their enemy when she was down-hearted and confused, their assault produced little they could have desired. Where a company of fusiliers might have fled, Mrs. James went on, first joining Amelia at supper, then returning to her husband's study to review the records of the estate.

Those accounts told her of a man destroyed by emulation, not of the extravagance of his rich neighbours, but of the generosity of his friend Squire Jones. That amiable blunder had undone Dr. James, who had rented his farms too cheaply; made his gifts too freely; and invested too often in projects rather from the hope of benefitting the projectors than from an expectation of profits. He had, moreover, upheld a crowd of dependents, including a son at Oxford to whom he denied nothing; and so, not a single disaster, but a steady outspending of income over many years, always artfully encouraged by clever Mr. Sinamore, had brought the Jameses to ruin.

It is perhaps strange that never once in her investigations did Mrs. James curse the generosity which had created her own difficulties; indeed, nothing more violent than a sigh escaped her lips, and the many debts marked "forgiven" not only cleared the painful mystery of her condition, but inspired tender memories of the late doctor. And yet, about two o'clock in the morning, when she at last felt composed enough to sleep, the walk up to bed was a long one, and very lonely.

In the morning, at breakfast, she said carefully to Amelia, "My dear, it is evident that I must leave Meadowlands very soon, and that I shall lack the means to provide for you. I do not envy you, returning to your brother, but if you would find it helpful, I would be happy to write him first, explaining that you spoke as you did out of sympathy to me; that I in fact biased your reply, which you now greatly regret. Would that help, do you think?"

"Madam, I should despise myself should I permit any such letter to be written to my wretched brother. It is rather he who must apologize to you, and until he does, I shall not return to Paradise Hall.

"Instead, let us put our energies into letters to my father, who will, I promise, set matters right very quickly."

This advice was so sensible, and so much better suited to the temper of both women, that it was immediately adopted, and they began at once with pen and paper to express in ink those passions which they could not (as they might have wished) express with cudgelsticks or law-suits.

When they had written and dispatched these letters, as well as notes to Charles James and Mr. Adams, they set out upon a walk, which was, however, cut short by the return of rain showers. The storm, growing steadily worse through the morning and afternoon, reduced them to a day of needlework, which occupied them until about four o'clock, when Mrs. James recalled they had neglected to write to Ireland.

Amelia, who had not quite forgiven her brother for (as she imagined) so enjoying himself abroad, replied shortly, "Rob Jones, madam, hath sent us not a single word since his departure. If he hath been too busy all these months to write a letter, he must now lose his chance to be a hero. I am very angry with my brother." She had no sooner spoken, than she saw something which intrigued her.

This was the massive figure of Mr. Adams, astride an extremely wet and unhappy-looking mare almost the size of a Clydesdale. He had, by the time Amelia noticed him, ridden nearly to the gate of Meadowlands, but was just becoming fully visible through the thick grey mist and rain. Amelia's shifting in her chair drew Mrs. James's attention, and the two women, pleased with the diversion, exchanged curious glances.

Several minutes, however, elapsed before Mr. Adams was introduced. He had in the interim removed his overcoat, and even replaced his riding boots with a pair of slippers he had carried; and this rather odd demonstration of his courtesy we mention even though certain persons will assail him for being ostentatiously good, and certain others, for being blind to fashion and *etiquette.*

If Mr. Adams was indeed blind, his eyes were still remarkably bright. I mean that they now sparked with righteous anger; and this, of all the angers, is the only one lovely to behold. (Yet righteous anger, tho' it perfectly becomes the human countenance, has this disadvantage: that we can never feel it on our own behalf; and to this flaw, I think, its great rarity may be attributed.)

Impelled by his strong feelings, then, Mr. Adams strode into the room, greeted the ladies briefly, and, forgetting his usual shyness before Amelia, began immediately:

"Ladies, I read your letter with shock and dismay, and yet, while I promise you those two unnameable rascals will hear correction from my pulpit, I believe we may allay, for the while at least, your fears of displacement.

"Your father, Amelia, has been generous in the living granted me; and I in turn have saved regularly from it, tho' I promise you I have held the money only as custodian, awaiting a proper object for its expenditure."

Turning to Mrs. James, Mr. Adams became almost gleeful; and, wiping away the rain-water which still dripped from his hair into his eyes, he cried triumphantly, "We shall confound the rogues after all. Surely, madam, your troubles are ended, and '. . . the desert shall rejoice, and blossom as the rose,' for the sum at your disposal is not less than . . . *eighty pounds!*"

The hopes raised by his tone were (as you may imagine, Reader) utterly dashed by the fortune Mr. Adams finally announced; yet Mrs. James thanked him gently before explaining the scope of her crisis. The longer she talked, the quieter and more solemn he seemed, but at her conclusion, he threw his arms into the air, and proclaimed that—let the world think what it might—he would have her and Amelia as his guests at the parsonage until Tom Jones should return to set things right.

"The Squire's arrival, madam, could surely not transpire long past the end of the month; and no scandal will accompany the brief visit of two very respectable ladies, with the added chaperonage of my own Mrs. Barnes.

"Yet we shall see whether those sad scoundrels Hacksem and Hastings retain any conscience public shame may touch. My sermon this Sunday shall be upon *Genesis,* iv, 9, 'Am I my brother's keeper?' and I promise you, ladies, I shall *answer the question.*"

——

Upon this declaration (which was made, I assure thee, with every bit of sincerity he possessed), Mr. Adams was about to take his leave, when his hostess reminded him that it still rained extremely hard, and was, moreover, time for supper. These considerations, which in any case would have influenced so sociable a young man as Mr. Adams, were seconded by being raised in a voice showing quite plainly Mrs. James's loneliness. When Amelia (who was generally a stranger to self-pity) echoed the invitation in similar tones, Mr. Adams surrendered. Thinking no more of the scoundrels than of the Man in the Moon, he smacked his lips and, with a cheerful smile, held out his arms to lead the ladies in.

# VI

### In Which Hacksem and Sinamore, Having Bested Mr. Adams, Grievously Insult Amelia

Mr. Adams's large heart, when swelled with strong emotion, tended oft-times to squeeze his brains. His sermon to reform the two scoundrels, though feelingly written and staggeringly delivered, suffered from a trifling flaw; namely, that neither Mr. Sinamore nor Mr. Hacksem bothered to attend the service. Although the six villagers who braved the downpour that Sunday declared he had never spoken better, the Parson was still disappointed in himself.

Despite their absence, Messrs. Sinamore and Jones were perfectly informed of all the parson's opinions. The vehicle of their information was that curious journal which, like the *influenza*, travels on the wind. I mean, of course, *Rumour*, and rumour had in this case blown as swiftly as a gale. (Indeed, I have always believed that if a rumour and a lightning bolt were to leave a cloud at the same moment, the rumour would reach the ground in ample time to be struck by the bolt—a fate, incidentally, I consider perfectly appropriate for all such troublesome stuff, which is generally inspired by idleness and propelled by malice.)

The two scoundrels therefore learned almost simultaneously of Mr. Adams's sermon and of his plan to take Amelia into his home; and these two bits of information, taken together, they deemed to constitute an attack upon their interests.

Mr. Sinamore in particular was a gentleman too high-minded ever to resent an injury when he could return it; and no sooner had word reached him of Mr. Adams's opposition, than he and his colleague began to spread a counter-rumour, that the Parson's interest in the well-being of Miss Amelia Jones was of a sort entirely unbecoming a gentleman of the cloth.

Finding, however, that Mr. Adams's high reputation perfectly protected him against such slanders within his own parish, Mr. Sinamore aimed his sights higher, and went to visit the bishop under whose authority Mr. Adams lay.

This bishop (whose name we shall conceal) was indeed an ornament to the church, for besides being one of the best horsemen and shots in the country, he drest extremely well, kept a fine table, and told comical tales with an unmatched wit. In his selfless campaign to become all things to all men, he had, alas, fallen a little behind in ecclesiastical matters. To say truth, it was some while before he could associate a face with the name of Mr. Adams; yet, his memory once being refreshed, he heard the two accusers with close attention; for he loved a well-spiced story, and Mr. Jones played the aggrieved brother, and Mr. Sinamore, the concerned parishioner, with consummate skill. No sooner had they completed their performance, than the bishop thanked them for their honesty, and promised he would write Mr. Adams a letter of warning, in which he would teach the sly dog (as he called him) some discretion.

The bishop's letter was, in fact, slightly delayed by his packing for a journey to Scotland, and did not reach Mr. Adams for nearly two weeks, or until the end of the second full week in October. By this time, in nearly daily meetings, the Parson and his two friends had about exhausted the plausible explanations for the continuing silences of both Charles James and Tom, and had almost reached that stage where concern becomes despair—tho' Mr. Adams would now and again suffer fits of his nearly-incurable optimism.

On the afternoon of Friday, the 18th, then, these three friends were taking tea together at Mr. Adams's, when Mrs. Barnes, with a solemn respect motivated by the seal upon the envelope, brought in the bishop's letter. This the Parson read with considerable gravity, until finally, with a firmness of tone quite unusual to him, he announced:

"I am afraid, ladies, that the bishop has absolutely forbidden me to offer you the hospitality of my home; and has, moreover, cast certain aspersions upon my motives which another sort of man—hearing them from another sort of man—might be inclined to resent."

"Oh, Mr. Adams!" cried Mrs. James sympathetically.

"It appears, madam, we have been outmatched in yet another quarter. Yet we may still prevail easily enough; for far less than £80 will rent you a handsome cottage; and, of course, we expect to hear from your father, Amelia, almost hourly now."

"Nay, sir," came Amelia's unexpectedly fierce reply. "We have done enough of passive waiting. I say, let us go on to find my father if he is in London; or, failing that, let us approach there one of his powerful friends, for there we have many persons of influence who may help us, while here we have none. My father, for aught we know, may have left already for America, or even—given his nature—gone instead to India, or Timbuktu, or anywhere else. Perhaps I should have written to Rob earlier, but we may now do that as well from London. Why should we wait here, at the mercy of Hacksem and Mr. Sinamore?"

It sometimes happens that an idea is not voiced until it has become, quite silently, the common belief of every person concerned. So it was now, for Amelia's proposal brought not a single objection from Mrs. James (whose sorrow was hardening into a hatred and a darker suspicion of Mr. Sinamore) and only a few pointless equivocations from Mr. Adams, who at last said:

"Well, Amelia, I begin to think you are correct; yet before undertaking such a journey, I must insist that you make a last effort to persuade your brother to relent."

"My brother, sir, knows very well where to find me," Amelia replied harshly, before softening, and adding with a smile, "Yet, I must return home to collect my jewelry and money; and, for your sake, I will ask him to break with the wretched Mr. Sinamore."

Very early the following Monday, therefore (having spent a considerable part of the day earlier upon her knees, requesting that patience which was, perhaps, the sole deficiency in her character), Amelia Jones appeared at Paradise Hall. The morning air was clear and extremely cold, and crows sat in leafless trees beneath a sun which seemed distant and weak; yet she felt, perhaps oddly, relief to be home.

Home, however, had changed, as was apparent from the frightened look of Mrs. Limeslices when she opened the door, and then, without a word, disappeared to find (as it turned out) Mr. Grimes. This toad-like gentleman, after studying Amelia with a superior, almost leering countenance, told her he would fetch *Mister* Jones, but—almost incredibly—did not admit her into her own house.

Her brother, with hardly greater hospitality, led her to a fireless parlour, where he posted Grimes as sentry in the doorway, and then took the sole uncovered chair for himself. Very graciously inviting her to stand as near him as she liked, he began, "I am glad, Amelia, you have decided to join me."

"You are, brother, entirely mistaken; for I am so far from joining you that"—here, remembering her promise to Mr. Adams, Amelia interrupted what might have become a denunciation; and when she resumed, her tone was more kindly—"that I fear I must present you with a choice; one, however, which I know your own goodness will help you to resolve correctly: Hacksem, you must turn away from this course, or else—"

"Sister!" cries Mr. Hacksem loudly. "Pray do not dictate to your superior. I shall demand, and you, relent. Ah, you will try my sense of mercy! I am prepared to take you back for all your wickedness, but ingratitude will defeat my generosity."

"Wickedness?" asked Amelia, in a despairing confusion which would have convinced the harshest judge of her absolute innocence.

"Nay, sister!" roars Mr. Jones. "Save your pretty tricks of purity for those who will be titillated; save them for those young London gentlemen who will find them worth paying extra for. But do not try them on your brother."

Reader, the horror and amazement which these words inspired in Amelia may scarce be described. Indeed, I can myself in no other way explain them, than to assume that Mr. Hacksem had become deranged from musing upon the stories he and Mr. Sinamore had spread about the village and to the bishop. Whether he had in some way been imposed upon by Mr. Sinamore, or whether he had suffered the worse fate of believing his own lies, I cannot at this point say—yet surely we must all be warned that, of the two great practical dangers of lying, the risk that others will disbelieve us is certainly less than the danger that we shall sooner or later come to believe ourselves; for, when we imagine ourselves the authors of reality, we are mad beyond words.

About the state of mind of Mr. Jones, however, we shall speculate no farther now, but only report the conversation which followed his accusation. Amelia, who was (after all) his sister, and an affectionate young woman, began to conceive a genuine alarm for his sanity; and rather than answer angrily, she endeavoured to soothe him.

"Indeed, brother, I believe you are tired. I suppose the business of the estate hath been too great for you; but you may believe we will find better help for you than that odious Mr. Sinamore. . . ."

"Amelia, I beg you!" says Mr. Jones, clasping his hands to his forehead. "Do not slander the one good man in all the world willing to forgive how our wicked Parson has debauched you, and to marry you, soiled as you are."

Astonishment had now made Amelia mute. Could a single word have expressed pity, anger and despair all at once, I believe she could have uttered it; but as it was, for a long moment, she said nothing. At last, seeing Hacksem grow calmer, she offered softly, "Let me go now, Hacksem, and collect my belongings. We shall speak again when you are better."

"Sister, you shall not leave. Only a marriage to Mr. Sinamore can restore that family honour which your public whorings have dragged through the mud. Until you accept him, your possessions shall remain with me."

"Brother, will you deny me what is my own?" demanded Amelia, ignoring Hacksem's most offensive words, but blushing wrathfully.

"Sister, until you accept Mr. Sinamore, you have *nothing* that is your own. Indeed, if you must be stubborn, you shall have only this engagement gift from me: an empty closet, without light or food. Let your wickedness and pride feed you there; and we shall soon, I think, have our wedding."

In saying this, I believe, Mr. Hacksem somewhat exceeded the authority granted him in law; yet I suppose he meant to hold by force what he could not gain by writ. As, moreover, he was now the most influential man in Somersetshire, I will not absolutely deny that the judges at Quarter-Sessions might have supported him.

Amelia, of course, was in no state of mind to consider this. Caring now only to make her escape from a place as mad as *Bedlam,* she began backing towards the doorway, while trying to ignore the feeling that neckless, black-browed Grimes meant to lay hands upon her.

Hacksem raised his hand in warning. Still hoping to leave peacefully, Amelia bowed her head, and, with pretended humility, asked whether she might go bid farewell to Mrs. James, and gather some clothing.

This gambit Hacksem met with a sneer. "Indeed, sister," said he, "you must have as much contempt for my brains as for the Christian religion and the progress of our nation."

"Name not the Christian religion, thou tyrant,"cried a frantic Amelia, who, drawing herself up to her full height, turned hastily to leave. She had just reached the doorway, when Grimes, grabbing her very tightly, spun her around, so they were both facing Hacksem, upon whose face there was a look extremely hideous.

Amelia, for all her bravery, might have now lost everything she valued, had it not been for a certain quiet "click" which sounded in the room.

This was the drawing back of the hammer of a pistol, which Mrs. Limeslices, slipping quickly through the doorway, had an instant before placed against Mr. Grimes's ribs, and which she now used eloquently, to press her demand that he raise his hands and stand absolutely still, for, "If you do not, I promise your lungs will have a shorter route to the open air."

Noble Grimes, tho' his courage was perfectly sufficient to oppress a helpless young woman, lacked quite that pitch of heroic virtue necessary to laugh away a pistol-ball through the chest. He therefore complied with this command immediately, and—to say truth—his knees then so lost their native stiffness that within a moment the only part of him still standing was the hair upon his head.

A certain look in Mrs. Limeslices's mild grey eyes hinted it would be unwise to interfere with her. Sending Amelia to open the front door, she said firmly to her erstwhile employer, "I suspect, Hacksem, that persons besides your father would be displeased to hear you held this young lady against her will; and so, for the sake of 'progress in the shire,' let's keep this tiff our secret. Pray, young sir, do not follow. We have had enough of hunting accidents."

In an instant, then, she and Amelia were running down the long drive toward the road. At Mrs. Limeslices's suggestion, they continued past the road, across some fields, and onto a little-used footpath through a wood. There, at last, they stopped to rest. Amelia, casting herself down upon a stump, and then catching her breath, whispered sadly, "Oh, Limeslices! My brother is mad."

"Not so mad as that, dear ma'am," replied Mrs. Limeslices, "for ever since your note came Friday, they have been plotting how to frighten you into submission; and, for all I know, this was but a part of their scheme. Yet, I concede that to be always near Mr. Sinamore would drive me close to madness, and it may be . . ." Here she ended, as was her habit, inconclusively, so that the last word belonged to her superiors; and idly she laid the pistol beside her, but with its barrel happening to point towards Amelia.

"Mrs. Limeslices!" said Amelia, in alarm. "Have care with that!"

"Oh, la, ma'am," answered the maid, patting her white hair. "You are perfectly safe; for, to be sure, it is bad enough to point a pistol at a man without the extra crime of loading it. And if I had shot Mr. Grimes, who do you suppose would have been obliged to get the stains from the carpets? 'Tis no wonder women so rarely kill." Laughing, she continued:

"Ifacks, I am very sorry to have startled the gentlemen; tho' in truth they have so often played the bully with me that I believe they a little deserved it. Well, ma'am, I am sure you need not stare at me so; for I promise you that if any other *he* places an unwelcome hand on my dear Amelia, I shall shoot him for all the carpets in England."

Finally, standing, she ended, "Well, dear Miss, we have a long journey ahead of us to London; and whether or not any of your friends plan to help, we should be going. Are you ready now?"

"Ready, indeed, dear Limeslices," answered Amelia, who viewed this change in her maid with wonder, and also (I suspect) with a certain shame for having always before thought her a silly, if very kind, old woman.

Amelia now leaped to her feet, but perhaps too hastily, for her blood did not follow; and the familiar scene of bushes, trees and Somerset sky seemed to spin upside-down. Mrs. Limeslices, however, caught her, and a moment later, the two women were moving briskly down the path.

# VII

## *Of an Escape Easy, Gentle and Amusing*

Amelia and Mrs. Limeslices, fearing interception if they tried to reach Meadowlands, made instead for Mr. Adams's house, which, very tired and dirty, they reached about two in the afternoon. As soon as he had heard their stories, the Parson sent word for Mrs. James, who arrived just as the sun was setting about three hours later, bringing with her some clothing of Amelia's and all the money she had. The air let into the house with her was the cold wind of October, and behind her, the stars were visible above the blue-white region of the sunset. She was shown into the dining room just as supper was being placed upon the table; and while they ate, the four conspirators discussed their situation, which, at length, Mr. Adams took the liberty of summarizing thusly:

"I suppose, then, ladies, that we must leave as soon as possible. I shall go in the morning to ask farmer Pickdell's son to drive us as far as Glastonbury; for we are agreed not to appear in Domney, if we can avoid it. Thence we shall easily find a coach to London; and so, if all goes well, we may by the week-end find our dangers at an end."

His summary being received with general approval, Mr. Adams then excused himself to write two letters, one to the bishop and the other, including notes for a sermon, to his curate. The theme of this sermon I have not been able to learn, but I have no doubt it was something touching the very core of religion, such as duty, or patience, or obedience to civil authority.

There remained behind Mr. Adams three women in a state of lively excitement. Each of them, having lived a rather dull—I do not say unpleasant—life, had now before her the prospect of adventure. Each, moreover, had personal reasons to wish Hacksem and Sinamore brought low; and though revenge may be poor morality, even the haughtiest moralists admit it spurs action wonderfully.

Mr. Adams left at first light, and reappeared about two hours later with wagon and driver. The company quickly readied themselves to depart, the ladies and Mrs. Limeslices aboard the wagon, and Mr. Adams riding his horse. Mrs. Barnes, meanwhile, only stood in her thin dress watching from the garden. Except for the white vapour of her breathing, she displayed no more life than a stone troll, until long after the riders had gone, when she finally permitted herself a pair of heavy sighs.

That time of year had come when the turnip wears the glowing smile of Mr. Jack-O'-Lantern; and the crows flew over a countryside brown with the cut remnants of the harvest and just mysterious enough to heighten drama without oppressing spirits.

They reached Glastonbury near sundown, the night air prompting the ladies to wrap their shawls about them; and, after parting from young Pickdell (who was to lead Mr. Adams's horse back with him), they took lodgings at the stage-coach inn. The end of the harvest business had left this building nearly empty, and so their landlady greeted them most eagerly.

To say truth, this landlady (whose name was Mrs. Custard) had another reason for attending our friends so carefully. She was, as it were, a *semi-widow*, which is to say that her husband's affections had died sometime before, tho' her husband, I fear, lived on in flourishing health—at least if we may judge by his energetic way with his businesses, or by his vigourous efforts, underway even as our friends arrived, to talk or wrestle pretty Nancy Chambermaid into his upstairs bedroom.

Mrs. Custard, a handsome, red-cheeked, richly-figured woman of a little under forty, had borne her bereavement extremely well. After a few years of sending her husband those little communications special to the conjugal state (such as throwing at him the contents of a china-cabinet, or emptying over his head the contents of a chamber-pot), she had at last found quieter consolation in the daily intercourse of business; and in this, I believe, she generally fared about as happily as her late husband.

A very pleasing supper of beef and broth was set before our friends; and after they had supped, Mrs. Custard begged leave to join them herself, more, I am sure, in the hope of learning some news than of selling some punch.

Her expectations were, however, disappointed, for, while the party did order a bowl of *negus*, Amelia had already warned Mr. Adams (who was as generous with his information as with anything else he possessed) that they must be discreet. When asked where they were bound, therefore, he replied simply that, "I am escorting these ladies to London; where they are to meet with this young lady's father, who is Mr. Thomas Jones, of Paradise Hall."

Tom's name being, of course, well known to the landlady, it was to her considerable credit that she now proposed no additional little luxuries which might thicken the bill in the morning. Mr. Adams's remarks had, however, brought him to her attention, and when he later excused himself to smoke his pipe out-of-doors, she said to Amelia:

"Well, miss, you could not have found a worthier protector, for I attest I have not seen so powerful a figure of a man—Parson's gown or no—in all my life. To be certain, Amelia (may I call you so, now we are alone?), we had here last spring Lord Cholmondeley, who, in London, the ladies cheer as "My Lord Athlete": I promise you, he was a frail, dry stick to this jolly parson of yours. I'm sure *I* should feel perfectly secure, so long as he was near. . . ."

When both Amelia and Mrs. James responded with cold stares to her smiling freedom, Mrs. Custard blushed, cleared her throat, and began a new topic; yet, Reader, she had done a curious damage. I mean that she had ended Amelia's habit of considering the Parson as a type of prayer- or commonplace-book upon legs, rather than as a man. The new version of Mr. Adams struck Amelia more with surprise than with any other emotion, but she fell asleep that night reviewing it, and in the morning, she had reached the breakfast table before her thoughts turned, as was their custom, to the charming son of Mrs. James.

With the usual punctuality of such conveyances, the morning coach departed from the yard of Mrs. Custard's inn (which was called the Stag and Dove) precisely forty-seven minutes late. Mrs. Custard herself, looking extremely downcast, had walked out to say good-bye; and as the coach was loading, she approached Amelia, who was standing beside Mr. Adams.

"I am sure, miss," said she, "that if I said anything wrong last night, I am heartily sorry. Indeed, I spoke only from a wish to be good company; for, in truth, it is very hard for a woman to amuse herself, or even to think well of herself, when her husband ignores her, as mine does. Do, miss, forgive me." This she said very contritely; and Amelia, who was really the best-natured young woman in the world, immediately replied that nothing had transpired to displease her, and that she rather looked forward to the accommodations of the Stag and Dove on her return. That this pleased Mrs. Custard, was evident from her expression. Her pleasure, however, was extremely short-lived, for almost at once her husband appeared in the yard, in the company, this time, of *Betty* Chambermaid; and something about Mrs. Custard's frown suggested that he might shortly discover a horse-shoe fitted to that part of his anatomy where the similarly-shaped *laurel-wreath* is generally set.

Just at this moment, however, there clattered into the yard a coach from Surrey. The first person to step down from it was a handsome young ensign of the Navy, his brown hair descending in waves to his collar, and his cheeks blooming with colour. No sooner did Mrs. Custard catch sight of him than her whole countenance brightened; indeed, I believe I may say that she *hugged* him with her eyes.

"Sweet miss," she cried, beginning already to edge from her old guests and towards this splendid new one, "you are kind to a foolish woman; and, believe me, you shall be very welcome whenever you return. Yet now I must greet my new arrivals! Aye, sir! Coming!" she concluded, as if responding to the young officer, who, in fact, had not yet noticed her existence.

Watching her sweep down upon the startled ensign a moment later, Mr. Adams declared, "How justly doth great Homer pronounce the virtues of the hearth to be the greatest excellencies of woman! And what a paragon is Mrs. Custard!"

Hearing this, Mrs. Limeslices placed her hand upon her jaw, and with a giggle told Mr. Adams he would make any woman a delightful husband. With what amusement Amelia received the Parson's words, I need not acquaint thee, Reader; yet, as she did not positively laugh aloud, we may, I believe, assume she still liked him pretty well.

A few moments later, our friends boarded the London coach, which, under threatening skies, was to carry them to just those adventures we shall display in our next chapter.

# VIII

## Containing Dreadful Events Certain
## to Interest the Reader

Mr. Custard being a very astute business-man, his coaches were of the narrowest possible dimensions. That in which our friends rode might have easily held four small persons plus, perhaps, a very thin King Charles spaniel, but now carried, besides Amelia and her companions, a large quantity of mail which would not fit on the roof (where two other persons rode), and a lawyer by the name of Caitlin.

Mr. Caitlin at first endeavoured to discuss with Mr. Adams various complex legal matters. As, however, the Parson's ignorance of jurisprudence nearly sufficed to make him imagine that a law-suit was what lawyer wore into court, Mr. Caitlin (who was really a convivial man, and only a little marred by being extremely greedy and ambitious) turned instead to the personalities of the law. In this he succeeded better, holding forth divertingly for above two hours, until, learning that our friends came from Somersetshire, he unfortunately asked, "Whether they knew a certain Mr. Sinamore?"

Without waiting for any formal response (for indeed he received only a vague, uneasy shifting within the coach, which I suppose the general roughness of the road concealed from him), Mr. Caitlin next lengthily reviewed Lawyer Sinamore's career, beginning, more or less, with the stars which attended his birth, and ending with his slaying of Medusa. In truth, this enthusiasm was unsurprising, for it is but natural to admire those who have done everything we wish to do; and, to give Mr. Sinamore credit, his reputation had by that date spread nearly everywhere that influence and wealth were blindly admired, which is to say . . . nearly everywhere.

At last, having concluded his tale, Mr. Caitlin asked his companions whether they could tell anything of the Great Man's most recent adventures. To this, Mr. Adams replied vigorously:

"As last I heard of him, he was, I believe, deep in the business of putting a widow out of her home, and helping a son steal an estate from his father."

"Aye, sir; aye, I understand you," rejoined Mr. Caitlin, with a wink. "Mr. Sinamore is ever ready to serve the interests of those who have ambitions, against the interests of those who have none. Well, this is how we progress; and, you may be sure, no man will do it more smoothly than Mister Sinamore, or with greater profit for all on his side. For my part, I salute him, for, as Plato saith, it is bold men who make the world go on."

Mrs. James frowned at this, and seemed about to interrupt angrily; yet a far noisier and more startling response now occurred, in the form of a crack of thunder which, although far off, bespoke great power. When this was, a moment later, followed by a bright flash and a second, louder crack much nearer, the lawyer began to turn very pale; and, sinking down in his seat, declared that he had but little love for the workings of a storm.

"In truth," said he, "I have been afraid of thunder and lightning since a boy; they are, I suppose, not much to the liking of any solicitor, as they suggest that Court before which all sophistical pleading is idle."

Mr. Caitlin then groaned (for the thunder continued very loud), and sank down still farther in his seat. This, however, lowered his eyes about level with the bosom of Amelia, who sat extremely near him. The proximity brought an expression both alert and contented to his formerly discouraged features, until Mrs. Limeslices, observing the fact, reached out (for she sat opposite him, and beside the Parson) to poke him sharply in the ribs, while bidding him to sit up and "be a good, brave *gentleman.*"

Perhaps luckily for Mr. Caitlin, this exchange had gone unnoticed by Mr. Adams, who was in fact still wracking his brains to discover where exactly Plato recommended ejecting the helpless from their homes. In truth, I believe he would still be looking to this day, were it not that, all at once, the storm they heard overtook them, with the wind, sweeping across the road, throwing the rain very hard against one side of the coach. That side happening to have a leaking window; the travellers began to be wet as well as cold; and Amelia, seated nearest the faulty pane, began to be the wettest of all. Observing this, Mr. Adams at once forgot Plato, and, endeavouring to trade places with her, induced a new oscillation to the motion of the coach to accompany the tilt of the wind and the bounce of the road.

So, indeed, might the philosopher, seeing the coach from without, have remarked how it suggested our world in miniature, full of lust, violence and gallantry, battered by the elements, and bound upon an uncertain journey.

Alas, Reader, I have often observed that, while good persons generally content themselves with remarks, bad ones usually favour actions; and so it was upon this occasion. Mr. Custard's coach had now begun to climb that very hill upon which Tom Jones himself had earlier come to grief, and which the Reader will find very handsomely described in our Second Book. Among the furnishings of this particular road were (as the Reader will no doubt recall) three specially blood-thirsty highwaymen; and it will surprise no student of the tenacity of human nature, that these three gentlemen are now to make their second appearance in our history.

In truth, Mr. Adams had barely risen from his seat, when these gentlemen rode into the path of the coach, and in loud voices demanded that it halt. The coachman's hasty compliance with this command had the unlucky effect of throwing Mr. Adams forward into the closest possible contact with Amelia, and especially with that charming part of her form which Mr. Caitlin had, a moment earlier, been warned not to admire. The young Parson's embarrassment soared beyond all bounds (including that of reason) and, having placed one hand securely upon the coach-door, he was about to pull himself modestly back when—oh, *misfortune!*—the burliest of the highwaymen happened to jerk open the coach-door, causing Mr. Adams to tumble out into the mud. In his desperate effort to save himself, moreover, he had gripped wildly to Amelia's garment, and so he had come loose with a rip, and now held a portion of her sleeve in his hand.

"Odso, Jack!" cries one of the highwaymen, "here's a fine piece of reverent clergy for thee. Wast hearing her confession, Father? Oh, and in a Protestant land, too!" There then followed several jokes upon respect for the cloth which, tho' amusing, shall be here suppressed. At length, having enjoyed their laugh, the robbers ordered Mr. Adams to his feet, promising they should let him return to his sport soon enough—at which words, Mr. Adams looked very black, and clenched a fist larger than the knuckle of an ox, but said nothing.

The chief of the highwaymen now thrust his head deep within the coach and called, "Come out, ladies!" and when, a moment later, these three and Mr. Caitlin were aligned sullenly (and a little fearfully) beside Mr. Adams, he continued:

"Now, gentle-folk, let's all be sensible. We'll have your money and your watches—and, ladies, your rings and such—and you'll have your lives."

Hearing this, Mr. Adams (who, I believe, had never before considered the consequences of a robbery) declared very earnestly, "Look'ee, sir: these ladies have great need of their money; and, moreover, *as* ladies they require and deserve the protection of all good men. Will you not content yourself with what this gentleman and I can give? For, here I have £80; and this gentleman, I believe, must have at least as much, since he is a lawyer and tells us he does prodigious business."

The results of this speech were several (the loudest being a moan from Mr. Caitlin), but the chief rogue, after taking the money from Mr. Adams's hand, answered with a leer that he supposed in some better world —which, as he was a Christian, he hoped to reach—robbers would take only from those who could afford it, but that for now, they must get by as they could, and so, "You must all strip, and be damned."

Indeed, I fear that Mr. Adams's mention of the defenselessness of the ladies had inspired certain ideas which we abhor too much even to mention; for the bare-headed rogue, declaring that Amelia had the finest eyes he had ever seen, stepped close to her and offered a certain insult to her person.

Reader, that epitaph commonly applied to unlucky gamesters—that "they did not quit when they were ahead"—might well be stuck to this nasty rogue, for no sooner had his finger-tips touched the barest fibre of Amelia's bodice, than Mr. Adams, forgetting entirely the pistol aimed at him, rose like a giant champion to her defense. Having, indeed, no lance to use, he made the target serve for the weapon; or, in other words, pushed the rogue's head through the side of the coach, a tactic which, tho' it is nowhere mentioned in Spencer or Ariosto, seemed—if we may judge by the screams which resulted—to have worked pretty well.

Alas, villainy is rarely friendless in this world; nor, I fear, are villains such brainless oafs as they are made to appear in old romances. Mr. Stumpling had some months earlier been saved by the misfiring of a rain-wetted pistol; but the gentleman who had failed to kill him then, had learned better since. The pistol, which he had all this time kept dry beneath his cape, he now aimed at the head of Mr. Adams, and fired.

There came an extremely loud report, and at once Mr. Adams grasped his head, the blood oozing between his fingers. Amelia screamed, Mrs. James fainted, and Mrs. Limeslices—who had been pummeling the trap't villain with the butt of her pistol—turned to look. The two rogues—certainly realizing to their horror what they had done—stared dumbly at each other a moment, 'til the handkerchief'd one, in the voice of Hamlet's ghost pronounced, "Hast killed 'un, Jamie." The villain in the coach now freed himself, and after surveying the bloody scene with pale visage, ran to his horse and galloped away; in which heroism, his two colleagues immediately seconded him.

Mr. Adams now began to stagger pitiably, and pulling his hands a little away from his face, he said to Amelia, "Mrs. Limeslices!" and to Mrs. Limeslices, "Amelia!" and then pitched forward into the mud.

Reader, it would be an epic in itself to tell thee how the three ladies (for the two roof-passengers and the coachman had long since run away) got the body of their fallen hero into the coach. Mr. Caitlin, it is true, helped them (and tho' he mumbled often that he feared the law if he did not, I believe he was at heart a good man, if not a great one). In about a quarter-hour, they had him aboard, and then, with Amelia at the reins, they drove him as fast as they could to the inn which they saw at the top of the hill, all the while believing, I suppose, that he might have done as well in a Viking ship with his dog at his feet.

# IX

## *A Chapter Which Begins Desperately, and Ends as Shall Be Seen*

Its horses frothing, the coach splashed its way into the deserted yard of the inn on the hilltop. The hostler had watched its approach sullenly from a chair at the stable door, but now, at the cries for help and a surgeon, he jumped galvanically to his feet, and waded as quickly as he could to aid our distraught friends.

Our friends beheld a dismal scene, for the Biting Whale had fallen wretchedly, with shutters hanging loose, cheap green ballast glass set into broken windows, and weeds growing high in the flooded yard. Though the short day was already far advanced towards evening, not a single cheerful light burned indoors. The Biting Whale (which seemed now whale-like indeed, being half-submerged in rain-water, and grey and shapeless in the late-afternoon mist) looked nothing like that happy place Tom had visited, and little enough like any human habitation at all.

The hostler, however, was unquestionably a human being, who, having first supposed from the blood that Mr. Adams was dead, soon discovered signs of his breathing; at which, without waiting for assistance, he draped Mr. Adams's arm around his own neck, and began dragging the Parson (whose feet kicked limply into the marshy waters) towards the inn.

When he had brought Mr. Adams indoors, the hostler opened another door an inch or two, and called softly, "Betty!" Hearing footsteps, he said to the others, "Here, gentles, I must stop, or I'll be dismissed; for the master will have none from the stable in the house. I hope the poor gentleman may live, especially as I believe that is a cassock he is making so bloody. Now I shall see to your coach."

The maid (who was indeed that Betty who had been so kind to Tom) now appeared, and, seeing Mr. Adams (who had been left prop't upon a chair), immediately begged the others to carry him upstairs, while she herself would send for the surgeon.

The others had complied only as far as to raise Mr. Adams from his chair (occasioning thereby a groan, the first noise Mr. Adams had made since falling) when a man at the top of the stairs demanded loudly and imperiously that they halt.

"Bodkins, people!" roared this person, whose identity we shall presently reveal. "What murders do ye perpetrate here? Believe me, I shall shoot if I must!"

"Sir," responded Amelia, with all that gentleness of which she was mistress, "here is a poor clergyman we fear is dying, who was robbed upon the road."

"Robbed?" replied the man up in the shadows, descending into partial view. "And brought here, I suppose, that he may cover my sheets with blood, and involve myself with the law, before he shall expire."

No answer was forthcoming.

"How? Wilst not explain thyselves? Then wilst tell me this? Who shall pay me for all the harm, the time, the trouble? Eh?"

So bizarre was this inhumanity that even Mr. Caitlin began to be appalled. Yet only Amelia had sense to act, by throwing a pair of guineas which the landlord caught as neatly as a frog catches flies. Sated, he then began an apology best characterized as beslimed, of which the following was the conclusion.

"Gentlefolks, you must forgive me; for a poor man is easily cheated; and if I seem cold, it is only because warmth is nowadays so dear. If compassion were not so costly, I believe I should be the most compassionate soul in England.

"Well, you may take the gentleman up, with my blessings and best wishes; and—shall ye have supper, and stay the night, gentlefolks?"

The others replied that they would think of this later; but for now, they begged his leave, and, pushing angrily past him, they took Mr. Adams to his room.

An hour passed before the surgeon appeared, a grave old gentleman, named Mr. Priestly, plainly drest and wearing a wig extremely rusty. Lacking fine clothes, eloquence, even that nonsensical Latin which persuades the ignorant, he possessed nothing to recommend him—except that he had perfectly mastered the job of a surgeon, which is to make the sick well without making them bankrupt.

Accordingly, having spent perhaps three-quarters of an hour with his patient, he joined the others in their parlour, and, after surveying their anxious faces, spoke thusly:

"It is common practice for members of my profession to raise at the outset of a treatment every frightening possibility, and to cast the situation in so grave a light that any failures may be forgiven as inevitable, and any successes celebrated as proofs of highest skill and genius.

"In this case, alas, I must break with my brethren, and tell thee directly the wound is inconsequential. A glancing pistol-ball hath torn a swatch of skin from the top of the Parson's head, and—as scalp wounds are always extremely *sanguinary*—bathed his face in blood. This blood, and the fainting shock attending it, caused your alarm, which I believe you may now lay to rest. To say truth, your friend is in little danger, except it be from fever, of which I see at present no trace. So, I fear, I lose a good income."

Ending with a smile (which was reflected upon every face in the room), he accepted a glass of punch, and shortly afterwards excused himself, saying he should return early in the morning to change the dressing.

Amelia (who had maintained a suitable decorum in the surgeon's presence) now grasped Mrs. Limeslices's hand and led her several dance-steps across the room. She then called for Betty, to whom she said, "We shall be staying the night. Will you please ask our landlord to have a bright fire, and the best dinner he can provide, set for us in this room as soon as may be?"

Betty hesitated before venturing, "Good madam, I shall be happy to do what you ask . . . only, ma'am, believe me, you shall pay for it most dearly; no less, I believe, than three times what you should pay in any other place."

"Lackaday, saucy miss!" intervened Mrs. Limeslices. "My madam cares naught for such trifles, for this is Miss Amelia Jones, daughter of *the* Squire Thomas Jones, of Somersetshire."

At this, Betty turned very pale, stammered that she had meant no offense, and left the room suddenly. About an hour later, she returned to say that their meal was ready, but that their landlord preferred to serve them in another room. Notwithstanding their surroundings (for they had been given a damp, low-ceiling'd room, lit only by a pair of candles and a fire mostly of green twigs), or their food (which was but soup, cold mutton and stale rolls), the company dined with an appetite bred of relief; and soon after, content to have heard no more from their landlord, they went up to bed.

# X

## Containing an Interview Between Amelia and Betty, and Several Lesser Matters

During the night, Amelia was awakened by Betty, who said that the wounded gentleman was delirious; running, however, into his room, Amelia discovered that he was merely dreaming, and that his "mad gibberish" was in fact the Fourth Book of the *Iliad*, perfectly recited.

In the morning, the surgeon, Mr. Priestly, found Mr. Adams to be still weak, but speaking coherently and with a considerable appetite; and, on returning downstairs, he informed Amelia that, "Nature hath her cure excellently in hand; and, as I do not suppose you wish to hire me simply to applaud her workings, I believe I may be now discharged from the case, especially since Mrs. Limeslices tells me she is capable of changing the dressings daily.

"Ideally, Mr. Adams would keep to his bed a fortnight; but as he tells me your business in London is urgent, I believe he may travel in a week, if he travels quietly—which, I gather, is not quite his habit."

So saying, Mr. Priestly took his leave, after charging Amelia a very modest fee and refusing the present she sincerely offered. This gentleman had in fact been many years before one of the most successful men in London, 'til his unorthodoxy (for he never made an unnecessary charge in his life) caused him to be cried down by all the surgeons, physicians and apothecaries of the town. As he was now ending his days in rural obscurity, let us remember him always for his skill, compassion and honesty.

Before departing, Mr. Priestly had said that a week of bed rest would make the Parson's recovery complete; but no sooner had this news been conveyed to the landlord, than he burst in upon Amelia (who was finishing her breakfast in the parlour) with a tirade even nastier than his first, the essence of which was that he must be sure of his money, if he was to have guests for a week. Otherwise:

"Tho' no man is eager to see another, injured, thrown out into the road; yet those who take from innkeepers without paying are nothing but thieves, and *hanging* is proper for them.

"As for the gentleman being a parson, well, as Christianity was begun in a stable, I suppose one or two Christians may as well *end* there, tho', by all that's holy, I have as great a reverence for the Faith as any man in England."

At her first meeting with this bully, Amelia had been shocked into a quick surrender, but, having grown a little wiser overnight, she now replïed, "In truth, sir, you have a right to look to your interests; and pray, how will they be served if you are dragged into the law-courts? That gentleman with us yesterday"—for Mr. Caitlin, after a very fond parting, had left a few minutes earlier on the revitalized coach—"was a solicitor who told us that an action may lie against any who contribute to a man's death; and as for prosecuting such a matter, my father's estates are the largest in Somersetshire, and our Lawyer may be known to you. His name is *Sinamore.*"

This pronouncement (and particularly its last three syllables) did much to brake the spinning brains of the landlord, who now said that so long as he was paid, all would be well, and he was extremely sorry if he had spoken out of turn. Amelia promised he would receive what was his due.

Immediately after the surgeon's visit, Mr. Adams had fallen once again into a deep sleep. Then Mrs. James (more agitated, I suspect, than she cared to admit by the prospect of a delay) had gone to her room to rest, and Mrs. Limeslices had migrated to the kitchen. So was Amelia left alone to face a grey, chilling afternoon in a room as welcoming as a grave.

For nearly an hour, Amelia sat at the table, reading, or rather holding, a volume of the *Spectator.* At length she noticed that the tablecloth, though very stained and dirty, was pink; and, reminded of her father's letters, she called in Betty.

"Betty, said she, "I believe I may ask you a question frankly. If this is indeed *Mr. Nautley's* Biting Whale, my father wrote of it with highest praise. Was he mad, or did something happen to make it as it is?"

"In truth, madam, we were once as fine an inn as could be wished. But about a month after your father passed through here"—Betty's eyes turned momentarily dreamy—"*our* Mr. Nautley was called to Scotland by the illness of his mother, who is, of course, a most aged woman. Before he reached Edinburgh, there was an accident, his coach overturning in a river. Mr. Nautley escaped, but on returning to free the postillion, he suffered several injuries, and swallowed, moreover, a great deal of river water, with the result that he came down a few days later with pneumonia. This he is presently so far from mastering, that we have been warned to expect his death hourly. Ah, madam, it doth seem hard that a gentleman who hath sailed all over the seven seas should die from a little brook where the children might drink."

Here she paused to wipe at certain rivulets wending down her cheeks. "This tyrannical Mr. Nautley you have met, madam, is but a cousin to our true landlord, who, having no other relatives, hath appointed him as caretaker 'til he recover, or as heir if he should not. In truth, ma'am, it scarce seems possible that the two men could share a drop of blood; for the one is as good a man as you will meet, and the other, as bad."

This struck very hard at Amelia, whose burdens were already fraying her nerves. "I fear, Betty," said she, "the bonds of common blood are everywhere diluted; for my own brother hath done such harm to me, and to those my father loves, as scarce could be believed."

"I am sorry, ma'am," sighed Betty, "to hear it. Yet I believe your father (who is the finest man I ever saw) will quickly make corrections; and, ma'am, you are far surer of his aid than I am of good Mr. Nautley's."

"Alas, Betty," cried Amelia softly, "I am no more sure of his aid, than I am of the weather on a day in April, for my father may now be anywhere upon the earth, and I have had no word from him in answer to my several anxious letters."

I have often observed, Reader, that generosity is independent of means. There is a shrewd person who will not give you the dead fly atop his stack of gold dishes, for fear he shall have need of a fly, or lest he lose a profit when insect prices rise, or for a hundred other excellent reasons; and there is a foolish person who will share whatever he hath, on the flimsy grounds that you need it, and he can, one way or another, spare it. You may generally find the former person by knocking at the finest home, or calling at the richest chambers, wherever you are, but to find the latter, you must ofttimes seek in small and obscure places; tho', to say truth, I believe the harder journey will reward thee better, whether thou borrowest or not.

Amelia had discovered such a paragon by accident; for Betty, seeing her distress, reached inside her own blouse, and withdrew, by a chain around her neck, Tom's ring. "This ring, madam," she said, "your father gave me some time ago. I should like you to keep it until you find him, after which you may, if you remember, send it to me, or not, as you see fit."

Betty now blushed scarlet. Amelia, however, was far too innocent ever to question Tom's generosity; and, after first refusing the ring, at last accepted it with thanks. Just then the landlord began to shout for his maid in language such as you shall not find quoted in this history (nor, indeed, in many a tawdrier one). Betty evinced great fright, and would leave, but Amelia would not release her, 'til rising, she had taken her hand, and promised her she would see her kindness repaid.

## XI

### *In Which Amelia Reaches Her Father's Door—and Has It Slammed in Her Face*

Mr. Adams so hated confinement, and so yearned to reach London (where he expected a quick end to the lunacies of Hacksem and Sinamore) that he endured his week of rest only because to do otherwise, would have been to make Amelia frown. As it was, he passed the final two days of the period pacing the inn, and explaining to any who would hear him how miserable he was to have caused the company's delay.

In truth, none of our four travellers much regretted the moment when, beneath a sky scarcely lightened by the dawn, they boarded the coach which was to carry them on to London.

They reached that great city two days later, amid a rainstorm very fierce, and in a mood very little brighter, as it was then the 1st of November, on which Mr. Sinamore was to take possession of Meadowlands. Having transferred from the stage-coach to a hackney, they allowed their bodies to be transported through bustling, muddy streets, tho' their thoughts (I dare say) never came nearer than the border of Somersetshire.

It was about one o'clock in the afternoon (tho' the sky seemed hours darker) when the hackney-coach reached Tom's town-house. They were at once shown into the drawing-room, where a few moments later Mrs. Guerdion attended them, speaking, however, with a coolness they had by no means expected. After the slightest of curtseys, she seated herself at Tom's desk, and spoke as follows:

"Amelia, I have not the heart to deceive thee by even a moment's false hospitality. I yesterday received this letter, which, I regret to say, you must now read."

Holding the familiar stationery with an unsteady hand, Amelia saw:

My Dear Mrs. Guerdion:

It sorrows me to be obliged to tell you that my sister Amelia has done something to displease me nearly beyond amendment. Knowing herself to be no longer welcome here, she has, moreover, taken flight with some persons as disreputable as herself. Whether these persons shall have the impudence to present themselves to you, I cannot say; yet I charge you, as you value your position, to offer them no succour, unless it be that my sister should express a wish to place herself alone under your protection, pending my arrival.

You will find enclosed herewith documents signed by my father and witnessed by Mr. Hastings Sinamore, Esq. attesting to the authority of,

Your obliged employer,
Mr. Hacksem Jones

Amelia composed herself carefully before asking, "And do you intend, Mrs. Guerdion, to honour my brother's wishes?"

"I believe, ma'am," replied that old woman stiffly, "they are rather commands than wishes; and, as his documents would show you, his commands must be obeyed."

"Pray, good Amelia, do not think me harsh. Your father's house hath been my home these thirty years, and I am more attached to it than are any of the furnishings, and most of the bricks. To leave it would be very hard, indeed."

"But surely, Mrs. Guerdion," asked Mr. Adams, "this young lady's father must have the final word?"

"Indeed, I hope he may—when we are able to hear it. But of what use is that now?"

"Ma'am?" asked the Parson.

"What help may you expect from Mr. Jones?" Mrs. Guerdion persisted.

"Why," said Amelia, a trifle frantic, "I expect my father to save me from the cruelty of mad Hacksem, and to resume control of Paradise Hall."

"And yet, Amelia," said Mrs. Guerdion in exasperation, "you cannot expect that anytime soon; for surely you know the Squire left two days ago for America?"

Seeing her dismay, Mrs. Guerdion continued more gently:

"Your father, miss, has gone to the colony of Maryland as aide to Lord Suffley. Last month he spent with the Suffleys in France, except for a day or two earlier this week, which, while awaiting ship for Baltimore, he spent with them at Edenfield.

"I had thought all this was known to you, Amelia, for I have forwarded to the Suffleys every letter of yours—and, indeed, of yours, Mrs. James —as soon as I have received it. Can it be that Squire Jones has answered none of them?"

Amelia answered softly, "We have heard nothing since learning he was to go to France. The trip to America my father did mention, but only as likely for—'sometime in late October, or perhaps early November' were, I believe, his words. We supposed he would write us when his plans were settled—and indeed, I believe he would have, were not something horribly wrong." (Here, Reader, we must indeed blame Mr. Jones, whose embarrassment concerning Lady Suffley had led him to communicate with his daughter in a style we may only characterize as *written mumbling.* )

Near-despondency had settled over the meeting. Our friends' alarm we need not explain farther. More subtle was the unhappiness of Mrs. Guerdion, who, having for thirty years willingly followed every order given her, could not bring herself to disobey the first one she thought immoral.

At last, Amelia asked, "What reason might he have had for silence?" and when, after a considerable time, no one had answered, Mrs. Guerdion said: "I hope, ma'am, you will not find it too inconvenient to lodge a while elsewhere. A letter to Mr. Jones in America will reach him within two months or less, with luck; and as much longer will likely bring us the happy solution to this unhappy mystery." As though propelled by this thought, Mrs. Guerdion stood quickly; and the others, rather dazedly, followed suit.

At the front door, she said hurriedly, "My dear miss, do be discreet. I should not wonder that other of your father's friends and retainers have received similar letters. Forgive me that I am so afraid. If—if you are very desperate, you may leave word with my sister, who lives in Russell Street. I wish you good luck; I am sure your resources are ample."

With that, she curtseyed our friends out the door, onto a walkway still slick with rain-water.

Mrs. Limeslices, who had been waiting in the coach with all the baggage, received the unhappy news most sensibly, by bitterly cursing Mr. Hacksem for his plotting, and Mrs. Guerdion for her cowardice. After this, she observed a polite silence, to allow her betters to conduct yet another council of war within the chilly confines of the coach.

Mrs. Guerdion had judged the wealth of the company by the richness of Amelia's clothes; and, in truth, as she wore a lovely travelling dress of dark blue, and a coat trimmed with soft fur at hem, sleeve and collar, it would have been difficult to believe how limited were her resources.

Yet the company had left Somersetshire with only about £300; and of this, Mr. Adams had lost his £80 to the robbers, and their gracious landlord, as promised, had charged them rampantly for their wretched lodgings. There remained in their common fund less than £190, a sum adequate, to be sure, for three persons living modestly two or three months, but scarcely sufficient to launch a campaign against the rogues of Domney and Paradise Hall.

Mr. Adams's contribution to the discourse in the coach was largely to blame himself again and again for the crime (as he conceived it) of having been injured during the robbery, and so having caused the fatal week's delay. When the others had ten or twenty times told him he was entirely forgiven, he at last brightened, and attempted to raise their spirits by saying hopefully:

"I believe, ladies, I may for once have the advantage of you; for while at university, I had ample opportunity to learn both the pleasures and the tricks of living on a little. We shall, I promise, survive quite handsomely for as long as need be; nor, after all, shall we be harmed by the experience, which shall teach us sympathy for others as well as confidence in ourselves."

This Mr. Adams said with as much assurance as he could muster. Alas, nothing in the circumstances of the company would second him; for the rain now began again to beat very hard upon the roof and windows of the coach; the coachman earnestly requested instructions they knew not how to give; and they could not, they now realized, in any direction be certain of a friend. They had, in short, some reason to envy the colliers who had been filling chutes across the street, and who must now shelter only 'til the rain should end. At last, Amelia called out the name of an inn she had seen on their first arrival, and which had appeared both decent and affordable.

The harm our companions had suffered by reason of Mr. Adams's injury was only now becoming apparent, and was likely to become much greater; for it sometimes happens that a small event is like the first snowflake dislodged from an alpine slope, a light thing which begins an *avalanche*.

With so high a metaphor, shall we leave our friends (for, indeed, to leave our friends when they are in trouble, is but the way of the world); yet we shall perhaps rejoin them soon. Just now our own business requires our attendance elsewhere, with Mr. Jones upon an ocean, the very waves of which I even now hear lapping.

# BOOK
# THE SIXTH

# I

## In Praise of Readers

Although, Reader, we presently have many solemn matters before us, I hope we may behave like the mighty gentlemen of the Court of King's Bench, who never let their business distort their tempers or their appetites; and that we shall, in short, make a good supper no matter how many life-deciding cases we are to hear.

I have often observed these legal gentlemen to relieve the strain of their duties by staging handsome dinners, at which they deliver eloquent testimonials to their splendid profession or their honourable colleagues. The healthfulness of such dinners is obvious; and, as I have earlier spoken kindly of two noble topics (this history, and myself), I shall now continue, Reader, by speaking very well of *thee*.

Know, then, Reader, that I consider thee to be no less than the chief magistrate of this history, entitled to deliver a verdict upon each of its characters, and in fact, upon the whole history itself. Indeed, Reader, methinks I see thee, even now, seated at thy bench in black robes and powdered wig, looking very grim—and commanding respect while inspiring love.

How, Reader, shall we praise thee? An author (whom I conceive to be a sort of mere attorney) is free to caper about the courtroom, saluting and condemning whomever he pleases. *Thou* art obliged to hear all with a calm demeanour, and a rigourous patience.

Whenever some villain—some Sinamore or the other—stands before thy bench, and a hue-and-cry is raised to dismiss the court and fetch a rope, thou must permit no riot, but stay to hear the last evidence presented —whatever instant pleasure it might cost thee.

Let there appear some figure (Mrs. Guerdion, perhaps) whose guilt remains ambiguous, and thy author, like some lazy law-clerk, is likely to throw up his hands, and defer entirely to thy Solomonic wisdom. Then, I fear, thou reasonest alone long into the night, while the streets fall still, thy rooms grow cold—and thy author snores in some nearby tavern. Oh, uneasy lies the head that wears a powdered wig!

In short, Reader, thou hast a harder job than any author ever born. If I shall now and again offer thee some small jokes, it is merely to ease thy difficult task. Never may I forget that final judgement is reserved to God at last, and to thee before. I may present the evidence, but thou must sift it; and I trust thee, even more than I would trust a Grand Jury at its Quarter-Sessions, to look closely, hear carefully, and decide with all the wisdom God hath given thee.

So, Reader, let us dry our eyes, and return to our deliberations.

---

# II

## In Which We Record a Letter Tom Received, and Describe the Start of His Great Journey

---

Our narrative must now regress a little, to follow Tom westward, and to correct a small error (accidental, I am sure) in the report of Mrs. Guerdion.

Tom and the Suffleys had indeed returned to England a few days earlier; and most of these days had indeed found them residing quietly at Edenfield. On the afternoon of the 28th, however, Tom had excused himself, saying he wished to stay the night in London, and would join them aboard ship on the morrow.

Tom slept that night in Hanover Square. In the morning, as he was leaving (to spend his last day in England revisiting persons dear to his heart), a letter arrived for him. Mrs. Guerdion having gone to visit her sister, the letter was handed him directly; recognizing the seal, he broke it eagerly, and read:

Deptford
28 October

My dear friend,
    By the time you receive this, I shall almost certainly have sailed for Boston, where I am to join the staff of General Gage.

---

You, more than anyone, will understand how ill this fits with my hopes and my convictions; yet, as you will know, it is an appointment honour obliges me to accept.

Dr. Johnson has kindly offered to oversee certain of my personal affairs (which the haste of my appointment has greatly disrupted), but I entreat also your aid, for anything my dear Becky may need.

I am sorry not to have heard your personal observations upon France, which has always seemed to me the loveliest country in Europe, especially in autumn. Your military observations, which arrived here yesterday, I have already forwarded to a gentleman close to Lord North, who will, I trust, see they do optimum service.

That, I believe, is everything, except to set in ink what I have long carried in my heart; namely, that my friendships with you and the Doctor, along with the love of my Becky, form the great joys of my life; and that to see you all again is the continual prayer of,

> Your friend and servant,
> Bob Askew

The nearness of his own departure had filled Tom (as it doth many travellers) with a sadness for the transitory nature of life, but this letter raised an anxiety as much sharper as it was more noble. He at once wrote begging leave to call on Dr. Johnson; and, as soon after as possible, he clapped his hat upon his head and, not bothering to bid the servants farewell or leave a note for Mrs. Guerdion, hurried out the door.

Dr. Johnson heard the colonel's letter with visible emotion.

"Aye, sir," said he, "the appointment came only after Colonel Phillips took ill. Nothing could have been less fortunate, for I believe our friend had meant to resign his commission within a day or two, in order to marry Miss Carlisle. Before the appointment, a resignation would have been simple; afterwards, it became impossible, since to refuse to serve abroad would have been to admit either a fear of danger, or a selfishness of joy, which, though any man may feel, no gentleman may indulge."

"But why," asked Tom, "did he not carry through with the wedding in any case, and take her with him to America?"

"The stated reason," replied the Doctor, sighing, "is that her father would not officiate 'til the banns had been properly read, which time did not permit. I suspect, however, that the Colonel did not wish to make her a widow so soon after making her a wife."

"Surely," cries Tom, "our situation in America is not so desperate?"

"Indeed, sir, that's as may be; the generals and politicians know more of such things than I. But I suspect our friend, who is as brave as any man I know, suffers somewhat from the Anglo-Saxon fault of *fæge,* which is a feeling of being fated to die."

This Dr. Johnson said without scorn, and indeed, with a kind of sympathetic patience he added, "That is a delusion which, as it harms no one but its believer, none of us may condemn."

Smiling with an effort, he concluded, "But let us now turn to your concerns. How may I help you? You know I pride myself as a man of affairs, and will undertake any business you wish."

Tom replied (for his spirits had fallen very low) only that he wished the Doctor to announce he was receiving correspondence for Mr. Tom Jones, to be forwarded as soon as possible; "For," says Tom, "I have lately had such bad fortune with letters addressed to me, that I scarce believe I still live in a civilized nation."

This Dr. Johnson readily agreed to do. He then pressed Tom to take lunch with him at the Mitre, but our hero, noticing the hour grew late, declined.

So the Doctor led Tom downstairs. At the door, he clapped him upon the shoulder, and said earnestly, "Indeed, Tommy, the dangers of America may be over-rated, but I would have you treat the Americans like the inmates of Bedlam. Why, sir, they are the freest people upon earth. When men reject membership in so great a nation as ours, we fear not for their patriotism, but for their sanity."

Tom's coach now appeared, and the Doctor, braving the rain without hat or coat, walked him to it. After the door was closed, he put his hand upon the window-sill and cried:

"Well, sir, I shall not wish thee luck. The virtuous must always be happy, for courage is a cardinal virtue, and the courageous suffer few insults and enjoy much praise; and above all, to the courageous all beauties of discovery, all foreign vistas, of earth or mind, are freely given."

With these axioms—which delighted him however much he might doubt their truth—ringing in his ears, Tom rode through the bleak streets to the barge which would carry him to Deptford.

A steady rain forced Tom to spend his river-voyage inside the deck-cabin of the barge, where, seated at a plain deal table, he was lulled by that soft pattering which rain makes falling upon water, and by the occasional rumpling of the sail, heard through the open window. The Thames, in short, soon had the same effect upon our hero which the river *Lethe* (in some stories) is said to have had upon certain Greeks: *viz.*, it made him forget first where he was, and then to be awake; and so, when his barge at last drew alongside the mighty *Nonesuch*, he had to be shaken into consciousness.

The Suffleys having not yet arrived, Tom was shown without ceremony to his cabin, which was one of those in a series in the aft-part of the ship reserved for junior officers. This porthole-less box (for only cannon are expected to breathe below-decks in a warship) was surpassingly small and crowded, but kept in the highest state of naval cleanliness and order.

About eight o'clock, the Suffleys hosted a dinner for the other civilian passengers, from which Tom (as was becoming his habit) excused himself early, saying (as was true) that his recent travels had exhausted him.

Tom's nature was extremely sturdy, and, once used to the slap of foot-steps running over the deck above him, he slept very soundly. Just before dawn, he was awakened briefly by a change in the ship's motion, as the *Nonesuch* met the first of the long Atlantic rollers, and began the steady rise-and-fall which would not cease 'til they were safe in America. About seven a.m., he rubbed his eyes and, drawing on his heavy coat, stepped out onto deck under clear skies, to inhale the chill salt air and watch the last dab of the English coast disappear astern.

Reader, tho' I hope some few chapters hence to show thee what I may do in a *nautical* vein (of which, I promise thee, the above "astern" is but a hint), our tale is of persons, not fishes. Accordingly, I shall spare thee any unneeded tossing upon the waves.

This principle I shall particularly observe because there occurred on this voyage nothing of note, except that Mr. Jones discovered himself to have a sailor's appetite for the ocean, while Lady Suffley discovered herself to have a—I know not what's—abhorrence of it. This temporary difference in their aptitudes produced, I am sorry to say, a new element in her view of our hero. I mean that she now, at least temporarily, began to hate Tom at least as much as she desired him. The resulting emotional confusion, however, she managed pretty effectively to discharge simply by expressing her tenderness for him only on those occasions when it was certain to enflame the jealousy, and ensure the vengefulness, of her husband.

The *Nonesuch* required above nine weeks to make a crossing which luckier ships have completed in only five. Such variations are, however, inevitable in ocean travel. More importantly, somewhere about mid-ocean her ladyship's stomach grew stronger, and her head more level; and so the voyage drew on calmly until the 21st day of December. Late that afternoon, as Tom lounged in his cabin, he heard a cry and stir above deck, and hurrying to see, found a crowd of passengers, in every careless sort of dress, staring excitedly in the direction of the Captain's glass, towards a faint, foggy smudge, which was America.

Innumerable *naval* authors (who shall themselves never go sailing, unless a *hurricano* as great as that blowing between their ears should one day catch up their study chairs) tell us of the great sentiments which swell in the breasts of landed travellers. *Our* travellers, I fear, felt nothing, except a general relief that they would now be able to place a little distance among themselves, and a little solid ground beneath their feet.

From this dullness, we must, however, exempt our hero, who, having enjoyed the vast expanses of the sea, now thrilled to consider that he had reached the home-land of his beloved. To be sure, he still had before him most of the task of finding her; yet (so, Reader, do we justly call him hero!) as the ship, under foggy light the colour of oiled steel, tacked into vast Chesapeake Bay, his only thought was that America did not seem such a *big* place, after all.

# III

## The Suffleys Land, Travel and Show
## Their Skills as Governors

The company slept that night in Baltimore, and in the morning departed overland for the capitol at Annapolis, where his lordship was to take up the reins of government. This journey they might have completed in a tenth the time, and in ten times the comfort, by small boat—but Lord

Suffley insisted he would have no more of watery dangers, even upon the calm waters of the Chesapeake.

His lordship demanded a coach for himself and his wife, but thought horses sufficient for Tom and their escort, Major Principes. This Major was a tall, ruddy-faced gentleman, just then exuberant because his sainted father's recent demise had brought him an estate, allowing him (at age fifty) shortly to return to England, "to live as a gentleman should—shooting at nothing capable of shooting back." He told many jokes and laughed very loud; he wore no wig, and his white hair poked from beneath his hat. His ethics and courage (to judge from his conversation) fell a little short of the highest standards, but he was genial and informative, and Tom welcomed his company after the weeks aboard ship.

A day's hard travelling brought the company at sundown no farther than a miserable inn called the Royal Dragon, about ten miles from Annapolis. The Suffleys immediately went off, complaining, to the inn's best room, and the Major, who had been very cooly treated by them during the day, began venting his feelings to Tom.

"We must all, by G__d," said he, speaking over his pewter mug of beer, "hope for better manners from this new governor than I've yet seen, or else, instead of the one red-coat escorting him in, we'll need a column of five hundred to escort him out. Why such a sour man? Is it something to do with that gorgeous-haired wife of his?"

This question Mr. Jones chose to ignore, instead answering with a query of his own. "If, Major, you wished to locate a certain woman—a woman from Boston, I believe, and with connections to shipping, or perhaps smuggling—how would you go about it?"

Major Principes was immediately interested. "Why, sir, now I know there's a man in Maryland with a mind like my own. Enough of politics! Now, your friend, Miss . . ."

"*Mrs.* Wilson."

"Mrs. Wilson, if she is any considerable merchant at all, will certainly be known to one of two groups of persons in our town: the merchants or the customs-house men. Tomorrow night, you and I will visit the two taverns where those gentlemen separately congregate. 'Til then, drink more; 'twill help you sleep."

The next mid-morning, they reached Annapolis, which, beneath blue skies, and with a few turned leaves still clinging to their branches, seem'd the cheeriest sight they had met since leaving England: a town of neat-laid brick and elegant white marble, surrounded by rivers and made prosperous by controlling both the trade, and the government, of Maryland.

Before the governor's mansion, an honour-guard of fifty men, with a band of fife-and-drum, had been hastily assembled; and the ceremonies (for the old governor and his wife were both good-hearted persons) were carried out with a warmth seeming to belie both the coldness of the ritual and the frostiness of the morning.

Tom spent his afternoon resting in a pleasant bedroom overlooking, not the water, but the mansion grounds. In the evening, the Suffleys hosted a dinner for about twenty, including the departing governor and his wife, and a number of prosperous planters and merchants. These last were rough, care-free gentlemen, who provided Jones his first taste of American life; for, about midnight, as Tom bid the company good-night, they were just clearing away the Suffleys' furniture in order to wrestle.

The next day being Christmas-Eve, every tavern in town was to serve an early and lavish dinner, and so Tom and the Major, as promptly as they were able (which was about one o'clock P.M.), met to begin their tour. As they set off—Tom atop a fine bay gelding of the Major's—a scattering of wet snow-flakes slipped about them, and the Major said:

"Remember, Tom, that, while the customs-house men are all ours, the merchants (if we wander as far as the Compass) will include many rebels. I get along with them because everyone knows I don't give a fig for politics; and if I did, I'd be on their side against the side of men like Suffley. But we all obey the rules—I don't ask them who burned the *Peggy Stewart*, and they don't ask me where the Army's going to bivouac next month. It may be they'll ask us to leave; if so, take no offense, and go quietly. Understood?"

"Perfectly."

"Damn it, Tom," continued the Major irritatedly, "no man joins the Army to shoot his friends; that's work for brainless young lords. Well, here we are, and let's be quick; I'd dislike riding home in a blizzard."

The Green Leaf, haunt of English customs-house officials, proved useless; and so, after a single tankard, they returned to their horses. The snow now dropt more heavily, though still not sticking where it landed.

The Compass, at the rising western end of the town, hosted in a single large room both rich American planters and merchants, and a great many backwoodsmen, who wore buck-skins and kept their long-rifles close at hand as they drank and quarrelled.

Major Principes paused near the door, surveying the room before guiding Tom to a table near the back, where five gentlemen smoked pipes and sipped punch. Each wore good linen, but sported the hardened skin of the outdoor life; they looked, indeed, like unusually sober country squires. All were Tom's age, except for one boy of perhaps eighteen, with fiery red hair.

"Friends," said Major Principes, "I come before you on a mission of the heart. This is Tom Jones, who is seeking a woman he met in England. Her name is Mrs. Wilson, and she lives, he believes, in Massachusetts."

Many years earlier, Reader, Tom had suffered terribly for naming his beloved (very respectfully) to strangers at an inn, but now he was amply compensated. Most of the company merely shook their heads, or muttered that Wilson was a common name, but the red-headed gentleman asked quietly:

"Could you mean Mrs. *Angela* Wilson? From Boston?"

"Aye!" cries our hero. "Aye, Angela! What know you of her?"

"Pray, sir, be seated," says the other. "I'll tell what little I may.

"If this be the same woman—she is rather tall, with a considerable mane of dark-brown hair, and as perfect a woman's figure as you may wish; and she is about thirty years of age—"

Our hero could scarcely retain his seat for joy, and the other gentlemen all listened with rapt attention. Indeed, I have generally found that, for pleasing adults, a story of love will out-do a tale of a hundred heroes, or of twice as many storms and dragons. Yet I digress.

"Aye, sir! The very woman!" cried Tom, hitting his fist upon the table. "What else?"

"Well . . . she is the widow of an immensely-successful merchant who, I believe, prospered by finding a shorter route between England and America—one, that is, not obliged to swerve into the customs-house. . . ."

The company replied with a laugh which was half a cheer.

". . . And in this he continued richly several years, until, one foggy autumn night, his craft would not answer the hail of one of the King's cutters. The warning shot went a little awry, and in fact carried over the deck, where it cut good Mr. Wilson clean in half, and made poor Mrs. Wilson one of the richest, youngest and prettiest widows in New-England. . . ."

"Poor lady," murmured the appreciative crowd.

". . . That very night she conceived an unshakeable hatred of English

---

rule; and all she has done since to aid the cause of Liberty in Massachusetts —well, I could not tell you half, did I dare. Pardon me, Mr. Jones, but if Mrs. Wilson desires you to know more, she will certainly tell you herself; and, if I have the right woman, you may enquire her whereabouts of any merchant or sailor in Boston. Ask for her at Faneuil Hall, or anywhere."

At this, Major Principes pounded Tom upon the shoulder, and demanded, "Whether Annapolis hospitality is not the world's best?"

"Indeed, gentlemen," replied our hero, "I am in your debt forever. Pray let me buy this punch, and the next."

Once the oranges had been squeezed into the bowl, Tom hoisted his glass and offered a toast to "The Handsomest Woman in New-England." This had, however, scarcely been drunk (with acclaim), before the young gentleman who had told the story set Tom back by declaring:

"Sir, it ill becomes a younger man to instruct an older one; yet I must tell you that I, like almost every other man Boston-bred, would give a left arm above the elbow for the love of Mrs. Wilson; and, sir, if you believe you have an honest claim upon that miracle, you are a very poor fellow to be spending your days here in a heap with us."

Not even our hero was so wild and foolish as to take instantly to horse upon such a prod. Yet, like all great men, he knew how to bear advice— particularly when it matched his own opinions. Although excited, he now look'd solemn, nodded, and stood.

"Gentlemen," said he, with a kind smile, "it is wisely written, that 'a little child shall lead them.' Young sir, I have now been three days in your country, and one in your debt. I hope I may sometime soon repay you. Major, are you with me?" Bowing, he turned quickly and left them.

Outside the Compass, snow was crossing the road in daunting flurries, and piling thickly upon the ground. Yet no two gentlemen could have donned their capes and mounted their horses more staunchly than did the Major and his friend. Major Principes had lived ten years in America. As for Mr. Jones? Why, Reader, he was a hero. The products of the storm bounced from him as lightly as—snow-flakes; and, indeed, so warm was his heart, I wonder they did not turn to steam as they touched him.

# IV

## Containing a Christmas Dinner, and
## a Most Alarming Letter

Jones arrived home about four o'clock, feeling brisk, and wearing a masculine version of that smile which adorns the portrait of a famed Italian lady. This smile, a frequent habit since his trip to southern France, was, I believe, singularly unwelcome to Lady Suffley, and a main cause of that hatred of him we have earlier attributed to the sea-sickness.

Whatever the cause (and we may shortly present thee, Reader, with yet another), Lady Suffley now greeted Tom by saying that she and her husband begged him to stay that evening in his room. This brutal snub afflicted our hero not at all; for he was then feasting upon a large *soufflé* of romantic thoughts, and could have spent his evening very happily in a *root-cellar*.

Christmas morning the bright sun shone in a sky very blue, and fell outside Tom's window upon a perfect carpet of white, marked only by the prints of a single deer.

In the company of half a dozen of the household servants (but without the Suffleys) Tom walked to a tall-steepled church, where much was said upon love. Tom (tho' he shivered from the neglect of his pew-warmer) heard all of it eagerly, and if his images of the sermon were unorthodox (for I recall no angel named *Wilson* in any of the gospels), yet he walked home resolved to do good for his fellow creatures—in which, I submit, he caught the purpose of religion as well as many a solemner spirit.

Tom returned to his room to find a memorandum of above fifteen pages, detailing his duties in the coming weeks, lying upon his desk. Such a packet was unsurprising; for, since the sea-voyage, Lord Suffley had spoken to Tom as rarely as possible, preferring to send him various notes and memoranda, all written in a style resembling those London porters, who are not happy unless they are elbowing you into the gutter.

Lord Suffley now announced that he himself would oversee taxes and the military, leaving Tom nothing to do but fend off any resulting complaints. "Those other colonial duties, such as the maintenance of roads and the building of schools, we must," his Lordship graciously concluded, "set aside until the present revenues crisis hath been resolved, by whatever means necessary."

Perhaps oddly, Tom read this *communiqué* not merely calmly, but with positive pleasure; and had no sooner completed it, than he lay contentedly upon his bed to meditate away the hour or so before the Christmas banquet.

Reader, we shall by no means pretend that our hero's mind was as precisely ordered as the Royal Observatory at Greenwich. Yet his contentedness with this letter was, I think, perfectly logical: Tom had not forgotten Mrs. Wilson once in the months since Marseilles; politics were, in his conception, the great obstacle to their reunion; and, while he could not instantly drop his toryism for her, he secretly welcomed whatever might let him move honourably towards sharing her views of English wrongs.

Tom had not lain many minutes thinking, before he understood his own feelings, and even offered silent thanks to Lord Suffley *for being such a rogue;* after which he very willingly rose to dress for his Lordship's Christmas banquet.

About noon, the first guests arrived. Excluded were all the good-natured private persons Tom had met the day before, and the party suffered for it. The dinner, however, was splendidly arrayed: the dining-room, overlooking the mansion's snowy garden, was deck'd with holly and mistle-toe, fragrant with cinnamon and cloves, and bright with hickory-fires and chandeliers. A trio played, the tables groaned; the guests cried, "Ahh-hh!" and hurried to their seats. Tom shook hands with Major Principes, bowed to several hungry-looking ladies, and took his place very willing to be jolly.

I believe all the sixty or so guests shared Tom's intention; yet the Suffleys ate little, and stopped frequently to whisper together, using their hands to shade their faces. Three or four times they took messages from military couriers, who then bent low to hear their replies. Tom observed this, and his appetite waned. Major Principes, who sat not far from him, ate steadily, remarking that the good soldier eats what is put before him, but looking often to the dais.

Alas, Reader, in dangerous times, our pleasures are rarely our own, and the good must suffer with the vicious—from whom, indeed, they are not always easily told. After the Duchess led the other ladies out, Lord Suffley rose to say:

"Gentlemen, I have called you here partly to celebrate a happy occasion, but largely to prepare you for difficulty and danger.

"I need tell no man here of the hazards confronting British rule in North America. We read nearly every day reports of arms smuggled, of taxes refused. Clashes between our troops and angry mobs never cease, and those between our troops and the colonial militias have—I dare say —been avoided only because of our commanders' super-human patience.

"In Boston, there is martial law; in every colony, a Committee of Correspondence lets new rebels learn the tricks, and support the crimes, of the nasty Massachusetts traitors. There even exists a movement in our own Parliament to abandon to the mob what wise government and the labour of many generations of gentlemen have built upon this unyielding continent."

Five or six waiters now began removing the remnants of turkeys and geese, three suckling pigs, roast-beefs and uncountable side-dishes.

"My good predecessor, gentlemen, met every affront with patience, every insult with kindness; and had as his reward a state of rebellion daily more apparent, and a rabble grown so mutinous as to burn a ship and seize a cargo not thirty miles from where we sit today.

"Gentlemen, the era of compromise *ends* today. I have this morning ordered the seizure of two hundred muskets, with much ammunition, and the arrest of four persons, at the"—Lord Suffley here consulted a slip of paper—"Compass tavern. This, I promise, is but a beginning, for what has been done to Boston, may be done to Baltimore, and Marylanders must learn that those who despise the *civil* authority must bow to the *military*.

"Gentlemen, we shall have a very simple policy. If there is a tax, we shall collect it. If there is an affront, we shall avenge it. If there is a rebellion, we shall crush it. Maryland *is* British, and Maryland will *stay* British, let it cost us what it may.

"I thank you."

Lord Suffley had sat again with features very flushed. Six or seven gentlemen quickly applauded in grim approval. The rest hung a moment as slack-jawed as children at a blood-stained puppet show. Uncertain what they had heard, disliking so violent a Christmas, they finally joined in a quiet clapping; and upon this clapping, the ladies rejoined them.

As for Tom, his confusion had now reached the pitch of anguish. Never was a man fonder of the good things of a holiday, of ale and beef, and kisses 'neath the mistle-toe. Against this, he felt horror and revulsion that his own government could have so treated the good gentlemen of the Compass Inn; and an equal horror and revulsion that those good gentlemen could have armed themselves against that government. In truth, Reader, the nature of rebellion exceeded his understanding (as, I fear, it doth mine), and he could not have been more despairingly alarmed had he that morning found the church he attended suddenly inverted over a flaming pit, and himself clinging for his life to the edge of a pew.

In his confusion, Tom let benevolence desert him, and began to consider those around him to be as evil, and as repulsive, as devils—and particularly to despise himself for accepting any part, even temporarily, in Lord Suffley's plan.

At meal's end, however, the guests were provided a sort of *musicale*. Two choirs sang Handel, after which, to the accompaniment of first *pianoforte*, and later, portable organ, all in the room began a spontaneous caroling; and Tom, although still angry with himself, began to think he had judged his colleagues too unkindly.

In truth, Reader, I hope he had: for in few of these candle-lit and loudly-singing persons did there grow any malice save that born of fear for place: they had come to America, and built their lives, upon the prospects of government jobs. Now that government was swaying, and knowing no better, they grip't 'til their nails bled.

So, at least, would I believe; and yet Tom's last experience that evening would argue against me.

While helping the Suffleys ease their guests toward the door, Tom was accosted by a customs-house official. Mr. Consyne—one of the few to have applauded his lordship willingly—stood about five feet tall, and weighed perhaps eighteen stone; his eyes were a good deal compressed by the plumpness of his cheeks, and yet the fabric of his suit (which was extremely rich) encompassed him handsomely. At his side, walked a lady as plump and satisfied as himself.

"Well, sir, Mr. Jones," began Mr. Consyne, "I believe we shall have some spirit in the government now."

"If by spirit," replied our hero (who, having been lulled by the caroles, was now recalled to this world), "you mean a form of bullying denial of the rights of Englishmen, then I think we shall indeed have spirit enough."

At this, the gentleman stared very hard and said cuttingly that, "He had not supposed the King was in the habit of sending out weaklings to administer his colonies."

Tom, reining in his temper, answered, "As, sir, I am sure you do not wish to provoke me, I will explain: I meant only we must not let a desire for revenge, or any personal spite, interfere with the proper workings of government."

At this, Mr. Consyne spread his thick arms and nodded wisely. "Oh, aye, sir, now I understand you." Winking, he continued, "You must not fear for that; for Lord Suffley, I assure you, hath already promised there shall be revenues enough to reward all honest labourers."

To what fascinating depths this discourse might have sunk, I cannot say, as Mr. Jones now excused himself. Major Principes had in fact signalled to him, and, on Tom's drawing nearer, now whispered to him, "None of our friends, I find, were taken. Yet you now see, I think, how dreadful is the situation here. Well, my boy, never mind that, and take all the pleasure you can; for our world, I fear, is not only fallen, but falling still. So a Merry Christmas to you, and a good night, and a better tomorrow."

When Major Principes, the last guest, had gone, Tom and Lady Suffley were left alone. Though her Ladyship had already hinted the age of tenderness was ending between them, our hero's low spirits required some inspiration, and he wished at least to give her a kiss of holiday joy. The Duchess, however, stood several paces farther from him than ever before (and this, Reader, is a very strong indicator of dislike in cultured persons, for when they begin to treat thee as a likely source of disease, thou mayst be sure they need thee no longer); and said coldly:

"I am sorry, Mr. Jones, but I must ask you again to deprive us of the pleasure of your company. If you will but once more spend the evening in your room, we shall, I promise, very soon put an end to the need to confine you there."

Mr. Jones responded placidly, for, besides the fact that he was a gentleman, and naturally gracious, he had now developed an abhorrence of the Duke, and a sense of shame to be in his employ, which made him very willing to have this time to be alone, and to contemplate a letter of resignation. Accordingly, not *very* sorry to have been denied a Christmas buss, he wished the Duchess good-night, and took himself upstairs.

Reader, I have no doubt that the behaviour of the Suffleys (and especially Lady Suffley) has, in its sharp alterations, greatly amazed thee. Lord Suffley had many years before, I believe, abandoned himself to the habit of profitless malice—and this, combined with his natural conservatism, had led him to answer the pressures of America with hasty and unwise force.

As for her Ladyship, in regard to Mr. Jones, we have already hinted that she was a little gnawed by the green-eyed monster; or that (in other words) she was one of those persons who, rather than let another touch what they desire, would prefer to see it sawed off and pickled in lye.

And yet, Reader, for all her jealousy, Lady Suffley (in the lonely wilds of America) might well have forgiven Tom as a Christian should, had it not been for a letter she had found waiting for her when she reached Annapolis.

This letter, which she no sooner saw than she secreted in the bosom of her dress (perfectly safe from her husband), had been sent her from London; she recognized the hand, and so soon as she was able, locked herself in her bedroom to examine it. Only then did she open and read.

8 November, 1774

Dear Madam:

Owing to our young colleague's error, Miss J\_\_\_\_\_s has now arrived in London, making it necessary to deal decisively with her father. Yesterday, dear madam, I found a means to do so, without bringing distasteful suspicion upon ourselves.

You may remember that last summer, some vicious person assaulted one Captain Whipsblood of the House Guards in a Smithfield tavern. The Captain hath recently established that his assailant was none other than our Mr. J\_\_\_\_\_s (abetted, it seems, by some Yankee strumpet), and hath since promised publicly to shoot J\_\_\_\_\_s through the heart at the first opportunity.

Calling yesterday upon the Captain, I was delighted to learn your ladyship knows him (for I took the liberty of mentioning your ladyship's name), and even more delighted when he kindly agreed to assist us. He must leave shortly for Boston upon secret business, and guarantees that if you can arrange for J\_\_\_\_\_s to be in that city on or about the first of March, our problems will be ended forever.

The Captain (a man after my own heart) hath proposed a refinement I consider excellent, which is that your Ladyship provide him with a document, bearing anything resembling your husband's signature, and accusing Mr. J_____s of theft of Government monies. The Captain plans to kill him in the simplest possible manner, but as dueling is nowadays somewhat frowned upon, he would feel better having some legal document enabling him to justify himself before any board of enquiry. He shall not, of course, make this letter public unless absolutely necessary—and no one will question your having engaged him in a private hunt for a thief, since we all understand the need just now to make our taxation system appear as well-run and honest as possible. If you would be so gracious as to send such a letter to the Captain, care of General Thomas Gage's command, Boston, I believe we may begin to think of J_____s as an extinct species.

I have already pledged to the Captain that minority interest he requested (very properly I think) for his cooperation; I am sure you will agree it was money excellently spent, if only for the joy it will bring to your dear self, and to,

Your ob't, humble servant,
H.S.

P.S. You will, of course, keep charge of Mr. J_____s's mail until the end?

Mr. Sinamore had written a fair number of words, but Lady Suffley contented herself with repeating over and over the single phrase "Yankee strumpet." At each repetition, her voice became notably more angry, until she rose and carried the letter to the fireplace; and she watched it with very narrow eyes until it was scarcely a puff of ash and vapour ascending the chimney.

In truth, Reader, Mr. Sinamore had not only kindled the fires of jealousy within her Ladyship, but suggested the means to quench them, for she had in fact once known Captain Whipsblood much as Lady Bathsheba knew a certain Captain *David*, and still regarded his marksmanship very highly. She therefore sat willingly to compose the charges against our hero—using her pen, I may say, as some other persons might use a dagger. As for her previous affection for Jones, well, she felt the lawyer had sealed his fate; and, being tender-hearted, she decided to spare herself the pain of any further association with a doomed man.

So, Reader, may we explain her coldness to Mr. Jones, and so explain the curious instructions given him in our next chapter.

# V

## In Which Jones Is Given a Mission, and Departs for the Wilderness

Reader, I had rather by far undertake to explain thee the secret plottings of the Court of Muscovy, the hidden actions of the badger in his hole, the innermost thoughts of the sea snail—nay! even (which are much harder) the public doings of our courts-of-law—than to chart even the simplest workings of the human heart. Indeed, this wiley organ doth treat the pursuing author as the hare doth the beagle; for no sooner do we close upon it, than it doubles back, passing close enough to touch us, but heading in the opposite direction; and so, too often, are we left with our noses in a bramble, our paws out beside us, and our reputations in the air.

By this profound speculation (for no other occurs to me) do I intend to introduce almost the last conversations ever held between the Suffleys and our hero.

Lady Suffley wasted no time in searching her husband's affairs for a mission to Boston. Such a mission (a most hazardous one, moreover) was in fact pending, and few will doubt Lord Suffley's joy at hearing his wife propose that his rival undertake it.

Therefore, a little before noon on the day after Christmas, his Lordship summoned Tom to his study, and, not troubling to offer him a seat, said:

"You have had occasion recently, Mr. Jones, to give some hints of your ability to judge military preparations."

"A very small ability, my lord."

"No doubt; and yet, my wife believes you are the best man for a task given me by the military command in Boston.

"I wish you to tour the forts of western Maryland and Virginia, studying whatever you think important in order to represent the Colony of Maryland at a conference on military preparedness to be held at Boston, Massachusetts, on the first day of March. It is not an easy job, or a safe one, but it must be done. Major Principes will accompany you, to provide a second opinion." (Indeed, Reader, in sending along the Major, Lord Suffley was preserving his own reputation, for to send a single, inexperienced person into the wilderness in winter, would have been viewed in every quarter as tantamount to murder.)

Our hero, who had many times calculated the miles between Annapolis and Boston, heard this with a pleasure he could scarcely conceal. "My lord," said he calmly, "I shall leave within the week, or as soon as Major Principes can be ready."

Lord Suffley stared with surprise at this whole-hearted response, and then said half-reluctantly, "I commend you, Mr. Jones, on your fortitude; for, in truth, I myself should dread to ride any farther than Baltimore with winter here." After a pause, he added:

"Indeed, Mr. Jones, we have had some reasons for disliking one another; yet, now you are leaving, I wish you a safe journey."

Reader, I believe his Lordship was sincere; for, despite his temper, he was not truly wicked, so much as simply overburdened. Had he been a handsomer man and a burlier one, I believe he would have been a better one; and, to give him his due, he was at least able to recognize those virtues he could not reach.

As for Jones, he was too enraptured with the prospect of an escape from Maryland to consider this peace-offering very carefully. He did, however, respond politely; and after several more compliments were exchanged, he left to begin his preparations.

During the next several days, Lady Suffley seemed very pleased with the prospect of Tom's departure, for (I suppose) the dangers of travel upon the frontier made it likely he would die in some accident, thereby removing all obvious guilt from her hands. At the same time, by getting him out of her sight, she hoped to remove the passion for him from her bloodstream; and as insurance, she was quite certain that if he were alive by the time Captain Whipsblood reached Boston on the 1st of March, he would certainly be dead immediately thereafter.

And yet, Reader, we have greatly misled thee if we have suggested that her ladyship, for all her tactical subtlety, had anything like great steadiness of mind concerning our hero. The war between vanity and lust was a very close one within her heart, and she was of different opinions concerning Mr. Jones, not merely every day, but every hour, so that she might wish to push him into boiling oil, and then drag him out and smother him with kisses, half a dozen times together before breakfast. She began to dream of him (when she could sleep), to catch her breath at his approach, and even to regret her plans for him. So high did this fever rise that, the night before his departure, she decided to visit our hero in his room.

Entering (perhaps for old time's sake) without a knock, she approached the bed where our hero (it being somewhat past the middle of the night) lay sleeping.

"Thomas!" whispered she. "Sweet Thomas!"

"Who's there?!" cried our hero, sitting bolt upright with alarm.

Familiar lips prest against his, then murmured, "Sweetest Thomas, speak softly. Have you missed me?"

"Why, madam," replied Mr. Jones groggily, "indeed I have done nothing but sleep these several hours."

"In dangerous times, Thomas, true lovers should be together."

Mr. Jones made a noise very like a snore.

Lady Suffley was always steadfast in her desire. Shaking him a little, she asked tenderly:

"But you must leave me tomorrow. Will you not . . ."

And here, Reader, she paused, and thought.

"Will you not reconsider? I promise my husband may find another emissary. Only say you want to stay with me."

I have often gratefully considered, Reader, how lucky are men that we have our virtue always in our own control. Indeed, Tom's protection this night was not his strong right arm, but rather *indifference;* and, in truth, I do not believe he could have obliged the Duchess for a kingdom. As, however, he was a civil gentleman, with no trace of cruelty in his nature, he answered gently:

"In faith, ma'am, for all my gratitude and affection, I must still tell thee that, during those days—not few!—when thy attachment seemed to wane, my own heart was given elsewhere, and, in short . . ."

What Mr. Jones wished to say was cut short indeed, for Lady Suffley now leapt suddenly to her feet, and, with sparks sufficient to set the bed ablaze flashing from her eyes, cried: "Enough! Know, sir, you have had more kindness from me than any man ever did; and much more, I think,

———

than you deserve. Well, all's one; my desire will soon enough be buried, and you forgotten; and so good-night!"

This last phrase was, in truth, somewhat muffled by the slamming of the door; yet Tom understood it well enough. Rather than inspiring any regrets, it reconfirmed (as thou mayst well believe) his conviction that he was departing scarcely in time. That comforting thought echoing softly in his brain, he returned to sleep, and to dreaming of a woman whose name, I suppose, is very easily guessed; for—as Lady Suffley probably meant to say—true lovers will always (one way or another) be together.

Tom's departure had been delayed so that Major Principes might take leave of a certain Miss Macintosh—a lovely girl (poor, but perfectly respectable) to whom, I fear, he had made certain matrimonial promises. On that very morning she was to begin packing, the Major appeared at her kitchen door to say blandly (while she cried) that he now believed "a penniless American lady" would never be happy with English country life —and that he deserved to be shot for having grieved her. His second sentiment, I entirely share; yet not an hour had passed after he left her, before the Major began to lament his own folly and cowardice—for the simple fact is that he feared nothing about the marriage but the loss of freedom he thought it would bring. Tom urged him to reconsider; but he preferred to hide in taverns for the better part of a week, until he imagined the crisis had blown over.

Very early on the 15th of January, however, Tom had been wakened, helped to dress, and fed a very good breakfast of bacon and eggs, biscuits and tea. He ate in the warm kitchen, surrounded by Suffley servants eager to know the purpose of his trip. Although Tom had lived in the house scarcely three weeks, he was already a favorite; for indeed, it doth not take vast experience to prefer wine to mud.

The morning still hung foggy and dark—barely a morning at all— when Tom and the Major, each well-armed, well-mounted, and leading a pack-horse well-equipped, rode away. They looked once about them in farewell, then, kicking at the flanks of their horses, knocked the ice of the mansion from their boots.

They moved slowly through the mist-softened town, then turned west beyond the ferry-crossing. No snow having fallen since before Christmas, the ground lay bare, except for some rut-ice, and a frost upon the meadows. Sun and fog rose together; the Major, with vapour puffing from his mouth, sang two or three Irish ballads unaccompanied, before throwing back the hood of his cape and saying kindly:

"Look'ee, Tom. We pass within a few miles of Baltimore late this afternoon. If you were to take ship there, you'd reach Boston before the weekend. I could bring you the report myself, and no one would . . ."

Tom, of course, shook his head to this.

"No, I suppose not. Well, consider, then, that you shall soon see some of the loveliest, least spoilt country upon earth: rivers and chasms, wild beasts and wild savages—tho', I promise, those savages are as good persons as you shall meet anywhere, besides being mostly allies of the Crown. Six weeks shall go all too quickly, I fear."

Major Principes, though he had said this firmly enough, now fetched a deep sigh, and began (as he would continue doing the entire journey) to glance longingly behind him. Jones, of course, understood the part Miss Macintosh played in this sudden nostalgia for Annapolis; yet he supposed the Major must pay the price of his stubbornness, and he had, moreover, strong reasons of his own for pressing forward.

Very uneasily, therefore, Jones answered that, "The beauties of this country are no doubt very considerable, and yet . . . could we not ride a *little* faster?"

The two friends (one very eager to retreat, and the other as eager to advance) had in fact already ridden beyond sight of the highest belfry in Annapolis; they now passed ever fewer farm-houses, and, as day wore on, they drew near the immense forests, where the true wilderness began.

So, Reader, shall we, trusting to their skills, and, especially, to Providence, let Tom and his friend plunge into the black, thick woods. I own I have not the Major's faith in the peacefulness of America; yet, if they should, perchance, survive, I shall be very willing to greet them again. Meanwhile, however, we are due again in England, whither we shall convey thee with all the speed of a turning page.

# VI

## Containing the First of Several Remarkable Conversations

After a single night at the Partridge Inn (to which they had repaired on leaving Mrs. Guerdion), Amelia and her friends had taken lodgings in Dart Street; or rather, Amelia, Mrs. Limeslices and Mrs. James had lodged there, with Mr. Adams two or three streets away.

No sooner had Mrs. Limeslices begun the unpacking, than Amelia and her friend started composing letters to Edenfield and Maryland. They next held conference to decide which of Tom's friends might be trusted, and settled upon only Colonel Askew, who had always treated Amelia as a favourite, if unofficial, niece. Amelia bemoaned her distance from Rob (whom, in fact, she missed very much), but brightened at the prospect of writing to Charles James. Indeed, I believe young Mr. James now became the great hope of both these ladies, who discussed what they considered his imminent arrival in terms of highest confidence—Mrs. James always hearing his name with a smile, and Amelia, with a sigh.

Alas, the morning brought a note from Colonel Askew's housekeeper saying the Colonel was abroad. Several cold days then produced not even a card, until Amelia and Mrs. James felt as empty as their letter-tray.

Our two ladies were obliged to wait these days in a sitting room very dingy, beside a fire extremely small. Despite every possible economy, they still found their expenses shockingly high, for a reason which, I think, does little credit to their fellow creatures.

The truth is, Reader, that young women of Amelia's evident fashion and breeding rarely take such obscure lodgings in London, unless they have been doing breeding of another sort, and wish for a period of some months to hide themselves from friends and relatives. The persons who cater to these distressed ladies seem nearly all to have extremely delicate consciences, which they cannot silence, except by stuffing their mouths with bank-bills. These persons are not, to be sure, such great friends of

Vice as to sing his praises in the streets; yet neither are they so proud as to refuse any gifts he might *privately* send them.

In short, Amelia, for all her purity, had been obliged to endure having her waist-line studied before a price for lodging was named; after which she was allowed to rent two very small rooms which, with meals, cost her nearly as much as the best inn in Somersetshire.

These drab rooms were, of course, only the latest in a series of blows to Amelia's self-confidence, of which the first had been her brother's behaviour, the next, Mr. Adams's injury, the third, her banishment from Hanover Square, and so on. These she had, however, survived pretty stoically, until, on the morning of the 6th of November, her landlady, whose name was Mrs. Blandish (and who, considering the way she earned her living, was not a very bad woman), brought her at last a letter.

This Amelia received greedily, and after thanking Mrs. Blandish read aloud to Mrs. James:

> Hanover Square
> 6 Nov. 1774
>
> Dear Miss,
>      Your brother is come to London with the intention of carrying you home. Please do whatever you can to stay clear of public places, and expect no more help from your affectionate,
>
>                     Honesta Guerdion

I have said Amelia read this aloud; yet in truth she finished in scarcely a whisper, and then let the letter drop to the floor before exclaiming:

"Oh, Mrs. James! What am I to do? I will gladly face any reasonable danger, only I promise this waiting to be found will very soon destroy me."

(In truth, Reader, I believe Amelia spoke very sensibly, for all miseries are relieved by action, and only when we dare not resist troubles, do we feel their full force.)

Neither Mrs. James nor Mr. Adams (who had come quietly into the room as Amelia read) could make any response to this, tho' Mr. Adams, I believe, was preparing to mention several excellent scriptures upon patience, when Mrs. Blandish returned to announce:

"Your son is here to see you, Mrs. James."

The company heard this with great satisfaction, Mr. Adams slapping his knee and crying, "How timely are Thy mercies, O Lord!" and the two ladies turning immediately to the looking glass to adjust their appearance.

If the good ladies had intended to outshine their guest, I fear they were disappointed, for not Kitty Kennedy herself was more gorgeous than the young gentleman who now appeared. Mr. Charles James wore a dark-blue satin coat, breeches to match, a shirt which cascaded ruffles, and shoes with thick gold buckles. Adorned with those rich curls we have earlier celebrated, he looked indeed like an angel sent down from the ethereal regions of—White's, perhaps, or the ball-rooms of Bath.

"Mother!" cried this young gentleman, stooping to embrace Mrs. James.

"Thank you for coming, Charles," she replied, the tears standing in her eyes.

"Indeed, Mother, I left as soon as I could." Mr. James had by now disengaged himself, and taken an offered seat. "You cannot imagine how shocked I was to read your letter."

"We shall do well enough, Charles, now that you are here."

"Indeed we shall," added Mr. Adams, dabbing at his own eyes.

Mr. Charles James looked rather blank at this. "How, Mother?" he asked, in some uncertainty.

"Why, Charles, we have only to support ourselves until Squire Jones returns to England. Your father, I know, sent you one last term's allowance of £300; with only half of that, we shall last very easily."

"Mother!" cries young Mr. James. "If only I could help. Alas, I have had many expenses, and some small reverses . . ." (for young Mr. James was unluckily fond of what are usually, and wrongly, called games of *chance*) ". . . and, in truth, I had come to ask you when I might have my next allowance paid."

A very awkward hush had now fallen over the room, for Mr. James knew not what to say, and the others, not *how* to say it.

At last, the young gentleman ventured to whisper, "Even a *hundred* pounds would help."

Suppose, Reader, the besieged garrison, its food gone, its bearded and bloody troops barely clinging to the ramparts, should spy in the distance the gaudy banners of a relief column. Suppose next that, no sooner had these relievers fought their way in, than they proposed to borrow half their colleagues' rifles and all their ammunition, and then to march away again. Might not indignation and disappointment struggle with gratitude in the breasts of the rescued?

So was it with our friends, for should I say either that they were too hurt to be amazed, or too amazed to be hurt, I should pretty fairly summarize their feelings. Mr. James had disappointed not only financial expectations, but the hopes of a mother and the prayers of a gentle admirer; and I believe nothing is more bitter than the loss of illusions.

Amelia now sat blushing and silent, while poor Mrs. James opened her mouth wordlessly two or three times, as part of a general trembling. At last, Mr. Adams (who, I suppose, least regretted any blunders by his rival) said quietly, "Well, young sir, I fear we shall have to disappoint you. We have little money enough to be passed around here."

Mr. James answered unhappily, "I had not, Mother, expected to be used so; I did not mean to fail you, and if I did, I am sorry." His words may have offered an apology, but his aggrieved tone seemed to demand one.

No apology was forthcoming; yet shortly, while the tea was poured, Mr. James began to talk merrily of Oxford. That the others scarcely replied, deterred him so little that he rattled on almost an hour, before withdrawing a large gold watch, and announcing with surprise that he must be going—an announcement which, alas, failed to produce any cries of regret.

This encounter might, however, have ended fairly happily, had it not been for one final unfortunate remark.

Mr. James had at his arrival placed his chair to face away from Amelia, and then, suffering either a medical, or a biblical, *stiff neck,* had looked directly forward during his entire visit.

Poor Amelia (who was, after all, a young woman, though a very brave one) had smiled hopefully at every muscle twitch suggesting Mr. James was about to look in her direction. It was only as he was leaving, however, that he finally addressed her, saying primly:

"I hope, Amelia, you will soon find means to submit yourself to the authority of your brother; for though I do not doubt he somewhat errs concerning your guilt, the authority of the male within the family is with me a cardinal principle."

Poor Amelia was too astonished to respond quickly; yet Mr. Adams at once jumped to his feet, snapt his fingers in the air, and cried forcefully, "I am pleased, sir, you employ the generic 'male,' instead of the specific 'man.' I cannot conceive how any *man* would speak as you have, tho' I imagine from your dress that you represent rather the genus *Pavo,* species *muticus,* in English, the *Peacock;* and I promise, sir, that, at your next such remark to this dear young lady, I shall *pluck your feathers.* "

His eyes very wide, Mr. James now made a single skip, which carried him from his chair to the doorway. With the stairs safely in view, he felt able to venture a retort, and said:

"Well, Mother, I suppose now I must make my own way in the world, since those who have nothing are always scorned by those who have a little more. Perhaps I shall yet make some tiny figure in this great world.

"Amelia, I find by your silent approval of this gross gentleman, that there is more truth in certain rumours than I would ever have believed. I am sorry for it, and sorrier still for certain fond thoughts I may once have enjoyed."

With this, Mr. James darted away, leaving behind three persons pretty well contented with his absence.

Reader, I have not often had occasion to quarrel with the actions of Mr. Adams, whose behaviour, if not always elegant, was in nearly every case morally exemplary. On this one occasion, however, I believe his fondness for Amelia, and his desire to look well in her eyes, led him to an action a good measure crueler than was necessary. I do not think he ought to have threatened Mr. James, for, in truth, there was within the silly little gentleman no harm—nor, indeed, very much of anything else.

And yet perhaps I am being over-scrupulous; for it doth appear that Mr. Adams succeeded in at least one, extremely important, quarter. To explain this requires that miraculous power of looking within human beings which authors (like surgeons) have enjoyed ever since it was first granted them by that incense-garbed deity, *themselves.*

Accordingly, Reader, let me tell thee that Amelia on this occasion first considered Mr. Adams with an admiration not many steps from beginning love. I certainly do not say that she loved him because she was weak, or even that she was as yet obliged to sit upon her hands to keep from embracing him—I only say she *admired* him. Indeed (so long as we do not confuse spirit with brutality), we may say that every woman prefers a man of spirit, since, as thou knowst, some things must be done energetically if they are to be done at all.

In thinking more warmly of Mr. Adams, Amelia was not only filling the void left by the ejection of Mr. James, but consoling herself for that misery which besets us when the loss of much convinces us we are fated to lose all. The failure of so many likely sources of aid—her father, Rob, Charles James—had convinced her everything would fail in time. Nor, indeed, could any of the others say much to brighten her spirits, or their own.

Soon after Mr. James's departure, the night arrived, with high, cold winds beating hard against the small window of the apartment, and perfectly completed our friends' misery. They now sat above two hours without speaking, subsisting only on the comfort of a mutual presence, and feeling, I think, like persons adrift upon a black river, who, if they missed the jagged rocks, would be swept into an ocean entirely as black, and infinitely larger.

This bleak interlude continued until about eight o'clock, when Mrs. Blandish, wearing that look of solicitous terror with which she habitually announced bailiffs, sheriffs, bill-collectors, fathers and brothers, stood shaking at the doorway to tell Amelia:

"Madam, a wild-looking gentleman downstairs demands to speak with you."

Amelia and her friends, all suddenly deathly pale, now exchanged glances of alarm, for who in their association could be called "wild," except for Hacksem? Indeed, I think their alarm was very well justified, for there now came upon the stairs a banging step which, by its slow, loud regularity suggested a damned spirit, a ghost, a—monster from the scalded brain of a *gothick* writer. There was next projected upon the far wall of the hallway a shadow so immense they immediately lost their fear of Hacksem in the greater fear that they were about to meet the Devil himself.

# VII

## Horror, Mystery and More

The steps upon the stairs now grew loud as thunder; the shadow upon the wall contracted enough to match the head—a huge, misshapen head —which rose above the top of the stairs; and in the distance, dogs howled.

If courage, Reader, is what makes us recall our duty when danger surrounds us, then Mrs. Blandish was the most courageous of women; for she now remembered her promise to attend a sick neighbour some blocks away. With the hairs upon her head for some reason springing up like spikes, she bolted suddenly into the hall, and thence into what appeared to be a closet, but was in fact a second exit down to the street—her business, I believe, requiring the ability to come and go with some secrecy.

Our friends, alas, had less courage (or different duties), for they now sat nailed to their chairs, their eyes very wide and their faces very pale, as the creature mounted the stairs.

At this moment, drawn by the commotion, Mrs. Limeslices stepped from the bedroom where she had politely hidden herself during the visit of Mr. James. No sooner did she see the apparition now shuffling towards them, than she dove back into her room, either to arm herself, or to commend herself to her Maker.

Indeed, no sight upon earth is more conducive to our terror and pity than that of innocence threatened, for when the innocent are allowed to fall into the claws of the wicked, what hope may we reserve for ourselves?

Alas, Reader, it is a slow business to compose such mighty sentiments! And in the time I have so spent (which a wiser author might have used to move our friends to safety), the apparition made its swaying way directly to the door-frame, where it stood a moment with the rain-water puddling at its feet, before opening its terrible maw to say:

"Amelia Jones? May I introduce myself?"

Amelia, her voice uncooperative, nodded weakly.

"My name is Samuel Johnson. I am a friend of your father's, and hope I will be a friend of yours.

Reader, this was indeed a person familiar to thee; and I hope I may be forgiven if I accidentally obscured what ought to have been a simple appearance—for thee, if not for our heroine.

Some moments now transpired before Amelia had sufficiently recovered to offer the Doctor a seat, and to make the introductions. Mr. Adams, discovering himself in the presence of *the* Sam Johnson, became ecstatic, but manfully restrained himself from any fawning praise, only declaring *Rasselas* to be both the finest satire, and the soundest piece of morality, composed in the past century.

The danger, not slight, that Mr. Adams would now attempt to discuss religion and philosophy until dawn, was averted when the Doctor, seizing the small gap of a pause for breath, said hastily, "I believe, ma'am, I owe you some explanation of this intrusion.

"Your father, before leaving England, asked me to collect and hold his mail until he should have a firm address in America. For reasons which are unclear to me, he had not received any important, expected letters since joining the Suffley household. I knew in particular he had wished to hear from you.

"The Post Office was kind enough to send me his mail. While sorting it, I noticed a letter from you, with a return direction rather unexpected . . ."

Amelia blushed, Mr. Adams shifted his feet.

". . . and decided to call upon you."

The Doctor now fell silent, while each person totalled his or her impressions. He then asked carefully, "Am I right in guessing you have written more than once to your father during these last months?"

"Why, sir, all of us, faithfully." Amelia looked closely at her friends, saw their approval, and began again:

"In truth, Doctor, we have written desperately, for something terrible has happened in Somersetshire, so terrible I lack the heart—even if I had the time—to explain it to thee in detail."

The Doctor—as fond of a story as any man alive—leaned forward eagerly, tho' he said nothing.

Amelia continued, "To be brief, my brother hath conspired with our lawyer, Mr. Sinamore, to drive this good woman from her home, and to steal my father's estate. There are more crimes we suspect, but of these, we are certain."

The Doctor groaned, then rose and strode twice across the room, before declaring, "Monstrous! Madam, are you positive?"

"I am, sir."

"Then we must hire a courier to go to America directly, while we—or I alone—confront your brother, the villain; and this lawyer, if he dare show his face."

"Sir," interjected Mr. Adams, "they are both very willing to show their faces; they are bold men. Yet we have suspicions of their ruthlessness which, though short of proof, make us wary of challenging them, and adamant against letting anyone else confront them for us."

"Why, sir," replies the Doctor, standing very straight, "villains may threaten us with pain, with death, and with ruin. I am sick and old, and have been most of my life very poor. They would be threatening a lump of coal with black paint. So let us hear no more of that."

Mr. Adams, as earnest as the Doctor, had now risen to his feet to continue the debate, when Mrs. James asked, "Are we not wrong to imagine that these criminals will be lured by any persuasion, or driven by any terrors, in our power? Will we not rather be exposing ourselves to superior force at a time when concealment will serve us better?"

The tactical sense of this struck both gentlemen very hard, especially as it was the first time Mrs. James had spoken.

"Well, madam," replied the Doctor, "you are very likely correct. We must not let our plans outrun our understanding; and there are many mysteries here, such as the involvement of the Suffleys, who must, unless we are missing something obvious, be a part of the conspiracy.

"What say you to this? I shall write immediately to Tom in a style sufficiently veiled that he—but no interloper—shall understand my message; and shall entrust it to some honest sea-captain to be delivered by hand. Will that work, do you think?"

This question the Doctor had directed to the others generally; and they, after a moment's thought, agreed that it might.

Indeed, Reader, I believe these four persons, unused as they were to violence or plottings, had acted as wisely as expertise and circumstance allowed.

A few minutes later, the Doctor stood to take a very warm leave. The others each pressed his hand in parting, and he in turn bid them to, "Stand firm and expect better times. We shall visit each other soon, and often." They watched him depart with, it seems, hardly any of their original horror.

The Doctor had no sooner departed than Mrs. Limeslices crept from her hiding-place, to be told what a great man she had missed. This news she took extremely hard, since, as she declared, the country held no finer author, unless it be some two or three writers of very sweet romances.

# VIII

## Containing Nothing but a Short Letter

The next day was Sunday, and Mr. Adams, having agreed for a guinea (though he would have done it for free) to accept the duty of a church near his lodgings, did not reach Amelia's until the mid-afternoon. As he entered her landlady's building, he encountered a middle-aged woman of vaguely familiar countenance walking in the same direction.

When Mrs. Limeslices had shown them in to Amelia, this woman handed Miss Jones a note, and said that she had been asked to wait for a reply. This note Amelia read with great interest, and then passed to Mr. Adams, who similarly discovered the following:

> 8 November
> At Hanover Square
>
> Dear Miss,
> A gentleman who refuses to give his name (but who says he is well known to you) claims he must see you upon a matter of life-and-death. I believe him not to be an agent of your brother's; yet you must decide for yourself whether you wish to risk seeing him, and depend no more upon the help of,
> Your devoted,
> Honesta Guerdion
>
> P.S. The gentleman is freest on Sunday evenings; my sister, Augustina Miller, will carry back your reply.

Mr. Adams raising no objections, Amelia said, "If you please, Mrs. Miller, will you tell your sister we should like to see the gentleman this evening at eight o'clock? And will you thank her for daring so much on my behalf?"

"Ma'am, I shall," said Mrs. Miller, pleased to be treated so politely; and with a smile very genuine, she went out the door, and about her business.

As did Mrs. Miller then, so shall we now, and rejoin our friends in about five hours, when, perhaps, items of interest shall be revealed.

## IX

### In Which a Plot Is Discovered

By eight o'clock, the clouds of anxiety had grown very thick around our friends, who were almost relieved when a knock upon the door interrupted their nervous chatter.

Mrs. Limeslices answered the knock, but even that perceptive lady did not recognize the small, sickly gentleman who stood before her.

"May I help you, sir?" said she.

"Do you not know me, Mrs. Limeslices? I am Will Stumpling."

This introduction produced a flurry of attention, with Mr. Adams being quickest to offer up his chair, Mrs. James quickest with tea, and Amelia quickest to ask him how he did.

Indeed, Reader, though I have sought to spare thee such tricks as lightened the recent appearance of the Doctor, Mr. Stumpling had undergone a most mysterious transformation, from a young person to an old one. Now he straightened himself painfully, set down his teacup, and began:

"I have a confession—which I fear will only anger thee—and a piece of information, which I hope may redeem at least some of the misery I have caused.

"Know, then, this:

"I was early a part of the plot against your father you now see unfolding. I will not defend myself, except to say that I never imagined at first that anything so foul was intended.

"The conspiracy did not originate in Somersetshire, but was first broached by a gentleman from the North of England, whose name is unknown to me, but who had, it now appears, a fierce hatred of your father. This gentleman hath, within the last decade, built a great fortune by manufacture, and easily convinced your brother that as much money could be made in Somersetshire—if only some persons were not old-fashioned. Indeed, I believe all true wickedness stems from this northern gentleman, since it was he who goaded Hacksem continually."

The others had now leaned forward upon their seats.

"Lawyer Sinamore was, I believe, long ago brought into the conspiracy, which was then obliged to wait for some proper opportunity—as when, of course, your father chose to go abroad.

"I had been a participant early, when it seemed your father would only be talked into modernizing Somersetshire; for Hacksem's arguments were persuasive; and, in truth, nothing upon earth is more persuasive than the prospect of wealth, to one so poor as I.

"The moment your father announced his departure, however, the plan turned more vicious; and I—after a hesitation of which I am ashamed—told Lawyer I wished none of it. After much pleading and threatening, I was at last allowed to leave for London with your father, but on a pledge of silence, accompanied by many dire warnings.

"For many weeks, I kept my word, since I believed Lawyer's threats. At last, however, my conscience became very bad; and when I learned of your father's plans to join the Suffleys—for Lawyer broke his promise, and came to London to demand my services as go-between for himself and Lady Suffley—I resolved to act.

"I wrote to your father asking him to meet me at an especially dangerous and crime-ridden tavern, where I thought we might talk unobserved, but Lawyer's agents followed me, and arranged to get me a beating, the marks of which I believe I shall carry all the days of my life."

Here Amelia said something extremely tender, but Mr. Stumpling only sighed, and responded:

"Madam, pray do not pity me, for your sympathy raises an agony of shame far worse than any blows I have suffered.

"Indeed, I know you will detest me, when I tell you my reason for acting was my—I must not say, 'love,' for I have no right to the word, but my desire for you, aggravated by knowing that you cared only for a gentleman who had everything by birth, Charles James. That was why I helped Lawyer at first and, heaven forgive me, briefly joined the darker plot: I wanted to hobble your fortunes and make my own; and I decided either to have, or to punish you.

"So, ma'am, find a better object for your sympathy than one who, in order to have you nearer his own level, would have brought you to ruin."

This frankness utterly daunted the others in the room, and for several moments there was more blushing than speaking, or even breathing. Yet a certain power in repentance lets it heal some of the wounds it makes. I suppose (for I would be frank myself) Mr. Stumpling benefitted from the recent decline of Mr. James. Moreover, Mr. Adams well understood the motive, if not the deed; and Amelia, though she had never had any hint of Will's devotion, could still not entirely hate him for it. Accordingly, she said (with an effort):

"Well, Mr. Stumpling, that's all a matter from the past; and we'll discuss it no farther. Pray, continue."

"Unfortunately, ma'am, your father left town while I was recovering from my injuries; and I was thereafter too frightened to make a further attempt.

"I very carefully kept myself ignorant of events in Somersetshire, until last week, when, in the course of a law-suit, I met a gentleman slightly known to you, by the name of Caitlin. On his informing me of your coming to London, I guessed the reason, and knew I must act."

Mr. Stumpling's features assumed a look of anguished haste. "Madam," said he, "I came here with another purpose than begging your pardon. I hope I may, if not reverse the crimes, at least prevent a worse catastrophe than any yet seen."

His listeners' faces mixed curiosity and alarm.

"You realize, ma'am, that Squire Jones could not have irrevocably given his estate to Hacksem: whatever the documents may say, the courts will always hear a claim of fraud or forgery; nor would an action to recover be especially complex."

"Well?" demanded Amelia.

"Well, ma'am," continued Stumpling, "if the guardian should *mortgage* the estate, the mortgage will be valid, whatever happens to the guardian. Alas, Amelia!—unless their plans have been changed, Hacksem and Lawyer Sinamore mean to mortgage the estate to that same evil third party from the North, whose name I do not know, but whom I believe to be utterly ruthless—and who will then foreclose, and claim all. Once that foreclosure is completed, the legal title is his, irrevocably—and he, Hacksem and Mr. Sinamore will be free to divide Paradise Hall as they see fit, damming the streams, displacing the poor, and building whatever manufactories they wish.

"In short, dear ma'am, if your father is not in England to enter his claim at the spring Quarter-Sessions on the 17th of April next, he will have no reason to return at all; for he will no longer have an estate to defend."

At this, Amelia sighed and fell back in her chair, Mr. Adams banged his fists against his temples, and Mrs. James and Mrs. Limeslices looked extremely grim.

It was, however, Amelia who spoke first, saying, "Why, then, we have one hundred forty days to find my father and bring him home. If we suppose that eight weeks will be required for each crossing of the ocean, we have exactly twenty-eight days to invest in our preparations here, and in our search for him there. 'Tis not trivial, but I believe it may be done."

Amelia had ended upon a note of some excitement. Yet Mr. Stumpling now replied, "Alas, ma'am, I fear your troubles may not end there."

"What mean you?!" cried Amelia, who was (with some cause, I admit) growing impatient with the young gentleman's hesitant manner of communication.

"Forgive me, ma'am, for a reluctance in admitting something so dark, and yet—and yet I must say it.

"Madam, that northern villain had always wished for us to deal violently with your father, but Hacksem and (less eagerly) Mr. Sinamore dissuaded him. Yet Lawyer when he called on me in London had grown a hundred times more ruthless than I had ever seen him before. Now, madam, I would believe anything of the conspirators, and with you free to seek the Squire, and America so wild and far away . . . ma'am, there is danger of an *assassin.*"

"Heaven protect us!" cried the Parson.

But Amelia only said, "Why then, I must leave as soon as possible. Mrs. Limeslices, we will go tomorrow to see about passage."

At this, Mr. Adams leapt to his feet and bellowed (fairly genteelly, I allow), "*Never!!*" Then, calming himself, he continued, "Madam, be sensible. This is a task far too dangerous—"

"*Mr. Adams,*" says Amelia. "Be sensible yourself. I am not the one standing and shouting. We shall speak of this later.

"Now, Mr. Stumpling, is there anything more you wish to tell us?"

"Nothing, ma'am. Except, of course, how wretchedly, abjectly sorry I am." This he said in a manner so evidently sincerely, that Amelia replied pityingly that, for her part, she entirely forgave him.

She also watched attentively as he rose to leave, which he did with motions sufficiently reluctant that she asked whether he felt well enough to go.

"Well enough, ma'am," answered Stumpling, "though I fear too poor. After tonight, I dare not remain in London; yet I have not money to escape. Well, a worse punishment would be too light for what I've done; and so, to all, good-night."

He had now huddled his great-coat about him and walked as far as the door, when Amelia stopped him.

Reader, it is a considerable virtue of the young that, whatever their tempers, very few of them have learned to hate *upon principle*. Amelia very naturally and smoothly unbuttoned a small gold-and-ruby brooch she wore and, holding it out to Will Stumpling, said, "This will bring you about thirty pounds, I believe. Please take it."

"Madam," replied Mr. Stumpling, rather sadly, "it would be to no purpose; for I could sell nothing so redolent of you."

At this, even the Parson sighed; Amelia, meanwhile, had whispered to Mrs. Limeslices, who disappeared momentarily into another room, and then returned with two or three folded bank-notes, which she handed to Mr. Stumpling. This the young gentleman accepted with trembling hands and then, bowing gratefully to Amelia, he departed.

# X

## *An Incident Which Some Will Think Contains a Moral*

Mr. Stumpling had no sooner departed than Amelia and Mr. Adams began to argue which of themselves was better qualified to seek Tom in America. The argument becoming extremely heated, Mrs. James at last declared that (however sorry it made her) they both must go. This Mrs. Limeslices seconded, saying, "I no more expect to see one of you succeed alone, than I do to see half a bird fly south for the winter." As for the two combatants, they signed the accord at once, for the very simple reason (I suppose) that it was what they both had wanted all along.

There remained but a single, dull impediment to action; namely, the lack of cash, for they swiftly calculated that, after leaving money enough for Mrs. James and Mrs. Limeslices to survive the winter, Amelia and Mr. Adams would have funds too scant for travel. After many minutes' thought, only Dr. Johnson was mentioned as a possible source, but was immediately rejected by Mr. Adams, saying, " 'Tis widely known the Doctor supports a crowd, including a blind woman and two or three broken wits, upon little income. The poverty of so great a man should be a national scandal. Yet I fear it is but the common fate of authors, who, having nothing to sell but words, are frequently paid in the same commodity."

Mrs. Limeslices shook her head at this, saying she was sorry to hear it, but that for her part, she would no longer think so well of authors as formerly, and thanked heaven there were none in her family; and so the conversation ended.

Amelia awoke the next morning with a cold, which persisted several days; and it was not until the morning of the fifteenth of November that the two friends, seeking to travel as cheaply as possible, made the rounds of Thames merchants' factors, shipping offices and quay warehouses—all, alas, to no avail. The need to reinforce Crown positions in New-England had placed a premium upon space suitable for human beings, although (on account of non-importation) space for hard-goods was plentiful. It therefore happened to our friends (as it often doth to the innocent) that, tho' their expectations were modest, reality was more modest still: they wanted little, and were offered nothing at all.

This searching continued until about four in the afternoon. Very discouraged, they were leaving the office of Lockwood & Sons, Ship's Chandlers, when one of the Lockwoods chased after them into the street to ask, "whether they had tried Captain Rising, of the *Glendower*, a tea-brig sailing for Maryland at week's end?" The Captain, it seemed, was a gruff man but an honest one, and sometimes carried passengers at very moderate charge. His ship was anchored and taking on cargo about two miles from where they stood. Having said so much, Mr. Lockwood shrugged apologetically, and then disappeared back indoors, for he had come out in his shirt-sleeves, and the afternoon was extremely cold.

There was, in fact, so chill a drizzle in the darkening air that three or four times our friends nearly abandoned their search for the tea-brig.

Yet a quarter-hour's hard walking brought them upon a tall, whip-like gentleman wearing a long black woolen coat and an old gold-braided captain's hat, who was supervising the loading of crates into a distressingly small ship. At their approach, he had been spouting above one oath for each two sentences, but seeing Mr. Adams's surplice, he tempered his language, and greeted them quite civilly. After some preliminaries, he offered to carry two passengers for forty pounds less than any offer they had yet heard, but warned them that, "They must eat salt pork and salt beef, and never mind the sea, for *Glendower*'s a pitching raft."

Mr. Adams was about to declare the price still beyond their means, when Amelia asked, "If sir, we were to bring you the money by noon tomorrow, would you be good enough to hold our places?"

The Captain, who had little enough to lose by agreeing, shifted his pipe in his mouth and answered, " 'Til noon, miss, but not a minute more."

Our two friends walked away, but not contentedly, for they were soon again in their now accustomed argument, with Mr. Adams warning they would leave Mrs. James impoverished and themselves underfunded, and Amelia insisting that Mr. Adams lacked . . . fortitude.

This argument continued with its usual tenacity all the way to Amelia's lodgings, which they reached after dark, and where Amelia was immediately seized by Mrs. Limeslices, who dragged her to the fire, untied her wet cape, and began chafing her hands as earnestly as if she had just pulled her from a river.

When Amelia had enjoyed five or six minutes of this, Mrs. James was able to give her a large envelope, which she said had been brought by Dr. Johnson's man-servant. Opening it, she found two smaller envelopes, and a note explaining that the Doctor had been called away by the death of a friend, but wished her to have the enclosed letters, which were (except for her own) the first he had received on her father's behalf, and which he hoped she would put to the earliest possible use, for, "in such a situation as yours, *punctilio* is wrong, and information is very valuable." He then closed with many kind wishes for her success, and a promise of any future assistance in his power.

Amelia (tho' a little tired of all this kind pulling and pushing by her friends) now held the two sealed envelopes towards the fire to read them. Upon the first envelope she recognized the handwriting of her brother Rob. Tearing the seal eagerly, she discovered:

Dearest Father,

If the scarcity of my letters has disappointed you, I hope I may now begin to make amends; for I perceive nothing to prevent my becoming the perfect correspondent.

I arrived here ten days ago, upon a morning cloudless and warm, to find the harbour filled with British and, especially, American ships. During my voyage, I became certain I am suited for no life but the sea, and so faithfully did I study the Captain's books upon navigation, that he immediately introduced me to several American merchants here, who have promised me I shall soon commence a voyage, I hope to China or India.

The talk here is everyday of the troubles in New-England. I begin to sympathize a little with the Americans, not only from their kindness to me, but from the evident harm our English policies have done to trade and liberty—and, I fear, from the misery I saw in Ireland. I shall say no more of a topic you dislike; yet, since you are attending to the family wealth, you might wish to avoid any cargoes twixt America and England. The Americans here are determined to arm privateers and raid British shipping, the moment war comes—as they are certain it very soon shall.

On a happier note, several of these Americans possess both good fortunes and beautiful daughters. I ask you, Father, to picture the charms of a young lady wearing a colourful silken dress, on a warm night, with sea breezes wafting among the palms, and waves falling along the beach . . . the natural desires of a young man are, however, properly tempered by the recollection that Jamaica is an island, and a *small* one.

Something of all this doth make it hard to continue my train of thought; I shall cease for the evening, and begin a new letter as soon as possible. You and my dear sister are always in my thoughts. I wish I could enclose a gardenia for Amelia! I trust, however, she is happy with traditional comforts, as I am with exotic ones; and I will write her directly, as soon as I may.

Until then, I remain, in all duty and fondness,

Thy loving son,
Rob Jones

P.S.: It may be that I shall volunteer to serve upon one of those privateers, but strictly for experience while they are training, and not to seek conflict; for my time in Ireland hath taught me how unsuited I am for aught violent or rough.

In truth, Reader, not even angelic Amelia could have looked up from such a letter and examined her own cold, dilapidated apartments without feeling some twinges of envy and annoyance. As, however, she loved her brother very much, her anger was directed not so much towards him of the gardenias, as towards her entire, frustrating situation.

So it was with shaking impatience that she seized the second, less promising letter, and read as follows:

Marseilles
29 October

My Dear Chevalier,

I imagine you little expected to hear again from your friend Bavard. (And is not "friend Bavard" the last phrase you might use? —and yet, Monsieur, you were the one trust-worthy friend Bavard ever had.)

All goes exquisitely for me. My father-in-law having discovered his work-load reduced to nothing now spends his days sleeping beneath a tree and his nights very sociably sleeping with his wife, and leaves all the business to Your Servant.

I am a true business-man! For who knows better how to catch a thief than one who has twenty years or more practiced every little trick which may be played upon an innkeeper? Better still, I may now quite legally cozen all my customers, who generally receive me like a lost relative indeed! I tell them they have the appetites of great Pantagruel, and they eat and drink three times what they intended, they are so flattered.

And so, dear Chevalier, to the theme of my epistle. A man, I believe, should experience each feeling once, for the sake of the novelty; and now I believe I shall display gratitude. I am returning to you half of the £100 with which you bound-up my marriage to my dear Lisette, and thereby saved at once my life, and my soul. I hope you may buy with it some token either to please a beautiful lady, or to remind you of your friends here; or, better, both. (If only you were here, I could show you how to make it go *three times* as far.)

———

231

But now I must end!—for I see that noble sentiments are less durable than ignoble ones, and £50 is a tempting sum for such a one as,

Your eternal servant,
Bavard

P.S. Lisette is preparing her own dear memorial for you, which she promises shall be named either Thomas or Thomasina—names chosen, I trust, from a purely philosophical gratitude. And both of us wish that we may see you again one day, or at least that you shall live many happy years before you are transported to a still happier place, on the occasion of which, I am sure, the angels will all stand and cheer.

Amelia, noticing the letter to be decorated with certain stains about the size of tear-drops but of a purplish colour, discounted most of what she read, until she saw in the envelope a last slip of paper, which proved to be a draft upon Coutts for £50. While she stared at this in joyous amazement, Mr. Adams read the letter, at which he expressed some satisfaction, "though, beyond the tone of gratitude, there are several themes which appear a little . . ."

But Amelia, knowing better than to let him mount his hobby horse, now ignored him, preferring to wave the bank-note in the air and cry, "Ladies, we are saved! I sail on Friday. Mrs. Limeslices, you will please begin the packing tomorrow: as few things as possible, and the warmest I own. Mrs. James, shall we have wine for a toast?"

These two ladies immediately signified their acceptance of these instructions, for youth at such moments may be denied nothing. Their faces, to be sure, reflected something less than the highest pitch of enthusiastic joy. Yet I have sometimes known persons to look most solemn when they were most pleased; and perhaps it was so with them.

# XI

*Containing a Storm as Violent as*
*Any in Homer—and Which None*
*Should Read Who Cannot Swim*

That Friday morning, our two travellers were rowed out, through a fog very thick, to the *Glendower*, where Amelia was given the deck cabin (a sort of hut six feet in each dimension), and Mr. Adams, a bunk at the stern of the ship, very commodious for a gentleman half his size. Neither, however, made any complaint, so grateful were they to be under sail— which, in fact, they were within thirty minutes, when the fog began to lift.

Alas, there fell out that first morning a little dispute between the Captain and the Parson. This started amicably enough, when Mr. Adams, full of high spirits, began striding about the deck and discoursing knowledgeably about the nautical life—concerning which, he had in truth read a great deal. Captain Rising, an altogether happier man once his feet had left dry land, noticed this, and asked, "Whether he had made many sea-voyages?"

Mr. Adams answered genially, "Sir, I believe I may say so, for I have been with Anson and with Cook—"

"Why, sir," cries the Captain, "you are indeed a sailor, then. Yet I would not have guessed you old enough to have gone with Milord Anson."

"With him 'round the globe, sir, and with Jason and the Argonauts seeking the fleece, and Odysseus seeking his home."

The Captain, though poorly educated, now sensed something amiss. "Indeed, sir, you jest with me; for some of these persons, I know, have not lived for many years, if ever."

Mr. Adams, smiling condescendingly, replied, "Sir, I do not jest, for what I have read, I consider myself to have done; and, indeed, to have done more profitably than many who have set their bodies in motion but left their minds at home."

"Well, Mr. Adams," cries the Captain, "this is fine nonsense, and would make me the king of Scotland because I once saw *Macbeth* acted upon the stage."

Mr. Adams, proud of his schooling, began to wax very hot. As he was meditating a tart reply, however, an unlucky burst of wind, combined with a need to tack slightly around some other traffic, caused the *Glendower* to roll sharply upon her axis. This sudden motion brought to Mr. Adams's face a look first of surprise, and then of decided queasiness. He now paused, swallowed hard once or twice, and said manfully, "I see, sir, I can say nothing of moment to one who has not read."

The Captain, drawing himself up and then gazing down with a superior expression, replied, "And I see that I *need* say nothing of moment to one who has not sailed. The railing, sir, is where your next eloquence must be directed." And with that, he left Mr. Adams to his growing discomfort.

Mr. Adams's discomfort grew considerably with the *Glendower*'s first ocean contact, and persisted (with decreasing ferocity) for about the next four weeks, during which, he was among the most miserable of mortals; and though he generally suffered silently, he once mournfully told Amelia that, "he now understood why the ancients had thought the dead went *to hell by boat.*"

What of Amelia? Why, Reader, she had her father's constitution, and moved easily about the rolling deck; nor, in truth, was she much saddened to find a point of superiority to the burly Parson. She was never cruel or gloating; yet (as thou knowst) it is as pleasant to be protective of, as protected by, those we like.

Aside from smiling sympathetically, Amelia filled these weeks by making plans for America, striding about vigorously, and studying the horizon as though that would bring land the sooner into view.

About noon of their sixth Monday at sea, as Amelia was in her usual place near the bow of the ship, Captain Rising, alerted by a drop in the ship's glass, appeared on deck to make his own survey of the horizon. Even before putting the 'scope to his eye, he saw that the surface of the water had changed, the swells augmented with smaller waves, faint as the shocks sent through a mattress when one corner of the straw is pounded. Looking carefully a few points off the stern, he at last perceived a black concentration rising above the water at the extreme limits of his vision.

He then turned restlessly to other business for half an hour. When he looked again, the black concentration had spread detectably. He called onto the deck his mate, whose name, I believe, was Boggins, and bid him see that, "the cargo is all doubly secured. We'll have hot supper served to all alike, and the cooking fire extinguished, in one hour. And see that the pump is manned once supper's over."

"Aye, Captain."

"And do it quietly."

"Aye-aye."

At three o'clock, opaque clouds filled two-thirds of the sky, leaving all the water below to seethe in false night. The winds then began to blow very high, and to scrape the round tops off the swelling waves. Through these roughening seas, the *Glendower* plunged faster and faster, tho' the Captain twice ordered her sail reduced.

Not long after dark, the hooshing winds rose to a howl; and the poor ship, toss'd by waves already higher than her bow, began to oscillate with each descent, her bow dropping momentarily in the free air. Now two sailors laboured at the wheel, and the cold rain and spray, battering down, made the deck like glass. Captain Rising ordered Amelia and Mr. Adams not to move from her cabin, where they sat close together, looked very frightened, and held each other's hands.

For nearly an hour (tho' it seem'd a hundred times longer), they heard only the wind and sea, and the Captain's shouts steadily fainter in comparison. When the ship's motion had turned so desperate that the cabin deck was vertical as often as horizontal, and an invisible hand swept the room's contents back and forth, there came from outside what sounded like gun-shots. Almost at once, the ship steadied and relaxed. This calm persisting some ten or fifteen seconds, Amelia and Adams (who had scarcely breathed in all the past hour) both exhaled at once and, believing a miracle to have occurred, began to rise from the floor where they had crouched.

They had no sooner reached their feet, than, with a rumble hardly to be believed, a gigantic wave burst against the cabin-side, twisting it, sending water dripping through the boards, and then crashing torrentially through the window-pane. At this Amelia screamed, and Mr. Adams fell to his knees in what he supposed would be a final prayer; and a moment later, Boggins pulled open the door, and shouted that they must come out at once, for the next wave would surely sweep the cabin away.

They had stept from the wretched box into a nightmare, as they now saw (dimly, for the rain fell in sheets, and the night was very black) waves towering above the top-mast, with their glistening ridges steeper, it seemed, than castle-walls.

Boggins had led them across the slick deck to the main-mast, where the Captain clung wearily, his face wild; and Amelia, looking behind her, could see no one at the helm. At once, the mate commanded them, "Hold on for your lives!" and, grabbing as strongly as she could, Amelia felt another massive wave break over her, its intense liquid grip almost tearing her arms from her shoulders and carrying her away.

Amelia now shouted to the Captain (tho' his face was not above six inches from hers), asking what they must do to save themselves.

"Why, miss," cries he, his voice cracking, "we must tie ourselves to the mast, and give our souls up to God, for we haven't a shred of canvas to turn us bow forward, and as we lie, we'll break with any wave."

Peering up, Amelia saw only bits of sails remained, and realized the shots she had heard, had been the canvas blowing apart. Now the stinging rain made her shut her eyes; yet in closing them, she pictured the ship with a single sail far forward. "But can we not," she asked, "do *something?*"

Before any answer came, Mr. Adams bellowed (tho' their three faces were extremely near), "Can we not put a jib-sail at the bow-sprit?"

"Why, Parson," shouted the Captain, "we've two overboard already. No man can cross that deck."

"I can!" replied both Adams and Amelia; yet the Captain heard only the Parson. After a single hard look (for indeed they had but moments remaining), he nodded, then said loudly, "Wait!" Opening the hatchway, he raced below-decks, to reappear a minute later (another heavy wave having pounded against the ship) carrying an immense bundle of cloth.

"Mr. Adams," cried he, "attach these iron ringlets, three along the mast, and three along the flying-jib-boom, then raise her no more than half way. D'ye understand?"

"*Viam aut invenium aut fascium!*"* answered the Parson, stuffing the sail beneath one arm and, with the other, launching himself across the pitching deck, while, behind him, Captain Rising shook his head and called to Amelia, "I know naught of these *viams*, but hope Mr. Adams will find a way to raise the sail."

Mr. Adams, meanwhile (crouching with one hand stretched before

*I will find a way, or I will make one.

236

him, so that when he fell—which was often—he might easily push himself to his feet again), had run nearly half the distance to the bow. Now, seeing yet another wave speeding forward through the downpour, he dove for the bow-mast, and, grasping it with his free arm, covered the sail with his body and held his breath while the water, barreling over him, swung him ninety degrees as easily as it doth a bit of sea-weed. As it ebbed, Adams rose swiftly, already struggling to spread the sail-packet. He set the first eyelets while the bulk of the cloth snapt and fluttered madly in the gale; then, using his body as a wind-break, he fought the others into place, and, at last, drew the line slowly. Almost at once the sail filled and hardened, and he strained to raise it each further inch.

Amelia (exceedingly annoyed to have been denied a part) had watched this from the main-mast, where she, the Captain and the mate were tied. At the first white flash of sail-cloth ahead, she slipt the horn-handled knife from the mate's sheath, and cut their ropes. The mate and the Captain dashed for the wheel, and so doing, entirely forgot Miss Jones.

Too fascinated to be much afraid, Amelia now followed them aft and, as they struggled to turn the ship about, threw her own weight to the helm. So obsessed were the men with their task (for the ship could not have taken another wave against her sides) that they neglected to dismiss her; nor, in truth, could they easily have found a place to send her, the wave before having carried her cabin overboard.

With a sail in place, and hands at the wheel, *Glendower* turned slowly to a safer posture before the waves, the next of which broke over her stern with little harm. She had taken water, the Captain declared, but perhaps not a lethal amount; and, "if these winds moderate, I believe we may live until morning, after all."

In truth, the winds had already fallen from their most terrifying pitch, and the heavens begun to clear, tho' the waves continued immense. Mr. Adams now lumbered back towards them, breathing very hard, and looking extremely weary but yet very pleased.

The Captain, taking the occasion to wipe the last of the rain-water from his own eyes, now studied Mr. Adams closely, then said, "Well, Parson, I believe perhaps you are a sailor, after all."

Mr. Adams, first looking to Amelia for approval, grinned to this, and then, more solemnly, urged that they all betake themselves to their knees to render thanks for their preservation, and to seek of the Almighty mercy for those who had perished.

When their service (which, by reason of the cold, was short, tho'
fervent) had concluded, Captain Rising and the mate, saying they would
watch the ship, urged Amelia and Adams to go below and rest. This they
did very willingly, being so tired they could not walk without staggering.
Water sloshed in the hold, and the bunks they found were narrow and
damp. They closed their eyes at once; yet I believe they enjoyed some
pleasant thoughts in the few instants before they slept; for Amelia had the
satisfaction of knowing she had played her part in the saving of the ship,
and Mr. Adams (besides a similar achievement), also felt (as he in later
years would often declare) that he never thought Amelia so perfect as
when at the helm of the *Glendower*. That Miss Jones could ever have had
any corresponding fondness, so unbecoming a young maiden, for the
heroic appearance of the Parson, we shall, of course, categorically deny
—unless it be that some future events prove us in error.

## XII

### In Which Amelia and Mr. Adams
### Go from the Glendower to the Fire

Those who had built the *Glendower,* had built her well. When, two weeks
later, the British frigate *Flame* overtook her, she was not only afloat, but
shipping so little water that four hours on the pumps each morning kept
her perfectly sea-worthy. Our friends, too, had survived better than had
been hoped, for, aside from being hungry, thirsty, wind-burnt, cold and
tired, they had suffered scarcely at all from their adventure.

The Captain of the *Flame,* whose name was Dashforth, very kindly
offered to take off all aboard the tattered brig, but Rising and Boggins
refused, saying they believed that, with the two remaining crewmen, they
could bring her safely into port. Yet both these gentlemen, arguing they
should save some weeks of travel, urged Adams and Amelia to make the
transfer.

Accordingly, as the *Flame*'s boat off-loaded its gift of supplies for the
*Glendower,* Amelia and her friend stood at the railing to say their good-
byes. Mr. Adams first lowered down the small trunk which carried the few

of their possessions (including, thankfully, Amelia's remaining cash) which the storm had not swept overboard. He next turned to second Amelia's farewell with his own, especially to the Captain.

During the *Glendower*'s two drifting weeks, a curiously strong friendship had grown between these two gentlemen, probably upon the ancient principle that opposites attract. Now Mr. Adams (who was impetuous), having first shook the Captain's hand, next grabbed him by the shoulders and kissed him upon the cheek, a gesture which the Captain took with a good forbearance, even saying that, "he would be sorry if they never met again."

Indeed, Reader, I believe their acquaintance had done them both good, for Captain Rising had gained a respect for education, and Mr. Adams had learned that the stars are not writ in *Latin*.

That night, while the stars (if any) shone outside, Captain Dashforth held in his cabin a dinner party, to celebrate his own birthday and to welcome his new guests. The Captain (who, indeed, was one of the most daring officers in the British Navy, tho' he had the complexion of unbaked white-bread, and a manner as retiring as the meekest country curate) estimated for them that the *Flame* would not reach her destination, which was Charleston, South Carolina, for another three weeks at the earliest, "tho' if the winds continue to oppose us, the end of February would, I fear, not be unreasonable."

In fact, the winds so continued to oppose the *Flame*, that Captain Dashforth, had he been of a heathen persuasion, would very likely have tossed our friends neatly overboard, as persons unpopular with one sea-god or another.

Instead, the gallant Captain became almost Amelia's greatest comfort during these long days of contrary winds. Amelia now had no other occupation than to pace the deck in endless recalculation of her schedule, with results daily more distressing; but the Captain regularly informed her of their progress, to make her efforts, if not more pleasing, at least more precise—a service Mr. Adams, to his noticeable chagrin, was unable to supply.

Our friends had passed Christmas and New Year drifting with the wrecked *Glendower;* now they lost above another month aboard the half-becalmed *Flame*, in better comfort, but no greater peace of mind—for time was moving much faster than the ship.

At last, one lightly-clouded afternoon in mid-February, as Amelia stood unhappily upon the quarter-deck, Captain Dashforth approached to say, with a smile, "You are, I think, a little too gloomy; for the winds, as you can see by the sails, are changing. We shall reach South Carolina within ten days. From there, you may easily make Annapolis before the first of March; and to be home from there within seven weeks, will be simple, since those very winds which have delayed us, will speed your journey then, and you may reasonably expect to reach the courtroom well before the 17th of April."

To say that Amelia heard this with delight would be excessive; yet at least the compass of her feelings turned towards hope. She felt able now to contemplate her prospects without any inclination to blasphemy, and she thanked the Captain warmly for his help.

So far as the Captain spoke of the sea, he was a very good prophet indeed, for on the morning of the 25th of February, Amelia went on deck to find the ship so near to Charleston harbour that the buildings ashore were individually visible. The day felt, in comparison with any winter's day in England, extremely warm, and she began to think the loss of most of her clothing during the storm would prove but a minor disability.

Mr. Adams now joined her, to observe the scene with considerable joy. Very swiftly, however, a forbidding sense of their task overcame him, and he said quietly, "Indeed, Amelia, we shall have our work well laid before us."

"Are you worried?"

"In faith, only a little; for when I consider how far we have come, and how thoroughly Providence hath protected us, I believe most strongly we shall prevail. Above all, I—am happy we have each other for support. Yet I see the Captain likes you very well; and he is an honourable man. If you should—prefer to remain here with him, I would be quite—willing to continue the journey alone."

"Indeed, Mr. Adams," replied Amelia, not so angry as she might have been, "you have acquired the habit of talking less foolishly upon some matters, but more foolishly upon others."

The Parson now found the waters extremely deep, yet paddled on as best he could, saying, "We have had some very considerable arguments upon a woman's place in such travels as these; and I should like you to know I was wrong."

Smiling, Amelia answered that she had known it a good while, but she was glad to hear him say it. "And yet, Mr. Adams, we have not yet come far enough to worry about sharing the credit."

*Flame* now dropping her anchor in Charleston harbour, Captain Dashforth appeared to invite them to stay with him at Government House.

They left Charleston by the first available ship, two days later, and arrived in Annapolis about noon on the 28th of February. Mrs. Pilloe, the generous wife of a wealthy planter, had provided Amelia with hat, gloves and coat, as well as several elegant dresses originally ordered from London for a daughter of hers, who happened to be exactly Amelia's size.

Miss Jones, therefore, made a very genteel appearance as she and Mr. Adams traveled by coach from the Annapolis, landing at the Grey Falcon, an inn not three doors from the Compass. There they bespoke a supper, and sat to compose a note.

"Secrecy," said Amelia, "may prove of some use. My father, if in trouble, may need allies known to himself, but not his enemies. Therefore, let us write to him under some name—Amelia Robb, perhaps—which shall be obvious enough to him, but a mystery to the Suffleys, should they intercept it."

Mr. Adams consenting to this small deception, Amelia took her quill in one hand (while still keeping her soup-spoon in the other), and composed a short letter, asking her father to join them as soon as possible. This she handed to Mrs. Party, her landlady, who (as she had previously been extremely friendly) greatly surprised her by frowning and saying angrily, "La, ma'am, I had not thought so charming a lady would consort with England. I am sorry to know it. Well, my son shall carry it for you, if he must, for a shilling."

It was not until they had seen this note dispatched, that Adams and Amelia began to exult, and to think their trials ended. Now they raised their glasses to bright *Victory,* and congratulated each other cheerfully upon what they supposed would be the happy ending of their mission, when Tom himself should momentarily stroll through the door.

Alas, they had barely ended their meal, when Mrs. Party's boy returned with the note in hand, to say, "he was very sorry, but the butler at the Mansion had told him Mr. Jones had left the colony many weeks ago."

At this, Amelia and her friend started from their chairs, exchanged looks of complete dismay, and both declared at once they must speak with the Suffleys, even if—as Will Stumpling had hinted—Lady Suffley was in league with Mr. Sinamore and the others. Finding the streets quite passable, they walked, and in about twenty minutes, reached the soldiers guarding the Suffley home.

Being civil and well-drest persons, they were passed through to the door, where, having explained their intentions, they were diverted to the library. Above half an hour then passed before they were shown into the drawing-room, to find, seated upon a small sofa beside a broad window, Lady Suffley.

Reader, I would not have thee think Lady Suffley one of those empty-headed aristocrats who keep honest suitors waiting solely to prove their own importance. In fact, she had been consistently busy, first in fuming and raging at the news of Amelia's arrival, then in breaking two or three china soldiers against the wall, and lastly in sending her butler to fetch Lieutenant Brawly, a powerful and ill-tempered gentleman who had lately replaced Mr. Jones in her recreations. Then she had taken two or three deep breaths, rubbed her hands along her cheeks and smoothed her hair, before, with a smile, sending for our friends, to whom she spoke as you shall see in our next chapter.

# XIII

*Showing What Interesting
Alternatives There Are to the Truth,
and Containing a Promising Change
in the Friendship of Adams and
Amelia*

It is a fact well known to physicians, that man is the only creature able to lie standing up. I myself have noticed how certain well-schooled persons may even lie before they speak, by smiling when they are angry, or shaking hands when they would rather fetch you a fleck upon the ear. Since, however, ours is an historical, and not a medical, work, such observations are very likely off the mark.

Lady Suffley, therefore, now rose as gracefully as a bubble from her seat, and came to receive our two friends, saying, "You, my dear, must be Amelia. Your father spoke of you often, very often. And you, sir, must be Mr. Adams. You are both very welcome."

Having eased them into chairs beside the sofa, she next assumed a look of utmost tenderness and pity, and said quietly to Amelia:

"Alas, my dear, I am sorry to be obliged to bring you such unhappy news; and you may believe that I myself have not had a moment's peace since learning of it."

"Why, madam," asks Amelia in alarm, "whatever may you mean?"

"Indeed, miss, you must be resolute, you must be brave; for your father and one of our officers departed two months ago to inspect fortifications upon the Western frontier and to attend a conference in Massachusetts; and we learned two weeks later that, somewhere near the border, they were ambushed, either by Indians, or by Sons of Liberty, so disguised; and, in short, you are now, dear miss, an orphan."

These words she accompanied with so sad a tone that Amelia no sooner heard them, than she burst into tears, while Mr. Adams, falling back in his chair, began trying to pull his hair out by its roots.

Observing this grief, Lady Suffley immediately rang for her maid, whom she ordered to run and fetch a strong cordial. This the maid, whose name was Louisa, did hastily; and on her return with the tray and glasses, she whispered discreetly to her Ladyship that Lieutenant Brawley had arrived, and awaited her in the library.

Lady Suffley made no reply to this information, but, after distributing the cordials to her guests, she said very softly that she would leave them a while to their thoughts, and, so saying, left the room.

This Louisa happened to be a tender-hearted young woman, whose natural sympathy was heightened by knowing (for gossip races among the members of such a household) who Amelia was. Accordingly, as soon as she saw Miss Jones growing calmer, she begged to know the cause of her unhappiness.

"Alas, girl," replies Amelia, "the hardest news that ever was. My poor, foolish father is dead, and his family ruined."

At this, the young woman stared with something mixing horror and dismay, then, clutching at her breast, asked, "Oh, ma'am, when can such tragic news have come? We have heard none of it."

"Why, miss, my father died nearly six weeks ago," replied Amelia.

Louisa then dropt her hands and said with amazement, "Oh, ma'am,

I believe you are the victim of a jest; either that, or we all are; for Roger of the kitchen received this week a letter from your father, written to thank us all for our kindness (tho' rather, we should have thanked your father), and saying that Major Principes had suffered a minor accident, but that they still expected to reach Boston by the 1st or 2nd. This letter, which was carried by a Virginia woodsman, was written not two weeks ago. You may see it if you wish."

Amelia and Mr. Adams were about equally quick in understanding this. Mr. Adams now set down his cordial glass; Amelia drained hers. Louisa said she prayed she had said nothing wrong.

A moment later, Lady Suffley returned, surprised, no doubt, to discover that her young guests had composed themselves so well.

Amelia asked, "Would it be possible, my lady, to see this letter concerning my dear father's death? 'Twould be a great comfort."

*Almost* at once, Lady Suffley answered, "I—alas, Miss Jones, so great was my anguish, that I no sooner read the letter, than I plunged it into the fire, and watched it burn."

Miss Jones and her companion now exchanged glances perhaps a little too obviously, after which Amelia said, "My lady, I understand perfectly. Now, if you will forgive me, I believe I should like to return to my rooms and lie down."

Immediately, her Ladyship was all solicitousness. "My dear girl," she cried, "you must take my carriage; and, as I suppose you will soon be returning to England, I should like you to stay here as my guest until you may find a ship. It would be the least I could do, for the memory of your father."

"Madam," replied Amelia, "you are extremely kind; yet I believe I should prefer the unsocial comforts of private reflection and"—she here indicated Mr. Adams—"spiritual consolation."

"Indeed, my dear," said Lady Suffley, rising. "You are wise beyond your years."

Very soon, therefore, Mr. Adams and Amelia found themselves upon the street again. The air, too, had turned extremely cold, and perhaps for that reason, our friends walked as rapidly as they could, with their heads down. That was unlucky, for, had they been more careful, they would have seen two red-coats following stealthily behind them.

Mrs. Party had not forgiven Amelia her consorting with the Suffleys; for, though she was by nature (and profession) a sociable enough woman,

her convictions—for liberty, and against English rule—absolutely domi-
nated her character. She was, in short, a political quarrel seeking its
occasion; and so, while she *did* bring up the hot cider Amelia had requested, she did not bring it quickly, nor did she smile or chat as she set
it clattering upon the table. In fairness, however, I believe her natural
kindness, though wounded by Amelia's letter to Lady Suffley, had only
received its death-blow from the two hard-looking soldiers now seated in
her parlour.

Amelia herself had scant cause for cheer. "Well, Mr. Adams," she
began, as soon as Mrs. Party had gone, "Lady Suffley has kept my father
ignorant of his troubles—or he would never have undertaken that frontier
journey. We must leave at once for Boston. With great luck there, we may
still take ship for home in time. Ah, but if we miss him, we shall not even
have money left to sail for England."

Mr. Adams, who was miserable to see Amelia glum, offered all the
gentle words he could, but just then, I fear, lacked the courage to offer
more. A few minutes later, they descended the stairs, with Mr. Adams
carrying their baggage—for they had agreed to save all expense of porters
and servants.

The Parson was about to call to the kitchen for Mrs. Party when a huge
gentleman in scarlet and white (who was in fact Lieutenant Brawley, and
nearly the size of the Parson himself) stepped from the parlour into his
path, and said gruffly, "You are Mr. Adams?"

The Parson, though disliking the tone, admitted this.

"I must ask you and this woman to come with me."

"Where?" demanded Amelia, thrusting herself into the discourse.

"Lady Suffley wants you," replied the Lieutenant, with little warmth.

Amelia then said that they could not, "for, in fact, we are leaving
Annapolis directly."

Reader, great affairs often turn upon small matters. Had this bullying
lieutenant chosen to arrest Mr. Adams, I believe the Parson would have
gone peaceably—such was his regard for authority, whether civil or ecclesiastical. Yet Brawley preferred to grasp the wrist of Amelia, at which
the Parson, stepping forward, delivered to that part of his anatomy known
as his "guts" a punch of very considerable force, one which (if we may
judge at all by the Lieutenant's expression) was received with as much
distaste and pain as surprise.

Indeed, the Lieutenant now quit his grip upon Amelia, and, letting out
a roar more noisy than informative, immediately returned to Mr. Adams

a very considerable salute upon the chin.

The topic having been so handsomely raised, Mr. Adams began to formulate a reply upon his opponent's breast. Alas, the Parson's lack of training told upon him (tho', in truth, I believe he fought infinitely better than the Lieutenant would ever *preach*); for the sad truth was that he had entered the room carrying a small bag of Amelia's which, as it was hers, he was loath to drop; and so he now fought, as it were, with one hand behind his back.

So it happened that our poor Parson, despite landing some blows which covered his opponent's face with blood, still received two hits for every one he delivered, and was soon hard-pressed, with his back against the wall. Miss Jones now began pounding upon the Lieutenant's back (to scant effect); and, far more ominously, the Lieutenant's aide, and co-equal in size, whose name was Sergeant Grind, now stood to join the battle, in order to share the glory of victory.

Yet, Reader, if the bright goddess of battle had declared for the Army, she had reckoned without the plump goddess of cookery, for just at this moment the kitchen door (which had, in fact, been open an inch or so since the fighting began) flew wide, allowing Mrs. Party to race across the parlour, leap upon the table, and address the top of the Sergeant's head with the bottom of an iron skillet of above eight pounds' weight.

Lieutenant Brawley had been playing the drums pretty roundly upon the breast of our good Parson, when the clash of this gong made him lose his measure; or, in other words, he very foolishly looked behind him, at which Mr. Adams (who was a quick study in all things) very expeditiously kneed him in the groin, and then delivered such a serenade of knuckles to his jaw, as sent him spinning back into the parlour, to crash over the table, thereby knocking Mrs. Party to the floor, and bringing the battle of the Grey Falcon to its end.

Mrs. Party (a short, round, solidly-constructed woman) had almost at once rolled to her feet, and now declared (dropping her skillet accidentally upon the head of the Lieutenant), "Madam, I owe you an apology; for I understand now that you are no friend of British government. Am I right in thinking that letter my son carried was in the nature of a challenge?"

"Indeed, ma'am," answered Amelia, "I believe it was—and a reckless one, I see; for Lady Suffley plays very roughly. Yet now we must leave you. We must sail from Baltimore to reach my father in Boston as soon as possible."

"Why, miss," replied Mrs. Party (who had a quick intelligence, much aided by experience in such problems), "you will be arrested if you try to board a ship in Baltimore; and you will never reach even Baltimore without a guide. If you will wait here, I will fetch someone from the Compass to lead you. Why, miss," she concluded, "I am glad I misjudged you; for you and the gentleman are much too nice to be damned, wretched Tories." And before Amelia could answer, she had gone out the front door.

Amelia, after the violent shock of the battle and the earlier false news about her father, now began to think how few days remained 'til Tom must be in England. Sighing, she said, "Alas, Mr. Adams, I almost fear we are ordained to fail, for who may gaze upon so bleak a scene as that" —she meant the view outside the window, which was of bare trees, blackening skies, and a faint snow beginning to fall—"and believe we are any of us meant for happiness in this world?"

Reader, the Mr. Adams of six months earlier would have, upon this provocation, unleashed a fusillade of scriptures, before counter-attacking with *Cato* and *Boethius*. I am very pleased to report, however, his *now* saying earnestly, "Indeed, dear Amelia, I am myself very frightened; yet we must remember that, as we are told nothing may be perfect in this fallen world of ours, it follows nothing may be perfectly bad. For all our difficulties—and I own they are daunting—I consider myself utterly reassured and compensated by being near to *you*."

This he swiftly followed with some actions well suited to his text; for (not to postpone our theme) he then took Amelia in his arms and kissed her, an action which, though many will condemn as overdue, was yet pretty well covered under the rubric "Better late than never."

Neither, may I say, was Mr. Adams's affection ill-received, as Amelia now responded to it, for many long moments, with considerable kind attention; at the end of which, tho' slightly flushed, they both looked very well pleased. Indeed, I have generally observed that such gestures are worth at least a hundred reams of good philosophy offered by one who stands away from us.

Whether this affection might have continued to any blameable length, we shall dismiss as speculation, admissible in no court. The return of Mrs. Party (whom, I fear, they had entirely forgotten) with her guide, soon obliged our startled friends to quit their activity and gather their belongings.

Amelia now asked, "How long, Mrs. Party, will it take us to reach Boston by land?"

"With good weather and no accidents, less than a week. Indeed, ma'am, I like you better and better, for there's no more patriotic city in America."

"Well, Mrs. Party," said Amelia, almost frantic with haste, "we will go, and thank you. You believe yourself safe here?"

"Why, ma'am, even these two are smarter than to provoke the ridicule of the whole Colony, by charging a lone woman with beating them senseless. In any case, I think the British Army shall soon have greater worries than me. Now, I beg you, go."

Amelia and Mr. Adams, recognizing sound counsel when they heard it, picked up their belongings and followed their guide out into the black night.

## XIV

### In Which Our Story Returns to London, to Disclose a Certain Letter

We must now, Reader, leave Amelia and Mr. Adams, and hasten to London to observe a situation at once distressing and promising; yet we shall not, from a tender regard for the inconvenience of our readers, dwell long upon the sadder aspects of the scene, tho' we understand that most persons are perfectly willing to observe misfortune, so long as they are not obliged to relieve it.

Mrs. James and Mrs. Limeslices had both sacrificed considerably to equip Amelia and Mr. Adams, and then steeled themselves to survive, indefinitely, and utterly alone, upon the little money they had left. Accordingly, they immediately removed themselves to the smallest, dingiest apartment imaginable, where, with scarcely a bushel of coal to warm them through the winter, they set to weathering, in darkness and hunger, the long months until spring—nor would their caution allow them to correspond with any in Somersetshire, or their pride, to accept help from Dr. Johnson.

When Mrs. James and her friend had endured above two months of this, and the English winter had grown to its gloomiest at the end of January (for the weather had never been colder or drearier, and the absence of news hung upon them, as the ice hung upon the lintels of the door-ways), the post brought Mrs. James a most curious large envelope, containing another, smaller envelope, and, upon the most expensive sort of paper, an unsealed note reading:

> Dear Mother,
>     Our late unhappy meeting drove from my memory the enclosed letter from father to you. What it may contain, I cannot guess; nor do I understand why he sent it to me first, unless some last illness had disordered his senses. I do not suppose it very important, but only my usual lightness of head kept me from forwarding it to you sooner.
>
> Regretfully,<br>Charles James, Esq.
>
> P.S.: I know that, if the enclosed should represent any considerable legacy, you will not hesitate to take pity upon your poor son.

Mrs. James had in fact long before concluded that her poor son's brains were such that, should he ever suffer head injury, only a carpenter might heal it. She therefore, with a sigh, forgot her son's letter, and opened her husband's.

This, dated three days before Dr. James's death, contained (besides some sentiments too personal to be repeated here) a brief paragraph stating that he believed some terrible conspiracy was afoot, and that he now sent her his final effort both to provide for her, and to honour his obligation to Tom Jones.

After waiting for her eyes to clear, Mrs. James unfolded the last document, a piece of heavy parchment, covered with frightening Gothic lettering, beginning:

# Codicil

> Know all men by these presents that I, Richard James, physician of Meadowlands, Somersetshire, being of sound mind and body, do hereby amend and revise my last will and testament.

There followed perhaps four hundred words of ever-denser legal prose, full of "Statutes of King Henry" this, and "II George, 19, plac. 8"

---

that. Mrs. James, tho' overwhelmed by these details, understood perfectly their essence: that her husband (from beyond the grave, as it seemed) had appointed her *his successor to the trusteeship of the estate of Mr. Thomas Jones of Paradise Hall.*

The emotions inspired by sudden shifts of fortune are, I have found, full as strong as those inspired by sermons, philosophies, and even well-written histories. If, therefore, Mrs. James now failed to leap into the air, or otherwise dramatically to signify her satisfaction, it is only because of a detail we have neglected to mention; namely, that her age, plus loneliness, hunger and fear, combined with a severe cold, had destroyed her health. We have already noted that Mrs. James was a tall, thin woman; but her recent hunger had reduced her to almost a ghostly, translucent relic of herself. She was, in fact, even now reading the letter in her bed, covered with all the blankets the poor apartment afforded, topped with her worn lace cap, and attended by Mrs. Limeslices.

Accordingly, she now said faintly, "My dear Limeslices, we have had remarkable news," and weakly extended towards her friend the copy of the codicil.

Mrs. Limeslices read this with a growing excitement we cannot easily explain, unless it stemmed perhaps from a reverence for the written word perfectly natural in the daughter of a clergyman.

"Why, ma'am," says she, shaking a clenched fist even as she reads, "here we have our way of hitting back. I know not whether the forms be entirely legal—we shall have to ask Dr. Johnson about that—but at least we shall put a memorable fright into the villains of Hanover Square. We must put it to them at once."

Mrs. James, who had meanwhile grown uncertain, only replied, "Alas, Mrs. Limeslices, my late husband was a good man, but how could he possibly have out-witted the Lawyer?"

"La, ma'am," answered the old maid, not at all deterred, "why may a woman not control an estate, if her husband chooseth? Or even," she added as an after-thought, "if he chooseth not—in a *civilized* country."

"Indeed, Limeslices," said Mrs. James, "I now recall that even Mr. Sinamore many times accepted my signature upon estate documents, when my poor husband was too busy, or too weary, to complete them."

"Why, ma'am," replied Limeslices, every minute more hopeful, "that's precedent, is it not? They have already accepted a woman's signature as valid; what objection may they make now?"

Mrs. James, after considering this a long moment, nodded and attempted to rise; but falling back, said weakly, "Dear Limeslices, I suppose you are determined to act upon this at once. I am grateful; yet I beg you only to speak with Dr. Johnson. Nothing would be more foolish than for you and I to confront Hacksem and Mr. Sinamore."

"Why, ma'am," replied Mrs. Limeslices, already reaching into the closet for her coat and hat, "I shall do, I assure you, nothing I consider unwise."

For the next half-hour of that late, grey afternoon, Mrs. Limeslices walked unassisted through the London streets, while hail-stones the size of large peas, driven upon a howling wind, slapped into her face, and stung her wrinkled skin a shiny red. When she reached the door of the Doctor's home, she was half frozen and entirely exhausted.

"Well, Madam," said the Doctor, once he had served her sherry, "I may guess from the look upon your face that you have some fortunate news to convey."

"Indeed, sir," answered she, "I believe I have, but it may be your opinion will differ from mine." So saying, she handed him the codicil to the will, which he had no sooner perused, than he clapped his hands together and declared, "Why, madam, here is just the opportunity we have awaited. Nothing could give us a better chance of delaying those rascals."

"Do you believe, then, the courts will uphold it?"

The Doctor, who was, I fear, no great friend to the authority of women, answered in measured tones, "That shall depend upon whether Dr. James is ruled to have been a steward (which is merely a job, having no rights of succession), or a *trustee,* which is a legal role *requiring* him to appoint his own successor—particularly where he believes the estate to be in danger.

"Any decision will likely require some months to reach; and so will extend our deadline from a very desperate, to a very reasonable one. Our only task now is to see that we do not unmask our battery too soon; this letter, madam, must remain our entire secret."

Mrs. Limeslices (who had, I suspect, hoped for a more dramatic outcome) heard this discontentedly, then demanded:

"Are you urging us, sir, to leave those two villains—or those three, if they really are in league with some extra figure, as Mr. Stumpling saith

—in control of Paradise Hall as long as another two or three months, despoiling it as they see fit, and perhaps mortgaging it beyond recovery?"

"I do not pretend it will be easy," replied the Doctor. "Nor is it ever easy, madam, to await the precise moment for a counter-attack—yet that is what makes an army succeed."

"Well, sir, what is difficult for an army, is impossible for me. As the world habitually asserts that a woman is too unstable for command, I believe I shall prove it correct, and confront those rascals—however many there may be—directly. We have been given an advantage over them, and I propose to use it."

"Madam!" cried the Doctor, rising from his chair. "This is recklessness! You cannot imagine these gentlemen will oblige you by stepping aside?"

Mrs. Limeslices said nothing; the Doctor, hugely alarmed, continued imploringly, "Reason carefully, madam; you believe them dangerous. Will you not force them into something violent?"

Mrs. Limeslices answered calmly, "For that, I believe I may prepare myself, if you will be so kind as to accept custody of the codicil, and then to give me a note in your own hand attesting to your having seen it. As soon thereafter as possible, I would urge you to get the document into some still-safer, and secret, hands."

The Doctor made one last endeavour. "Are you absolutely certain, madam, that there is no problem which may not be relieved by a temporary loan of funds?"

"I thank you—but, no."

The Doctor received this with a look of disappointment, but little surprise. After a moment, he nodded, and, taking up pen and paper, produced the desired statement.

"I have often wondered, madam," said he, handing over the note, "that those of our young gentlemen who yearn for adventure do not simply give up their estates and move into some wretched City apartment, since poverty, I believe, hath killed more persons than all the tigers that ever were.

"Well, Mrs. Limeslices, no one will ever doubt your courage. I hope that you will use this discreetly; but as that is probably a vain hope, I will add a second one; namely, that you succeed in whatever wild thing you attempt."

Mrs. Limeslices accepted the note with thanks, heartily shook the

Doctor's hand, and a moment later was upon her way again.

As the world is universal in declaring that what is bold, decisive and heroic in man, is idle, vain and reckless in a woman, we shall not trouble to join the chorus of condemnation which, assuredly, is now arising concerning Mrs. Limeslices's initiative. We shall therefore simply accompany her, in righteous silence, on her venture of the next chapter.

# XV

### Describing Mrs. Limeslices's Adventures, with a Form of Hospitality in Other Than the True English Style

The afternoon had declined nearly to evening, and only faint remnants of icy mist still hung in the dark-blue air, when Mrs. Limeslices, with a disregard for her own well-being we scarcely know how to condemn, began her second walk, towards the house in Hanover Square which still, in her mind at least, belonged to Tom Jones. Safely within her coat she concealed the letter from Dr. Johnson, which she clasped to her breast as she hugged her arms about her for protection.

Mrs. Limeslices had often before visited the house in the Square, and had always associated it with the highest measures of charm and refined gaiety, and especially with light and music. This bleak evening the building was nearly black, so dismal, indeed, that she almost turned away. At length, however, fortifying herself by several gulped breaths, she knocked at the door.

The surly doorman at first refused her admittance, but finally showed her into a tiny room directly off the hallway, where she found, seated before a tea-service and wrapped in a woolen shawl, Mrs. Guerdion, who immediately sprang from her chair, and said in alarm:

"I fear, my dear Limeslices, you have picked the worst possible night for a visit. For days, the fiends upstairs have hounded us to prepare for a gentleman's visit. A pair of warlocks—if one believes such fulsome nonsense—could not take more frightened delight in a meeting with the devil. His coach is to arrive from the far North momentarily. I assure you I have grown heartily to hate the thought of him, and have instructed the servants that I am sick this evening, and will not attend the door."

Mrs. Limeslices instantly guessed this northern visitor to be the villain described by Mr. Stumpling. Her knees began knocking together; yet she stood her ground. Wishing to encourage Mrs. Guerdion (who, despite her protests, had several times proved a friend), she replied, "If, madam, your visitor is—as I suspect—part of the conspiracy which displaced the true rulers of this home, he may find something here to gall him; for these villains' claims are now, I think, as gossamer as spiders' webs." And so saying, she held forth the Doctor's note.

"Well, madam," admitted Mrs. Guerdion, after a moment's reading, "it may be you will raise some excitement here yet this evening. I believe I shall be happy enough to spend the time here quietly by myself, yet I wish you all the success in the world; for as you know, there are many things we may wish to come about, tho' we dare not act to advance them."

Mrs. Guerdion next led the brave Mrs. Limeslices into a small parlour directly across the hall, and promised to fetch the two gentlemen for her. It was only natural that, as she waited in this room, formerly so cheerful but now cold and illuminated by only a pair of tapers, Mrs. Limeslices should tremble, and that she should two or three times consider whether she might yet get safely out the door.

When she had sat a short while mustering her courage, Mrs. Limeslices heard (for the small study was directly off the hallway, near the front door) another knock at the door, answered by one of the servants in most deferential tones, followed almost at once by footsteps and the voice of Mr. Sinamore purring, "My dear sir! How very good of you to oblige us . . ." and a few more lines of this ilk, finally fading down the hallway, towards the staircase and the finer upstairs rooms.

So it began to seem to Mrs. Limeslices that she had been entirely forgotten, when, five or six minutes later, the door opened, admitting Messrs. Sinamore and Hacksem Jones.

"Madam," said the Lawyer, glancing first at his companion, and then speaking with great smoothness, "you surprise and honour us. How may we assist you?"

"You may assist me, sir," declared Mrs. Limeslices, unwilling to be lulled, "by resigning without protest your stewardship of Paradise Hall; by breaking off whatever negotiations you may have begun with the gentleman upstairs to alienate the estate from its proper owner—and by accepting until his return, the authority of a woman whose signature you have often honoured on estate documents. I mean, Mrs. James."

"Why, madam," interjected Mr. Hacksem, sneering, "we long accepted the Doctor's habit of employing her signature upon documents—for who is to be more malleable to our purposes than such an old woman as she? Madam, we know you both too well . . . and it is idle to pretend an old *woman* will stand against us."

"Well, good young sir," answered Mrs. Limeslices, boldly throwing Dr. Johnson's note upon the desk, "malleate this, if you can."

Looking at once annoyed with his colleague, and bored with everything else, Lawyer Sinamore took the sheet from the desk, and glanced upon it with one raised eyebrow, one closed eye.

In a moment, however, this thick black eyebrow became the central cloud of a storm, which overspread the Lawyer's face until at last the thunder burst forth:

"Madam, you will push me too far! Whatever sort of foolish charade or fraud you imagine yourself to be undertaking, I warn you, madam, you will find yourself at the barrel-end of the law—I might almost say, 'the rope's end.' "

"Oh, Lawyer," answered Mrs. Limeslices cooly, "do not frighten me with the law; for that's my protection: the law will vindicate me, as soon as the matter may be tried—this spring will not be too soon for me."

"You, madam," replied Mr. Sinamore coldly, "have neither friends, money, nor energy—and the law, you know, does nothing on its own prompting. We, on the other hand, can afford to be generous—especially with *you* who has done nothing against us. Give us the codicil, and take whatever terms we offer."

"Why, sir," says Mrs. Limeslices, "you must not imagine I am so foolish as to have brought the original document; that, as the note declareth, is far away, and very safe: have no fear of that."

The Lawyer's heavy eyebrows now cast shadows like small horns upon his forehead. He raised his fist suddenly and angrily, then, with an effort, lowered it, all a-tremble. "Madam, you provoke me exceedingly. Still, you shall find me slow to anger. Now, I pray you, excuse me, while I consult with my colleague." His forehead having become very moist,

Mr. Sinamore wiped at it with a large handkerchief, and backed towards the door, to confer with Mr. Hacksem. A moment later, without further comment, they departed, and Mrs. Limeslices heard their footsteps ascending the stairs.

Perhaps two minutes passed before footsteps returned, now descending nearly at the run. These steps, however, stopped not at her room, but at that across the foyer. A new voice—vile, high-pitched and demanding —roared, "Madam, I will have that codicil!"

Mrs. Limeslices, terrified and curious, crept to open the door, and, peering across the gloomy foyer, discovered that a gentleman, presumably Mr. Sinamore's mysterious visitor, had, in a natural mistake, begun threatening Mrs. Guerdion, who still sat to her tea in the parlour opposite.

Reader, some gentlemen habitually enforce their will by brute strength; and tho' we may find little to recommend the ethics of this tactic, we do concede its occasional successes—providing, of course, that the person attempting it possess a sufficient quantity of brute strength. Alas, this stranger (tho' he had otherwise much of the brute about him) was a trifle lacking in vital strength—indeed, his black-cloaked body appeared so frail that, were it not for his voice, Mrs. Limeslices might easily have taken him for Mr. Hacksem Jones.

This spider-like creature cast himself upon the settee beside Mrs. Guerdion, and, after half a dozen sharp threats, began to reach toward that part of her person where he imagined the great document to be concealed.

Now, Reader, Mrs. Guerdion was a woman of some experience, who knew very well how to receive both the welcome, and the unwelcomed, advance. Accordingly, while crying some words which insulted his sense, morals and parentage all at once, she reached to the low table before them, and dumped the steaming contents of the tea urn onto her assailant's lap, after which she grabbed his wig, and tossed it entirely across the room, at which he, opening his mouth very wide, began roaring extremely loud, imploring the aid of Mr. Sinamore, as certain persons of better principles are supposed to implore the aid of the Deity.

It happened that this altercation exposed to Mrs. Limeslices the entire profile of the mysterious gentleman—a revelation of absolutely no use to her, but one which will permit us (as we are bound to present thee, Reader, with all information possible) to offer thee a fact likely to provide but scant cheer; for this financier from the North, this great spur to wickedness, was none other than—Reader, we are pained to admit it—our hero's own half-brother, and whole-nemesis, Mr. *Blifil!*

We are ashamed, Reader, not to have detected sooner the hand of this monster. And yet some villains, like the dragons of old sagas, surround themselves so thickly with smoke, and lie so deep within their caves, that one may no more anticipate them, than read the letters within a bottle of black ink: their plans, like the hidden words, must be allowed to spell themselves out.

Mrs. Limeslices was spared the shock of recognizing this worst of villains—whose deceptions had so nearly cost Tom first the affection of Squire Allworthy, and then his life upon a false charge of murder. She understood, however, that whoever he was, Mr. Sinamore would easily correct his misunderstanding, and that if she tarried, her life—to use the ordinary phrase—would not be worth a farthing. So, her heart beating wildly, she slipped the door closed, and retreated to the nearest window, which, she remembered, looked onto the small garden at the back of the house.

This she opened, even as Mr. Sinamore's boots began again pounding the stairway. Cold air swept over her; from the hall, Mr. Sinamore shouted, then the door flew open. She crawled out the window (the sill now quaking with the Lawyer's thudding strides), and let herself drop onto the shrubbery below.

Having scarcely three feet to fall (and that well cushioned), she was instantly upon her feet and running towards the front gate, while the Lawyer, his moon face stuck out the window, yelled after her that she would greatly regret what she had done.

In that manner, Reader, ended a battle having, it may be, little in common with those of the *Iliad* or the *Aeneid,* and yet still in their tradition of single combat by great champions. The final result of it, we shall, perhaps, be obliged to defer a while longer; yet I may tell thee very clearly that Mrs. Limeslices had made an impression not soon to be forgotten. Indeed, I suspect the appearance of the meek Limeslices bearing the (if I may speak so) poisoned codicil, had a sort of shock value not equalled since the Greeks entered Troy stuffed in a pony.

Indeed, so furious was the Lawyer that I believe he would have very willingly taken off after the poor maid, were it not for an unfortunate complication, which was that the rain had begun again, and he happened to be wearing a new coat of some 100 guineas' purchase, suitable for a Lord Mayor; and so it was that he chose to send his deputy, and, grabbing Mr.

Hacksem by the scruff of the neck, threw him out the window after Mrs. Limeslices, with orders to pursue.

We must now, alas, leave Mrs. Limeslices and Mrs. James, and return to America. It may be we shall have no further occasion to rejoin them until the very conclusion of our tale; but at least we are content to have assured our reader that the two ladies are untroubled by over-indulgence, and entirely free from what the youth of our nation universally declare the greatest of all afflictions; namely, *boredom*.

# BOOK
# THE SEVENTH

# I

## Showing What Part Politics May
## Play in Such a Book as This

We are now, Reader, like explorers who, having passed the last dot of civilization, must strike alone into the wilderness.

I refer not merely to natural dangers, for we who have survived ship-wrecks and robbers, may pretty confidently face bears and angry natives. Rather, we must now endure a sort of moral wilderness, that strange land of *revolution*.

I have heretofore said little of politics, of orators and ambassadors, congresses and committees; for, in truth, studying politics resembles watching an egg hatch: you must stare a long time at a plain white shell before anything results, and then you are as likely to discover a vulture as an eagle. Indeed, I have generally considered politics to lie outside our mandate, which is to show thee human beings trying to live in the world as it is, and not the entirely different matter of human beings trying to make another world. We are eager to know what it is which makes a good squire, and not what makes a good squire obsolete.

And yet, an almost magnetic influence appears to be drawing our characters to Boston, which (as Mrs. Party hath already observed) is the most political city in America. As it is the nature of true histories to shirk no issue shaping the lives of their characters, we shall, therefore, ourselves take up musket and bayonet, and follow the Boston road, let come what politics there may.

Reader, if politicians were content to govern only each other, and leave the rest of us in peace, the world, I suspect, would get along very much better. Yet politicians, like unwelcome guests, tend to force their interests upon us, whether we will or not—and so, I suppose, we must be ready to throw them out when they grow obnoxious; or (as this is too easy an image), citizens must always reserve the right to banish the corrupt and oppressive, and to unmake those who would make them less than human.

Rebellion, when rules are corrupt and rulers deaf to correction, may therefore be defensible, but it remains a dreadful business; for, besides the innocents who suffer, rebel leaders, like the victims of a robbery, are usually in the greatest danger from the persons they are enriching. Even the noblest rebels too often end like Marcus Brutus: killed, with thanks, by their countrymen. From top to bottom, therefore, we must foresee only danger for our friends.

Would that our friends were bound for Switzerland! Yet a history must display its characters as neither wiser nor more prescient than they are in life: ours have *carte blanche* to approach their own destruction—at the run, if they wish. We may only hope that they fight (if they must) upon the right side, and that, if they fight, they may survive—for (moralists notwithstanding), I have never noticed a funeral much cheered by the recollection that a *good* soul has been lost.

Alas, Reader, politics are matters of the highest importance—perhaps even higher than comedy. Yet they drip with danger, violence, chaos. Our friends are racing towards a city stuffed with politics—armed, blockaded, and soon to be at war from politics. Shall we, like naturalists, cooly mount and study the contending parties? Are we to choose sides randomly, or to wait until Fortune hath made her choice, and then (like true politicians) second it with our acclaim and profound reconsiderations? Reader, we have now half our characters dancing upon a powder-keg, and the rest rushing to join them. What are we to do?

What indeed—except perhaps to pray they all be done dancing before the keg explodes.

---

## II

### Our Hero Arrives in Boston in a Condition Very Sad

---

On the 15th of March, travelling alone, Tom reached Boston, that city where, in the estimation of Lady Suffley, Captain Whipsblood was to decide Tom's fate. Writing from Pennsylvania to his friends at the Suffley mansion, he had somewhat understated his difficulties, for the "minor accident" he reported had in fact left Major Principes with a concussion and a broken leg.

Tom, with considerable courage, first transported the Major some twenty miles through hazardous territory to the nearest settlement, and then stayed with him for as long as his injuries seemed threatening. During these five weeks, they spoke most often of Miss Macintosh, about whose claims Tom waxed so eloquent that the Major at last resolved to propose to her before leaving America, "Tho'," he concluded, shaking his head, "it doth seem a pity to have my friends say, 'Poor Principes; he was nearly home safe, when a Yankee got him as he was boarding the boat.'" The resolution itself Tom heartily endorsed, both from its morality, and (I suppose) from his own respect for American ladies.

When the Major was at last out of danger, he and Tom had a very warm parting, and Tom, racing to make up the lost days, continued North. By travelling every daylight hour, and collecting his notes every evening, he did in fact recover all but two weeks of the delay, tho' the report he finally produced (which argued the complete insufficiency of English forts to police so large an area as America) would likely have produced only a wave of apoplexies in London—had it ever been delivered.

In fact, his last morning in New York, while waiting to be ferried to the Boston boat, Tom had seen a girl of about six slide from the dock into the water, and had (first tossing his *porto-folio* heedlessly away) dived in to rescue her. For his kindness, he had received the cheers of all about him, the gratitude of the girl's parents (the girl herself being too occupied in shivering and turning blue), and not many hours later, a sore throat and gasping cough, accompanied by chills and a fever extremely high.

Reader, we have followed a very ancient literary tradition in once or twice hinting that Mr. Jones burned with love for the American lady; but I fear that burning (noble as it was) could not much compare with the fevers which had then begun to consume him in earnest. The entire trip from New York to Boston, he had sat sweating in the freezing cabin, clenching his teeth and fighting off delirium.

The quarantine of Boston Harbour, begun in response to that famous Tea Party, was now entering its second year, with the British Navy prohibiting all cargoes and all persons not connected with the government. Jones, of course, was among the acceptable few; and so, after having his papers examined by a young lieutenant from a boarding party, had been allowed to land a short distance from Faneuil Hall. Finding that famous meeting-place locked and guarded, he hurried through the Quincy Wharf district, a region now dismal, half-deserted and troop-laden on account of the blockade.

How Jones kept his feet during that long day, I am unwilling to guess; yet he did, for he not only walked the length of the waterfront (with the winds off the water redoubling his misery), but visited half a dozen merchants' taverns. At each one, he asked the same question—where he might find Mrs. Angela Wilson—but at last, on reaching the Golden Crown, he exhausted his strength, and allowed some concerned gentlemen (who saw by his manner and clothing that he was respectable) to help him to an inn not far away, and to send for the physician.

This physician, whose name was MacFee, hearing the case was desperate and the patient likely rich, came at the run, and indeed left his hat upon the stairs, so quickly did he climb them. He then examined Jones with lightning speed, before asserting categorically that the case was nearly hopeless, and that, except for the patient's native strength and spirit, he saw absolutely no grounds for encouragement.

Reader, I have sometimes had occasion to mistrust the direst predictions of the medical profession; yet I believe in this case, Dr. MacFee was correct, for Jones, after the examination was completed, only begged the gentlemen who had helped him, "that they tell Mrs. Wilson where he was," before falling back onto his pillow, and into a delirium which continued four days.

So might our tale have ended (and, indeed, would have, were this one of those absurd and gloomy German fables). As, however, Mr. Jones was a sturdy Englishman, he fought very hard for those four days and nights, and at the end, broke the fever's back—tho' at such a cost to his own energies, that he awoke scarcely able to move, as well as very sore from his exertions.

Even heroic Mr. Jones might have been a little inclined to moan, or to curse his fate, were it not that he opened his eyes (when he finally did, after all that struggle) upon the one sight in all the world he most desired. I mean, of course, the face of Mrs. Wilson, who was then sitting quite close to him, as, in fact, she had been (so often as her work allowed) over most of the past two days. After Jones's staggering tour of Boston, his quest for her had been a secret about as well kept as the direction of the sunrise;

and it had not been long before, returning from a trip to Salem, she had been given the message.

We have heretofore, Reader, said very little concerning the mind of Mrs. Wilson. Yet no figure of our story is more complex, or more difficult to explain.

I have always considered human beings too rigidly bound to a creed as resembling travellers speeding through strange country with their noses (from arrogance or fear) stuck in a guide-book. Such persons often make excellent time upon the road, but never hear or see anything of value—and are, moreover, very likely to run down the innocent, or even to careen into a tree or over a cliff. Such persons, in short, are exactly as great a menace to themselves as to others.

This, I believe, was nearly the case of Mrs. Wilson. Confronted with a choice between Mr. Jones and her business in Marseilles, she had chosen to ignore her own natural wishes, in favor of what was politically correct.

Yet the impression made by Jones that evening in Marseilles had not only been strong, but had grown stronger upon reconsideration; so that now she had, I believe, chosen to close up her political map long enough to consider her own feelings. In simpler words, she had now concluded she must listen to her heart, or be deaf forever, and so had grabbed her cape and run out the door.

Now she leaned close to our hero and whispered, "Tom? How do you feel?"

Our hero, his eyes only slowly bringing him back into this world, now wet his lips and answered slowly and faintly, "Alas, ma'am, I fear I am a dead man."

"Oh, do not say it!" cried Mrs. Wilson.

"Oh, aye, ma'am, it must be so—for I see an angel has come to get me," said our hero, sinking (with what may have been a smile) back upon his pillow.

This brief exchange (besides proving that, in a good person, the sense of humour is very durable) marked the turning-point in Tom's illness. His recovery was thenceforth so notable that within two days, Dr. MacFee (who was not a bad soul, for all that he admired wealth) declared himself to have witnessed a miracle, at which, Tom and Mrs. Wilson smiled upon each other very fondly.

Alas, it was but an hour later that the landlady's son, a sprightly lad of about sixteen, carried up to Tom a note, which, he said pleasantly, had been given him by a liveried servant not fifteen minutes earlier. Mr. Jones dismissed the boy with a shilling, and, with a look of apology to his friend, now read these black words:

> 21 March 1775
> Boston
>
> Sir,
>
>     I know you have courage enough not to deny satisfaction to one who, as you must admit, has suffered injuries which no charity may forgive, nor any apology amend. I shall therefore call upon you tomorrow morning at 5:30 A.M., in company with my second, and a gentleman capable of certifying the outcome of our meeting. Your choice of sabre, single rapier or pistol will be acceptable to
> > Your obliged servant,
> > Capt. Desmond Whipsblood
>
> You will, of course, keep all of this in strictest secret.

Reader, I am happy to say that our hero's complexion grew not one shade paler as he read this—tho' whether from courage, or because his recent illness had already left him ghost white, I cannot say. Mrs. Wilson, however, had no sooner been handed the note, than she began to tremble very violently, before saying, "Alas, sir, you must come away with me at once."

Jones looked back in amazement. "Why, ma'am," says he, "surely you do not expect a gentleman to run from a challenge?"

"A gentleman may run from a murderer," replied Mrs. Wilson, "and I promise you, the Captain has no interest but to kill you as conveniently as he can. And to kill me, as well."

"Then, madam, I have twice the reason to wish to face him."

"Aiee, sir, thou art a fool indeed! This is no private duel; the Captain is an agent of the British government, and hath more resources than you can imagine. If he dislikes his prospects in a duel, he will have you murdered in an alley—or launch some other scheme to take both of us together. Do not argue with me, sirrah; I have known him far longer than you."

Alas, Reader, our hero, having had his vanity prick'd by this vague intimation of Mrs. Wilson's past, now spoke extremely foolishly:

"Indeed, madam," Tom said, "why exactly must I avoid this Captain?

And how precisely is it that you know him so intimately? And am I wrong, or are you now protecting him?"

Mrs. Wilson, who had risked much to visit Jones, could scarcely tolerate being accountable to him—particularly when his questions were so clearly mad.

"Look'ee, sir," said she, almost pleadingly, "I would not be here, if I did not—care for you. Have patience, and I shall clarify everything; but if you refuse to trust me, you must look out for yourself. One last time: will you come with me?"

"Madam, I cannot," answered our hero, very curtly—yet I think, very sadly.

"Well, then, I believe we have nothing more to say to one another," replied Mrs. Wilson, taking up her cloak from the bed, and standing.

Poor Jones watched her depart. She looked fixed in her purpose, and not eager to be recalled; yet, perhaps, had he spoken at once, she might have listened. As it was, she paused at the doorway, but had reached the stairs, and was beyond hearing, when he finally raised one hand, and cried softly, "Angela . . .!"

No beginning could have been more heart-rending, yet nothing followed; for immediately after, he fell back against his pillow and slept, a course of action very wise for one expected to fight for his life early the next morning.

---

# III

*Containing a Duel Very Bloody*

---

The cold night waned, and the pale sun, like a frightened child, peered out on frigid Boston.

Mr. Jones, having been wakened well before dawn by his landlady's son, now stood upon unsteady legs and tried to dress himself. Every motion oppressed him by its unfamiliarity, and he was once obliged, because of dizziness, to sit upon the bed. At length, looking by no means ill for a man who had been dead some weeks, he picked up the candle, and made his way down the dark stairs, just as the first light was appearing out-of-doors.

His landlady had very kindly prepared him a light repast, consisting of a roll, some tea, and his bill (this last, I suppose, included so that she might have something by which to remember him). He ate very slowly, his fright making swallowing difficult, and had in fact finished only a few mouthfuls when the door opened, admitting the grey morning light and the bleak Captain Whipsblood.

This gentleman, looking down at our hero (who, I am sorry to say, required both hands to hold his tea-cup steady), now said with a sneer that he was pleased to see Mr. Jones looking both fit and eager, "for an event I am sure we have both long sought."

Our hero answered that he was at the Captain's service.

"You have, I suppose," says the Captain, accidentally rattling his sword, "said farewell to those you value? Especially to the lovely Mrs. Wilson? I shall look forward to seeing her, later this morning." His voice much resembled a blade drawn across an oiled stone, being at once smooth, and grating.

The Captain stepped back a pace, and gestured for our hero to precede him. Jones, with a cough of exertion, stood.

Tom was now a faint print of himself; for, besides his weakness and natural fear, he knew in his heart the indefensible wickedness of dueling. Indeed, his constant prayer since waking had been (the fine language removed), "Oh, Lord, I go to do a thing very wrong. Please help me to do it very well, and then forgive me." Though this prayer (in all its variants) must certainly be among the commonest prayed, its beauty is not, perhaps, greatly enhanced thereby. Nor shall we defend him, except to observe that, in his own confused way, he believed himself to be protecting Mrs. Wilson.

Captain Whipsblood, his coat and breeches perfect upon a body very straight, his hair, moustache and boots all gleaming a spotless black, glared down upon our hero as he passed. So great was the contrast between these two, that Tom's landlady, falling to her knees before the Captain, begged him, "For Heaven's sake, do not kill this poor gentleman, heathen-fashion, in my parlour, but go outside, and shoot him neatly, like a Christian."

Mr. Jones, pausing a moment at the door, now rediscovered how lovely is even the bleakest morning, while we are alive to enjoy it. The crows sang, and the dirty snows glistened; and he felt surrounded by hints of the approaching spring—tho' at the end of the path waited the Captain's coach, black as any hearse. As he walked, with a pace slower than a Tyburn convict's, he heard the rhythmic crunch upon the snow of his own boots, echoed swiftly by those of the Captain.

The Captain's steps had, however, scarcely begun, when they were marred by a sound like two wooden blocks colliding. This clunk (which interrupted our hero's profound speculations upon mortality) was followed at once by the thudding of something heavy onto the snow beside the walk.

Turning, Jones discovered the Captain resting peacefully upon the snowy grass. Near him stood Mrs. Wilson, holding a pistol like a club, and looking extremely grim for one whose arrival had been so timely.

"Well, Mr. Jones," said she, staring past him, "we are even."

"Angela—" began our hero.

"Nay, sir, talk later. Can you run?"

"I can try."

"Well, look behind you, then follow me."

Glancing back, Tom saw an Army lieutenant, Whipsblood's second, vaulting the fence into the yard. Mrs. Wilson fired in his direction, and he dove for cover.

They hastened around the side of the inn, down a narrow brick-walled arbour-way to an alley, and through a maze of court-yards ending in a burial ground, across which a carriage waited. They ran past two rows of grave-stones; then Mrs. Wilson helped Tom aboard the carriage, and, seating herself beside him, cracked the whip above the horses' heads. The chariot lurched forward, rounded the corner upon two wheels, and was soon headed south-west, skirting the mouth of the Charles and leaving Boston far behind.

When they were safely in the country, Mrs. Wilson slowed the horses to a walk. The sun now shone in earnest, and the musical coursing of the freshets carried on an air scented with melting snow.

About eight-thirty, emboldened by the cheerful sight of geese flying north, Mr. Jones returned more rationally to a question he had the day before asked too angrily; namely, "What business it was that had made Mrs. Wilson an enemy of Captain Whipsblood?"

Mrs. Wilson tied the reins about the whip, and shifted to face Tom. "Why, sir, 'tis a reasonable question. We are nearing Roxbury, and if you will have patience 'til we reach my house there, I promise to explain."

Tom, very weary, said that he would wait, and that he thanked her for the rescue.

Mrs. Wilson answered that she was happy to have helped, and only regretted using the less lethal end of her pistol and not finally doing the Captain's business; for, "You may be sure, sir, we have not heard the last of him."

## IV

### Showing What Happened to Amelia and Adams in Boston

Mrs. Wilson's rescue of Mr. Jones had several noteworthy results.

One of these was negative. Captain Whipsblood, having been injured in the second tenderest part of his body, which was his vanity, not only declared publicly his intention to turn the city—nay, the colony—upside down in order to find his assailants, but told several of his fellow officers (in confidence) that Jones was wanted in Maryland for theft of government monies—a crime making him automatically an enemy of the Crown.

One effect was, however, luckier, since the whereabouts of Mr. Jones became of interest to a set of political persons who otherwise would likely have cared little about his existence; and this, in turn, was potentially useful for those of his family seeking him. . . .

That is to say, Miss Jones and (peripherally) Mr. Adams, who after a journey extremely slow, miserable and cold, reached Boston by horseback on the 23rd of March, or about as the story of the rescue was appearing in gazettes and news-papers being cried from every street-corner in the city.

Amelia immediately seized the first copy she saw, to learn with considerable astonishment that her father was being praised (and in some circles, d——ned), as a rebel of the extremest militancy. She read this to Mr. Adams as they walked (for they had upon their arrival taken rooms at an inn, and left their horses at its stable); and he, on hearing it, blessed himself audibly, and then begged her to read it again.

Most daunting to our friends was the knowledge that, instead of sim-ply calling for Tom at Army headquarters, they must now avoid all governmental contact, and enquire secretly for one who might well have departed the colony. For Amelia, this seem'd almost a fatal complication; yet, since Captain Dashforth had told her Atlantic crossings had been made (once or twice) in as few as twenty-one days, she persisted in hoping, and declared they must begin their search in the taverns near Mrs. Strutt's Inn, which had been named by the news-paper.

Boston in those days had fallen to a state scarcely to be believed. The blockade having ruined trade, most docks were empty, most shops locked and boarded, and most streets, where not deserted, points of confrontation between red-coats and angry, jobless men and women. Not a sermon, speech or news-paper article ignored the question of independence; and citizens wishing to argue what they had heard or read, met in the taverns, which alone remained centers of angry prosperity.

Those taverns near Mrs. Strutt's were, as we have earlier noted, popu-lated by merchants and sea-captains, all inclining to the cause of *Liberty*, and many deeply bound in political conspiracy. Amelia and Adams there-fore found themselves ignored—and in such a way as to suggest that their enquiries, if pressed, would lead to violence.

There exists, however, a momentum in our actions, which makes us loath to abandon them, even if they prove useless, until some clearly better way shall present itself. Amelia and Adams, having spent their morning being rudely treated at half a dozen taverns, finally paused for a lunch (scanty but costly), and then betook themselves to yet another smokey, beer-scented tavern. This was, in fact, the Golden Crown, at which Mr. Jones had some days earlier collapsed.

The reception here was no kindlier than elsewhere, but later, as our friends stood in the street trying to decide their next tactic, they were approached by a gentleman who had followed them out of doors. This gentleman appeared about thirty years of age. He was short, plump, freckled and red-headed, and dressed like the greatest fop and coxcomb in Boston; for, along with a silk shirt lavishly frilled, he wore dark-blue velvet coat and breeches, and a burgundy waist-coat heavily chased with gold. Stuttering very badly, he asked whether he had the pleasure of addressing, "M-m-m-miss Ahahahah-melia Jone."

Amelia had recently been disappointed in another well-drest young gentleman, and now only reluctantly answered, "Yes."

The young gentleman, whose stutter (though we shall no longer reproduce it) was in fact permanent, and not a result of tension, resumed:

"My name is Bateson. My father was one of those who carried *your* father to Mrs. Strutt's inn. Did I understand correctly that you are now trying to locate him?"

Mr. Adams, tossing himself into the conversation, now eagerly declared, "Indeed, sir, we must do so, at once!"

Amelia, however, amended this cautiously, saying, "My friend is correct; our need is urgent. Yet, may I ask why you choose to help us, when none of your associates will?"

"Madam, that is something of a tale, and the street is cold. A chop-house lies at the end of the street, where we may be comfortable. Will you join me?"

Mr. Adams endorsing this hungrily, they began to walk. Along their way, they passed several soberly-dressed gentlemen, to whom Mr. Bateson attempted stumbling greetings; these gentlemen (Amelia saw) always answered him with the same blend of fondness and condescension. When they were seated, Mr. Bateson selected a letter from a small packet before beginning:

"My friends, madam, are cautious with good reason. A dangerous man named Whipsblood, being a great enemy to *Liberty,* wishes badly to find Mrs. Wilson—"

"Pray, sir," interrupted Amelia, "who is this Mrs. Wilson with whom my father's name has been tied?"

"Why, ma'am," answered Mr. Bateson, "she is a very wealthy merchant, and a patriot. She and my family have sometimes done business; but what her connection with your father may be, I cannot guess, beyond what the news-paper saith.

"But to continue: Captain Whipsblood wishes desperately to find her, and he is not above using agents, including one . . ." (here he blushed so fiercely that his freckles appeared to swim in beet-and-milk soup) ". . . so beautiful as yourself. Suspicion in such times as these, while still ugly, is probably inevitable—yet we must not let it drive us from our natural friends.

"Now, as for myself: this letter is from my brother, who represents our trading-house in Annapolis. I shall not tax your patience by reading it; but, having told me in January of meeting a Mr. Tom Jones, he now mentions in this most recent note, that Mr. Jones's daughter and a certain massive Parson came seeking her father in Maryland, and, having fought splendidly with two Grenadiers, are thought to be following him to Boston.

"In short, ma'am, I believe you because I believe my brother."

Seeing Amelia growing restless (for the waste of even a minute had lately become a torment to her), he ended contritely, "Ma'am, forgive my wordiness. I should like to help you."

"And can you?" asked Amelia.

"Ma'am," said Bateson, "I cannot promise; for I have never taken much part in the activities of our Committee of Safety. My speech, you see"—here he smiled sadly—"is thought to lack a *Ciceronian* fluidity."

Sighing, he continued, "Yet I have met Mrs. Wilson, and know some who know her better. Will you give me twenty-four hours to seek? And will you, please, stay as much in secret as possible?—For I promise you, this Captain Whipsblood will learn very quickly who you are, and after that, I should not wish to be in your place."

Mr. Bateson having yet to speak a single implausible word, Amelia now said gently (and was instantly seconded by the Parson) that she would be happy to wait.

A bill for their wine lay upon the table. Amelia was about to reach for it when Mr. Bateson intercepted her, saying with yet another genial smile:

"Nay, ma'am, a stupid tongue doth not keep a man from writing shipping orders or bills-of-lading. I believe you shall find few merchants warmer than Bateson & Sons—of which I am the second Bateson. Please allow me; for I find my money speaks with an eloquence my speech shall never have."

He then stood and begged to be excused, saying that anything they cared to order would be added to his account; and that, if they agreed, he would meet them at the edge of the nearby Old Granary burial ground at six o'clock the next evening, bringing with him whatever news he might.

Amelia and Adams both promised to appear; and as Mr. Bateson departed, they looked upon each other and sighed with relief, for this seemed the single time in all their travels that Providence had not behaved like a boxing-instructor, lifting them up only after first knocking them to the ground.

The next day, Adams and Amelia remained indoors, while outside the watery sunshine, melting a considerable quantity of snow, turned the streets nearly impassable.

If, Reader, we have lately recorded not a single quarrel between Adams and Amelia, it was simply that, since their discovery of mutual affection after the battle of the Grey Falcon Inn, our friends (tho' very chaste) had sweetened their troubles with so many smiles and kisses and hands gently held, as would make one wonder whether Amelia was (as a heroine should be) every moment of the day obsessed with her duty to her parent.

This morning, indeed, Amelia had some difficulty persuading the Parson to content himself with his former beloved, a copy of Aeschylus. When at last he had obliged her, she turned to writing to Dr. Johnson and Mrs. James, to tell them that she regretted having no way to receive their letters, but hoped very shortly to find her father and begin the journey home.

About five o'clock, our friends began to pace; and about forty minutes later, as the shadows were growing long, they left the inn, and walked the half-mile to the cemetery. There, in the gloomy shelter of an oak, they saw what almost seemed a gorgeous, shimmering scarab, but proved to be the exposed waist-coat of Mr. Bateson, who was this time decked in an iridescent green silk, its gold and silver threads catching the very last of the day's light.

"Friends," said he, without preface, "I hope my trust in thee is not misplaced; for I have information which, in the wrong hands, may do harm, not only to Mr. Jones, but to the security of New-England.

"Your father, Amelia, is indeed with Mrs. Wilson, at a country inn which she owns, but which is kept by a person named Southwark, near the village of Roxbury. Given the lady's need of secrecy, they will probably not stay there long, but the information was certainly accurate as of this morning. I hope it may help you. I have arranged for a person to guide you safely to Roxbury tomorrow night, if you wish. He will call for you at your inn—which, forgive me, I happen to have discovered."

Amelia and Mr. Adams began to thank him, but he held up his hand, and continued:

"You may be less happy to learn that your own actions have become generally known. Several journals this morning carried Maryland dispatches naming you as fugitives because of your fight with the soldiers in Annapolis. I do not say anyone searches for you actively, but you might be well advised to avoid day-light and public places. Mr. Adams . . ." (he now asked diffidently) ". . . I do not suppose you would temporarily change your cassock for another style?"

"Sir," replied the Parson, not unkindly, "that I never could do."

"Nor, in truth," said Mr. Bateson, equally gently, "had I expected it. Well, my friends, I believe we have concluded our association. I pray it may prove lucky for you." This, though nominally directed to both our friends, was in fact spoken to Amelia, who had (we must say) entirely captured the heart of poor Mr. Bateson.

"Well, sir," said she, "I hope we may someday very soon have opportunity to repay your kindness."

"Indeed, Amelia, I should rather thank *you;* since if you really do have an important message for a friend of Mrs. Wilson's, I will have had my chance to contribute something other than my money to the cause of Liberty—and that, I promise you, delights me immensely, even if we three are the only ones who shall ever know it. 'Mr. Bateson hath played his part.' And so, good-night."

With that, Mr. Bateson slipped away from them, and into the twilight. They were sorry to see him go; for, despite the foolish splendour of his waist-coats, and the sad halting of his speech, he had proved such a friend as few of us can spare in this life.

# V

## How Disaster Struck Our Friends at Roxbury

Mr. Bateson's promised guide appeared the next evening about eight o'clock. John Chauncy was a tall, broad-shouldered, talkative person of about twenty-five, and a gentleman despite his servant's clothes, which (he immediately explained) he had donned before leaving the offices of Bateson & Sons, where he was senior clerk. Always chatting freely, he took the role of porter, carrying down for Amelia and Adams those few items destined for their saddle-bags.

Until they reached their horses, he spoke genially of everything from his work ("the prospects for a person of spirit are unlimited") to Mr. Bateson, whom he praised as, "the most under-estimated gentleman in Massachusetts." Once they had mounted, however, he led them quite silently over a dizzying course of back-streets, by-ways and overgrown paths. This journey exceeded twelve miles, and required nearly three hours; and so obscure were its roads that (despite Mr. Chauncy's skill) it would likely have been impossible without the assistance of a full, white moon.

These three figures, then, (one hooded, and the other two with their tricorn hats pulled low about their ears) reached the village of Roxbury a little before eleven that night. They found the inn-keeper asleep in a parlour chair, and roused him by shaking his arm persistently.

Wakening in a foul mood (which was, indeed, habitual with him), the inn-keeper grunted at our friends; yet Mr. Chauncy (who knew him well) began patiently, "Mr. Southwark, these good people are seeking the gentleman travelling with Mrs. Wilson. This young lady is his daughter, Amelia Jones, and the reverend gentleman with her is Mr. Adams. I will vouch for them; now, pray, where may we find Mrs. Wilson and her friend?"

Mr. Southwark replied indifferently, "You may answer that as well as I, since Jones and she left here above six hours ago. They rode east, but with my employeress, that means nothing."

To Amelia and Mr. Adams, he continued more eagerly:

"Well, gentlepeople, I regret disappointing you; but as you're here, what could be better than rooms? Mrs. Wilson's are always reserved; yet we have some others, most elegant, to be let. . . ." He then rubbed his hands together; for Mr. Southwark was one who, meaning to prosper in life, only embraced political matters so long as they paid better than any others.

Amelia and Mr. Adams, utterly discouraged, looked to Mr. Chauncy for advice.

This good-hearted gentleman took them aside, and said charitably, "You may guess how sorry I am. I was supposed to ride on tonight to Concord, but if you refuse to stay here, I'll escort you home; we won't reach Boston before the moon sets, but we'll make it reins-to-saddle, if we must."

Amelia thanked him for his offer, but said that they would stay overnight, and decide in the morning what to do next; "For, in truth, I believe we are both unwilling to conclude our day by back-tracking to our starting-point." This she said quietly, in a voice revealing the fall of her hopes over the last few minutes.

Mr. Chauncy, first urging them to be brave, then took a kindly leave of our friends, after which Mr. Southwark offered them a light meal while their rooms were made ready.

It was nearly mid-night before they were shown upstairs by the chamber-maid, while their host resumed his explorations of the mighty land of *sleep.*

His ship of dreams had been under sail barely half an hour, however, when it was destroyed by thunder; or—to speak less nonsensically—when he was wakened by a voice outside his door, roaring that he must open up, or face the wrath of the British Army.

We have already hinted that Mr. Southwark's devotion to the cause of Liberty fell a little short of fanaticism; in truth, it also fell a little short of his devotion to the King of Siam, and was, indeed, non-existent. Accordingly, he now roused himself instantly, and, crying, "Coming!" as hospitably as he would have in answering a call for rum punch, hurried to unlock his door.

There poured into the room six angry persons. Four of these were vicious-looking savages, two wearing the costume of the Pequot Indians, and two, of the 62nd Light Infantry. Leading them were a muscular-looking lieutenant named Snipps, and a towering, black-haired Captain named Whipsblood.

Having received these gentlemen courteously, Mr. Southwark may well have expected gentle treatment in return. If so, he was perhaps mildly disappointed when Captain Whipsblood, stepping forward, suddenly grabbed him by the shirt-front, jerked him close, and placed the edge of a razor-like knife against his exposed throat.

"Look'ee, sirrah," says the Captain in a voice very low and menacing, "you are now but two inches from hell-fire. Answer me quickly. Have you a person named *Jones* staying here?"

Mr. Southwark was, I believe, far too good a Christian to make other than a meek reply. Accordingly (speaking very softly, so that the blade might not be *vibrated* through his Adam's apple), he now answered, "Top of the stairs."

Reader, let this be a lesson to us all to be steadfast in the truth!—for our trials never last so long as we fear. In a moment, Mr. Southwark—

---

who not once during that moment had even considered offering a false-hood—was free, to catch his breath among the dust-balls upon his floor. The Captain, replacing his knife and drawing his sword, now ordered his two Indian soldiers to guard the back of the inn, and led the remainder of his force, with notable clatter, up the stairs.

In the room at the top of these stairs, as Mr. Southwark had correctly observed, a person named Jones was readying herself for bed. (That she was alone, need not, I suppose, be mentioned; for there never had been anything blameable about her behaviour or that of Mr. Adams, nor anything we should at all blush to record. Yet, let us say it; for, if this must be the end of our heroine, we should wish her reputation, at least, to endure forever, unsullied.)

Our innocent heroine had barely slipped beneath the soft covers, when there came the loudest imaginable banging upon her door, accompanied by a demand to come out at once, or to prepare to die without mercy.

Reader, no heroine of antiquity—no Deborah or Antiope—ever responded to danger more bravely than did our own Amelia. Leaping from the covers, she armed herself by holding the chamber-pot high above her head; and only then cried as loudly as she could for Mr. Adams to come and help her.

Next door, meanwhile, the noises of pounding and shouting had some-what disturbed the contemplations of Mr. Adams (who had been reading, with the tears standing in his eyes, of the final reunion of Odysseus and Penelope). He had, therefore, already set the book down, when there reached his ears Amelia's call for aid; at which, not pausing to consider that he wore only his night-shirt, he bolted into the hall-way, and seeing four scoundrels pummeling Amelia's door, barrelled into them with sufficient force to knock them all down the stairs.

Without surveying the damage, or even reviewing his own situation, Adams now rapped softly at Amelia's door, and announced himself; at which the bolt was immediately cast back, and he was let in.

Reader, thou must remember that our two friends had assembled in some haste; and now, after bolting the door behind them, beheld each other in attire entirely new. In truth, tho' the lighting, consisting of but a pair of candles, was not especially good, I believe neither of them had ever before seen anything which quite so interested them. Certainly Mr. Adams, gazing down at that significant portion of the beauty of Miss Jones revealed by her shift, began to conceive an idea of what was meant by the phrase "a happy death."

Never, indeed, had our friends been in graver danger of the blameable; and it might have gone ill with them, had there not very luckily appeared the far wholesomer menace of four blood-thirsty soldiers, who, having regained their footing, were now, like their ancestors at Agincourt, charging once more unto the breach.

These gentlemen were done with talking; instead, linking their arms, they threw themselves mightily against the door. Twice, three times, the oak planks held. Then they groaned, and at the fourth blow, they collapsed, the door tearing away from the wall like a ramp, over which the Captain's minions stumbled into the room.

They did not find the fortress undefended. Amelia brought the chamber-pot squarely down upon the first; and as for the unlucky second, Mr. Adams caught him as he fell forward, and, holding him like a battering ram, ran him across the room, and threw him head-first out the closed window. Shattering the pane with the top of his skull (which nature had wisely made extremely thick), and letting out what may have been his battle cry, this warrior dropt upon his Pequot colleagues in a rain of splintered glass, much as Zeus is said to have visited his beloved within a shower of gold—tho' the love-struck deity perhaps landed more softly.

Alas, Fortune (as is her wont) now reversed herself; for, having first stood by our intrepid friends, she now embraced their better-armed opponents. The fickle goddess—it doth pain me to say—now allowed Captain Whipsblood (who, tho' fearless, did not despise the cheap advantage, providing it was his) to press the tip of his sword against the soft side of Amelia, and to warn Mr. Adams he must throw up his hands, or else "see this wh——re . . ." (for such was his language) ". . . skewered like a roasting-pig."

Reader, we have often before made jests of sorrows and dangers; for which our only excuse may be that we intended thereby to lighten miseries, and to instill hopes where none seemed possible. But who would now, by joking, insult the humbled and defenseless? There are some occasions, Reader, which defy even our efforts to be brave; and which leave us no choices but silence or lamentation.

Such is our occasion now; for Captain Whipsblood (though he would not for several minutes understand the nature of his victory) had by this raid arrested every reasonable hope of saving Tom's estate. Indeed, since Captain Whipsblood, like a certain boneless form of sea-creature, was ever driven to greater cruelties by the sight of injuries he had already inflicted, his success in capturing one, unexpected, *Jones,* only redoubled his determination to take the other; and so this night boded very ill not only for our young friends, but for those two older adventurers we shall in our next chapter rejoin.

# VI

## In Which Certain Mysteries Are Clarified

Our story must once again retrace its steps, to show how Mr. Jones and Mrs. Wilson escaped the net which caught up Amelia and Mr. Adams.

The explanations Mrs. Wilson had promised our hero were in fact delayed by nearly thirty-six hours, the reason being that, shortly after they reached Roxbury, Mr. Jones had excused himself to rest a few minutes, and then gone upstairs and slept without interruption until the next morning; after which, he had eaten breakfast, and then fallen fast asleep, only to wake shortly before supper-time.

His wakening, however, had found him in far better condition than at any time since his arrival in Massachusetts. Indeed, he felt so much improved that he insisted upon Mrs. Wilson's joining him for supper in his room, where (once the food had been brought, and they were alone) she finally satisfied his curiosity.

"You have very kindly," said she, "borne with my need for secrecy these many months; and now, I believe, deserve the answer to at least two questions: Why Captain Whipsblood is my enemy, and How it was I so often met and avoided you in Europe.

"My husband, Jonas Wilson, was a Salem-man, a merchant, and, later, a smuggler. Five years ago, he was killed by the British Navy. Not long after—since he had left me quite rich—I began to draw suitors, of whom the most persistent was an aristocratic, widowed Army officer, named Desmond Whipsblood. Nay!—Do not stare; I was very young, and he, tho' you will deny it, has a kind of charm—a charm, perhaps, most appealing to those who think themselves weak, as I, in those days, certainly did.

"I will not say I loved the Captain; I even wonder why I admitted his attentions; yet we had come near to an engagement, for which he declared himself very eager. Then I learned—never mind how—that he had designed the policy of brute force against New-England smugglers, and was therefore (as I conceived it) almost the murderer of my husband, who had been a better man, and dearer to me, than a hundred Captain Whipsbloods."

Anger and regret had entered Mrs. Wilson's voice; she paused and drew several deep breaths before continuing:

"When he called upon me the next evening, I confronted him bitterly. Whipsblood, sir, is a very reciprocal man, who always throws back what he receives, and as much more as he can. He told me angrily he knew (as was in fact the case) that I had resumed my husband's smuggling ventures, and swore he had protected me only out of (as he called it) love; but that he would thenceforth be as harsh an enemy as he had been loyal a friend.

"He departed that night in a rage, and was soon after recalled to England, where (as I heard) he continued his rise in the Secret Service. He had always been hard, but his wickedness (I am sorry to say) dated from our separation. That night, I made a very bitter enemy—and a very dangerous one, too; for, believe me, his reputation as a bully, while deserved, is nothing compared with his talent as a ferreter of secrets, a builder of files and dossiers. I remember that, as he left, he flung the door open wide. It was snowing hard outside, and the cold blast of air he let in chilled me to my bones. Why sir, 'twas an omen indeed—for there is such a grip of mortality in that man's enmity, as scarcely can be put in words."

Calming herself by refilling their glasses with the last of the wine, she continued:

"For nearly five years, I avoided the Captain; yet three close associates of mine met horrible deaths—"

At this, Jones reached for his wine, his hand somewhat shakey.

"—and I several times detected his influence in reverses I suffered. During those years, however, I gradually abandoned my ordinary business, to work for Liberty and American rights—which, like most noble causes, had use for a criminal or two.

"Those causes brought me, seeking arms, to England last summer. I landed in the South to avoid the Secret Service, and was at the Biting Whale only by chance that night we met."

Mrs. Wilson, though not a laughing woman, now laughed delightfully. "Indeed, Tom, I treated you unkindly; yet, beyond my need of secrecy, I feared you belonged to that wretched class of gentlemen who, thinking themselves irresistible to women, consider all women their lawful prey. I thought you handsome but shallow, and am happy to have been only half right."

Mr. Jones smiled with satisfaction; Mrs. Wilson smiled in reply, and then returned to her story:

"After leaving you, I rode north, avoiding London, but visiting tens of small manufacturers between there and Manchester—one of whom, I guess, betrayed me; for, not long after, I was lured to London, supposedly to meet a gentleman whose failing iron foundry could be converted to the casting of artillery.

"I was to meet him at a tavern near Smithfield, but what I met, of course, was Captain Whipsblood, who, after whispering that he had evidence enough to confine me to Newgate or some worse prison 'til I rotted, next offered, with a leer, to preserve me, in exchange for certain private favours which I scorn too much to mention."

Our hero, who had heard all the story with horror and amazement, now clenched his fist and declared, "Madam, I shall not rest until the Captain has paid for his disgusting rudeness!"

"Sweet friend," replied Mrs. Wilson, with a kind smile, "you repaid the Captain almost the moment he spoke; for, if you remember, you treated him to an entire bottle of wine."

" 'Twas only a first payment," answered Jones, very gallantly.

"It may console you, dear Tom," continued Mrs. Wilson, "to know you made another conquest that night. I had always held I would care for no man who was not also (as my husband had been) an ally. After that night, I began to hope you were he. No one 'til you had made me feel what I felt with my poor, dear Jonas."

Poor Tom had been suffering the last effects of his illness; yet now his spleen, or his marrow, or some other puissant organ had redoubled the production of his blood, restoring at once all his energy, and his colour. He therefore was inspired to offer a response, such as a very warm kiss, and some very suitable compliments here and there about the person of Mrs. Wilson.

Mrs. Wilson had, however, herself momentarily risen, to transfer some of the dishes to a nearby dresser, move her own chair closer to Tom's, and set upon the table a plate of candied fruits. Again seating herself, she chose from this plate a cherry, which, bringing sweets to sweets, she slowly and daintily consumed, while now and again shining upon our hero those brilliant brown orbs whose beauty we have often commended.

Our hero (who was, I suppose, very fond of candied fruits) now placed his arm around Mrs. Wilson and kissed her. This she returned eagerly, but then, pulling herself away, said tensely, "Nay, sir, I have not altered my opinions since Marseilles; and you must realize that we are—unless some miracle occur—only weeks or months from war with England.

"The arms which I and others have acquired are massed in Concord and its neighbouring village of Lexington. The British know this very well. Soon, they will advance from Boston to seize what we have; and we will try to stop them, and—so—our war. If you stay with me after the fighting's begun, you will have pledged yourself beyond withdrawal."

Mrs. Wilson had, I believe, express'd herself very clearly; and our hero seemed to understand. He now looked away, as if in deep thought, before gazing deep into her eyes, and asking, "Since, dearest lady, we seem now bound upon a long campaign together, how do you suppose the action may begin?"

Mrs. Wilson, who imagined Jones to be as lucid as herself, now relaxed, and leaning very near him, whispered, "Why, sir, first with words, but soon enough with deeds."

"Such as?"

"Well . . . once the parties are closely engaged, there is generally much light skirmishing, and a seeking for soft-spots."

"And then?"

"And then, when preparations are complete, and weapons drawn, there is a thrust, which is properly met with a counter-thrust . . . and so on."

"And is it such a simple matter, then?"

"Well, sir, it may begin simply, but tends to complexity; for the parties, once they are engaged, are usually unwilling to leave off—and, indeed, generally wish to press the action forever."

Alas, Reader, so closely have we attended this conversation (for one can never learn too much about military affairs), that we have neglected to inform thee how, while talking, our two friends had drifted from their table by the fire to Tom's four-posted bed; where (for they are surely almost done with speaking) we shall leave them perfectly safe in each other's arms.

# VII

*An Astonishing Discovery by Jones,*
*and a Conversation Ending in a*
*Manner Which Some Will Find*
*Shocking, and Others, Very Natural*

Thou has no doubt often considered, Reader, the strange phenomenon of *simultaneity:* by which, upon, perhaps, the same afternoon, and within a very few miles of one another, the child may play with jacks-and-ball, while the murderer awaits the hangman's noose, the architect reviews his plans, the gentleman contemplates his roses, and the Minister pens a letter which shall plunge his country into war; and each of these considers his own actions alone, not merely in indifference, but in complete ignorance, of the activities of all the others.

So it was this morning with Mr. Jones, who, while his son was stealing his estate, and his daughter strove desperately to reach him from Boston, woke peacefully about mid-day, as the bright sun-light shone upon the curtains, to muse gratefully (and by no means wrongly) upon the return of his entire health.

His cheerful mood was, however, demolished by a note lying next to his wash-basin. Written in a familiar hand, this read simply:

> 7:15 A.M.
>
> I find I must go at once to Concord upon business, but shall certainly return before sun-set. Have all ready for immediate departure.
>
> A.W.

Something of the plainness of style here—for the note was a trifle lacking in "dearests," "angels" and "beloveds"—suggested to our hero (tho' it seem'd unlikely) that the night before had lacked perfection. More worrisome (for he felt himself ready to amend any disappointments) was the urgency of the message, which reminded him how dangerous were the times. Dressing quickly, he hurried downstairs to ask Mr. Southwark where Mrs. Wilson had gone.

"That, sir," replied the inn-keeper, "is a piece of information she prefers keeping to herself. You are, however, asked not to leave the grounds of the inn, and especially to avoid the village. If you must stretch your legs—for I see you are looking alive again—we have some acres of woods behind us; only do not cross over the stone walls."

Jones, though disliking the tone of this, contented himself with ordering his breakfast. As he ate, he was treated to a sight at first novel and then (upon consideration) frightening: a crowd of forty villagers, marching in column-by-two's down the muddy road outside his parlour window, with the bright sun beating down upon their muskets.

This martial impression was soon reinforced. The Friday *Gazette* arrived, and for half an hour, Tom listened to his host repeat its accounts of threats, troop movements, and resolutions.

"Well, sir," Mr. Southwark finally concluded, "certain persons may soon discover how all this talk of *Liberty* hurts business; and perhaps they shall be sorry enough, once it's too late."

Wishing to hear no more, Jones answered curtly, "As we are speaking of business, Mr. Southwark, you will please see that fresh horses are ready for Mrs. Wilson and me this evening at six."

Mr. Southwark replied cooly, "I am sorry, sir, to have raised politics with my betters; to be sure, your horses will be waiting." He then departed, leaving our hero, feeling very grim, to stare out the parlour window for near three-quarters of an hour.

At last, Jones called in one of the maids, and, giving her two guineas, asked whether she could find him some clean shirts, and the barber. This young woman being both efficient and courteous, Jones within the hour stood freshly shaved and attired.

His mood, however, was no better. Happy as he may have been on waking, Tom now suffered great tension and alarm: for there was a gathering storm of political violence which, though he could not understand, he could sense; and rigidly selfish Mr. Southwark appeared the emblem of all the dangerous ignorance around him.

About three o'clock, as the crisp winds were pushing in the rain-clouds, he ran out the inn's back door, to seek some place of rural quiet, where he might be alone, and think.

The grounds rising behind the Roxbury Inn were a blend of copse and substantial trees, through which several natural pathways suggested themselves.

Jones had climbed perhaps two hundred yards, when he noticed a doorway, more than half concealed by brush, cut directly into the hill-side. Its pad-lock had been wrongly set, for it now opened at a tug.

Leaving the door open for light, and walking down six or seven rough steps, Jones found a room about fifteen feet square, containing above a dozen large powder-kegs, quantities of shot, and no fewer than two hundred racked muskets, along with packages of naval biscuits, a cot with blankets, and a square lantern for use near explosives.

Nothing shocks us more than what we have willfully forgotten. Jones, now forced to admit what work Mrs. Wilson actually did, sighed loudly and cast himself down upon the bed with a moan of despair. In a rush, he despised himself for having, by the worst recklessness of his life, entangled himself in schemes of violence he but dimly understood, for a reason he might have called love, but which many others would have given a *lower* name.

And yet, the moment Tom began wondering what amends he might make for this wicked association, it began to seem infinitely less wicked. He started thinking, in other words, how repugnant it would be, not only to betray Mrs. Wilson (something he could scarcely bear to contemplate), but to return to working for the wretched Suffleys.

The longer Tom considered the matter, the more he knew that he abhorred not only the Suffleys, but all those English plans for North America he had a year before so eagerly endorsed. He would not now have returned to help rule Maryland, or any tiny fragment of it, for any price upon earth.

In sum, Reader, Jones now realized what he had earlier feared to consider (but what we have several times hinted): that he had, since first meeting Mrs. Wilson, undergone a complete revolution in his thinking, until he at last saw the need for a similar revolution in America.

When he had reasoned thus far, Tom (after some initial amazement) began to consider his own situation almost with complaisance, even congratulating himself upon his fortitude and free will (for he still knew nothing of the arrest of Amelia, or of the plottings back in Somersetshire; and so believed a return to his former life would only require facing Whipsblood in a duel). Quite joyously, he schemed how to persuade Mrs. Wilson to come with him to England to join the Parliamentary movement for the peaceful release of the colonies.

It is not, however, often the fate of persons who live so recklessly as our hero, to be allowed to savour their thoughts in quiet satisfaction. Tom, recollecting that Mrs. Wilson would be returning soon, now rose from the cot and went to the open door, only to discover a sky as dark as his mood had been, and a heavy rain just beginning to fall.

This unhappy circumstance would have meant little to Jones, had not his recent ill health made him unusually cautious. He therefore pulled the door partly closed, and was about to return to his cot to wait out the storm, when he heard Mrs. Wilson calling his name.

This hail he immediately answered, while stepping into the clearing in order to be better heard—with the primary effect, alas, of getting himself thoroughly wet in just those few seconds before Mrs. Wilson reached him.

She now embraced him intently, and they kissed before walking together down the steps to the shelter of the arsenal. As both had been soaked, and as a fire was impossible, Tom removed his coat, and Mrs. Wilson, her cape; and they then huddled together upon the cot, using one of its blankets as a tent over them both.

They had scarcely done shivering, when Mrs. Wilson began, "You were not at the inn when I returned; and Mr. Southwark—who I begin to mistrust—was very vague. Indeed, sir, I nearly thought—feared . . ."

"Madam," replied Jones, "I shall never desert you."

Mrs. Wilson now studied his face patiently before saying:

"Alas, sir, we have had news much worse than you know. A ship docked this noon in Boston, with instructions to General Gage that he must take absolute control of Massachusetts with those troops already in his command. He shall be given no reinforcements; and so, instead of being able to intimidate with numbers, he will be obliged to strike with force. Parliament has, moreover, declared Massachusetts in rebellion; a second Provisional Council is even now being assembled at Concord, to draw our war-plans. These matters are yet secret, but shall tomorrow be generally known."

"But how, Angela, can you be certain of so much?" cries Jones, dreading to lose his scarce-born hope of bringing her peacefully back to England.

"Why, sir, never mind our means—to stay with me, you must henceforth be prepared, not only to live upon the run, but even to face your countrymen upon a battlefield."

Jones (who, though developing an attachment to the American cause, was not yet prepared to kill for it) now forgot a part of the pledge he had made only a minute before. Seizing Mrs. Wilson's hand, he earnestly appealed:

"Dearest angel, you have already done more than many dozens of men will accomplish. Will you not come away with me?"

"Why, sir," she answered quietly, "this is my country; and if I love her in straw-berry time, I must stand by her when the cold winds blow."

To this, Mr. Jones said nothing; nor, indeed, was there any sensible reply to be made, except to hold her very close, which he did.

This closeness soon began both to reassure them, and to suggest further consolation, which, starting with their hands upon each other's cheeks, and their lips pressed together, they did take.

We shall never, Reader, condemn Tom and Angela for seeking amorous comfort upon the outset of so dangerous a venture. If our heroes, cold, hungry and frightened, could find ease so simply, shall we, who have so much more, begrudge them? As we will each of us, sooner or later, confront some parallel crisis, let us rather pray to be, in our turn, content with so little.

And let us, therefore, simply observe that, perhaps an hour later, when the rain had ended, and the clear sky lay only a hinted dark blue from full night, they walked back down the hill together. Mr. Southwark had their horses ready, and they were swiftly mounted. In a minute they were through the village, and into the open countryside, shadowy figures beneath a rising full moon. They rode very fast, with Tom, so anxious to be gone, never guessing how his daughter would soon pay for his wrong-doings.

BOOK

# THE EIGHTH

# I

## The Last of Our Prefatory Chapters, in Which We Discuss Jones, Justice and Hope

Reader, we are now come very near to the conclusion of our story; and we should be very false with thee were we to say that any ending seems likely but a *tragical* one.

In truth, as no sailor takes ship with the hope of being storm-tossed and drowned, so no author (I warrant) undertakes a story meant to end in disaster. Still, we must present thee, Reader, with an honest history; nor may any comments of ours (however deeply felt) prevent suffering, any more than philosophy or religion may prevent it in life.

We had once, many years ago, occasion to lament an earlier crisis in the life of our hero, when his own foolish heart (and the designs of one Lord Fellamar) had brought him near to hanging. That boyish folly, grievous as it was, offered one point in extenuation: namely, that our hero then injured no one but himself.

Consider the change the years have made in the powers, if not the judgement, of our hero! Now, for his folly, we have an estate stolen, an old woman dispossessed, a daughter and a Parson in chains, and enough other injustices to fill a list as long as a bankrupt lord's Auction Catalogue. Indeed, should Mr. Jones now be brought (without a chance to make amends) to a Tyburn hanging, I believe half the country would volunteer to drive away the cart, and the other half, host a party in their honour.

Consider lastly, the sad condition of our hero (who hath not, in truth, yet forfeited *all* claim upon our sympathies) and of Mrs. Wilson, trapped in a country upon the brink of war, and pursued by the wicked Captain Whipsblood. Who shall find, within all this, any grounds for hope?

Yet, Reader, it would be a poor business for us to despair; for what is faith, when it is untested? Our friends are now upon that storm-bound ship; the ship may not turn back; yet might not our friends still find safety, by great labour and the mercy of Providence? Let us continue to believe, so long as possible, that virtue and innocence shall prevail, and that even foolish Mr. Jones may be spared long enough to amend the worst of the harm he hath done—after which, he may even (tho' in truth, I doubt it) be spared any of the usual fates of repentant knaves, such as to hang himself, or throw himself upon his sword, or be carried away by the devil in a vast cloud of smoke and flame. At least we may hope—and, Reader, without hope, which of us would choose to live another day, or read another chapter?

## II

### In Which We Return Briefly to Adams and Amelia

Captain Whipsblood had no sooner ascertained which Jones it was he had in custody, than he was forced to decide whether to return to Boston with his prisoners (to be certain they arrived), or to entrust them to his lieutenant (to gain valuable hours in his own pursuit of Tom and Mrs. Wilson). This was, in short, the choice of pleasures, which is perhaps the most difficult of all choices to settle.

The Captain at last resolved (upon, I suppose, the proverb of a bird in the hand) to escort his prisoners back himself. After allowing his henchmen to rest until dawn, therefore, this mighty *hunter of men* began the long road back to Boston, which he reached about ten in the morning.

Amelia and Adams were charged with assaults upon officers in both Annapolis and Roxbury—the Captain delightedly stressing their *habitual* criminality—and scarcely three hours elapsed before they were thrown into a military gaol.

Mr. Adams found himself in the common cell with about thirty other prisoners (most charged merely with drunken brawling), while poor Amelia was confined alone in the smallest imaginable brick cubicle. Lacking even the sad consolation of fellow human beings (however depraved), she was obliged to sit, with no company but rats, insects and a trickle of foul cold water which leaked along one wall. Thus did our most innocent friend suffer most—not nearly so much from her surroundings, I believe, as from her concern for Mr. Adams, her father, and the poor ladies back in England.

For four days (which seem'd as many months) she waited so, until, in the late afternoon, when her tiny cell had already lost the only bit of direct sun it received during the day, her gaoler appeared, leering, to tell her to prepare for interrogation by an officer.

Amelia now endured forty minutes of anxiety, before the cell door was opened. At once her heart leapt into her throat, for there stood framed in the corridor light a military figure, of whom her dazzled eyes could discern no details.

Amelia, tho' very frightened, jumped to her feet and clenched her fists. What dreadful fate she imagined for herself, we dare not say; yet she stood boldly, and called, "Well, sir, you may try your worst."

After standing a long moment in seeming hostility, the figure before her asked emotionally:

"Amelia? Do you not recognize your Uncle Bob?"

At these words, Miss Jones, who had been steeling herself for yet another trial, raced forward to embrace the gentleman before her, who was not, of course, her real uncle, but her father's closest friend, Colonel Askew.

These two persons now held each other tightly, while Amelia shed many tears, and the Colonel, not a few. At last, the Colonel, sitting beside her upon the pallet which was the room's only furniture, apologized for having misled her about the interrogation—which had appeared, however, the only way to see her without alerting certain persons that she had a friend.

The Colonel then continued, "I did not believe the arrest report when I read it; nor have I in my life beheld anything so bleak. How, Amelia, has such a thing come to pass?"

Growing calmer as she talked, Miss Jones related, in the space of about an hour, the story of her troubles in England and her travels in America, until she ended with the alarming news that fewer than four weeks remained in which to bring Tom home.

Askew heard all this gravely, only once or twice sighing, and never interrupting. At last, he said uneasily, "I fear, Amelia, that while your situation is difficult, your father's is nearly hopeless. If only I had known

who this Mrs. Wilson was he wished to find in America—I promise you,
I should have dissuaded him. 'Tis one thing to argue for independence;
and quite another to kill for it."

Seeing Amelia turn pale, he paused, and then said, "And yet, much
here is suspicious; for, while I might believe Tom wild enough to join a
woman he loves in such a scheme, a bloody-minded officer here—named
Whipsblood—is said to be pursuing him upon a charge of theft from the
Maryland tax revenues; and that, of course, is a lie. A rebel, Tom may be,
but a thief—never."

"Some trap is being laid for him, I promise you!" cried Amelia. "Tho'
I cannot quite see what it is. Will you not release Mr. Adams and me? My
father must be found, while we have time."

Askew shook his head, then rose and paced several times across the
narrow cell. Halting, he placed his hand upon Amelia's shoulder.

"I shall ask Perry, my valet," said he, "to bring you better provisions,
and shall try myself to learn whatever else I can about Tom. If you wish
to write him a brief note, it *might* be possible to have it forwarded; for we
still have occasional contact with the rebels. But to do more would be to
warn the Captain you have a protector. Do not worry for yourself;
Whipsblood can have no interest in you but as bait for Tom."

"And my father?" asked Amelia.

Askew drew a deep breath. "That, alas, is a different matter. May God
protect him; I assure you I should not know what to do if I were he.

"Yet some revelation, or some bold stroke of Tom's, may solve this.
I shall do whatever I can to help. Meanwhile, do not expect to see me for
several days, since all the light infantry are to be sent into the field very
soon . . ."

Amelia barely concealed her alarm.

". . . and such actions always prove harder than expected."

Amelia nodded firmly, thanked the Colonel, and asked him that she
might be given paper and quill. Then (with special vehemence) she
begged that he might visit Parson Adams, who was very dear to her.

That the Colonel promised to do, and then he departed, leaving behind
a young lady as remarkable for bravery as for all the other virtues.

# III

## Of Jones's Short Life as a Fugitive, and the Choices He Was Obliged to Make

For above two weeks following their flight from the Roxbury Inn, Tom and Mrs. Wilson lived as fugitives, never staying two nights in any location, but fleeing from safe-house to barn to hidden arsenal. Their travel was nearly always at night, and in every case upon the most obscure and desolate pathways.

Tom, therefore, spent the first two weeks of April in a blur, accelerated by ever-darker news from Boston. At the start of the month, General Gage had begun assembling his light infantry and Grenadiers into a force all Massachusetts knew was soon to be used for raiding the arsenals of the militias. Jones was barred from the private discussions of the Americans; yet he understood from the steps they were taking, that they intended, if attacked, to surrender their ammunition *one round at a time.*

One of the most considerable advantages of constant activity, is the suppression of introspection; persons busy running for their lives rarely feel a need to review the *metaphysics* of their condition. So it was with Jones during those two weeks, until Saturday, the 15th of April. While he and Mrs. Wilson were resting in a farm-house several miles from the village of Bedford, she, after dismissing a courier, called him to give him a weather-beaten envelope bearing his name. The handwriting was familiar; the seal had already been broken (not, he assumed, by Mrs. Wilson); and so he opened it and found, in an unnaturally tiny hand:

My Dear Father,

Colonel Askew, who will attempt to arrange delivery of this letter, tells me I shall have but one chance to write, and must be very brief, and very frank. Therefore, although I would not wish to alarm you, I would have you know, first, that Dr. James is dead, second, that Hacksem and Mr. Sinamore have conspired to steal your estate, third, that you will be able to prevent them only if you are able to reach England by the 17th of April instant, and fourth, that Mr. Adams and I are presently under military arrest here in Boston.

Mr. Adams and I are, I assure you, in no danger. Colonel Askew tells me that your enemy, Captain Whipsblood, intends us only to draw you in; and it is imperative that you go at once to Salem, and take ship for England—since, even if that April dead-line should be somehow postponed, every hour is still of the greatest possible importance. Once you have left for England, we will almost certainly be released—or so the Colonel believes.

I pray that you will forgive my waiting so long before contact-ing you; indeed, I have tried every means available before this to reach you, but many misfortunes have prevented our contact. Mr. Adams and I have been pursuing you since November last, under conditions very bad; and that we failed, was the fault not of our indifference, but, I fear, of the innocence and inexperience of,

Your loving daughter,
Amelia Jones

In truth, Reader, I believe Amelia failed a little in her desire not to alarm her father, for Jones had no sooner read this than he emitted a loud scream and, crossing the room, banged his head against the wall with a violence which astonished Mrs. Wilson, who at once ran to his side. Jones, however, shook her off, and cast himself down into a chair, to bury his head in his hands and then remain as still as one shot dead.

Mrs. Wilson now attempted to rouse him, but, receiving no response, said quietly that she would leave him alone a few minutes. Then, retriev-ing from the floor the note (which he had tossed into the air in his first anguish), she left the room.

Alas, Reader, an author may not be so respectful of privacy as is an ordinary friend. Private anguish is the forge of character, and we now present thee with a guided-tour of the foundry.

Know then, that Mr. Jones in those minutes experienced some of the worst agonies of his adult life. He felt a tearing guilt that Amelia had suffered upon his account, and a terrible fear that Captain Whipsblood would never release her, except possibly in trade for Mrs. Wilson or himself. Above all this, was a black cloud of shame at having abandoned his estates, his duties and his friends.

Poor Jones!—now forced to choose whether to stay with Mrs. Wilson, or to rush to Boston, or to sail for home. It seems slight wonder that he sat unmoving in his chair. Indeed, he most resembled a gentleman being drawn and quartered by stallions: presently very motionless and taut, but likely at any moment to go off in several directions at once.

When Jones had suffered several minutes of anguish, Mrs. Wilson returned. Although we have (perhaps to our discredit) concentrated our attention upon our hero, I believe this lady's dilemma deserves consideration.

To be sure, Reader, Mrs. Wilson's fondness for our hero was strong; yet so were the risks she had taken to act upon it. She had not only shown faith in a gentleman who had at first declared himself her political enemy, but admitted a novice to a complex undertaking. Now to encounter an excuse for him to leave her, when he had learned so much about her operations, must have excited some anger and suspicion in the least subtle person (which Mrs. Wilson assuredly was not); and so, in reintroducing her to the room, we must credit her with enough intelligence to have had doubts, and enough trust and love to have dismissed them—for certainly she had resolved to help Jones if she could.

"Well, Tom," said she, "I am sorry to learn of all this; and of course I release you from any obligations. I shall help you to reach Salem, and in any other way I can."

Jones, at last able to raise his head, answered, "Surely you cannot believe I will leave my daughter?"

"Did you not read her letter? Captain Whipsblood has locked her away, where, I assure you, we could not retrieve her in a dozen years."

"Well, I must try."

"Look'ee, sir, I warned you the Captain was a deadly man; if you simply wish to have yourself killed, go downstairs and ask one of the farmers to shoot you; 'twill save a ride to Boston."

For a long while, Jones made no reply; yet I believe he needed only a moment to decide, and the rest of his time to lament his decision. At last, with a sigh, he asked, "I shall never desert Amelia. Is there nothing we may do?"

Mrs. Wilson, with an even greater sigh, answered, "I have bested the Captain once or twice before; if the present military crisis should pass, you and I may be able to mount a rescue. And then, there is this Colonel Askew—he is your friend?"

"Except for you, my best."

Mrs. Wilson could not resist smiling faintly. "Well, Tom, if he is a clever gentleman, and affluent, he will be able to keep Amelia from being mistreated—at least while the Captain is chasing you and me." Suddenly brighter, she continued, "So long as Amelia is safe, and you are determined not to sail for home, will you at least wait a few days before taking any other action?"

Poor Jones still found it hard to speak; for Paradise Hall had been the site of most of his joys, and he loved it with an unmatched tenderness. The notion of its lying even temporarily unprotected in the hands of Sinamore and Hacksem sickened him. And yet, there seem'd no reasonable alternative.

Accordingly, he conceded, in no very happy tone, "I suppose, Angela, I must stay here with you."

If Mrs. Wilson was hurt by this (as, indeed, I believe she was), she gave no sign, but only put her arm around him, and so the conversation ended.

Tuesday night, Tom and Angela rode to Lexington, which, with nearby Concord, had served since October as the arsenal and meeting-center of the provisional Massachusetts congress. They found assembled a dozen rebel leaders, including Mr. John Adams and Mr. Hancock. Jones, as always, waited outside the tavern with the sentries, but this evening he was not lonely. Some forty Minute-men stood restlessly upon the Green, and riders in teams of three came and went regularly, amid a level of tension he had never in his life beheld. The British Army in Boston had all that day been assembling special forces and gathering boats to transport them across the bay; and so the great crisis seem'd upon them at last.

Now and again a phrase would drift out over the commons, fiery words on the chill April air. Just at the close, John Adams said ringingly, "The British know as well as we where the guns are being massed, and they shall soon enough come to get them. Let us be ready to give them a loud reception, and a *warm* one."

There followed fierce cries of approval, with some pounding (it seemed) upon table-tops; then Mr. Hancock, the first one out the opening doors, took aside the Minute-man captain, and after requesting help with the transport of secret papers, said excitedly, "We shall, I suspect, have our light from Christ Church this night or the . . ."

But Jones caught no more; for at that moment, Mrs. Wilson collected him, to walk with her across the Green to the private house where they were lodged. The hour was one in the morning, the day Wednesday, the nineteenth. The moonlight gave each of the milling would-be soldiers a long shadow; and later, once they had left the crowd behind, Tom and Mrs. Wilson heard the wet grass rustle as they crossed it.

Our heroes had returned to their room extremely fatigued; yet they had slept in each other's arms scarcely an hour, when they were wakened by a loud knocking upon the door, and a cry that they must come out, to receive news of the greatest possible importance—with which we shall begin our next chapter.

# IV

## *Of a Battle Very Brief, but Perhaps Important*

Jones and Mrs. Wilson hastily drest, and had no sooner opened the door than one of the youngest daughters of the house, a girl of about seven, told them earnestly, "Father says you must go at once to Buckman's tavern; for the Red-coats are coming in force, and we are certainly to have a war."

Our heroes now regarded each other anxiously, then, without speaking, withdrew to gather their coats and weapons. In a moment, they were out upon the dark Lexington Green, in time nearly to be run down by a galloping rider, who cut the reins aside only at the last instant. Across the Green, the Minute-men had drawn up in ranks, but, the moon having set, were scarcely more than a darker form against the grey-painted tavern.

There was held a very short conference, no persons being excluded, from which Jones gathered that the British Army had crossed by boat from Boston to Charlestown, and was now marching in force towards Concord, a path which would take them first through Lexington. Little more was known, since British patrols (which had been riding every lane in the region since sun-set) had arrested above half the American scouts. "And so," said the Minute-man captain, whose name was Parker, "we must assume that the British are acting swiftly and wisely, and make our counter-moves accordingly."

"Why, sir," replied Mrs. Wilson, "then we must see to our cannon at Concord, for, tho' we have removed the smaller pieces, the largest and most valuable are still there."

"You may be certain, ma'am," answered the Captain, "those guns shall soon be hid in furrows; for we have already dispatched riders to Concord."

"I shall be certain, Captain," replies Mrs. Wilson, "when I have seen it myself. Where are Mr. Hancock and Mr. Adams?"

"Gone in a chaise to Woburn, ma'am, above ten minutes ago."

After glancing briefly to Jones, Mrs. Wilson said with finality, "I shall visit Concord. Will you spare me an escort?"

"That I cannot, ma'am," says the Captain, by now very eager to return to his own preparations. "We must reserve all the force we may to hold this ground."

"In that case, Captain, I pray God protect you all. Tom, come with me."

"God bless *you*, ma'am," replied the Captain, turning then to shout something unprintable at a sleepy drummer about twelve years of age.

Jones and Wilson found their horses in the stable (reaching there just as a rider, a bloody bandage upon his head, was dismounting), and were in a minute away and riding hard.

The trip from Lexington to Concord, even shortened by their often leaving the road to cross fields and meadows, still required above forty-five minutes. They travelled during the coldest, darkest part of the night, every minute afraid of British patrols, three or four times hearing (or imagining they heard) shots in the distance.

They did indeed hear, as they neared Concord, the frantic pealing of the Town-House bell. By a torch-light as they entered the town, Jones examined his watch: the time was a little short of four A.M.

Rumours abounded in the town, no facts having arrived since a Dr. Prescott had, an hour earlier, brought word of the British advance. Mrs. Wilson halted only long enough to ask at the meeting-room of the Committee of Safety, "Where is Barrett?" and, being answered that he was at his farm-house, refused an offered glass of wine and departed, with Jones following.

"James Barrett," said she, as they rose again to their saddles, "has in his care the whole of our gun-powder, some ninety barrels. He is a friend of mine, and trust-worthy, but has been Colonel of the Concord Minutemen only a few days. Let us pray he is ready for his command."

Jones, though very grateful for information (which, in truth, had been scarce to this point), made no reply, and they then rode extremely fast about a mile north-west of the village.

Colonel Barrett was a short, stocky man with receding hair and something of a hawkish nose, but very intelligent and sensible. His work was nearly complete when Jones and Wilson arrived: Tom helped to carry one of the heavy gun-powder barrels into the loft of the barn, and to disguise it with tar and straw; after which, with the rest of the volunteers, he joined the Colonel's family for breakfast. Their meal was interrupted (to their considerable satisfaction) by a report that the rest of the Concord weapons had been safely hidden in the surrounding woods.

A little after six, they rode back to the village, which was boiling with the news of a clash at Lexington, with many (some said five, some fifteen) dead upon the American side, and none upon the British. The British, fast advancing, were expected to reach Concord momentarily. In the full daylight, the American force was now assembled, and a few minutes after the arrival of Jones and Wilson, this force marched out, with fife and drum at their head, along the Lexington road.

They had gone a scant half-mile, when they saw a Red-coated column at least three times the size of their own, marching rapidly towards them. The junior officers now conferred in haste, and decided to fall back to Concord, which they did, with fife and drums still playing spiritedly. The British continued forward speedily, with their flankers, moreover, occupying the ridges south and west of the village, and threatening to surround it entirely.

Colonel Barrett now appeared again, his horse rearing almost uncontrollably with excitement, and, without dismounting, said that they must abandon the village and move north, "for we have left nothing here of military value, and have too few troops for its defense."

Mrs. Wilson (seconded by Jones, who had begun to feel something of the lust for battle) demanded, "Why can we not hold here, and fight, whatever the odds?"

"Madam," replied the Colonel hastily, "if the reports be true, we have martyrs enough already at Lexington; let us here have soldiers, and a victory."

Half convinced, Jones and Wilson followed the militia up the ridge north of Concord, to raise a Liberty Pole, and then to watch, ashamed, as the Grenadiers stormed the village. Minutes later, seeing British light infantry (the morning sun glinting yellowly upon their bayonets) advancing from the village towards him, Barrett led the Americans west, down to the North Bridge over the Concord River, then across that and up a hill called Punkatasset.

The pursuing infantry, meanwhile, had cut down and burned the Liberty Pole, and then halted; so that now, for above an hour, the two forces faced each other from atop their separate rises.

On Punkatasset, Barrett refused every demand to attack, and waited for his reinforcements, which arrived steadily, singly and in small units. Jones and Wilson were therefore free to observe these rough, unshaven recruits; to stare across the placid country-side at the menacing Red-coats; or to endure their own thoughts, amid a tension growing ever worse.

Poor Jones!—like old Squire Western, he still wished that the worst deeds could be avenged with a clout to the jaw; yet, looking at Mrs. Wilson (who, in a dark-green dress of Quaker plainness, resembled a woman of granite), he knew that some crimes demand greater measures, and that there would need to be at least a battle, and perhaps a war, to gain recompense.

These unhappy thoughts ended as the British resumed their advance, moving in a small column towards the river.

"Well, Colonel," cried Mrs. Wilson tensely, "surely we must act now."

"Madam," replied Barrett, "only mobs engage from impulse. We are an army, and must behave orderly."

"Why, sir," interjected Jones, who could feel the agony within Mrs. Wilson, "better a mob which fights than an army which does not."

Before another word was said, two junior officers, who had been leading reinforcements from Bedford, ran breathless to the Colonel's side and by frantic gestures pointed out white smoke billowing from the direction of the village.

At the sight of this, Colonel Barrett turned first very pale and then very red. All around him, others of the Minute-men, having seen the smoke, raised four hundred groans and cries, of which the loudest was an anguished shout, "Are we to let them burn the town?"

Barrett, looking extremely wild, surveyed the forming ranks, then, after glancing at Mrs. Wilson, answered in a blaring general command, "We shall stop them if we can. But let no man fire unless first fired upon."

The fife and drums struck up "The White Cockade," and the column, in ragged form, started down the hillside.

Below them, the British, allowed by the narrow North Bridge road to march no more than five abreast, resembled a scarlet river joining the Concord. The few troops already over to the western bank retreated at the Minute-men's advance, leaving but a small party to rip up the bridge-planks.

Two hundred feet from the bridge, Colonel Barrett cupped a hand to his mouth and called to these men to cease working and withdraw, at which they cast down their implements and, scrambling clumsily to re-cover their muskets (which they had leaned against some bare trees), kneeled at the front rank of their column, and took aim.

Now all happened swiftly, the Americans rushing on, the air filling with a forest of martial sounds—swords snicking out and musket-ham-mers clicking back, and Barrett roaring that they must not fire first. A pair of British shots splashed into the river; then there came a short British volley, at which three or four Americans screamed and fell; and lastly, the Minute-men, spreading into a wide firing line, returned an infinitely louder volley of their own, the smoke of which bloomed instantly and then dispersed like fog over the river-bank.

For Jones, there was only chaos: first the whistling British rounds, at which the man beside him, shot between the eyes, crumpled to the ground; then the roar and acrid smoke of the American reply; and last, amid the haze, a feeling almost of isolation as his fellow soldiers, shouting bloody oaths, began to charge the bridge.

Jones, his sword out, his eyes burning with the powder, was stumbling to follow, when he heard Mrs. Wilson cry his name and turned, in horror, to see her upon the ground.

Mrs. Wilson was (despite Tom's fears) uninjured, but had stopped to aid a farm-boy, who, his rifle still in his hand, was twisting upon the ground and begging for her help, while she in turn begged him to be calm.

"Shot through the leg, and pretending to be hurt," she said with affected ease as Tom approached; and the boy, assured he was not about to die, mastered his pain and lay still. The British, having been unable to fire effectively from their narrow quarters, had already begun to flee. Indeed, their withdrawal was now so rapid, and the road so narrow, that only the fleetest Americans stayed with them; nor would the day's truly bloody fighting begin for several hours, when the rear-guard of the retreating British would ambush another militia at a place named Meriam's Corner.

Jones and Wilson therefore saw that they might fairly remain to help the boy. The tall spring grasses seemed almost to cradle his body, but were stained with droplets of blood around his knee. Mrs. Wilson now tore a strip from her petticoat (a sight very interesting to our hero), and made a tourniquet which quickly staunched the bleeding.

In truth, the pleasure Tom now took from Mrs. Wilson's charming limbs was but a single token of his returning satisfaction with life. At great cost to his reputation as a hero, I must tell thee that a feeling of immense relief had gone through him as the sounds of gun-fire and the screams of anguish faded. He was, I fear, the sort of poor spirit who is (except when provoked) content to enrich the cause of liberty by keeping alive those who are meant to possess it—and I have no doubt that those readers who believe heroism to be an outgrowth of ferocity, rather than of simple conviction, will now lose all interest in *Jones.*

Mrs. Wilson (who was, for all her past activities, no more blood-thirsty than our hero) declared the young farmer's wound to be but moderately serious. "We may safely," said she, "carry him to the Reverend Emerson's house, and then go ourselves for the physician."

By placing the wounded boy's arm around his own shoulder, Tom was able to lift him into a standing position while keeping the weight off the injured leg. Mrs. Wilson assisting, they began a slow collective hobble toward Concord bridge. There, with the swift water bubbling beneath them, they passed the English dead in their red coats and mud-spattered breeches, but noticed too that the trees, which had seemed bare, were in fact dotted with innumerable new buds.

So ended our heroes' only active moments in the events of that momentous day. Nor, Reader, shall we here introduce any false touches of the *epic.* A hundred other authors may better show thee (if thou wouldst see) the bloody clashes, the courage and despair, of the British retreat to Boston. Let us only mention that, among the nearly three hundred British casualties, one of the last was a kind-hearted officer of the House Guards, who led out the covering party from Bunker Hill, and whose name was Robert Askew.

# V

*In Which Several Persons Yawn—but
Not, We Hope, Our Reader*

When our heroes (having left the boy with Mrs. Emerson) at last reached Concord, they discovered that the British had in fact destroyed nothing but a few captured supplies; the two other fires they had started, some non-combatants had persuaded them to extinguish. The Meeting-House was entirely undamaged, and it was there that Jones and Wilson went once they had dispatched the physician.

While Jones, as usual, waited outside, Mrs. Wilson conversed with several persons, and then returned to say, "I have left word that we are going to Roxbury, to make ready the supplies there. No doubt they shall be needed soon, for our next step will certainly be to close off Boston from the land, as the British have from the sea. We shall be safe; the countryside is all ours now, or will be very soon."

Jones, who had hoped that a single battle might bring England to negotiate, heard this disappointedly, but said nothing; and so they continued to the inn upon the tattered Concord Green, where the landlady, whose husband had gone off to fight, agreed to prepare a basket lunch for their journey. Jones, who had not slept for two nights, faced the prospect of a fifteen-mile ride with dismay, but a sympathetic smile from Mrs. Wilson was sufficient to persuade him, and soon they were riding east from the village.

They rode during the warmest part of that pleasant April day, and when they had completed about half their journey, Mrs. Wilson suggested that they detour towards a low knoll, topped with a single oak tree, a few hundred yards from the road. There, upon a blanket, they spread their modest picnic, while the sunlight danced, and the birds played, in and about the branches above.

Mrs. Wilson had all this while appeared preoccupied; now, seeming almost distracted, she drew a deep breath, and began:

"I have lately, Tom, begun to fear you are being led into a war you hardly understand. And so—although I dearly love your presence—I would not complain should you—choose to withdraw.

"Our fight, Tom, is not yours; nor is this your country."

Before looking into Mrs. Wilson's eyes, Jones gazed a long moment at the dappling sunlight upon the grey blanket.

"Madam," replied he, at last, "as one of your orators hath said, 'Where is liberty, *there* is my country'—to which I will add, 'Where you are, is my home.' "

Our hero, Reader, had never lacked for graceful language (or, indeed, for grace itself, in most forms); yet never, we must say, had he spoken more effectively. Mrs. Wilson first sighed, then sniffled, and lastly seemed willing to express her gratitude in a manner which, tho' it be as old as the human race, hath never yet been refused as out of fashion.

Had Jones but remained silent, he might have enjoyed a perfect afternoon. Alas, it is in the nature of heroes (or at least of ours) to press their advantage when they have it. Now he continued:

"Dear Angela, as we are already bound by so many other ties, will you not complete my happiness, and consent to be my wife?"

Mrs. Wilson had lately endured several hard rides, a battle, and her offer to abandon her lover, on barely an hour's sleep. Curtly (yet not unkindly) she answered, "Why, sir, as much as I care for you, I shall not marry anyone until the cause of independence is won, or so well launched as to be certain of victory. If you will wait, so will I; if you will not, well . . ." Having said so much, she immediately experienced, and expressed, intense fatigue; in short, she yawned pronouncedly.

Here, Reader, was a clear challenge to the romantic mettle of our hero. Jones, very gallantly for one whose eyes were crossing with fatigue (he was as weary as Mrs. Wilson), now begged her to name a time-limit.

"Why, sir, I shall know when the time has come," answered Mrs. Wilson, for whom the noises of birds and breeze and Mr. Jones had all become one pleasant hum.

"Will you at least promise we *will* be married one day?" pleaded our hero.

"Sir, I shall not."

"Why, then, madam, perhaps you would prefer that I go," said Jones, in sleepy dudgeon.

"Sir, you are foolish," answered Mrs. Wilson, lying back upon the blanket, with her eyes closed.

"Madam," asked Jones, lying beside her, but still annoyed, "do you forgive me?"

Mrs. Wilson answered, "Yes," and some three or four seconds later, they were both sound asleep.

When they awoke, the afternoon was nearly gone, the air very cold. They cast long shadows as they galloped over the meadow, and, despite riding hard, did not until twilight reach the inn at Roxbury, where Mr. Southwark greeted them by asking curiously, "What truth may lie in these horrid rumours we hear of bloody fighting all along the Concord road?"

Mrs. Wilson (who rarely spoke shortly to anyone but Jones, and then only in jest) answered simply:

"The rumours may be horrid or fine, as you wish, but they are almost certainly true.

"Now, sir, I beg you that we may have hot water as soon as possible, and then some soup or other light food sent up, with bread and wine, and no other disturbance."

"Madam," replied Mr. Southwark, with an oily smile Jones found very hard to stomach, "I shall be delighted to send someone up to you."

Jones and Wilson went up to their room, completed their washing, and then waited above twenty minutes (full darkness having meanwhile fallen) without receiving any food. Tom, in fact, was about to enquire when there came at last a knock at the door.

Mrs. Wilson, answering this, suddenly exclaimed in dismay, then fell back several paces as a tall, shabbily dressed, black-haired person forced himself into the room. Seeing Jones reaching for his sword, he cried sharply, "No idiocy, sir!" while pulling from his breeches a pistol, which he leveled at Mrs. Wilson.

"How . . . ?" asked Mrs. Wilson in a whisper.

" 'How?' " replied this gentleman (who was, in fact, Captain Whipsblood, though not then in uniform). "Why, madam, field glasses are common enough in armies, and your form stood out handsomely at Concord. I have followed you all day, until you chose to nap, and I rode on ahead to plan your welcome.

"Now, madam, you may begin to pay some of the penalty for all your deeds. Our dead litter the road from Concord to Boston this night; for which you shall soon answer to God Almighty, but sooner answer to me. Gather your clothing, both of you, and walk slowly before me down the stairs and to the carriage. Consider, too, madam, the satisfaction I should take in shooting you."

So, Reader, might a less noble author introduce certain speculations upon the nature of *Fate*, and the futility of resisting it. Our heroes, who had so recently behaved with such gallantry in the face of hot lead and cold steel, were now led off prisoners by a single officer, without even the chance to raise a finger in their own defense. For, in truth, they walked, frightened and dejected, down the stairs, past a very contented-looking Mr. Southwark (who, I believe, now considered himself the proprietor of the Roxbury Inn), and out to the cold night and black carriage, where Whipsblood's lieutenant waited to drive them to Boston, and to gaol.

## VI

### Filled with Black News, Folly and Kindness

Had Captain Whipsblood not needed our heroes to get safely through what was now rebel territory, he would probably have committed a pair of murders that very night. As it was, he merely seated himself in the coach beside Mrs. Wilson, with the tip of his knife against her ribs, and warned her she must cooperate to live. Having been twice challenged by American patrols and passed upon Mrs. Wilson's word, the coach reached Boston Army headquarters a little before one A.M.

Jones and Wilson were locked in a nearly-subterranean former powder magazine, whose single room had been divided into two facing cells separated by a narrow corridor. In these cells, just far enough apart that their outstretched fingertips could not quite touch, they were left until the building's single, high and tiny window had displayed daylight for above three hours.

It was then that Captain Whipsblood returned, looking very cheerful, to address himself first to Mrs. Wilson.

"Well, madam," said he, "now perhaps you understand the price of all your independence. Nay, do not trouble yourself to act self-confident.

You must abandon all hope of support from your rebel friends; for you are to be returned to England, where, as sure as God is just, you shall rot in prison until you are very old, or very dead. Last summer, madam, I gave you your chance to abandon your precious Yankee vermin. You were too proud to listen then. Let that pride comfort you when the gaol fever strikes as it did last year, and is killing every prisoner it touches."

Mrs. Wilson would certainly have replied very spiritedly to this, had not the Captain forestalled her by turning to Mr. Jones, to say:

"As for you, sir, I believe you shall regret my not killing you last night. Even that would have been preferable to being hung for treason."

"*Treason!*?" cries Jones.

"Aye, when a gentleman upon the King's business takes arms against the king's soldiers. My own evidence, I promise you, would have been enough to set you swinging—even without the other matter."

"Other matter?" asks Jones, staggered almost beyond speaking.

"Surely," answers Whipsblood, with a leer, "you did not think to escape justice? I have already charged you, upon the deposition of Lady Ellena Suffley, with stealing £2,000 from the Crown revenues of Maryland Colony. Why, sir, you know we hang thieves as willingly as traitors. One way or another, you shall ride the cart to Tyburn gallows—and then be dissected by some eager surgeon."

It is a mystery to the painter, not the *psychologist*, whether there be shades of black. Despair is never so deep that it cannot go deeper; yet Jones now plunged as low as any of us, not immediately facing the noose, shall ever descend. Speech eluded him; he only stared at Mrs. Wilson, who looked back in amazement.

A minute or two later, his knife-like features aglow, Whipsblood departed, and the prison door slammed behind him.

Indeed, I believe the Captain had won a great victory. During the next six days, living upon watery porridge in virtual darkness, Jones and Wilson grew steadily thinner and paler. Jones, meanwhile, never ceased complaining about his fortunes, lands and own unhappy fate. Not even Mrs. Wilson was forgiven for what he was pleased to call her coldness in refusing to marry him. In short, Reader, never had Jones been less of a hero—never had he been less pleased with his situation, or we less pleased with him—and it was for his un-Jones-like self-pity that we pronounce this the most tragical part of his saga.

The last of these wretched days had ended when the door above them opened, to reveal a hoary old guard, his face clotted with a lifetime's drinking, using a lamp to lead down the silhouette of a gentleman. This outline gripped the guard's shoulder, and descended each step with agonizing slowness by turning sideways to lower his stiff left leg, before following it with his more agile right. His right arm was heavily bandaged and set into a sling.

Jones and Wilson withdrew to the rear of their respective cells at the approach of this sad figure, and only came forward when he dismissed the guard (after claiming his lantern), and kindly called Tom's name.

Nothing would have been more proper than for Tom now to throw himself upon his knees in a rapture of gratitude and joy—for the visitor was in fact his friend Colonel Askew.

Instead, Jones introduced the Colonel and Mrs. Wilson with barest civility. Askew, after some kind words to the lady, continued to them both:

"I bring you news. Captain Whipsblood has gone to Maryland to gather the last bits of evidence. He and the Suffleys will be accompanying you back to London, to give evidence at your trial—but at least for a while, you shall be spared his threats and bullying."

Mrs. Wilson sighed with relief, but Jones only said it hardly mattered what else was heaped upon him, as he had little but indignities left to endure in life.

Askew, his smile slightly forced, continued: "I have saved the best for last. When the two of you sail for England, you will not travel alone. I am bound for Dorsetshire, and retirement. I shall go with you. And so," he added with a larger smile, "will Amelia and Parson Adams."

Jones, cheering slightly, begged to see his daughter.

"Impossible, I'm afraid. Whipsblood's own men guard her—as they guarded you until this evening, when, with assistance, they took sick. Yet I promise you will find her aboard the ship."

Fatigued with standing, Askew gripped the bars for support. At last, Jones—not yet utterly lost to common humanity—asked, "How, my friend, did you come to be injured?"

Askew (who would have more welcomed this question some minutes sooner) answered shortly, "I was hurt in the fighting outside Boston, sir, but 'tis nothing to speak of; pray let us not mention it again."

This brevity suited Jones pretty well, for he was then interested in nothing which diminished the luster of his own sufferings. Conversation lagged, until Askew—who had never before done anything so friendly for our hero—forgot his annoyance, and said, with all the spirit he could muster, "Why, my boy, you have before this faced dangerous times; you are, I know, innocent of the worst charge" (this, to the Colonel, meant theft), "and it would be a sad business if one gentleman in America should be hanged for acting upon principles which ten thousand in England have endorsed."

Mrs. Wilson seconded this heartily, but our hero (who had lately become a *sodden lump* in his behaviour), made no reply. Askew, after studying him, merely shrugged, and turned to Mrs. Wilson, to say, "Madam, there is little I may do for you, unless there is some family member to be informed that you are well."

"There is no one but Mr. Jones," replied she, "who is likely to take a personal interest. Yet I thank you for your kindness. I—do not suppose you could tell me about the military situation?"

"Only, madam," answered Askew, "that it is exactly as you must wish. Perhaps soon, I may be able to tell you more.

"Meanwhile, do not lose faith. If I am able to visit you again, I shall; if not, we will meet aboard the transport *Rose of York*, six days from today."

So saying, and seeming as if he would have said more, Askew bowed awkwardly to them, and began his slow, shuffling progress back up the stairs.

Reader, the moment had now arrived at which, in most domestic circumstances, Mrs. Wilson would (with very good cause) have given our hero what is generally known as a piece of her mind. That she refrained from upbraiding him, must remain one of the great mysteries of our story. To be sure, the superficial answer is that she loved him; yet we are more inclined to credit her long history of standing by good causes when they look'd entirely lost.

# VII

## Containing an Important Change

The spirits and behaviour of Mr. Jones only worsened during the remainder of his imprisonment. By that perfect late-April day when he and Mrs. Wilson were led aboard the *Rose of York,* even that lady's affections were beginning to thin.

Under guard at the ship's stern, Jones and Wilson stood as far apart as their chains would permit, while he stared at the deck, and she raised her face to enjoy the bright sun, blue skies and steady breezes, for about forty minutes, until the doleful arrival of Amelia and the Parson. Humiliated at seeing his own daughter being led along like a common criminal, Jones might then have done something desperate, had not Amelia and her friend been followed immediately by Colonel Askew, who, the moment he had mounted the deck, ordered the prisoners unchained.

At once Jones deserted Mrs. Wilson, pushed rudely past the Parson, and threw his arms around his surprised daughter.

Poor Amelia had stumbled boarding the ship; and, after embracing Tom, was glad to sit. Having lain three times as long in gaol as her father, she was now three times as weak; nor had she been spared mental suffering.

Since writing the note which Colonel Askew had seen carried to her father, Amelia had undergone a hundred alterations in her thinking: now supposing Tom would come to rescue her, now fearing he would surrender himself; one day imagining he had already sailed for England, another certain he had died in some distant clash with Whipsblood or the British regulars. She was often angry with her father for deserting her, and with Mrs. Wilson (whom, of course, she had never met) for having lured him into trouble; indeed, she was one time or another furious with everyone except Mr. Adams—and even he, I fear, scarcely escaped the mental lash.

In all this, Amelia had been perfectly human. Such was her love for her father, however, that she would never have mentioned her anger to him, had he not, while she was still exhausted, pressed her for details. She had hardly rested, when he began:

"Dearest Amelia, tell me now exactly what you meant by your note."

"Meant, sir?" asked Amelia, somewhat surprised. "Why, exactly what I said."

"But then, Hacksem hath seized my estates?"

"Aye, sir, and Dr. James is dead—under circumstances very ugly. We believe it to have been a murder."

"Alas, poor doctor!" cried Tom, staring into the distance, and speaking with theatrical melancholy. "How shall I make amends now? You were the best of friends."

"Aye, sir," answered Amelia sharply, "and he was left sadly over-matched."

Startled, Tom cried, "But what of poor Mrs. James? Surely Hacksem hath taken pity upon her?"

"My brother, sir," replied Amelia, passionately, "hath shown Mrs. James all the pity which the wolf shows to the bunny-rabbit. He and Mr. Sinamore have already seized her home for debts, and sent her to live, impoverished, in some wretched London room, where her remaining friends have been too poor to assist her, and where, I suppose, she shall soon expire from hunger, cold or disease. Her one powerful friend—having chosen to travel for his amusement—hath meanwhile forgotten her existence; just as he hath been pleased to forget the loyalty of a Parson named Adams, who risked his life in order to warn him of his danger."

Reader, I suspect thou art very willing to condemn Amelia for this un-daughterly behaviour. Yet she had charged Tom with few of the results of his negligence, concealing, for example, the insults and violence she herself had suffered from Hacksem.

Above all, we must judge Amelia's words by their effects. In truth, I, myself—tho' I trust I have disguised it supremely well—have lately felt scant sympathy for Jones, who, in all his suffering has undergone only *regret*, and expressed nothing like true *repentance*.

Amelia's frankness had at last made Tom realize the harm he had done, not only to her and the Parson (which time might allow him to repair), but to Dr. and Mrs. James—one, and perhaps both of whom were beyond his aid forever. Only then, with a rushing sense of helplessness, did Tom begin his trudge from the pool of self-pity.

Repentance, like many wonderful medicines, is of the kill-or-cure

---

313

variety. Jones's native strength allowed him to consider Amelia's charges almost calmly, only looking her wildly in the eyes and nodding. Yet he then hastily excused himself and sped below decks, with Colonel Askew ordering the guards to permit it.

Amelia bowed her head in dismay, but Mrs. Wilson sat beside her and told her she had done nothing wrong; and Colonel Askew, after drawing a breath, added, gently, "These were truths Tom was obliged to hear."

The ship, having raised her sails, began to move smartly before the breeze. In the distance, a battery of artillery, testing its guns upon the Dorchester Heights, made a noise very like a giant firing-squad—a matter which certain moralizing authors might, I suppose, consider portentous. As if the guns had struck their mark, Jones from below-decks emitted the first of many heart-felt screams, resembling the cries of six or seven thousand frenzied sea-gulls.

Mrs. Wilson turned paler than ashes; and the Colonel, nearly as pale. Some great catastrophe appeared at hand—and only Amelia now had any great faith in the outcome.

The screams persisted, with diminishing violence, until about high noon. When the ship had scarcely cleared Boston Harbour, our hero reappeared, looking extremely weary, yet calmer than he had for many weeks. He approached the others, and began, with unmistakable sincerity, "Amelia—my friends—I have led all of you into considerable miseries for my sake; and have in thanks treated you all extremely cruelly. I have compounded impositions with ingratitude; but now I tell you I am very sorry, and very grateful."

He continued in this vein some time. In truth, such humble words were never heard from a hundred of the doughty knights of Mallory or Ariosto; nor from the great drunken brawlers of French romance. As heroes go, our Mr. Jones was sad stuff—yet his daughter and his friends seem'd inclined to keep him; and that is our opinion as well—especially as his remaining days are now so likely to be few, and full of sorrow.

# VIII

## In Which Our Story Begins to Draw
## to a Close

Reader, we should never tell thee anything so false as that Mr. Jones, simply by beginning to repent, had cured himself of all his earthly woes. His burdens remained extremely heavy; yet his heart, I believe, was soon infinitely lighter. And so the short voyage to Maryland, surrounded by his daughter and his friends, did wonders to restore his old optimism and willingness to fight the villains who beset him.

Two days later, however, the respite granted our friends ended abruptly with the arrival of Captain Whipsblood, who, along with the Suffleys and two or three of their servants, was rowed out to the *Rose of York* as she lay at anchor in the Chesapeake Bay. Reader, thou hast no doubt often heard at the theatre that deep and threatening music which, announcing the arrival of some villain, is meant to stir in the audience feelings of alarm and detestation (and, in many cases, to end that pleasant *nap* which a preceding love scene hath inspired). Thou mayst (if thou pleaseth) now imagine such a menacing tune played *fortissimo*—for certainly Colonel Askew, who greeted these arrivals, met a line of villainy *well doubled*.

The characters of Whipsblood and Lord Suffley had by no means been improved by their close association; nor, indeed, would the most benevolent observer have expected much friendship between two gentlemen who would gladly have cut each other's liver out, excepting only that one lacked the courage, and the other, the opportunity.

Lest thou imagine, Reader, that these two gentlemen had quarreled over anything so trivial as politics or religion, I must tell thee their dispute concerned nothing less than Lady Suffley. In truth, from the instant Captain Whipsblood had crossed the threshold of the governor's mansion, her ladyship had hinted openly that she wished to revive their old *amour*. The Captain (who was possessed of very strong animal spirits, and an equally strong contempt of Lord Suffley) had at once flashed sparks from his eyes; and, in short, before the lamps had been extinguished that evening, Lord Suffley had discovered yet another incentive to grind his teeth to little nubs.

Lady Suffley herself was now brought aboard by means of the ship's chair, from which she had no sooner escaped, than she smiled very charmingly upon her admirers, and expressed an intense desire to see that notorious criminal, *Tom Jones*. This wish (as may be imagined) inspired no great satisfaction in the breast of either gentleman; yet they commanded Colonel Askew to bring the prisoner to the small deck cabin, where he might be interviewed—his Lordship thoughtfully adding that, for the sake of Lady Suffley's *safety*, the prisoner must be very thoroughly manacled during the interview, and thereafter.

When, in this pitiable condition, Jones was at last brought to her Ladyship, there ensued nothing but a long silence, interrupted only by her once or twice drawing audible breaths.

We must now, Reader, reveal to thee a small secret, which was that Lady Suffley, despite her best efforts to rub out the memory of Mr. Jones, had succeeded in the previous few months only in enflaming and enlarging it. Under such circumstances, it was almost impossible that she should be unmoved by their reunion, for, had he looked entirely wretched, she would have been moved at least to pity; and had he looked extremely well, to admiration.

In fact, Jones possessed one of those happy constitutions which recover rapidly from misfortunes, and the two days spent travelling with friends and family aboard the pleasant *Rose* had largely restored his customary vigour and colour—especially after he had found the grace to seek *privately* Mrs. Wilson's specific pardon for the unkind things he had said while in prison. So wholesome did our hero now appear, indeed, that Lady Suffley was inspired to speak to him as follows:

"Alas, my dear Tom," says she, placing a soft hand upon his forearm, "how much I feared this end! And how earnestly I tried to dissuade you, that night I visited you."

Jones replied that he remembered very well all her tenderness.

"Why, sir, you were very foolish. And yet a woman may forgive much, where she is certain there is repentance." So saying, she looked searchingly at Jones with her pale-blue eyes, and placed her other hand on his, before whispering, "Well, sir, is a time of repentance upon us?"

Jones, with a certain awkwardness, now stammered that he hoped he was heartily sorry for all his sins.

"Very well, sir," replies Lady Suffley, "but what of the particular sin of neglecting those who would be close to you?"

"Ma'am," says Jones sincerely, "now that I am near to my daughter and my friends, I pray I may never again be parted from them while I live."

"I believe, sir," answers her Ladyship, "you are willfully misunderstanding me. What of myself?"

"Why, ma'am," cries Jones, "now you go to the very heart of repentance, for sure I am very sorry for all the wrongs I have done your husband."

"My husband!" cries Lady Suffley in astonishment.

"Indeed, ma'am," says Jones, with what was certainly a kind of sincerity. "I am as sorry as yourself for all the wrongs I have done him. I pledge henceforth to follow the paths of righteousness—and, as you are certainly aware from Captain Whipsblood, there is another person to whom I have the strongest possible obligations."

"*Obligations!*" cries Lady Suffley, angered and perplexed beyond words. "Why, sir, to this *person*, you are obliged for your ruin, and nothing more. Mr. Jones, I believe you are as obstinate and foolish in love as in everything else. I am glad you have not arrogance enough to name this hated *person* to me, but for all else, I despise you entirely. Look'ee, sir, one last time: I offer you your freedom and lands to replace your estate, or the claim upon a better one when my husband shall be gone. What say you?"

Something extremely final and dangerous in Lady Suffley's tone would have deterred anyone less heroic than Jones. As it was, he, with considerable gentleness, replied, "Madam, I am grateful for your friendship, but I fear I love only Mrs. Wilson, and I regard you far too highly to deceive you in a matter so touching upon your feelings."

Lady Suffley's features now grew extremely dark, and, withdrawing her hand, she said in a voice trembling with anger, "Why, sir, pray do not speak to me of such stuff as love and friendship and feelings. You know nothing of such things. As for Mrs. Wilson, I pray you shall make her as happy as you have made me. May she enjoy your embraces after you have been turned off the Tyburn cart upon hanging-day."

So declaring, Lady Suffley stormed from the tiny cabin, intending, I believe, to see for herself this Mrs. Wilson who was so irresistible to our hero. (This meeting proved unsatisfactory, for Mrs. Wilson refused to speak, and Lady Suffley, having in her quest for fortune lost the taste for virtue, found nothing remarkable about her. In truth, Lady Suffley would not have understood Angela Wilson's attractiveness had they spoken an hour or more; for her Ladyship, like most fashionable people, cared little for courage, or for anything else which could not be imported at great cost from France or the *Orient.*)

Lady Suffley's departure left Tom to wait nervously for the guard to take him back below decks, where, once the ship was underway, Colonel Askew visited him with the short message that the Suffleys now insisted he be confined as dangerous the whole duration of the journey. "You have," said the Colonel, "brought all our new passengers to agree: they shall hate you, instead of each other. Whether that pact shall last the entire journey, I cannot say, but for now, you must wait here, and be patient, as always.

"I hope I shall still be able to arrange for you to see Mrs. Wilson and your daughter. Perhaps tomorrow morning. But we must be careful. I— am sorry."

Askew, indeed, examined his friend with a gaze of unspeakable pity, before turning to walk away.

Then, with a mournful glance at his departing friend, Jones cast his head into his hands, and resumed his contemplations of the unhappy state into which he had fallen.

# IX

## *In Which Our Story Draws Even Nearer to the End*

The following morning at dawn, Askew fulfilled his promise, releasing the prisoners from their rooms, and allowing them to meet in a small, dank storage area in the ship's hold, where he promptly left them alone, saying he would return in fifteen minutes.

They had scarcely gathered, however, when there came from every direction at once the sounds of intense disturbance: running feet, shouted commands, and then, from the distance, the bang of a cannon-shot.

Adams now said in alarm, "G—d protect us! What can be happening?"

To which, Mrs. Wilson, slamming her hand upon a convenient cask of salt-pork, replied, "Privateers, as sure as you live; or if not, some worse trouble for this vessel."

Pausing an instant, and changing her tone, she added fiercely, "Look-'ee: we are bound for hanging, if we allow it. But I say we may, if we are brave, seize this ship, and be free. Are you with me?"

"Why, madam," says Adams, in dismay, yet perhaps with some approval, "we shall surely hang for such an effort."

"We shall surely hang without it," replies Mrs. Wilson energetically.

"But how, madam, may four prevail against an entire crew?"

"Look'ee, Mr. Adams: if we can but get these English Lords and their lackeys locked below-decks, I can promise the ship-captain's help. Captain Lawrence is a New Bedford man, and once worked with my husband. He has not much courage, but is a patriot."

"But what," asks Amelia, "of this Captain Whipsblood? He is very dangerous, and may easily defeat us."

"Why, miss, if we fail, we shall at least have sought Liberty. What say you all? Quickly, before the chance passes!"

Having said so much, Mrs. Wilson now held her hand out before her. Jones (who, I believe, would have followed her straight past the Pillars of Hercules) took it; then Amelia placed hers atop theirs, and, lastly, Mr. Adams covered all three with a paw the size of a bear's.

Our hero now began to open his mouth, but the fine sentiments with which he intended to sanctify the pact were unfortunately lost to the clap of nearing footsteps, at which Mrs. Wilson whispered to the others to withdraw into the darkness, and ordered Mr. Adams to take a station behind the door.

Mr. Adams now raised over his head a salt-beef cask of above fifty pounds' weight, with which he might (despite his more moderate intentions) have done immeasurable damage. Yet even as the door opened, Tom cried, "No!" and Colonel Askew adroitly stepped back from certain death.

Askew, very easily guessing the source of his danger, said calmly from the passageway, "You may drop your weapon, Mr. Adams. Come with me, please, all of you, as quickly as possible."

As they raced up to the deck, Askew (wincing with pain from his injured leg, but moving very fast) hastily continued, "We lost our escort in last night's fog, and as the sun rose, the only ship on the horizon was a sort of light frigate, almost certainly a privateer or pirate. You heard their gun; we're hove to, and if the Royal Navy does not appear in the next few minutes, we shall certainly be boarded.

"Lord Suffley has ordered that you shall be given weapons, on your words of honour to defend the ship."

"Lord Suffley," replied Mrs. Wilson, "be damned."

They had now reached the fresh air of the early morning. The privateer's ship lay perhaps four hundred yards off the port stern, and, under full sail, was closing fast upon the immobile *Rose of York*. Her black guns had been run out, and among the mob upon her deck, a vast array of cutlery gleamed in the morning sun. Even Mrs. Wilson began to quail a little.

Standing on the *Rose of York*'s small quarter-deck with two pistols stuck in his belt, Whipsblood was bellowing orders to his two privates and promising to shoot Captain Lawrence if he surrendered the ship. As our friends approached, he shouted to Mrs. Wilson, "Well, madam, perhaps now you'll see there are worse things in this world than the British Army." Besides him, one looking very wild, and the other, very frightened, were Lord and Lady Suffley.

Mrs. Wilson's reply was lost, for, the privateer having now closed to within some forty or fifty yards, Colonel Askew asked with great urgency, "Do I have your words of honour to fight solely in defense of this ship, and to surrender your weapons if we prevail?"

Jones, seeing a look of extreme excitement upon the face of Mrs. Wilson, answered that they could not promise.

"Then," replies Askew, "I must ask you to step as far back from the line of fire as possible."

The Colonel had no sooner said this, than the privateer arrived near enough to cast her shadow upon the deck of the *Rose of York*.

The situation aboard the *Rose* was now absurd, for while Captain Lawrence, being sensible, had ordered his sailors not to resist, Lord Suffley (a gentleman whom birth, not talent, had appointed to command all the others) was shouting to his few soldiers to prepare to die fighting. Captain Whipsblood—who would certainly have fought with or without instructions—instantly drew one of his pistols and cocked both the barrels, while the two privates knelt upon the deck and raised their muskets.

Colonel Askew, while making some motion to draw his sword free of his scabbard, cried to Lord Suffley, "My Lord, resistance here is madness." Alas, before his Lordship could make his reply (which, we have no doubt, would have lived forever in the annals of Naval glory), the discussion was ended by a remark from the opposing craft, in the form of a single cannon-shot, which bursting high in the *Rose*'s rigging, neatly splintered the top third of her fore-mast.

The last fragments of wood and rope had scarcely crashed, smouldering, onto the deck, before a person aboard the raiding ship leaped upon its railing and, cupping a hand to his mouth (which, like the rest of his face, was obscured by a dark-blue tricorn hat, pulled low), cried boldly that they must at once throw down their weapons, or be blown from the water.

Captain Lawrence, a short, fair, plump man of perhaps thirty, now seconded this advice by jumping up and down upon the deck, and begging, "Do, do surrender!" In truth, Reader, the necessity of a yielding was now so obvious to all, that even Captain Whipsblood, after the scantest of pauses, raised his hand in acquiescence, and then slowly bent down to place his pistols upon the deck. The two privates (with relief very evident upon their faces) followed suit, after which Colonel Askew unbuckled his sword and added it to the pile.

With what trepidation did our friends await the boarding! Jones and Askew now took a step forward, the ladies each took a step back, Amelia and Mrs. Wilson placing their arms around each other for support, while Lady Suffley encouraged herself by quietly blaming his Lordship for everything.

Upon the raiding ship, the hatted commander (who was, I grant, a very dashing figure, for all that he was a pirate, and probably much worse) now swung several times a length of rope with a boarding-hook at its end, and launched it towards the *Rose*, where it caught over a yard-arm. Giving the line one hard tug, he next placed a pistol in his teeth and, making an overhand grab upon the rope to raise himself as high as possible, lifted up his legs, and began sailing alone over the water toward our helpless friends.

Oh Reader! Could I now divide that pirate's arc into Mr. Newton's *infinitesimals*, and devote to each of them a chapter upon the marvelous, I could not convey to thee half the sensation this boarding created, for:

The pirate Captain completed his flight by landing neatly upon the deck of the *Rose of York*, dropping gracefully to his knees, and then rising quickly with a look first of victory, and then of utter amazement, upon his face.

Indeed, this rogue and Mr. Jones now stared at each other a long moment in wild disbelief, and then:

"Father!" cries the pirate, throwing his arms wide, and, in the process, throwing his pistol overboard.

"My boy!" cries Jones, stepping forward into the sunlight.

"Brother!" cries Amelia, and faints.

"Great Heavens!" cries Mr. Adams, speaking, perhaps, for all the others.

Indeed, Reader, how are we now to disguise our own amazement? By what dry observations shall we hide our own sense of awe at the wonders of Providence? For, in fact, the handsome young pirate seizing the *Rose of York,* was none other than that lost soul, that worst of prodigals, Tom's own younger son, Rob Jones.

The sensation created by this discovery stopped nothing short of chaos, especially as it was accompanied by the arrival, *via* many other ropes, of above a dozen of Rob's associates, who, with little ceremony, arrested and led away Whipsblood and his troops, but, at Rob's instructions, left all the others perfectly safe.

Captain Jones, with the tears of joy still standing in his eyes, ordered that the ship be searched for valuables, and then went to embrace his sister, as a prelude to that longer reunion which, Reader, we shall endeavour to describe for thee in our next chapter.

# X

## *In Which Astounding Secrets Are Revealed*

Rob reached Amelia as Mrs. Wilson was helping her to her feet. The day having grown extremely hot, he no sooner embraced her than he offered to lead her into the deck cabin (a proposal supported by Mr. Adams), but this she refused, saying she had suffered only a momentary surprise, and was now perfectly fine.

These two (who really were immensely fond of one another) had scarcely ended their embrace, when Tom demanded eagerly, "You must now, Rob, perfect our joy by explaining how you came to be here."

"Indeed, sir," replied Rob, very anxiously, "with the Royal Navy so near, I have not leisure to tell my entire story; I hope you shall hear it another time.

"You may say, however, that my friends and I are privateers in training; for, when war begins—which we expect very soon—we shall ask our papers of the Continental Congress; and 'til then, we shall trouble Great Britain upon our own behalf."

Hearing this, Mrs. Wilson slapped Mr. Adams upon the arm (thereby first shocking, and then amusing, him), and declared, "That surely she had found a *wonderful* family."

Rob, however, restored the solemnity of the occasion by asking fiercely, "Now, Father, pray answer *me:* how do I find you all prisoners, and whom shall I punish for this most-monstrous offense? "

Tom, blushing to explain, at length began, "You must realize, son, that most of this is the result of a mistake, which I intend to correct—"

"*Correct!*" cried Lady Suffley, who to this point had been forgotten (a circumstance, I believe, new in her experience). "Why, sir," said she, "your mistakes were treason and thievery, and you shall see very soon how England treats those who betray her."

Reader, do not think Lady Suffley was practicing an idle malice. In truth, she never missed an opportunity to make herself look well, or her enemies, ill; and Jones was now, unequivocally, among her enemies.

And yet, in all matters under the sun, opinions may differ. Young Rob declared with sudden joy, "I believe, Father, we have begun to think very much alike. Well, then, you shall all come with me, and we shall be privateers together, for the best of causes."

"Aye, sir," said Lady Suffley, disdainfully, "do run off with this boy, and leave your estates to a son with the sense to improve them. You shall not be missed in Somersetshire, I promise you."

"How?" cries Rob. "What can she mean by this, Father?"

Before Jones could reply, Lady Suffley answered triumphantly, "Your brother, sir, has claimed your family's estate, while this clever gentleman" (meaning, of course, our hero) "was squandering his wealth, and risking his life, with this wh__re" (pointing now to Mrs. Wilson), "and, worst of all, stealing the tax-monies of the Colony of Maryland to support his vice and wickedness. Indeed, Mr. Jones, from what Captain Whipsblood tells me, I do not doubt that you and your wh__re" (pointing now very

---

323

emphatically to Mrs. Wilson) will turn next to piracy and murder to maintain yourselves. Very well—let the British Navy do the work of the British courts."

There are some words, Reader, which do not, like new tunes, grow more welcome by repetition. Among these words, I believe "wh__re" to rank very high; or at least it seemed to be so with Mrs. Wilson, for, at first hearing herself so named, she started and looked very surprised, but at next hearing it, she turned very red and clenched her fist.

Indeed, Lady Suffley might have received one of the greatest lessons of her life, had the school not been interrupted by a great clamour, as three or four of Captain Jones's lieutenants, having first tried to force their way into his presence, now demanded loudly that he attend them.

Rob, perhaps realizing how close the two ladies were to blows, commanded these lieutenants to state their business, whereupon they ordered brought forward (in the hands of several grinning sailors) Captain Whipsblood, and a chest measuring perhaps two feet in length and one foot in each other dimension.

The chief lieutenant, a short, black-bearded, immensely broad-chested pirate named Cobb, announced with a grin, "Why, Captain, let's hear no more about the poor pay of Army officers. Behold the rich stiffening we found beneath this gentleman's bed." So saying, he threw open the chest (the lock of which had already been broken), to let glitter in the sun as many gold guineas as any of us is likely to see in his or her life.

This dazzling display produced many remarks, of which Lady Suffley's was perhaps the most interesting:

"I am shocked beyond words, Captain!" said she. "So brave a soldier to have been a common thief! And to steal from those who have so long and so faithfully advanced your interest! We shall have more hangings than ever, this year. They will need a special volume of the *Newgate Calendar,* to list them all."

We are, Reader, a little embarrassed to record this, which we must consider a softening of Lady Suffley's memory in the heat of events; for the treasure was certainly her own; or rather, represented the earnings of a partnership between herself and the Captain—which, I suppose, her Ladyship had now decided to dissolve.

Alas, in so deciding, Lady Suffley had underestimated the Captain, who, with extraordinary strength, suddenly tore himself loose from the two sailors holding him, and with equally extraordinary dexterity, snatched from the bosom of her dress (for he was well familiar with both her habits of concealment, and her more intimate charms) a small note-book. Thrusting this toward Tom and Rob, he shouted, "Look, gentle-men, and then decide who is the thief, and who the patriot!"

Reader, it is very wisely written that, "The wicked flee where no man pursuith." At first glance, none of our friends had imagined the money from under Captain Whipsblood's bed to be anything but his private fortune. Had Lady Suffley been less rash about shifting the blame away from herself, I believe the result would have been nothing worse than Rob's pirates carrying away what was, after all, no great amount of money to her.

As it was, she had provoked the anger of one who never let up his assault until the city was ground into rubble. In other words, the Captain now continued:

"Know, gentlemen, that, immediately upon reaching Maryland, Lady Suffley began a little scheme of collecting monthly fees from those of her husband's employees who wished to linger in their jobs. These fees were not large—perhaps four hundred pounds per month, in total—yet this lady, I believe, hath never considered any crime beneath her notice. This . . ." (meaning the tiny volume he clenched in his fist), "was her ledger book, which I discovered during an intimate moment."

A cry of amazement now went up from all assembled, tinged (I think) with anguish on the part of Lord Suffley, and joyous anticipation on the part of all the others.

"Why, sirs," continued the Captain (who had, I believe, missed a great career in the courtroom, if not upon the stage), "such extortion would have been bad enough, had it ended there; but then she contrived a new wickedness; for it was, I now see, when this gentleman" (meaning Jones) "was dispatched to Massachusetts, that she contrived to steal £2,000 from the government revenues, and charge him with the theft. He is, I promise you, a traitor—but innocent, I now believe, of the theft. There, gentle-men, is your thief."

There now arose another gasp, but this time Lady Suffley used the opportunity to begin raising certain charges of her own—which, how-ever, were too implausible to be recorded here. The simple truth of the matter was that her Ladyship had no sooner written the Captain her initial letter accusing Tom of theft, than she realized (such was her excellence with numbers) that she had created a dangerous surplus in the government funds—in short, that if Jones were to be charged with a theft, it would be better that some money be missing. The appearance of the muscular Captain had suggested a way to cart the gold from the customs-house, and so may we understand her revived affection for him at his arrival.

In truth, Reader, I cannot easily explain why one as rich as Lady Suffley would stoop to such deeds; yet perhaps the very number and diversity of her crimes argues that an inventive mind, having few real or useful tasks, had inspired much of her folly.

Such speculations are, however, better suited for another time; for just now, the abusive charges traded between her Ladyship and the Captain (which had, indeed, reached the level of fingernails and fists) persuaded Colonel Askew he had heard enough.

"Madam and gentleman!" cried he, forcing a silence. "You have both been very helpful. Perhaps the courts will wish to consider your actions more closely. For now, I believe I may say neither of you possesses sufficient character to testify at any trial save your own; and I hereby declare, in my capacity as Dorsetshire magistrate, that the charges against Wilson, Jones, Jones and Adams, are dismissed."

Thou mayst wonder, Reader, whether the Colonel had authority to dismiss these charges. To be sure, the county of Dorsetshire doth not on most maps extend across seven-eighths of the Atlantic Ocean. Yet he had only hastened the inevitable; for, without the testimonies (or rather, perjuries) of Whipsblood and Lady Suffley, there were no cases against any of our friends, except Mrs. Wilson—and that but a weak one, full of hearsay and surmise. Indeed, if Colonel Askew *had* committed a small procedural error in order to help four worthy persons, I believe he acted upon principles as honourable as any in the works of Blackstone or my Lord Coke.

Mrs. Wilson now threw her arms around Tom in joy, and Captain Lawrence, who previously had said not a word, declared he believed him correct, and would himself give evidence in England that he trusted Mr. Jones and "the lovely American lady" (for so he carefully called Mrs. Wilson); and that he considered Captain Whipsblood and his friends, "the biggest liars upon the earth."

Rob Jones had heard all this with delight because his father and sister were now free to come and go as they chose—and yet with alarm because it had detained him long in a dangerous place. Accordingly, he now declared, "Well, Father, this hath been a happy day for you. And now I believe I may offer you, Mr. Adams, your lovely friend and my dear sister, a choice entirely free: whether to come with me, and take your chances with the American cause; or to return to England, and to rescue our estates from my scoundrel brother. Whichever you choose, I heartily wish you well. . . ."

Rob's kind offer, however, died in his throat; and, indeed, the flow of good spirits which followed Colonel Askew's announcement was brought to a sudden and confusing end, in the shocking incident which we mean to present to thee, Reader, at the very start of our next chapter.

# XI

## *In Which We Draw Still Nearer to the End*

We must tell thee, Reader, that friendship, as great a beauty as it is, is not in this world eternal or unchanging. The sad truth is that the hasty words exchanged between Captain Whipsblood and Lady Suffley had somewhat cooled their bond; which had, I suppose, always contained more of heat than of true warmth.

Even more to the point, I believe both these persons now began to regret having addressed each other so freely before an audience—for, after all, many little lovers' secrets lose their charm when publicly shared. Lady Suffley could, I suppose, take some comfort in knowing that the wife of a peer of the realm would never be punished for such trivialities as perjury and theft of government funds; but the Captain—who probably had less reason to expect charity to guide the hand of the law—now seem'd to think himself obliged to act on his own behalf.

To be brief, the Captain, in the midst of Rob's kind offer to his family, suddenly pulled a knife from the belt of a sailor, and, moving very quickly, grabbed Lady Suffley about the waist, and held the blade to her throat.

"Hark'ee, rogues!" cried the Captain. "This Lady and I are leaving, or we both shall die where we stand!"

Reader, no panorama ever drawn could have shown thee the amazement now etched upon every face. A full half-minute passed before the surrounding sailors, and those still lining the railing of the privateer, raised their firearms or drew their swords, after which, another, tenser silence fell.

Who can tell what mischief might next have befallen, had not Lord Suffley, to the amazement of all (and especially, of Lady Suffley), stepped forward and said:

"I should prefer, Captain, that I be your hostage."

Reader, I do not believe nobility to have formed a great part of his Lordship's character, yet this one display of it prevented disaster; for Whipsblood, absolutely staggered, fractionally relaxed his grip, allowing Lady Suffley to escape.

Whipsblood now seemed as good as a dead man; yet before anyone could lay hands upon him, Rob Jones said clearly, "About a year ago, Captain, you declined to kill me for an imagined injury to your family. I now return the favour. Take any of the boats" (for two or three small craft had been lowered from the privateer, to ferry back treasure), "and row due west; you will find land, or some fishing vessel, before sunset tomorrow."

Captain Whipsblood, still holding the knife before him, and bearing the expression of a trapt animal, back'd slowly to the railing, and lowered himself down by the rope ladder. A few minutes later, they saw him rowing away, his back very straight, and the oars moving very fast. They were not unimpressed by his courage or composure; yet I promise thee, Reader, such martial visions are far more pleasing on their departure, than at their arrival.

"Well, Father," says Rob, "I have spared an enemy of yours. I hope you can forgive me."

Jones answered, that he hoped he should always applaud mercy, though Mrs. Wilson whispered under her breath something about a fool.

"Then I must ask you all to choose quickly," continued Rob, "are you with me, or bound for England?"

Tom replied, meaning to speak for all, that he believed England was the universal choice.

Reader, nothing so confounds the human intellect, as to be found publicly wrong in a cherished assumption. It had never, I believe, occurred to our hero that he and Mrs. Wilson might ever be separated again, except perhaps by those terrible accidents which, tho' every mortal's fate eventually, are generally as far out of our minds, as they are out of our hands.

Accordingly, he was now rendered entirely speechless when Mrs. Wilson declared, "I, Rob, should like to go with you."

Mr. Macbeth when he saw the Dunsinane forest come a-marching towards him was not more certain nature had gone mad than was our hero on hearing these words. Having turned very pale, and looking like one who had received a near-mortal blow, he now begged the others to excuse him a moment.

"For heaven's sake, sir," cries Rob in considerable alarm, "be quick. We have already tarried here far too long."

Jones, nodding vaguely to this, took Mrs. Wilson to the back of the cabin, where he said to her, "In what, madam, have I offended you?"

"Why, sir," answered she, "in nothing of consequence."

"How, then," asked Jones, "can you destroy my every hope of happiness, my every dream?"

"Why, sir, if you mean, 'how can I return to America,' the answer is that I must. My fortune, beliefs and duty all require it. Why will *you* not come with me?"

"Why, madam," cries Jones wildly, "my estates shall be forfeited! A pack of scoundrels will claim all that is mine!"

"Well, sir," said Mrs. Wilson quietly.

"Madam," begged Jones, forlornly.

After a moment's silence, she replied, "Believe me, Mr. Jones, we shall meet again, if I have anything to say about it."

"When, dearest madam?"

Mrs. Wilson now shrugged, by no means happily, and then, as if making the greatest of concessions, added, "As soon as may be; for, foolish Tom, I do love thee." So saying, she kissed him, and without adding anything more, returned to the others.

And so, very sadly, did our hero follow after her a moment later, having learned how swiftly the wheel of fortune may spin in this uncertain world. In truth, Reader, I hope he may, upon further consideration, have found some small consolations in the love of a woman so sensible; but it would have tried the patience of a saint to think of them just then.

Tom returned to find the privateers had reboarded their own ship, excepting only his son, who fairly bounced with impatience and alarm. "Why, Father," says he, very fondly, "we may not, I fear, see each other for many a long year. Yet you and Amelia shall be ever in my thoughts."

Finding further talk impossible, and hearing no reply from his even-more-emotional father, he desisted, and they threw their arms around each other, after which he turned to shake hands with Mr. Adams and the Colonel, and then to hug Amelia.

"Brother," says she, not forgetting the sisterly duty to offer advice, even through her tears. "To write not once in a year is shameful. Be more loyal, or I shall forget thee entirely. And do not worry for the estate; we shall see it is returned to father."

This last she said in perfect good faith; and indeed, I believe the sudden collapse of Whipsblood's and Lady Suffley's conspiracy had made her think a few additional miracles would be the simplest things upon earth.

A moment later, the two ships having drifted very close together, Rob helped Mrs. Wilson make the transfer, and then himself leapt across unassisted. As the privateer raised her sails and moved away, Mrs. Wilson walked to the stern, where poor Jones could see her waving until she grew invisibly small in the distance.

Alas, poor Jones! While Adams and Amelia (finding him inconsolable) went into the deck cabin to confer with Colonel Askew upon plans for reclaiming the estate, he stood alone at the bow of the ship, watching his hopes sail away from him, perhaps forever.

And yet, Reader, of all our reasons for loving and admiring Tom Jones, none is greater than this: that he had, in full measure, the true hero's disregard for his own success. He had already that morning (and the hour had not yet reached nine o'clock) found a son, escaped a hanging charge, and seen two of his deadliest enemies brought low—and yet, such was his noble contempt for worldly affairs, that he still considered it almost the wretchedest day of his life.

# XII

## In Which Our Story Returns to England, and Draws Very Near Its End

We have often, Reader, celebrated in the character of our hero that native toughness which let him rise above his sufferings, and triumph when others would not even have tried. Never was this toughness more apparent than on the voyage home to England. So effectively did he convince himself of the need to regain his estates (for Rob and Amelia, if not for himself), that when, after a swift passage, the *Rose of York* at last sailed up the Thames on the 30th of May, he was once again a lion of energy and determination.

The ship had no sooner dropped her anchor than our friends, leaving Captain Lawrence to look after their goods, had themselves rowed immediately ashore, from whence they took the first available hackney coach to Hanover Square.

Having been warned by Amelia and Adams, Jones stood ready for angry words with Mrs. Guerdion—ready, indeed, for nearly anything except the tones of affection and relief with which she greeted him.

"Glorious heaven!" cried that stiff-laced woman, as she opened the door upon our hero. "Surely I have lived to see a miracle. From this day forward, they may preach every Sunday whatever foolishness they wish about devils and angels, and I promise I shall believe every word! Oh, Squire, you are, I hope and pray, in time to prevent the wickedest crime in the world—to rescue Mrs. James, and stop the dastardly theft of your estates!"

Jones, who had supposed his wealth already gone, might have heard this news with soaring hopes for himself; yet we are delighted to record that he only answered, in a voice of great concern:

"What fiends, Madam, have threatened Mrs. James!?"

"Oh, sir, forgive me my small part in it, but your son and wicked Mr. Sinamore are even now trying (if they have not already succeeded) to bully Mrs. James into signing away your estates."

"*Egad!*" cries Jones—by now, I suppose, a little aware of his own interests. "What, madam, hath *Mrs. James* to do with my estates? We had heard all was lost weeks ago."

"So, sir, the wicked villains had intended; but at the Quarter Sessions, Mr. Stumpling, backed by the magnificent Dr. Johnson, brought an action showing an error in the proceedings. It doth appear that the late Dr. James, who had an inordinate faith in his dear wife" (at this, Jones, for several reasons, fetched a sigh) "had attached a codicil to your agreement with him, naming her as his life successor. This codicil, if sustained, will void every action of Mr. Sinamore's since the doctor's death, and will—"

"Indeed, madam," cries Colonel Askew, "we understand what follows. But what is this about *bullying?*"

"Why, sir," says Mrs. Guerdion more calmly (for she really was a sensible woman, only presently overwrought), "you are correct: time is everything. My young master and that monster Sinamore learned of the codicil last winter, but never imagined Mrs. James would apply it effectually until the case was entered last month. Since then, they have hunted unceasingly for her, and two days ago, they found her. One of them, at least, hath been with her every moment since, to try to force her into waiving her authority. So they mean to claim all, and save themselves vast legal costs. They sit every night beside your fire-place, Squire, and discuss their stratagems; and last night they swore, 'that they would be done with the useless woman'—for such were their words—'this day, by one means or the other.'

"In truth, Squire," concluded Mrs. Guerdion, on a note almost of despair, "from what I have heard, the pitiable woman is now virtually their prisoner, besides that she is desperately poor, and ill. Dr. Johnson is himself too sick to help her, and I—I dare not. I should not be at all surprised if her will is broken this very day; for I promise thee, that living with those two mad gentlemen hath nearly broken me myself."

Our friends now exchanged looks of wildest alarm.

"What, madam," cried Tom, "may be Mrs. James's address?"

Mrs. Guerdion named one of the most squalid and dangerous streets in London.

"We must go at once," cried Amelia, tugging at her father's coat.

"Why, may G—d help you pull the rascals down!" shouted Mrs. Guerdion at the back of Mr. Jones, who had already, with the others pacing, turned and begun speeding down the walk, to where the hackney-coach still waited. Indeed, by the time she remembered to tell them of the third conspirator, they were already far beyond hearing.

The four of them had not even reached the street, when Colonel Askew, taking a gold sovereign from his pocket, threw it up to the coachman and called, "Down from there, sirrah, at once!" in a voice so commanding that the old fellow immediately pitched himself to the ground. Tom and Askew now leaped up into the vacated box and, scarcely waiting for Amelia and her friend to take their seats within, cracked the reins and began—with Tom driving, and the Colonel drawing his sword to warn off any who might insist upon their traffic rights—a blazing dash through London.

The Colonel having once traded swipes with an irate gentleman of the Navy (neither suffering any injury), our friends reached the poor lodgings of Mrs. James in a little less than twenty minutes, with the horses exhausted, and themselves in a condition to fight all comers.

Had any last small measure of insult been lacking to provoke Tom to the very pitch of combative furor, he now received it in the sight of his own coach, with some new and preposterous coat of arms carved upon its doors, standing directly before the entrance to the lodging-house.

While Tom and the Colonel paused to examine this material crime, good Amelia, thinking only of her friend, Mrs. James, flew up the lodging-house steps.

Having learned in her travels something of the dangers of the ill-considered charge, Amelia, on reaching the top floor, tip-toe'd very quietly down the foul-smelling corridor, and placed her ear softly against the door, through which she heard the most menacing of words:

"Look'ee, madam," warned the hard voice of Lawyer Sinamore, "we have have been far too patient with you."

"And far too generous," added a second voice, equally harsh, and yet unfamiliar to Amelia. "Sixty pounds *per annum*, madam, is not to be sneered at, by any person in your situation. All for a signature, madam. Give us that, and we shall see you have a doctor, good food, and all else you need, after which you may leave at your convenience for Scotland and a retirement in tranquillity. Otherwise—well, madam, it grieves me."

There was to this second voice a vileness which nauseated Amelia, and, in truth, she might have hesitated, had there not come simultaneously the muffled sounds of a struggle within the room, and the clatter upon the stairs of her arriving friends.

Certain that she must act, Amelia first pounded upon the door, and then (hearing no reply) rattled the handle fiercely.

The door, however, responding no more than the persons inside, she, seeing Mr. Adams approaching, shouted to him to break it in.

Reader, so heated were the feelings of our friends, that I believe, had anyone suggested it, Mr. Adams would have gone straight through the wall itself. As it was, he merely threw his shoulder against the door, which, with a splintering crash, gave instantly away.

There now rushed into the room (stepping around Mr. Adams), Amelia, followed by Jones, followed by the Colonel. Three of the persons they surprised were known to them all, but the fourth was familiar only to our hero, who, after staring a moment in wild amazement, at last cried in consternation:

*"Brother Blifil!"*

# XIII

## *Virtually the End*

For the first time in thirty years, our hero and his great nemesis, his wicked half-brother, looked upon each other—while rage and dismay distorted both their faces.

As our rescuers entered the room, this rogue, Blifil, and Mr. Sinamore towered above Mrs. James, who cringed upon a battered settee. Reader, I could not easily portray the wretched state of that lady, who was dressed almost in rags, and so undernourished that the cords of her neck stood out like reeds.

Mrs. James had, at the instant of the door's collapse, screamed, then, seeing Adams and Amelia, cried, "G__d be praised"; and now, at Tom's appearance, she rolled back her eyes, and fainted dead away.

While Adams and Amelia laboured to revive the poor woman, Tom noticed his own wretched son struggling to confine in the bedroom some other person, by bracing his back against the bedroom door.

"Stand away from there, sirrah!" roared Tom, pointing towards Hacksem with a finger trembling in anger.

Hacksem obeyed, and the door sprang open, admitting Mrs. Limeslices, whose own momentum carried her tumbling into the room.

Mrs. Limeslices had no sooner recovered her legs, than she kicked Mr. Hacksem solidly in the shins; after which, she spied Amelia, and, rendering thanks unto Heaven, scurried to embrace her with all the affection of a mother recovering a long-lost child.

Such scenes are not, I fear, to every taste. Mr. Sinamore made some motions to depart, at which, however, Tom and Askew immediately drew their swords—with the Colonel looking particularly willing to make use of his.

Tom now enquired how Mrs. James did; and, being told she had regained consciousness, but was very weak, asked Mrs. Limeslices, "Madam, are you well enough to perform a service?"

"Sir," replied she, a little tartly, "I am, but that's by God's grace; for, had some persons arrived a moment later, we might all have suffered for it."

"Madam," said Tom (who had no patience to attend a lecture), "I apologize. Yet you will now render great service to your friends, if you will take this money" (he here handed over one of the five gold sovereigns he had earlier borrowed of Colonel Askew), "and fetch the physician and the nearest magistrate's officer. You may mention my name, if necessary."

"With all my heart, Squire," answered Mrs. Limeslices, looking fondly at Amelia, and then glaring at the three villains, as she left.

Our hero now faced one of the most painful duties of his career. Mr. Blifil had not moved from his position near Mrs. James. To see this worst of all villains standing over the old woman like an executioner, and holding a legal document like a sword or noose, was almost too much for Tom to endure.

When, three decades before, Blifil had been banished at last from Mr. Allworthy's house, it had been Tom who had pleaded for mercy for him, and who had secretly provided him the money on which he lived. Never had Blifil shown the faintest gratitude; and Tom, after several spurned attempts at reconciliation, had at last put the rascal from his thoughts. Yet now—for such is the permanence of wickedness in this world—he was obliged to recall what he would have infinitely preferred to forget.

"How, Brother Blifil," cried he, "can you have returned after so long, only to do harm? Are not the troubles of the past behind us?"

"Why, *Brother*," answered Blifil, with a sneer, "when one lives in comfort and ease, surrounded by beauty and one's own family, past troubles may perhaps be forgotten. But when one lives in a cold Northern hut, forever toiling to replace that fortune which should have been one's own; why, then, past troubles only gall and chafe—as you would have learned, had not some cursed fate brought you here five minutes before the perfection of my plans. Look'ee, sirrah!" he ended, moaning loudly, and raising the sheet of vellum. "A signature here, and your properties were lost, forever."

Reader, we must say that there was almost something pitiable in this, since Blifil, for all his holdings, really did conceive himself to be extremely poor. Yet we must not let pity outstrip sense; after all, this devil, if he did not weave every evil we have recorded, at least stitched the corruptions of Suffley, Sinamore and the others into a single black garment.

Yet now his schemes were tatters; and he, a pale gentleman shrinking within a frail body, had little with which to protect himself.

---

Jones, knowing Blifil to be ruined, sheathed his blade and said mildly, "I am sorry, Brother, that you have never forgiven me; or rather, allowed yourself to be forgiven. Others may wish to see you charged with some crimes; for myself, I only demand that you leave us, forever."

Blifil, tho' at first very furious, now drew himself up coldly and declared, "Well, sir, I have cost you great suffering, and that shall comfort me long. As for any legal retribution, do not expect it. The courts are cheese, through which one such as I may run and chew as long as I like. You shall never have me there—tho' you may someday have me where you wish me not."

And so, having sent shudders through Amelia, the finely-dressed gentleman crumpled the sheet of vellum he had held, tossed it into a corner, and, slipping past Tom and his daughter, left the room, and our story.

Mr. Sinamore seemed very eager to follow him, but was stopped by Jones's saying commandingly, "Lawyer, I have words for you!" When he halted, our hero went on more calmly, "My brother, sir, imagines himself to have been injured by me; but you have enjoyed at my hands, not only the making of your fortune, but all the trust which one gentleman may bestow upon another. What on earth led you to betray one who always treated you kindly?"

"Why, wretched dog," answered Mr. Sinamore, very proudly, "I disliked eating the crumbs of your table, when it was I who kept it set; and more than that, I had a very great taste for that proud beauty of yours, who . . ."

(Here Mr. Sinamore made some remarks concerning Amelia which we should rather die than repeat, and which—given the temper of Mr. Adams—Mr. Sinamore might have died for offering in the first place.)

"That will do, sirrah," roars Adams. "Look'ee that I do not forget the cloth I wear."

Mr. Sinamore, who was very much of a boxer and wrestler, met this threat with disdain—but then, seeing the Colonel and our hero eager to support their friend, he subsided, and answered:

"It matters little. You gentlemen, I suspect, have not the natures to set three upon one; and, as your estimable brother hath said, *Mr.* Jones, we have been too careful for the law. What have we done, except to use the authority you abandoned; and, perhaps, to try persuading this silly old woman" (meaning, of course, Mrs. James), "to relinquish a document she had neither earned, nor understood?"

"How!" cries Jones. "Will you deny the murder of Dr. James?"

"Why, Squire," the Lawyer answers, with a sneer, "never mind what nonsense that nasty girl of yours must have spoke; I long ago convened an inquest which pronounced his drowning *accidental.*"

Tom, stunned by this last, looked wildly to Mrs. James, who reluctantly nodded; and then appealed to the Colonel, who, as reluctantly, shook his head. At last, mastering his shock and rage, he said:

"I find, sirrah, you may not be held. Yet I warn you never to return to Somersetshire. And more: seek the business of the gentry anywhere in this realm, and I will unmask you; boast to anyone of the crimes I know you have committed, and I will see you hanged.

"Now, sirrah, go, and consider whether it shall not be worth even a confession to save your immortal soul."

"Why, Squire," replied Mr. Sinamore, as brazen a soul as any in the Devil's camp, "I leave you gladly, and shall later do whatever I please. Gentlemen, your servant; and now, Squire, I suppose you wish to speak with this promising boy of yours."

Indeed, Reader, Mr. Sinamore (who now pushed his way past Miss Jones, and out the door) had delivered one last hard blow to our hero. When a time comes to punish those we love, Justice may, as always, be blind-folded, but less, I think, to show her impartiality, than to hide her tears.

"Now, sir," says Jones to his son, while trembling and thinking the room very dim, "you must be dealt with. What, sir, are we to do with you? Will you not, at least, make the judgement easy by an apology, or an asking for mercy?"

"Well, sir," answers Hacksem, very calmly, "I see nothing for which to apologize: indeed, I like nothing better than to be tied with those two gentlemen who have just left you. I have no more taste for begging than do they. I do not need your money, Father, and I do not wish your mercy."

Having begun so calmly, Hacksem now burst out in high emotion, "Indeed, Father, you have some vanity in even addressing me now; for where, sir, were you when I needed you? When did you receive me as you received my brother and my sister? When did you consider my ideas? Nay, sir, when you were tired of even pretending to hear me, you gave the job to poor Dr. James, and went off to amuse yourself. Why, sir, your mercies are very late now; and I should far prefer to be the favorite of my uncle, such as he is, than to be the last choice of my nearer family. Good-bye to you all."

The estimable younger Jones had not even completed this, when he began striding from the room, with his eyes meeting neither his father's nor his sister's.

If, Reader, a lie is an arrow, then a dab of truth is the poison upon it. Within this wicked defense by Mr. Hacksem, there was just so much truth as to injure our hero deeply—or at least so I must assume, since, immediately after Hacksem left, he went to the room's small street window, and from there watched his son for several minutes, 'til a hackney-coach had driven him away.

It was then that Mrs. Limeslices appeared, bringing the doctor and an officer, as well as some wine, roast chicken and bread, which, she declared, would cure all that ailed Mrs. James or herself.

The food being set before Mrs. James, and the physician beginning to examine her, it fell to the officer to ask (with some impatience) whether he was to make any arrest.

"Alas, friend," replied Colonel Askew, "we have had here but ordinary wickedness, which, I believe, you may no more arrest, than you may the spinning of the globe."

The physician, having completed a very brief examination, now said (looking sharply at Jones), "I find nothing to ail this gentlewoman but hunger and neglect; for which, perhaps, certain persons shall someday think themselves ashamed."

Why, Reader, it was very much in the fortune of Mr. Jones to be blamed for the condition of a woman he had just rescued; yet, while some may consider this a very sound warning against the doing of good deeds, our hero accepted the rebuke mildly, and, giving the doctor a guinea, promised, "I shall do my best to see the good gentlewoman recovers."

In truth, there had been about the whole day something a trifle disappointing to Tom; and he now, being in the privacy of his family, sighed aloud, and said, very heart-brokenedly, "I am sorry, Mrs. James, to have failed you."

Reader, I believe generosity and kindness may appear in some very unlikely places—even in a widowed old gentlewoman. At least, I know that Mrs. James now quietly responded, "You have done as kindly by me, Tom, as any son could have; and, as we are now all restored to one another, we must all be utterly ashamed if we are not both joyous and grateful, instead of self-pitying and morose."

For above a full minute, our hero stood silently, wondering how

---

precisely to be at once contented and sad; then—for even paradox must fall before a true hero—he smiled, and said:

"Madam, you are right, and a celebration is due. If you will all follow me down to my coach, I believe we may find a fitter place to dine. Mrs. Limeslices, if you will see this food is given to some worthy poor person in this building" (for, in truth, Mrs. James's apartment was a dreary place), "we shall await you downstairs."

In a moment, the others were gone, and Mrs. Limeslices was left to gather up the meal. This she did pretty willingly, tho' all the while muttering what sounded like, "Marry come up—poor persons, indeed."

## Chapter the Last:
## Some Final Scenes, a First Improbability and Our Farewell to the Reader

Our friends remained in London only another two days, just long enough to visit Dr. Johnson, then scarcely recovered from the influenza which had disabled him all the preceding month. "I am extremely glad," said he, "to hear you have saved yourself, Tom; but if you will forgive me, I believe you have been too merciful. Charity is a glorious thing, but so, too, is a well-placed *boot.*" Jones promised he would in future keep the principle well in mind.

The next morning, being assured that Mrs. James was well enough to travel, Tom and the others bid farewell to Colonel Askew and boarded Tom's coach—its exterior having been repaired—for home. About sundown, they reached the Biting Whale, which, to their surprise, they found perfectly restored: Mr. Nautley, it seemed, had survived his pneumonia and, after returning to dismiss his worthless cousin, had wisely married the loyal Betty—who now received several lavish presents for her past, if rather dissimilar, kindnesses to Tom and Amelia.

The Nautleys having become staunch advocates of the wedded state, they were ecstatic when Mr. Adams, with the strong prompting of

Amelia, summoned all his courage and (while hemming, hawing, and turning very red) asked Tom for Amelia's hand. Tom, after making several jests more amusing to himself than to the poor suitor, at last bestowed not only his blessings, but a dowry entirely completing the modest Parson's pleasure and amazement.

So it was that, late upon the warm afternoon of June 3rd, the coach bearing Amelia, her husband-to-be and the others, at last rolled into sight of Paradise Hall, inspiring in them all the highest joys of home-coming, only a little tempered by fear for the harm Hacksem might have done.

Before sundown that long evening, Mr. Grimes, the former chief servant, was kicked onto the road, having first been obliged to surrender from his luggage several hundred pounds' worth of items he had taken upon the doubtful legal grounds *that they were not nailed down.* His former privileges were added to the position of housekeeper, which Mrs. Lime-slices (who had previously refused a generous pension) happily accepted.

In the morning, Tom and Amelia went to survey the woods and fields Hacksem had assaulted. Our friends found, besides many beautiful trees destroyed, and streams dammed, two entire hillsides dug away in the search for coal. By dusk, they had ordered the first restoration work begun. Several scars, they knew, would fade only with the slow passage of years, if ever—yet I believe they were properly thankful the damage was no worse.

All parties expressing themselves very eager, Amelia and Mr. Adams celebrated their marriage the first Sunday after the final publishing of the banns. To say truth, the news of this engagement somewhat stupefied the more fashionable part of Somersetshire, to whom it seemed that a poor clergyman like Mr. Adams—aside from combining height, strength, sweetness of personality and excellence of mind with education and the tenderest possible affection for her—could offer Amelia virtually nothing.

On Amelia's remaining firm, however, opinion began swiftly to change (for Miss Jones was not only right, but rich, and beautiful), and the joy upon her wedding day was, we may safely declare, universal; nor, indeed, was anyone happier than Tom Jones, not only from the occasion, but from two letters he had earlier received.

Reader, we must now ask thee (for the first time, and much against our instincts) to accept as true one fact which, we freely admit, smacks a little of improbability. This was that Mr. Jones received, on the Friday before Amelia's wedding, not one, but two letters answering the great remaining wishes in his life. As both letters were brief, we shall here recapture whatever credibility we may have lost, by presenting them unaltered:

Port-au-Prince
June 5, 1775

Dear Father,

I am writing solely to assure you, first, of the triviality of certain injuries which I suffered earlier this month in an action off the coast of the Carolinas, and, second, of my absolute determination to end a sort of life for which, I find, I have insufficient ferocity and devotion. It is now my intention to pursue a life nautical but not military: and I hope, after recuperating in England for some reasonable time, to undertake a career in the China trade; a plan which I know will appeal to you as much for its gentility as for its profitability. So I hope at once to entertain myself and aid my family, by launching a venture for which my year here in the West Indies hath, beyond a doubt, perfectly well qualified me.

You will consider me very rude (now that I think of it) to have held to the last any mention of your friend Mrs. Wilson, a woman for whom I must say I have the highest regard, and who, incidentally, always spoke of you with noticeable fondness. I hope, Father, you will try to maintain a friendship with her, once the present troubles are over; for, despite her youth, such a person would, I think, make a very suitable acquaintance.

Please pardon, as always, the excessive length of this; I imagine you are already tired of reading, and you shall anyway within a month or two have the livelier companionship of,

Your loving and
dutiful son,
Rob Jones

P.S.: I beg you to excuse the clumsiness of my pen, for one of the aforementioned minor wounds happened to go cleanly through my writing arm—an injury, as you may imagine, of no small inconvenience to so eager a correspondent as myself.

Our hero had little time to enjoy the noble variety of sentiments raised by this letter, since Mrs. Limeslices (who had imagined she was handing him his correspondence in order of decreasing interest) now put before him an envelope from Massachusetts which, upon discovering, he could

341

not hold calmly. Instead, his heart in wild palpitations, he leapt from his chair, and hastened out onto the terrace for privacy. There, after drawing two or three great breaths, he tore open and read:

> At the Red Boar,
> Salem, Mass.
> 17 June, 1775

Dearest Tom,

Communications being so very irregular, you may already have heard of our victory (for so we call it) at Bunker Hill. The fighting there hath pretty well assured the independence of this colony; for the British Army may no longer advance from Boston, and shall soon (I believe) lose even that.

I write, however, to another purpose; for the Continental Congress, having been shown its duty by a woman, hath determined that duty can only be completed by a man; and, in short, I am no longer to supply weapons to the militia. (This, in truth, is a business which, as it hath at last become profitable, hath at last become popular; and I can today count more competitors than I could last year count patriots.)

Let this not sound bitter. Sooner or later I will be needed for some task—perhaps in France, where my connections are very strong. I wish as much as ever to serve the cause of independence; and very likely I will seem more valuable to the gentlemen in Philadelphia if I show some independence myself.

I mean, therefore, to place the balance of my holdings in trustworthy hands, and to visit England (in particular, Somersetshire) to settle a matter of great importance to me; namely, whether that sweet music we heard in each other's arms was love indeed, or only the after-ringing of the cannonade.

Between now and the middle of August, therefore, I shall remain as near to Salem as may be; and, hearing no objection, shall sail for London as soon thereafter as practicable. 'Till then, know that you are safely in the heart of,

> Your affectionate,
> Angela Wilson

P.S.: I do not require it, but any small items about yourself, your family or your activities, would, I find, be very congenial to me.

Our hero, understanding this to be a very great concession to sentiment by the unsentimental Mrs. Wilson, now dashed back to his study, broke one quill entirely in half, and then blotted several sheets of paper in preparing his reply, which Mrs. Limeslices (who began to guess the nature of the business) saw posted that very afternoon.

So the wedding of Amelia and Adams, held upon a perfect summer's morning two days later, seemed to Tom, not only a joy in itself, but the type or intimation of his own; nor, I believe, did the youngest person there dance longer, sing louder, or drink more, than he.

That wedding of his in fact occurred upon a crisp afternoon in late October. Mr. Adams, having harvested vast wisdom during his several months as *pater familias,* offered from the pulpit a granary full of sensible advice which (tho' it made Amelia smile) was heard patiently by Tom and Angela, who understood very well the solemnity of the occasion; after which they all walked home (for Mrs. Jones would hear of no carriages) amid a swirl of autumnal leaves very lovely to behold.

There followed an evening of celebration, ending with a feast extremely magnificent, which our two heroes attended in body, even if their thoughts were (as I suspect) elsewhere. About nine o'clock, the new Mrs. Jones was led by her step-daughter (whom she had already come to consider, after Tom himself, her closest friend) to the bed-room. A few minutes earlier, Amelia returned to announce quietly to our hero that his bride was ready to receive him—at which Jones, his eyes sparkling with fire, bid the company a good-night, and went to enjoy all the happiness he had so long desired. That night, they were very likely the two happiest persons upon the earth; and to this resolution, I believe, no objection may be raised, for certainly the rewards of goodness, tho' not always swift, are very sweet, and lasting.

It may be, Reader, that thou hast a curiosity to know something of the later fortunes of certain of our characters. We would gladly oblige thee in anything; yet, as our characters have been numerous, we shall mention only a few, choosing (as doth Fame herself) to honour some, and neglect many others of equal, or even far greater, merit.

The villains of our piece, who were so mercifully treated by our heroes, fared far worse at their own hands. Mr. *Blifil* returned almost at once to the complete obscurity of his northern hamlet, where the memories of his expensive failure are his closest companions. Mr. *Hacksem,* finding himself deserted by both the gentlemen he had wanted for his friends, very soon suffered a complete nervous collapse: he is presently confined in a private mad-house in London, where recent symptoms give hope of his recovery, tho' at no very rapid pace.

Mr. *Sinamore* never dared appear again in Somersetshire, but began a life of wandering criminality, during which his vices so overmastered him that he at last began to rot in advance of death; and when (which was not many years later) he was in fact buried, it was as much an aid to the sanitation, as to the morality, of the country.

The *Suffleys* endured all those punishments usually inflicted upon the rich and powerful, which is to say—none at all. Shortly after arriving in London, however, *Lady Suffley*, rushing to halt a duel being fought over her, was unluckily shot at by both gentlemen. Tho' uninjured, she thereafter altered her views of life, attending church regularly and clinging almost faithfully to her husband. Indeed, she now seems likely to become in time one of the greatest moralists of the fashionable world—a world which hath need, I believe, of all the moralists it can get.

Mr. *Stumpling,* who had made what amends he could, first by confessing to Amelia, and then by taking the case of Mrs. James and Tom's estate *pro bono publico,* became once again a trusted aide to the estate, and may soon, I believe, succeed his former employer as its steward.

As for the woman Mr. Stumpling tried to aid, Mrs. *James* stayed as a guest of the Joneses only until Tom could arrange for her to return to Meadowlands, between which residence and Paradise Hall, there continues the liveliest friendship.

*Colonel Askew,* perfectly recovered from all his wounds, resigned his commission, married his beloved Becky, and returned to Dorsetshire, which he is nowadays persuaded to leave only for semi-annual visits to Tom and his family; and where, I am told, his fields are very green, his days are very quiet, and his books are very many. They have at present two children, both boys, who, he promises, shall be bred as clergymen, statesmen or anything they wish but soldiers.

*Rob Jones* remained in England only until his wounds had entirely healed. One extremely rainy morning in January of 1776, as he stood looking out a window, he began thinking of warm Jamaica, of the opportunities for a young man of spirit—and, perhaps, of the cause of Liberty. Before that month was gone, so was he; and in early March, the name of Jones was once again enrolled among the privateers, where it remained until some weeks after the signing of the peace, six years later. Only then did he begin that trading firm which now seems likely to earn more money bringing silks from China than Paradise Hall could ever have earned cutting coal from the earth. In this he has gone partners with his sister, a Boston gentleman named Bateson, and his step-mother—

Mrs. *Angela Jones,* who waited nearly three years for her chance to return to France. This mission (which was available mostly because of its extreme danger) was at first opposed by her husband, as being entirely unsuitable for the recent mother of twin girls. After several rather spirited discussions, however, this gentleman was persuaded to see the moral necessity and good sense of her going; and it was shortly after this last journey that she was persuaded to settle down and lay the plans for the merchant firm of Jones and Bateson.

As for *Tom Jones,* he knows well enough to leave business to those who understand it. His new family and the lands of Paradise Hall now content him perfectly well. High upon one of the hillsides he used to wander in his restless years, he and Angela have lately constructed a pleasant arbour. There, in the shade of some alder or linden trees (I forget which), you are likely to find them, extremely pleased with each other, and equally pleased to have visitors, on nearly any fine day of the year.

So hath our story reached its end. Reader, farewell!—and a blessing go with thee. May you be wise as Dr. Johnson, and brave as Mrs. Wilson; as loving as Amelia, and as faithful as Mr. Adams; and may you at last— for then you will well deserve it—be lucky as Tom himself.

# AUTHOR'S NOTE

In writing *The Later Adventures*, I have played so freely with historical dates, places, persons and customs that, as Fielding might have said, "a traditional bibliography would too much resemble a thank-you note from the Visigoths to the *City of Rome.*"

Still, many readers will recognize Ben Franklin's wonderful *Autobiography* as the source for the story about the rice and fire engines: nothing I was able to invent conveyed the great man's character half so well. In addition, I tried to be fairly scrupulous in my use of information published by the National Historical Society, and the Chamber of Commerce of Concord, Massachusetts, concerning Revolutionary-era Boston and the Lexington-Concord Battle Road.

I gratefully acknowledge the personal help of Thomas Lockwood of the University of Washington; Peter Ginsberg of Curtis Brown, Ltd.; and Ms. Virginia Renner of the Huntington Library. Lastly (whatever silly turns I may have given to their discoveries), my thanks to all those fine scholars and historians who have kept alive our knowledge of the eighteenth century.

# ABOUT THE AUTHOR

BOB COLEMAN, Ph.D., wrote his dissertation on Henry Fielding and received his doctorate in eighteenth-century literature from the University of Washington in 1982. *The Later Adventures of Tom Jones* is his first novel.

Mr. Coleman lives in San Diego, where his other adventures include employment as vice president of a small-business brokerage and consulting firm.